RIGHTEOUS PREY

JOHN SANDFORD

RIGHTEOUS PREY

SIMON &
SCHUSTER

London · New York · Sydney · Toronto · New Delhi

First published in the United States by G. P. Putnam's Sons,
an imprint of Penguin Random House LLC, 2022

First published in Great Britain by Simon & Schuster UK Ltd, 2022

Copyright © John Sandford, 2022

The right of John Sandford to be identified as author of
this work has been asserted in accordance with the
Copyright, Designs and Patents Act, 1988.

1 3 5 7 9 10 8 6 4 2

Simon & Schuster UK Ltd
1st Floor
222 Gray's Inn Road
London WC1X 8HB

Simon & Schuster Australia, Sydney
Simon & Schuster India, New Delhi

www.simonandschuster.co.uk
www.simonandschuster.com.au
www.simonandschuster.co.in

A CIP catalogue record for this book
is available from the British Library

Hardback ISBN: 978-1-3985-2384-5
Trade Paperback ISBN: 978-1-3985-2385-2
eBook ISBN: 978-1-3985-2386-9

Printed and bound in Great Britain by CPI Group (UK) Ltd, Croydon, CR0 4YY

MIX
Paper from
responsible sources
FSC® C171272
FSC
www.fsc.org

RIGHTEOUS PREY

ONE

Bitcoin billionaire, amateur art historian, onetime farm boy George Sonnewell sat on a concrete abutment in a sour-milk-smelling alley near Union Square in San Francisco, the cement rough against his jean-clad butt.

The night was chilly, a good excuse for the long-sleeved work shirt and nylon Air Force jacket, heavy jeans, and boots, although a neutral observer might have been puzzled by the translucent vinyl gloves he wore on his hands.

The clothing had been worn only this once, the better to minimize the transfer of DNA to a murder victim.

And he waited, a predator in plaid.

Overhead, between the buildings, he could see exactly one star, surrounded by roiling purple nighttime clouds that reflected the kaleidoscope of city lights back to earth. Though he rarely used alcohol, Sonnewell had three-fourths of a jug of Burnett's peach vodka by his hip.

Bait.

His hands trembled. Nerves, he thought. He was scared, but he was going for it.

And here came Duck Wiggins, right on schedule, down the alley that he considered *his* alley. He spotted Sonnewell and the jug. Wiggins was a battered man, his face a collection of fleshly crevasses, eroded by his years on the street. His beard might almost have been mistaken for religious expression, so twisted and solid with filth it was.

Wiggins said, "Hey! This is my street, bitch!" and a moment later, "Whatchagot there?"

Sonnewell, matching the aggression: "What the fuck is it to you?"

"Gimme a taste."

"Why should I?"

Wiggins: "Give me a taste and I'll blow you. Later." He was lying. He was the top of the food chain, not this dweeb sitting on the wall like Humpty Dumpty.

Sonnewell pretended to think about it: "Bite me and I'll kill you."

"I don't bite."

Sonnewell pretended to think about it some more: "Okay."

They sat together, a yard apart on the abutment, silent except for the steady gurgling of the vodka—Wiggins got on it and never let up. It occurred to him at one point that the other man was neither drinking nor complaining, but if he wasn't complaining, then Wiggins wasn't complaining.

Sonnewell turned as if to say something, but instead cocked his arm and struck Wiggins at the base of the skull with a scything forearm blow, knocking the other man off the wall, facedown in the alley. The bottle fell backward, still on the wall, but didn't break.

As Wiggins hit the ground, Sonnewell dropped all his two hundred and twenty pounds on his back. Too drunk to fight, Wiggins tried to push up and then to roll, but the other man forced him down to the broken concrete.

Wiggins, face to the side, mumbling into the dirt: "Wha . . . t' . . . fuck?"

Sonnewell pulled a short hard-finished nylon rope from his hip pocket. The ends of the rope were knotted around four-inch lengths of dowel, like an old-fashioned lawnmower starter rope, the better to grip it. He dragged the rope past Wiggins' forehead, nose, lips, and chin to his neck, and pulled on the dowels for a long three minutes as Wiggins thrashed and kicked and pounded the concrete with his fists.

Sonnewell cursed and looked up and down the alley as he rode the other man, fearing a witness, but he'd chosen the kill site carefully and there were no other eyes. The alcohol was too much for Wiggins to overcome; Sonnewell won in the end.

When he was sure Wiggins was dead, Sonnewell untangled the rope from his victim's neck, put it back in his hip pocket, looked up and down the alley. Then he crossed Wiggins' feet and turned them, rolling the dead man onto his back.

Wiggins' forehead was wet with sweat and maybe vodka, and air burped from his lungs, creating a stench compounded of alcohol and old meat. Sonnewell took a black Sharpie from his shirt pocket and wrote a careful "1" on Wiggins' forehead. He retraced the "1" three times, to make sure it was perfectly clear. When he was satisfied, he stood, looked both ways, and left Wiggins as he lay.

Sonnewell was a half mile from his car and it was dark, and the San Francisco streets were mean. He touched his hip, where he'd tucked a compact nine-millimeter handgun. He was not to be fucked with, not on this night. Before he left the alley, he pulled on a dark blue Covid mask; he shouldn't get close enough to anyone to get Covid, but it was a useful disguise.

As he walked back to his car, he passed a row of tents inhabited by homeless people. He left the remains of the vodka there, next to a tattered plastic POW flag planted in a bucket of dirt.

When he got to his Mercedes SUV, unharmed, he locked himself inside, took out a burner phone, and called a memorized number. The phone call was answered by a woman. Her name was Vivian Zhao. She lived somewhere in Southern California, but he wasn't sure where. One thing he did know for sure: she was crazier than a shithouse mouse, and smart.

"How did it go?" she asked.

"Done. Alley near Union Square. As we discussed."

"You're my hero," she said. "Don't forget to throw the phone away. And your rope."

She hung up.

On the way out of town—Sonnewell lived south down the peninsula, in Palo Alto—he asked himself how he felt about killing a man. He was interested, but not surprised, to find that he was now genuinely frightened.

He would be frightened for a while, he thought. Accompanying the fear was an unfamiliar and growing exhilaration.

Sonnewell had grown up on a Central Valley corn farm, one of the four abused children of a hard-faced descendant of Okies who'd actually made it in California. His father believed, as his parents and grandparents had, in the fist and the razor strop. Sonnewell, his two brothers and his sister, lying on the banks of a local creek, had talked of killing the old man. They'd never done it, or even tried, though the talk had been serious.

Through strange and unrepeatable circumstances, Sonnewell had once invested fifty thousand dollars in a thing called Bitcoin. When he'd sold out, with Bitcoin at $46,000 per coin, he was a billionaire. He'd ripped off ten million dollars for each for his siblings and they unanimously told their father that he and his farm could go fuck themselves.

Yet, in his heart, Sonnewell was still an American farm boy, and believed in an America he saw dissolving around him. Half the people in the Central Valley couldn't speak English; the crazies who ran the California government had jacked taxes so high that ordinary hardworking people could hardly make it without abasing themselves before the assholes in the statehouse. The assholes who stood by as the great coastal cities of California were swarmed under by the unclean, the unhealthy, the addicted, the grasping.

Like Duck Wiggins.

The product of beatings since he was a toddler, Sonnewell was not quite right in the head.

He knew that. He was willing to use his difference.

AS SONNEWELL WAS pushing down the peninsula, U.S. Marshal Lucas Davenport was pulling into his driveway in St. Paul, Minnesota, half a continent away. Snow was falling: more than a flurry, less than a blizzard. There were two new inches of snow on the driveway, and he knew, as he drove across it, that he'd leave frozen tracks behind himself that wouldn't come off with a snowblower. He'd either have to laboriously scrape off the tracks in the morning, or they'd be there until February or March.

Though it was late, there were lights in the windows. He pulled into the garage, got out of the car, walked back outside and turned his face up to the snowflakes. They were like feathers, caressing his face; cold, tender, refreshing.

From well down the street, he could hear the faint tingling of recorded Christmas music coming from a house that must have had six hundred red, blue, and green lights hanging from it, and a sleigh with eight plastic reindeer in the front yard, along with a crèche. It was far enough away that he didn't mind, but he suspected the nonstop jingles were driving the adjacent neighbors nuts. Christmas was two weeks gone. In his opinion, it was time to can the Christmas tunes.

As the snowflakes evolved from refreshing to cold and wet, he went back into the garage, dropped the overhead door, and walked through the access door into the house, where his wife, Weather, was burning toast.

"You're burning the toast," he called.

Weather ran back into the kitchen and popped up the toast. "Mmm," she said, "Peanut butter–covered charcoal."

"Do anything good today?" Lucas asked.

"Skin grafts on a guy who got fried trying to fix a high-tension wire," she said. She was a plastic and reconstructive surgeon. Her tone was routine because the work had been routine; it was what she did. "Blew most of the fat off his body. He's got the face of a thirty-year-old angel, but everything below his neck is a mess of scar tissue."

"Nice image," Lucas said, shucking his coat. He hung it on a hook in the hallway between the kitchen and garage.

"How about you? You catch him?" she asked.

"No, but I've got a better idea where he might be hiding. Not that I care much. He's not exactly Al Capone."

"What are you going to do now?" Weather asked. She was a short slender woman, with blue eyes and an oversized, slightly bent nose, which Lucas had found instantly attractive when they first met: gave her a craggy aspect. Her hair, originally a dishwater blond, was showing the first hints of gray, and now was being managed by an enormously expensive hairdresser named Olaf, though only Lucas considered him enormously expensive.

"Get a beer, and either watch some basketball from the West Coast or roll around in the bed with my old lady," Lucas said.

"I'll meet you upstairs in fifteen minutes," Weather said. "My breath will smell like peanut butter and burnt toast."

"Mmm. Peanut butter." He patted her on the ass on his way to the refrigerator.

LUCAS WOKE AT ten o'clock the next morning, pleasantly relaxed after the moderately athletic sex. He got up, yawned, scratched his stomach and wandered downstairs in his undershorts and tee-shirt, made himself a cup of cocoa with tiny marshmallows, turned on his laptop and brought up the Google news feed.

The headlines weren't all bullshit, but most of them were; his eyes hooked on a short story about a man strangled in San Francisco, the strangulation having been announced in a press release by the killer. The press release was attached to the story as a sidebar.

A vertical wrinkle formed between Lucas' eyes. A killer was sending out press releases?

We are all, he thought, *going to hell.*

THE FIVE

If you have money, a lot of money, as all of us do, how do you get your thrills? Skydiving? Fight clubs? Orgies? Gambling? Fly your own jet, sail your own super-yacht? Well, of course you do. All of that. But it gets old, doesn't it? It has for the Five.

So now, to liven our lives, we're going to murder people who need to be murdered. We're doing a service to the American culture at large, and at the same time, enjoying the extreme thrill of being hunted by the police, by the FBI, by whomever takes the time to chase us. Yes: we are going to help rid America of its assholes. We invite others to join in. Really. Please do. We can't get this done alone. So many assholes, so little time.

As for us, we've already killed the first of our designated victims, Duck Wiggins. Wiggins lived on the streets of San Francisco. He was a disgusting piece of human trash. He stole, he raped, he precipitated fights, he attacked innocent elderly Asians, and the San Francisco police believe he stabbed at least three of his fellow denizens of the gutters. And, of course, he defecated on the sidewalks whenever he felt the urge.

One of the Five strangled him this morning. We put a numeral "1" on his forehead and San Franciscans will no longer have to put up with Wiggins' vicious insanity.

To complicate the moral matters for all of you, each of the Five have put an anonymous, untraceable Bitcoin (worth $44,123.23 apiece at the instant of this writing) into a Bitcoin wallet whose

address we've already sent to Street of Hope, a San Francisco orga-
nization dedicated to helping the homeless. Will Street of Hope accept the $220,616.15 (as of this instant) to do good? Or refuse to do
$220,616.15 of good on grounds that it's blood money? We shall see,
shan't we?

The Five

(Next up? A politician! Stay tuned to this station.)

A WEEK AFTER the Wiggins murder, an almost cartoonishly hand-
some dude—and a dude he was, with big shoulders, square teeth, a
chin he could have used to chop wood, a thousand-dollar sport coat,
loafers worn without socks—snuck out the back door of the Asiatic
Hotel in Houston, Texas. He planned to walk around the corner to
where he'd parked his car.

His simple plan was sidetracked by a bottle blonde, a beauty,
maybe thirty, maybe a little older, medium tits, small waist, tight ass,
the whole alluring package. She was leaning against the wall of the
theater building across a narrow brick walkway from the good-
looking guy, next to a door used by the stage talent. She was wearing
a black silk blouse and dark skinny jeans. She was smoking a cigarette, like one of those '40s stunners in the black-and-white noir films.

The good-looking guy was not bashful. He pulled up, nearly stumbled, and said, "Whoa! Howya doing, girlie? All alone in the dark?"

"Taking a break between sets," she said. He could hear the faint
sound of music behind her, coming from the partially open door.
She frowned, stepped closer to him, said, "Say . . . are you Jack
Daniels?"

He gave her his best whitened-tooth grin. "Maybe. You from around here, or are you traveling?"

"From Austin," she said. She looked out of the alley toward the street. They were alone. "Are you sure you're really . . . let me see your face."

She reached out a slender hand, as if to turn his head into the light. Daniels let her do it, the grin still on his face. She didn't touch him, though. She had the blade of a straight razor tight between two fingers, snatched her hand back toward herself, nothing gentle about it, and Daniels felt a streak of cold pain, like a lightning strike, across his neck.

The woman stepped away and he realized, as blood gushed across his thousand-dollar sport coat, that she was wearing translucent vinyl gloves.

Andi Carter's father was the executive vice president of the LaFitte National Bank in New Orleans. He'd never be president, nor would he ever be less than the exceptionally well-paid executive vice president.

When Andi Carter's father was thirty-eight, his wife had run off with a building contractor to begin a new and better life in the Florida Keys. Her father was left in a middle-management bank job with not much in the way of prospects and with no notable assets . . . with one exception.

Her.

A smoking-hot thirteen-year-old, she'd caught the eye of several LaFitte executives and board members. They'd collectively made a deal with her father, and thereafter taught Andi the ways of the world, along with several uncomfortable sexual acts. They eventually (under some duress) pooled money to send her to Wharton, at eighteen, to study finance. Her father, in the meantime, had been promoted into the do-nothing executive vice president position. From which he'd never be promoted or demoted. That's just the way it was, in New Orleans, if you'd whored out your teenaged daughter.

At Wharton, Carter had been told about this extraordinary investment opportunity in a thing called Bitcoin; all the smart kids were talking about it. She'd extracted the necessary money (under some duress) from the bank executives and board members, and though she'd gotten in a little late, it wasn't *too* late. A few years later, she was worth more than all the executives and board members put together. She could have bought the bank, if she'd wanted it.

She didn't.

Now, in the alley with the slightly crazy Andi Carter bending over him, Jack Daniels bled to death, but not instantly. When cut, he'd staggered in a circle, grasping at his neck, his carotid artery slashed open by the razor and furiously pumping out his lifeblood.

When he finally fell, Carter had again looked out toward the street, then dragged the body to the end of the walkway and behind the dumpster there, leaving a long bloody streak on the bricks. It was hard work, made easier by the jolt of adrenaline that was surging through her.

When they were out of sight from the street, she squatted and watched in the harsh illumination of a LED penlight as the last of Daniels' blood trickled out on the bricks. Trickling, not pumping: his heart had stopped.

She gagged once, not because of the blood, but because of the rotten-tomato-sauce and spoiled-banana odors that lingered behind the dumpster. When she was sure he was gone, she took a Sharpie from her purse and wrote a loopy "2" on Daniels' forehead. She packed the penlight in her purse, along with the tissue-wrapped straight razor and the Sharpie, and removed a compact 9mm pistol, just in case—she was not in a good part of Houston.

She walked three blocks to her Panamera, which had a splash of mud across the license plate, obscuring the number. Still wearing the gloves, gun in hand, she made it to the car unmolested, looked at her watch. She'd be back home in New Orleans well before dawn. She took a burner phone from under the front seat, punched in a memorized number, and said, "It's done. Straight razor, his body's behind a dumpster at the side of the Asiatic Hotel."

The woman on the other end said, "A dumpster? That's so delicious."

"The best thing of my life, Vivian," Carter said. "I want to do another."

"That can happen—but we should leave some room for Three, Four, and Five before we go all Lizzie Borden."

"I guess. But move them along, huh?"

"I will."

Carter clicked off. The phone would be dropped on a dark portion of I-10, its parts run over a thousand times before first light. She'd stop on a side street to wipe the mud off her license plate, so a cop wouldn't stop her for that violation, and maybe remember it, if her car had been photographed as it passed near the murder scene. She giggled as she pulled off the blonde wig, threw it in the back seat, and settled down to drive.

That whole thing with the executives and the board members? It had left a mark on her psyche, one not easy to rinse out. Not that she tried too hard.

THE FIVE

We're pleased to announce the death of the second of our designated assholes, U.S. Representative Clayton "Jack" Daniels of Brownsville, Texas. He was a real turd: a man of no morals, a liar, a racist, a deeply corrupt rabble-rouser who opposed the timely imposition of Covid-19 protective measures, a man whose vote in Congress was openly for sale to the highest bidder. He needed to go, for the safety of us all.

One of us cut his throat with a straight razor early this morning—those are not easy to come by, in this day and age—and left his body in the alley behind the Asiatic Hotel in downtown Houston. Note to Houston police: look behind the dumpster. Another note to police: look for Bunny Blue's fingerprints. They should be all over the bed.

We put a numeral "2" on Daniels' forehead and Americans will no longer have to put up with his political and sexual debaucheries.

Again, to make the murder more interesting, each of the Five have placed an untraceable Bitcoin in a wallet with the address sent to the Texas Poverty Law Center, which leads the fight against Texas hate groups. At the time of the donation, each coin was worth $42,320 U.S. dollars for a total of $211,600. Will the TPLC accept the blood money? We shall see. Fun, isn't it?

The Five

(Next up? We're killing a real greedhead!!)

AS CARTER WAS rolling through the night toward New Orleans, Virgil Flowers, an agent of the Minnesota Bureau of Criminal Apprehension, was working late in front of a Lenovo computer. He

looked up from page 388 of a 500-page printed Microsoft Word manuscript that had been edited in red ink, to the same manuscript on the
computer screen. He corrected an on-screen typo and . . .

Quit for the night.

"Jesus." No one awake to hear him. He'd been crouched over the
screen for five hours and his back ached like fire. He stretched,
scratched his head, yawned, and printed out the chapter he'd just
edited.

The printer ran for a while, stopped, signaling that it was out of
paper. Virgil put more High Bright Boise Multi-Use copy paper in the
printer and it started grinding away again. When the last page came
out, he moved the edited paper manuscript to the "done" box on his
desk and saved the electronic manuscript to his local drive, to the
cloud, and to a thumb drive.

He didn't want to do it, but he'd need to print out and read the
whole paper manuscript one last time after he'd edited all five hundred on-screen pages. Doing that, he'd probably find another five
hundred small changes.

He'd learned that if he read the novel on paper, he could more easily spot problems. It was a pain in the ass but had to be done. He
kicked back in his chair and looked at the stack of paper: this one was
good, he thought.

His first effort, the beginner novel, had been naïve. He hadn't
known what he was doing, but he *had* been learning. The second
novel, the practice novel, had been better, but was rejected by a New
York literary agent, though she'd been encouraging.

"You write well," Esther had said, in a thirty-two-second conversation. "You need more complications, more characters, and you need
to spend more time developing them. You need to keep the velocity,

but you do have to spend enough time with the characters to make them three-dimensional."

He'd done that with this third novel.

THE NEXT MORNING, he woke late—he'd been up until two o'clock—and found his girlfriend, Frankie, sitting in the kitchen, feeding the twins and simultaneously reading the *Daily Mail*, the American edition, as she did each morning.

"How'd it go?" she asked.

"Got up to page three hundred eighty-eight on the rewrite. I'll finish the inserts tonight." He got Cheerios from the cupboard and milk from the refrigerator. "One more trip through, and it's gone."

One of the twins poked a Cream of Wheat–covered spoon at him and said, "Da," looked confused for a moment, then went back to her Cream of Wheat. Frankie said, "Good. You're gonna sell this one."

"From your lips to God's ears," Virgil said, settling across the table.

The *Daily Mail* was voracious in its search for the very worst things that happened in the United States each day, and now, Frankie said, "A Texas congressman got his throat cut last night. Somebody wrote a '2' on his forehead."

Eyebrows up: "Like the '1' in San Francisco?"

"Exactly. Press release came out before the cops found the body."

"Fuckin' cops," Virgil said.

"This is gonna be something," Frankie said. "Actually, it already is something. I'll bet you ten American dollars that CNN is all over it this afternoon. *Breaking News!*"

"Fuckin' CNN."

The late nights on the novel left him feeling grumpy.

A WEEK AFTER that, it was Jamie McGruder's turn, the Minnesota ninja warrior in training.

McGruder slipped over the brick wall and duckwalked across ankle-deep snow and past a line of dormant bridal wreath bushes that edged the swimming pool. He was leaving tracks, but the front two inches of his size thirteen boots were stuffed with paper to make them easier to control on his size ten-and-a-half feet.

McGruder was a tall young man with dark hair, gray eyes, and long, feminine eyelashes. He was wrapped in a dark green Givenchy down parka ($2,990 from Nordstrom) along with black gloves and a black ski mask. He was wearing a black Tumi backpack. He was a hard body who worked out an hour every day under the eyes of a personal fitness coach. Until six months earlier, he'd never considered murder, not that he personally had anything against it.

He'd scouted the mansion, inside and out, and knew where the security cameras were located. The closest one was at the corner of the empty swimming pool, but on the far side of the bridal wreath.

The half owner of the house, Anson Sikes, was in New York. His wife, Hillary Sikes, the other half owner, should be on the move, coming home; she rarely left her office later than six o'clock. The housekeeper was in her apartment at the back of the house. He'd seen her shadow on the window shades.

McGruder had never served in the military but had taken a dozen courses from the wannabe tactical schools. He'd trained in knife fighting, sniping, pistol shooting, scuba diving, and evasive driving. He'd learned to spot enemies who were following him, in cars, on motorcycles, or on foot, and he'd learned how to lose them.

He'd spent a year in a boxing gym, where an instructor lied and told him that if he continued to work out for another three years, he'd be ranked in the top ten light-heavies. He'd jumped out of an airplane with a tac pack dangling below him; he had a brown belt in karate and would be a black belt within a year.

In stalking Hillary Sikes, most of that training had proven to be useless, although, he thought, maybe he could use it someday. And he had a pistol in his pack. He was an excellent shot, even if he said so himself.

All that training, but never yet knowing the thrill of an actual kill. Yet.

McGruder moved slowly through the expensive snow-covered landscaping, mostly duckwalking, but sometimes on his stomach, as much for the thrill of it, the ninja vibe, as for concealment. He took a full minute to cross the last open space to the corner of the garage and settle there in the soft snow.

In January 2011, in McGruder's first year at Harvard, he'd turned eighteen and had received the initial payment from the trust set up by his grandfather: one million dollars. He would receive another million at age twenty-one, another at age twenty-five, and the last million at thirty.

At eighteen, the twelve years to age thirty seemed like an eternity, and a million, well, it wasn't really all that much, was it? Not in this day and age. You couldn't exactly go crazy with it, or you'd find yourself broke. His stingy wastrel parents made him pay his college costs from his trust, but okay, he had that covered. What should he do with the rest? Could he use it to make more?

The boy had a gambling gene and he'd heard about this thing called Bitcoin. Some ultrasmart computer nerds told him it was going to be big. In February 2011, Bitcoin reached parity with the U.S. dollar and McGruder thought, what the fuck, what else are you going to do with your money? Buy more shoes? Another guitar? He put a hundred and ten thousand dollars into Bitcoin at $1.10. A hundred thousand bitcoins.

In November 2020, Bitcoin reached $18,000 per coin and he dumped the whole lot, only to curse himself later when Bitcoin got to $60,000. Still, his original investment was worth better than a billion dollars even after he paid his taxes, which he carefully did, and being a self-made billionaire at twenty-eight wasn't all that bad.

Until he got bored.

The band was particularly disappointing. McGruder sang and played rhythm guitar—rhythm guitar because he'd only learned the chords A, C, D, E, G, plus E minor, A minor, and D minor, because they were easy. He simply couldn't do bar chords, which the B and F required, because the strings fell in the cracks of his index finger.

He also wrote some songs, three or four chords each. He thought they were pretty good, until he overheard the bass player, in discussing the music they were playing, refer to him as "the dipshit."

He'd fired her that same night but hadn't since been able to escape the secret feeling that he might *actually be* a dipshit. Even with all the money, the tactical stuff, the karate, the jumping out of airplanes, the high-end pussy. When he was at Harvard, he'd never been one of the guys invited to go out and drink until they were projectile vomiting, or to drive a rental car to Miami and back on a four-day weekend.

Because, he suspected, nobody liked him. Not even his parents—his parents least of all. He couldn't imagine what his mother was thinking when she bore him. Must have thought she was getting some kind of stuffed toy, like you'd win at a carnival.

So here he was, a simmering human soup of resentment, creeping across Hillary Sikes' yard, dressed in dark green and in black. Halfway across, it occurred to him that dark clothing might not be the best camouflage in a snow-covered landscape. Whatever. At the corner of the garage, he pulled off his backpack, slowly, slowly, and extracted a Japanese chef's knife with a fat nine-inch blade. The knife was sharp enough to cut through a thread floating in the air.

McGruder was wearing cross-country ski gloves made of leather and nylon fabric, the better to handle the knife. They were uninsulated and his hands were very cold. He touched his pants pocket and the Sharpie was there. He pulled it out and slipped it into his parka's handwarmer pocket, along with his hands, and waited.

The frigid Minnesota air held no water and he could feel the hair prickling inside his nose as he breathed. Not since the day he'd cashed the Bitcoin had he felt like this, so alive; the tension, the engagement, gripping him like a fist. He could still back out, but everything had gone so well that he didn't believe he would.

There would come a moment, though, when he'd either have to commit, or not. If he didn't, he never would. That moment was coming.

Then it did.

Down the driveway, he saw a flash of light through the inch-wide gap in the security gate panels. A moment later, the gates were fully open and the Lexus SUV rolled up the curving stone driveway as the garage door started up and the interior lights came on. Hillary Sikes slowed as she approached her parking spot. Her summer-only Ferrari

Portofino crouched in an adjacent stall like a crimson bullet; not something she'd want to ding, McGruder thought, so she shouldn't be looking into the rearview mirror.

But you never knew, did you? That you *couldn't know* was part of the thrill. If she saw him, locked the car and called the cops, he'd be in real trouble.

With that thought blundering through his brain, McGruder pulled the pin.

As the car edged into the garage, for a second it blocked the camera that covered the driveway. McGruder lurched forward, duck-walking, at first beside the car. Then, as it drove deeper into the garage, he moved behind it, holding his breath against the exhaust. The garage door rolled down behind him.

The garage was heated and Sikes swiveled and stepped down from the seat of the Lexus, scarlet Manolo Blahnik BB pumps flashing below an ankle-length silver fox coat; the coat was hanging open.

Sikes walked briskly around the back of the car, jingling her car keys, and then opened her mouth to scream as McGruder lurched up and slipped the chef's knife into her chest below the breastbone, angled upward to slice through her heart. He simultaneously slapped a gloved hand over her mouth to smother any scream.

Through the thin leather of his knife-hand glove, he could feel her heart thrashing against the blade. He pressed her against the car and the scream never made it out of the garage. She died there, lying like a murdered silver fox in a puddle of purple blood. McGruder extracted the blade from her chest, wiped it on her blouse, swiveled, dropped it in the pack. Took the Sharpie from his coat pocket and wrote the numeral "3" above Sikes' half-open eyes.

He stood, looked down at her, awaiting the rush: and oddly, he didn't feel much. A deceased woman, lying on a concrete floor. Nothing to do with him . . .

One of her pumps had come off. He picked it up, looked at it in the overhead light, turning it, and then impulsively pulled the pump off her other foot and put them both in his backpack. For the trophy room he'd someday build. Ten seconds later, he was out through the garage access door; moving slowly across a short open space and then behind the bridal wreath, to the wall and over.

The neighborhood, part of the lake country west of Minneapolis, was heavily treed. His car was a quarter mile away, in a lakeside parking lot with two dozen others, kids and parents out on the ice, whacking a puck around. The road was actually a lane, barely wide enough for two cars to pass, trees right down to the edge of the tarmac, with almost no traffic.

He stayed at the very edge of the lane except when a car went by—there was only one—and then he stepped behind a bush where he would be invisible. At the parking lot, he waited until there was no one walking toward a car, then hurried across the lane to his Subaru Outback.

He drove a mile out, stopped on a dark back road to pull the stolen plates off his car. They went across a fence into a snowdrift. Another few miles, he was on I-494, following the loop around the Twin Cities to an intersection with I-94 east of St. Paul. On the way, he took a burner phone out of his pocket and called a number he'd already entered.

The woman on the other end asked, playfully, "How's my boy?"

He said, "Done. With the knife. She was wearing a silver fox fur coat, if you need a detail for the press release. It was soaking up her blood when I left." He didn't mention the shoes.

"How do you feel?"

He thought about it for a moment, then came up with the word: "Ebullient."

AT I-94, MCGRUDER turned east, crossed the St. Croix River into Wisconsin. Forty minutes later, at Menomonie, Wisconsin, the first flakes of snow began bouncing off his windshield. Hadn't counted on snow. He peered up at the sky but could see nothing at all.

By the time he reached Eau Claire, he was driving thirty miles an hour on the interstate, through a tunnel of snow defined by his headlights and by the winking red taillights of a semitrailer ahead of him. He could see an occasional flash of lightning in the sky. He eased around the exit at Eau Claire and headed north.

Driving was still difficult, but he was only going a few blocks up the hill. Now moving at ten miles an hour, alone on the street, he took a left, stopped to look at the street sign to make sure he had it right—he did—and then continued through the business park. Slowing again, he found the building he used as a landmark, then turned onto a dirt trail. Another hundred yards and he saw a pile of broken blacktop, another landmark.

Head down, he got out of the car, took a flashlight from his pack, and checked his location. He needed to pull forward another ten feet, and then make a left turn. He got back in the car and did that.

With the car now wedged between two fifteen-foot piles of dirt, he parked, and again got out into the storm. He had two two-gallon plastic containers of gasoline in the back seat. He got them out, and, hunched against the wildly blowing snow, poured the gas through the passenger compartment.

When he'd finished, he threw the two containers onto the back seat, opened all the windows and doors, took a wadded piece of computer printer paper out of his parka pocket, lit it with a BIC lighter, and threw the burning paper into the car.

The gasoline flashed into roaring flame, singeing his eyebrows. He stepped away, then hurried on foot back the way he'd come. He had a good long trek ahead of him, but he was wearing the world's warmest parka, and with his head bent against the wind, he trudged toward the University of Wisconsin campus.

Overhead, there was a flash and a peal of thunder. Thundersnow usually didn't last long; it hadn't been snowing twenty miles west of Eau Claire, and he believed that like most thunderstorms, this one would be moving east. He'd get to his car, wait the storm out, and then head back to the Cities.

If he pushed it, he might have time to drop by a club. He was well known at a couple of them and they all had security cameras. If he could get his face on a camera, the night of the murder, that'd be icing on the cake.

And he would greatly enjoy himself, and enjoy the mental image of the asshole lying on the cold concrete of her garage floor. He might even try walking around in her shoes that night.

TWO

Murders done by Night People often aren't found until the Day People begin to stir. That was the case with Hillary Sikes. Her housekeeper, who lived in an apartment at the back of the house, got up at 6:30, took a shower and dressed, and headed for the kitchen.

Sikes usually ate two scrambled eggs with Canadian bacon and a cup of vanilla yogurt with strawberry, raspberry, or blueberry jam stirred in. Sikes was an early riser, and the housekeeper could usually hear her thumping around in the bedroom suite—she had a heavy tread.

This morning, the housekeeper heard nothing at all . . . what she thought (later) was a foreboding silence. She went to the bedroom door and knocked.

"Miz Sikes? You know what kind of jam you want in the yogurt?"

No answer.

She tried again: "Miz Sikes?"

No answer.

She pushed open the door, far enough to peek into the bedroom, and saw the bed had been undisturbed since she'd made it the day before.

When she thought about it for a moment, she hadn't heard the television the night before, she hadn't seen lights come on or off . . . though she thought she'd heard the garage door going up and down.

Confused, she went to the garage and looked inside, and saw the Lexus in its normal parking space. She later told the cops she didn't know exactly why she did it, but she walked past the Ferrari to look in the Lexus . . .

And saw the body in its puddle of blood.

She didn't immediately scream. Instead, she walked back into the kitchen, got her cell phone, dialed 9-1-1, and when the operator asked, "Is this an emergency?" she opened her mouth to say "yes," but instead, she began screaming uncontrollably.

She was sitting on the front porch, in minus-ten temperatures, wrapped in nothing but a quilted housecoat and already suffering from hypothermia, when the cops arrived.

VIRGIL FLOWERS WAS hard asleep at 7:45 when his cell phone rang and Frankie groaned, "Damnit. Somebody's dead and it's ten below."

Virgil crawled across both her and Honus the Yellow Dog, who snuck up between them on cold nights, to the nightstand. He picked up his phone and looked at the screen: Jon Duncan, his nominal boss at the Minnesota Bureau of Criminal Apprehension.

He put the phone to his ear and asked, "What?"

"Minnetonka, right now," Duncan said. "You'll need to bring some working clothes in case you have to stay a few days. I'll get you an address and the rest of it as soon as I can."

"Man, I . . ."

"Number Three was killed in Minnetonka."

Virgil could hear the capital letters, but they didn't register for a second. Then he lurched upright: "Not here."

"It's real," Duncan said. "The newsies started getting press releases right after midnight. The feds are on the way, we're on the way. The locals are there but standing back. We need you. I'll see you in Minnetonka."

Virgil had been up late, putting the final touches on his novel. At one o'clock that morning, he'd punched the computer key that would send the manuscript to New York, then lay awake for two hours assailed by thoughts of writerly inadequacy. Now this, with four hours of sleep.

Mostly because of Frankie's interest—she was a news junkie and had an instinct for things that were about to blow up on the media—Virgil had been following the investigations into the two "Five" murders, as they were now being called.

When the first press release had landed in the emails of fifty selected journalists, several of them had called the San Francisco cops on the off chance there was something to it. The San Francisco police spokesman said it was unlikely that anybody would have time to search downtown alleys in the middle of the night, based on an anonymous press release, but they'd get to it as soon as they could.

When they finally did, at six o'clock in the morning, they admitted that there was a dead Duck Wiggins lying in an alley with ligature marks around his neck and the numeral "1" written in black ink on his forehead.

On the second killing, the Houston cops had at first denied knowledge of a murder at the Asiatic, and then—whoops—admitted that there might have been a body there, behind the dumpster.

They refused to identify the body before notification of next of kin, but reporters for the *Houston Chronicle* were told, privately, that the dead man did, in fact, resemble U.S. Representative Clayton "Jack" Daniels. There had been no political meetings at the Asiatic that night; no real reason for Daniels to be there . . . at least none until the police took the tip from the Five. They found the fingerprints of Bonnie "Bunny" Blue, a sometime actress, on the headboard of the bed in the room rented that night by a "Bob Brown."

Blue was mostly known for her pneumatic breasts and a full-frontal nude scene in the Texas thriller movie *Chainsaw Shark-A-Palooza*, in which she was eaten (by sharks).

She didn't deny being in the room Daniels had rented, for cash, under the name Bob Brown, but had no knowledge of what had happened to him after he left the hotel room. The *Daily Mail* was the first with the story, followed by the *Chronicle* and, simultaneously, for some reason, the E! network, which may have paid for a first-person interview. Blue claimed she'd been exploited by the dominant male paradigm of Houston and she planned to sue Daniels' estate.

Daniels' wife said Blue could go fuck herself, if she wasn't too busy fucking everybody else in Houston, and she wasn't getting a dime. In Hollywood, a screenwriter thought the murders might be a concept. He noted the liberal tendency reflected in the press releases and began trying to sell it to Amazon and Netflix as a series to be called *The Antifa Assassins*.

The sensation had not abated when Three was found dead in her Minnesota garage.

Virgil had the best clearance rate in the BCA. Sometimes, when the suits got nervous, his reputation jumped up and bit him on the ass. Virgil told Frankie what Duncan had said and she scrambled off the bed and down the stairs, calling, "It's really cold outside. You'll need a hot breakfast."

Virgil kept a bug-out bag because he often travelled on short notice. After a fast shower and shave, he added a dressy blue cashmere sweater he'd gotten for Christmas, and a Glock semi-automatic pistol, to the top of the bag, pulled on a pair of Vasque winter hiking boots, and headed down the stairs.

The farmhouse had been built in the 1940s, a couple of years after World War II, and the kitchen smelled like all the soups that had been made there since; it currently still held the lingering odor of the balsam fir they'd put up for Christmas and left up until after New Year's. In his spare time, Virgil, along with Frankie's older kids, had done some modest modernizing, mostly out of sight. The well water no longer smelled of ancient cow manure.

"Eat," Frankie said. "Cream of Wheat with brown sugar and half and half. I made extra coffee and got out the Yeti bottle. Three! I mean . . . You're gonna be famous."

"We're not there, yet," Virgil said.

He was a tall man, lanky, casual, blue-eyed with blond hair worn too long for a BCA agent; he had smile lines on his cheeks and a few worry lines on his forehead. He might have been a surfer, if Minnesota had surf.

He worked out of his home office, covering the southern third of Minnesota, with the authority to call on the St. Paul headquarters for backup when he needed it. He ate three-fourths of the Cream of Wheat and gave the rest of it to Honus, who sat quietly drooling on the floor next to his boots.

Frankie said, "Number Three. I'll probably be on the network morning shows—Virgil Flowers' paramour—to tell them how modest you are and how you broke it. Maybe that red silk blouse with the cleavage. Something hot."

Frankie was a short, busty blonde with the face of a fallen angel, who salvaged old buildings for a living. She and Virgil, cooperating, had produced the set of twins, one of each, and someday might get married. Frankie insisted on hearing about Virgil's murder cases, in detail, with an emphasis on the blood shed by the villains, as she called them.

"Everything you wear is hot," Virgil said, "Because you're in it." He got his parka, ski hat, and winter gloves, kissed her goodbye. "This is gonna be a mess."

One of the twins began to cry in the second upstairs bedroom and then Sam, Frankie's twelve-year-old son by another father, came out of his first-floor bedroom rubbing his eyes, looking cranky, and asked, "What the fuck is going on?"

"Say 'fuck' again and I'll kick your ass up around your ears," Virgil said. "I'll see you guys when I see you."

Sam scratched his stomach and said, "Shoot somebody for a change, huh?"

"Don't forget the Yeti," Frankie said, and Virgil snagged the bottle as he went out the door.

A thermometer on the back porch said it was seven degrees below zero. Virgil crunched across the crystalline snow to the garage, backed his Tahoe out, and pointed it north toward the Twin Cities.

The farm had recently been expanded to include a stable, a barn, and two horses. A forever-uncelebrated side effect of the Three murder was that Virgil wouldn't be shoveling horseshit on this particular morning.

Which was good, because it was frosty. A weather forecast from a local radio station predicted temperatures would rise to three degrees above zero by noon, before falling again. The fields around the house were covered by a thin coat of snow, with a shiny, frozen surface that glittered orange when the sun peeked over the horizon.

They hadn't had snow for three weeks, and not much then, just missing a storm that had hit the Twin Cities two days earlier. The drive north to the Cities was uneventful, on mostly clear highways, much of it following the Minnesota River north, the river marked by a bosque of barren gray trees. At one point, outside the town of St. Peter, he saw a murder of crows dive-bombing one of the trees, and assumed an owl was lurking there, the mortal enemy of corvids everywhere.

The snow had gotten deeper as he drove north, showing signs of drifting by the time he crossed the I-494 ring highway. Duncan called again, with an address and information about the victim, Hillary Sikes, and told him to drive faster. Virgil arrived at Sikes' home at nine o'clock, an hour and a half after the first call from Duncan. At a checkpoint a block out from the house, a local cop checked his ID and waved him through.

Sikes' driveway looked like a police union convention, a dozen cops in and around the driveway in groups of two and three, all wearing Covid masks, and pumping gouts of steam into the frigid air as they talked. Virgil found a parking spot up the narrow street, put on a mask, and walked back.

Lucas Davenport, an old friend and a U.S. Marshal, had his butt propped against the front fender of an SUV. He was wearing a blue Patagonia parka with the hood down, jeans, boots, sunglasses, and a mask. He nodded when he saw Virgil coming.

Virgil said, "So?"

"Crime scene still at work," Lucas said. "Body was found by the live-in housekeeper who got up at six-thirty and wondered why nobody had slept in the victim's bed. She looked in the garage and called the cops. The cops called the BCA, and the BCA called the FBI. Looks like Sikes was stabbed to death by somebody who knew where the security cameras were. He came over the side wall, crawled along the bushes by the swimming pool and then waited by the garage door."

"Tracks in the snow?"

"Guy had long, narrow feet. Or long narrow shoes," Lucas said. "Might have been dropped off and then picked up by the wall, so there could be two people involved."

"Other security cameras?"

"Looking into it, but the houses here are set back in the woods and have driveways that curve up through a lot of trees. The cameras are on the houses, and don't monitor the road."

"You look pretty relaxed," Virgil said.

"I'm not standing in front of a media firing squad, like some people," Lucas said, with a grin. "This is gonna be a shit show."

Lucas was as tall as Virgil, with a heavier build, blue eyes, dark hair shot with gray at the temples. A scar tracked across his forehead from hairline to eyebrow, then continued on a cheek, the result of a fishing accident.

Like Virgil, he'd been a college jock, a hockey defenseman versus Virgil's third-baseman. They'd both gone to the University of

Minnesota, Lucas twelve years earlier than Virgil. Lucas had once been Virgil's boss at the BCA, a status that had never impressed either of them.

"Okay, I know why I'm here," Virgil said. "Why are you here?"

"I got a call from Porter Smalls," Lucas said. Smalls was a U.S. senator from Minnesota. He and the other Minnesota U.S. senator, Elmer Henderson, had conspired to get Lucas appointed as a deputy U.S. Marshal, partly because they liked him and considered him a law enforcement asset, and partly because they could use him. "Sikes was one of his larger donors."

"Good to know this is going to be a clean, well-run operation without political interference," Virgil said.

Lucas nodded at the cluster of cops in the driveway and said, "Here comes your boss."

Jon Duncan shouldered his way through the crowd. Like Lucas and Virgil, he was wearing a parka, jeans, boots, and a mask. Unlike them, he sported a Russian-style fur-trimmed hat with the side flaps tied down over his ears, which exponentially increased his nerd factor. He knew that, and it bothered him not in the slightest, because he was warm. He nodded at Lucas and said to Virgil, "We might turn you around and send you home—the feds are being obstreperous. Anyway, you ought to look at this."

"What is it?"

Duncan handed Virgil a piece of paper that had been folded over twice, and then sat upon in a car, so it held a butt-curve. "A press release from the Five. You need to read it to get the full favor."

Virgil unfolded the paper and glanced at Lucas. "You've seen it?"

"Yes," Lucas said. "It'll piss you off. Fuckin' posers."

THE FIVE

We have struck again, as Batman might say, and another asshole is on his—Did we say *his*? We meant *her*—way to Hell. This time, we visited the Twin Cities, as we're sure our beloved Twin Cities law enforcement community will discover tomorrow morning.

This particular body is in her garage. We stuck her in the heart with a butcher knife and left her lying in a puddle of blood, currently being absorbed, or possibly, sopped up, as the vulgar might say, by her silver fox coat. Pity the poor foxes, we pray you, but not this particular asshole. She was well known both for her insatiable greed, single-handedly putting dozens of workers on the streets, and for her right-wing-crazy politics.

So that's Three. We're tracking Four as we write. Good day to you gentleman and gentlewomen, and please, try to be fair—these people really are gargantuan assholes.

The Five

P.S. Once again, the Five have donated one Bitcoin each, now worth a total of $218,050, and have sent the wallet's address to the Northern Reach Garden Co-Op, for reasons that will become apparent.

Virgil finished reading and nodded. "It's like the *Washington Post* says: snide, college educated, politically liberal, knows the difference between 'lying' and 'laying,' capitalizes 'Hell' as a proper noun. Probably rich if he can tell the difference between a mink and a silver fox on the fly. Or, it could be a 'she,' I guess."

"Doubt it," Lucas said.

"The FBI probably has fifty experts arguing about the difference between 'lying' and 'laying' right now," Duncan said. And, to Virgil, "You want to look at the body?"

"Will I learn anything?" Virgil asked.

"No, but . . ."

"I know. 'Always look at the body.' I think Lucas is responsible for that particular commandment," Virgil said, tipping his head toward Lucas. "I first heard it at the BCA."

"That was me," Lucas said. "Gets your heart rate up. The murder stops being theoretical. Look in their eyes, if they're open."

"Then we should look," Virgil said.

"I already did. I didn't learn anything," Lucas said. "There's a tank of hot coffee in that Minnetonka squad. I'll get you one, if you want a cup."

"I got a bottle of it in the truck," Virgil said. "Don't go away."

Duncan led the way through the crowd to the garage, which was built of gray limestone from ground level to shoulder height, and from there up, was finished in wooden shingles. The back wall was covered with pegboard on which were mounted rakes, hoes, a sickle, manual hedge cutters, and an empty golf club travel bag.

Four cars were parked in a line, with two side-by-side overhead doors: a gunmetal-gray Lexus SUV, a red Ferrari, a black Mercedes SUV, and a reddish-orange Porsche Carrera Turbo. A group of cops were discussing whether the Ferrari and Porsche should be seized as evidence, and if so, who'd get to drive them to the impound lot.

Sikes' body was on the concrete floor behind the Lexus, a lush fur coat open beneath her, a congealing puddle of blood beneath it. Her face was almost paper-white in death, strong rather than pretty, with blunt features and a mouth that naturally turned down into a grimace. Her teeth were just visible between pale, slightly parted lips; she had a diastema. She had hair the color of last year's wheat straw, cut efficiently, rather than fashionably.

"She was stabbed, once, big knife, below the sternum, angling up to the heart, like the press release said. The guy knew what he was doing," Duncan said.

Virgil looked at the body for fifteen seconds, learned nothing useful. He could smell the blood. He'd once worked with a female homicide cop who described the scent of drying blood and the off-gassing of dead-body odors as "icky." Virgil had never come up with a better word for it: a sickly, fleshy smell, with a hint of copper.

He found the sight of her depressing and felt the first stir of anger. As an investigator who did murders out in the countryside, he'd seen far worse—decomposed bodies not found for days or weeks, crawling with flies and maggots. Still, he felt a touch of nausea from the sight and smell of Sikes, the icky odor of death mixed with a hint of a flowery perfume and the grate of car exhaust.

Lucas and Virgil were each other's closest male friends, in the way men form friendships around shared traumatic stress and a predilection for jockstraps. Though they were friends, they were not alike.

Lucas could look at a body and become immediately absorbed in the technical details of the death: how the killing had been done, possible motives, who had the opportunity. He saw murder as a puzzle. The body was a detail, but not the only one. Murder signaled a competition that he was determined to win.

Virgil sought balance, rather than a victory. He wanted to wrench his world back into what it should be, a peaceful place where people cooperated to create a civilization. He disliked violence and rarely resorted to it. Murder was always a shock to his system.

He was angered and disgusted by the sight of Sikes sprawled on the cold concrete of her garage. Lucas was . . . interested.

As he stepped away from Sikes' body, Virgil said, "We're gonna have to deal with the feds. They got the gun, here."

"Sometimes I hate those guys," Duncan said.

"Yeah, well . . . I saw a couple guys in long overcoats by the front door. Like movie Gestapo. I assume . . ."

"Yeah. FBI," Duncan said. "If you got to play with them, please, play nice, Virgie. They've got all the details from One and Two, which we might need, if we get involved here."

LUCAS WAS DRINKING coffee from a plastic cup when they got back to him, and he asked Duncan, "Did Sikes have any protection? Bodyguards? She's really rich . . ."

"Not as far as I know," Duncan said. "There were pump shotguns inside the front hall closet and a back closet next to the door from the garage. Another one in a second-floor dressing room. All three were loaded but had empty chambers."

"Do we know if she'd been warned of anything coming?" Virgil asked.

"The FBI contacted her husband—he's in New York, now on his way back—and he says they were not," Duncan said. "No indication that she was a target."

Lucas: "What about the political thing?"

"Snowmobilers for Trump on Facebook. She's said some pretty goddamned outrageous stuff," Duncan said. "She thought Trump was going to be reinstated as President as soon as Biden was convicted of child molestation. That's what she said, anyway."

"Any reason to think the killer is local?" Virgil asked.

"All three killings have a local feel to them—like the killer knew his way around. On the other hand, they could have come from New Jersey or Utah," Duncan said. "She was hated by a lot of people and they're not all local."

Virgil: "Because . . ."

"Her business. She created SPACs, S-P-A-C," Duncan said, spelling it out. "SPAC stands for Special Purpose Acquisition Company. It's like a free-floating bunch of money that investors give you. Then you go out and buy something that's worth a lot more than you're paying for it and you split the eventual take with your investors. Apparently, somebody always gets screwed."

"I know one of them," Lucas said. "There was a warehouse kind of place in St. Paul, off West Seventh Street, that was used by a Korean company to assemble small electric appliances."

"I had a shooting there when I was working for St. Paul," Virgil said.

"Yeah? Anyway, it's the only piece of private property on that side of the road, and it's right above a lake . . ."

The warehouse had a long history of manufacturing different small appliances, mostly junk, Lucas said. Sikes' lawyers found that she could buy the business, and the zoning would allow her to replace the building with anything she wanted, as long as it was less noxious than an assembly plant. She created a SPAC, got thirty million together, according to the *Pioneer Press*, bought the plant, tore it down, and was in the process of putting in four lakefront apartment buildings when she was murdered.

"Although," Lucas said, "It's really more like swamp-front."

Virgil: "And?"

"Kicked three hundred low-income, twelve-dollar-an-hour people out of their jobs," Lucas said. "Just, 'Hit the road.' No compensation, no nothing. There was a media fuss at the time, but that went away soon enough."

Virgil: "Then it probably is local."

Duncan: "Maybe. She's had heavy attention in the social media, both for the SPACs—there were several of them—and the snowmobiler stuff. They had a 'Circle the Lake for Trump' thing up at Mille Lacs, the last two Decembers, supposedly a thousand snowmobilers. I haven't seen it, but I've been told there's an anti-Sikes Facebook page. Maybe it's still there, I dunno."

The cops who'd been looking at the Ferrari and Porsche suddenly broke into laughter, and then just as quickly stopped, looked around, mildly embarrassed to be laughing at a murder scene with the body still uncovered and basically underfoot. Only mildly embarrassed.

"What's this Northern Reach that's supposed to get the Bitcoin money?" Virgil asked.

"The victims of another SPAC deal," Duncan said. "She bought up a big parcel along the river north of Minneapolis that was being rented to a truck-garden co-op. Fifty-some farmers out of business, the ones selling at the farmers' markets around town."

"Oh, boy." Virgil rubbed his nose, looked at Lucas: "The killer could have come from anywhere that has Facebook. He leaves no trace of himself as far as we know, except that he has long narrow feet. Or shoes. So, basically, after an in-depth analysis, I'd say we're fucked."

"Not us, so much, as the feds," Duncan said. "They've taken over. They might need somebody to do the scut work, but they'll be doing the heavy lifting, brains-wise."

"Brains-wise. I wish I'd said that," Virgil said.

"We need to talk to them," Lucas said. "Maybe they won't want us around. They're good at all kinds of things—better than we are."

"But we're better at other stuff," Virgil said. "Like the scut work that usually makes the case."

"There is that," Lucas agreed.

One of the FBI agents came out on the home's wide stone front porch and called something down to another agent who was sitting in a black SUV. Duncan, watching him, asked, doubtfully, "They can do things better?"

"Some things," Lucas said. "Who's running this circus? Has anybody seen St. Vincent?"

"He's inside," Duncan said. "That'd be our best shot at a quick meet."

David St. Vincent was the Minneapolis agent in charge. Lucas, Virgil, and Duncan ambled over to the porch, looked up at the FBI agent, who was wearing a knee-length wool coat nowhere near as warm as a down parka, and Lucas called, "We need to talk to David."

The agent looked down at them: "You're Davenport."

"Yeah. And this is Virgil Flowers, BCA, and Jon Duncan is coordinating for the BCA."

"Let me talk to Agent St. Vincent," the agent said. "I'll be right back."

And he was: thirty seconds after he went inside, the agent was back and said, "Give him five minutes. He's on the phone to Washington. He wants to talk with you."

While they waited for the agent in charge, Virgil, Lucas, and Duncan went back to the garage to watch the crime scene people work.

Duncan said, "They've been all over the car. Doesn't look like the killer touched it."

One of the crime scene techs, a middle-aged woman named Cheryl, turned and said, "If one more of you jerkoffs steps in that snow, I'll shoot you myself."

"You looking for DNA?" Duncan asked.

"Of course. I've got low hopes," Cheryl said.

"Can you get it off snow?" They all looked at the body-sized depression in the snow at the corner of the garage.

"Gotta say that's unlikely," Cheryl said. "I mean, if there was blood, or snot . . . or if he drooled in the snow. I don't see anything obvious. He did lie down in a couple of places and melted into the snow a little. We're trying to document the impressions."

She nodded at a guy with a LED light panel and a camera with a wide-angle lens.

Lucas turned, looked up and down the street, and said to Duncan, "You know what? We gotta knock on doors."

"Yeah."

"Gotta be a camera somewhere that sees the road," Virgil said. "My navigation system says it's a half mile along the lane, on either side of the house, before you get to an intersection."

They were still chatting when David St. Vincent came out on the porch and called, "Jon Duncan: bring your guys up."

St. Vincent was a short man with a fifties-style flattop, tortoise-shell-framed glasses, a chiseled chin, and a missing pinky finger, which Lucas happened to know was congenital, rather than the product of an accident. He was wearing a blue wool suit, white shirt, burgundy necktie, and a mask.

When Lucas, Virgil, and Duncan climbed the porch, he said, as they all shook hands with him, "C'mon inside, get warm."

They followed him inside, down a short hallway between two coat closets, and into an expansive living room with a bloodred carpet, mid-century furniture in colors coordinated with the carpet, and a bookcase built in sections on both sides and above a bar. One wall had an expressionistic oil painting of a horse, and from the way it was displayed, Lucas assumed that it was what art people called "important."

Two masked FBI agents were perched on a beige sofa with briefcases by their feet; one was typing on a laptop, the other was on a cell phone.

St. Vincent said, "We need your help—mostly with crime scene."

"Everything we've got," Duncan offered.

"Thank you. We'll reciprocate. We're coordinating the results of the investigations in California and Texas and we'll be adding yours to it. Plus we're doing our own research with the serial killer team."

"Do we know for sure that Sikes isn't a copycat?" Virgil asked. "That it's the Five group?"

"Yes. I assume you've seen their so-called press release? It came in to their list of reporters at midnight last night, seven hours before the body was found. They included a copy to the moderator of the Five channel on Facebook. She got so excited she tried to call the White House. Already got more than a million followers, or whatever you call them. I got woken up at one o'clock to warn me that this was coming. Didn't mention Sikes' name, but the rest of the detail is right," St. Vincent said. "With this, I'll tell you, things are about to get seriously ugly."

"It's already ugly," Lucas said.

"About a three on a scale of one to ten. This will push it to seven. If there's a fourth murder, the ugly will be off the scale," St. Vincent said. "Thank God this wasn't another politician, or the wingers would be going nuts. Get 2020 started all over again."

Lucas: "I got a call from a politician."

"I'm not surprised," St. Vincent said. He knew about Lucas' relationship with the Minnesota senators. "In any case, this is what we propose: everybody does everything. Don't worry about conflicts. If you're about to do something that will attract media attention, we'd appreciate a heads-up. Then go for it."

"I'm not sure at this point what we can go for," Duncan said. "I've read the reports out of Houston and San Francisco, and they were mostly notable for not coughing up any leads at all. No video, no DNA, no witnesses, no known connections between killer and victims . . ."

"That's correct, but we haven't dug deep enough," St. Vincent said. "These people are more reminiscent of a terrorist group than an ordinary gang. One thing seems clear to us: the victims were not only researched, they were scouted. Stalked. The stalker was seen, by somebody. They might not realize it, but somebody saw this guy."

"Have your computer people been looking at the sources of the emails?" Virgil asked.

"Of course. We're holding this close, but the emails come from a never-before-used Gmail account. They use it once and then not again. The next email comes from a different Gmail account and there are literally millions of Gmail accounts. The emails all come from the same computer. Unfortunately, it's an old Apple, sold long ago, then traded at a defunct used-computer place where nobody kept track of who bought what. It's a very cleverly crafted dead end."

"They've been thinking about this for a while," Virgil said.

"Yes."

Lucas: "Their press releases say they're all rich, and there's a hint the money might have come from Bitcoin investments. Have you guys . . ."

St. Vincent was nodding: "The problem is, one of the chief characteristics of Bitcoin is its anonymity, which is why criminals like it so much, and tax evaders. And IRS confidentiality rules don't help . . . we want them to cough up whatever they have on big Bitcoin winners, but they won't do it. We have to specify a name and then get a subpoena to get his or her records. Of course, a lot of the Bitcoin winners aren't hiding, they're bragging. We've got a list of those guys. There's more than a thousand names on it right now."

"That's tough," Duncan said. "Especially since you know the list is incomplete, and the ones you're missing are probably the biggest crooks."

St. Vincent nodded: "Yup."

"VIRGIL AND I will be knocking on doors," Lucas said. "Because that's all we got."

St. Vincent ticked a finger at him: "I believe that's about the best thing you could do right now, Lucas. We need cops talking to local residents. *Somebody* saw the killer. Somebody did. I'd rather have local law enforcement pushing that angle, than my agents."

BACK OUTSIDE, LUCAS said to Virgil, "Never heard anything quite like that, not from the FBI."

"Don't give him too much credit," Duncan said. "He wants local law enforcement to do it because his agents are too valuable to be knockin' on doors."

Virgil looked back at the porch, where St. Vincent was watching them go; he raised a hand and Virgil raised his. To Lucas: "We knockin'?"

"We knockin'," Lucas said. "Doesn't seem right for cops as high-powered as us, but that's what we're doing." He looked at the crowd of cops in the driveway. "We can get some local uniforms to walk with us."

Virgil checked his iPhone for the time. "Ten o'clock. Meet you back here. Get lunch."

"If you guys get the slightest sniff of anything, call me," Duncan said. "I'll be wired into everybody by then. Now, I gotta go kick some crime scene ass. They need to produce something."

"If they can't?" Virgil asked.

Duncan, grim-faced: "Then they're not working hard enough."

THREE

Vivian Zhao was short and thin with intelligent dark eyes and a way of talking to a person with her head half-turned away, but her eyes cut back to the person's face. She wore one tiny piece of silver jewelry, a simple loop that pierced the side of her left nostril. Her nails were always chewed short.

Zhao's hair fell to her shoulders and she did nothing with it: she called it her witch hair and most mornings, however it was when she woke, was the way it stayed for the day. She had tattoos never seen by anyone but her few lovers: they started below her collarbones and stopped above her knees. Her body between her collarbones and knees was a tangled universe of Japanese manga cartoons, a little color but mostly black, white, and gray.

Zhao had been a PhD candidate in economics until the process had become too boring to tolerate further. Everything was boring except, perhaps, money, of which she had little.

And murder. Murder wasn't boring.

It had become apparent during her economics coursework that much of the sand in the gears of America—and the grit in ordinary life, for that matter—was created by assholes. Specifically by assholes.

She could think of no more salient term for them. They were human scum who went through the world hurting others, with not a whit of conscience to be stirred. They weren't necessarily criminals, because the assholes in state legislatures, the Congress, and the presidency had bent and twisted the criminal laws to protect themselves. Everybody knew it; nobody knew what to do about it. The assholes held the levers of power.

They kept the American mushrooms—the people kept in the dark and fed bullshit—struggling toward all their individual concepts of freedoms: the right to own any gun you wanted, for the gun nuts; the right to abortion, for the feminists; fetal rights, for the anti-abortion crowd; the right of universal equality, for the progressives; the right to smoke weed, for the dopers.

It was all bullshit, Zhao thought. There was only one thing that got you real freedom: wealth. Money. With enough money, you could get anything you needed, anytime you needed it. You could get away with actual crimes for years, if you had enough money to protect yourself.

Zhao's money hunger had led her to a Bitcoin convention in Los Angeles. She'd gotten a low-paid speaking gig, in which she'd been introduced as "Dr. Vivian Zhao," although she had never finished her thesis. She hadn't corrected the convention's organizers. She hadn't bothered to tell them that her objective was to find somebody rich, cut him or her out of the crowd, and get some of that cash.

Her speech—"Get Out! No Taxes and the Good Life Elsewhere!"—had been well attended. During the cocktail party at the end of the day, she'd encountered George Sonnewell.

Sonnewell was standing alone, a big man with hooded eyes, a powerful neck and shoulders. A bull. He had a glass of bourbon in his hand, looking solid as a rock, and at the same time, innocent and lost. She'd approached with an inane comment about the attendance. He ignored that and told her he never wanted to leave the United States, not even to save his Bitcoin fortune.

"I love this country too much. I'd never leave. I admit that it doesn't work anymore," he told her. "The assholes are tearing it down. They're everywhere. I'll tell you what needs to be done: we need to start killing them. If we kill enough of them, maybe the rest will get the point."

With an impulse that she never quite understood, Zhao reached out and grasped the coat sleeve of this nerdish ex–farm boy and said quietly, "I totally agree. What you said . . . I've been waiting for somebody to say that. It's so obvious, but I never really thought of it that way. Maybe we should . . . begin."

He'd looked around and instead of fleeing, he'd asked, "Have you met Andi Carter?"

That was the beginning.

By chaining through the members of the ABC—American Bitcoin Council—they'd found two dozen members who had reached the same conclusion and seemed ready to act on it. But most weren't, not really. When the talk grew specific, about tactics, weapons, and targets, the recruits began dropping out. Two at first, then three more, then another, and another.

The talk, the planning, had been done inside dark web chat rooms set up by Zhao, using a software package called DesKreet. As members dropped out, she'd delete the old room and set up a new one, unknown to those who'd left. When they'd gotten down to five people, plus Zhao, it seemed they'd reached the necessary level of commitment in all of the members.

For security reasons, none of the five knew the identity of the other members of the final group except Zhao, and Zhao knew all five of them by name. When they'd gotten deep into their planning, they'd asked her to prove her commitment. That she wasn't simply hustling them, maybe setting them up for blackmail. Of Zhao and her five recruits, she was the only one who wasn't unreasonably, Bitcoin-filthy rich.

Zhao suggested a victim, a hedge fund operator named Josh Roper, known for his investments in West Coast slums, which, he bragged, returned sixty-five percent annually. The other five agreed he should be dealt with.

After weeks of research, scouting, and discussion in the chat room, Zhao killed him in his driveway on a cool Sunday morning in April. The six knew many things about the victim, and one really interesting thing: he got up at dawn on Sunday mornings, put on a dressing gown, walked out to the gate that protected his driveway, opened it a crack, stepped through, and recovered the *New York Times* from where the delivery man had thrown it.

The gate opened to the left. Zhao was standing to the left, behind the gate as it opened. The victim stooped to pick up the paper and Zhao shot him three times in the back of the head, and then twice more to be absolutely sure he was dead. She filmed the killing with a GoPro camera and posted it in the chat room.

Then the other five believed. None of them mentioned death, or murder. Their questions tended to the technical: "Where'd you get a silenced pistol?" and "How'd you choose a .22? Wouldn't a nine-millimeter have been more certain?"

"Suppressors are not hard to find, thanks to the assholes," she answered. "Those of you planning to use guns should ask around. You'll see."

The other five:

George Sonnewell hated what the street people had done to San Francisco. Andi Carter hated the greedy, grasping redneck politicians who'd played games with the bankers who'd taken her to bed a hundred times over. Jamie McGruder wasn't strong enough to hate but wanted to try killing someone because he was crazy. Killing an asshole seemed like a good idea and he picked one that made Zhao and the others happy. Bill Osborne was a black man, made rich by a timely investment in Bitcoin, who hated the gun dealers who were turning his beloved hometown of Cleveland into a war zone; and he knew of one who assembled ghost guns, and sold them to children. Marty Meyer's great-grandparents and most of their offspring had died at Auschwitz; he hated fascists and saw them everywhere on the rise. He had his eye on a right-wing talk show host known for his incessant promotion of every absurd right-wing lie.

Since the five recruits had decided not to reveal their real names to each other, they'd chosen airport codes as pseudonyms. SFO was San Francisco and Sonnewell, JFK was New York and Meyer, CLE was Cleveland and Osborne, MSY was New Orleans and Carter, MSP was Minneapolis–St. Paul and McGruder.

When their group had been reduced to the final Bitcoin five plus one—Zhao—with everyone committed to killing, they spent hours online together, working out methods of murder. Their watchword was "analysis," as in "We need more analysis" of this or that. They talked about weapons, about getaways, about evidence, about the tactics used by prosecution and defense attorneys so they could manipulate their killings to the benefit of the defense, should they get caught.

They looked at one another's choices of victims, suggested changes and dangers. They read thriller novels, most of which were useless, though some made interesting points about gunfire. They reviewed true crime stories, looking at the failures of other murderers, and how those failures might be avoided. They read police reports and learned how to buy dark web police scanners that could hear encrypted digital radio traffic.

While all five recruits knew Zhao, none of them knew for sure who the other four members of the Bitcoin group were, even though they'd all met at ABC conventions at one time or another. Meyer thought Osborne was a member and Sonnewell was almost sure that Carter was. The other three members had no idea of who anyone else was, and Meyer and Sonnewell were only guessing.

At the end, they felt . . . itchy. Carter had used the term. "I'm feeling . . . itchy. Got the urge to actually do something. If we're really going to do this, who's going first among the five of us richies? Somebody has to be first."

"I'll do it," said the man they knew as SFO.

Then he did.

And Carter followed.

Then McGruder.

FOUR

T he Minnesota murder had taken place on the frozen banks of
Lake Minnetonka, in the tiny town of Woodland, covered by
police from the neighboring tiny town of Deephaven. Lucas and
Virgil found the Deephaven police chief and got uniformed officers
assigned as partners in the door-knocking expedition.

The Sikes place sat at the outside of a ninety-degree turn in the
lane, with iced-up lakeshore behind the house at the bottom of a
shallow slope. Lucas and his partner took the west leg of the lane,
while Virgil took the north.

They were plodding and they both knew it but couldn't take a
chance of missing something. Since it was a workday, most of the
houses were empty. The others were occupied by people who worked
at home, retirees, and women who wouldn't have identified themselves as housewives.

Lucas' partner was named Mark Corian, a tall bulky man with pink cheeks and blue eyes, whose layer of fat would help protect him from the winter chill that might claw its way beneath his police parka. He asked, "We walkin'?"

"Think it'd be faster to drive?" Lucas asked.

"No, but it'd be a hell of a lot warmer."

"Good point."

Lucas was driving a Porsche hybrid SUV, and they took that. The first stop was a half block down the street. "Louis and Betty-Anne Carpenter. Both lawyers. I know them. Nice folks," Corian said.

They weren't home. There were cameras on the house, but they didn't cover the street.

Next house. "Don't know these folks, sign says Bartley," Corian said. They left the car at the bottom of the driveway, walked a hundred feet up to the porch. The house was buried in what amounted to a forest. They knocked: nobody home.

Lucas said, "Camera." He pointed at a camera mounted on the corner of the garage. "Can't see the street."

Back in the car, Lucas said, "Damn good thing we took the car. I got cold walking up the driveway."

"Told'ja," Corian said. "Supposed to be cold all week. Then we fall off the edge. Could be twenty below, middle of next week."

"I'm looking forward to it," Lucas said. "I plan to stay inside."

In an area that had about one reported crime a year, all of the houses had cameras and some of them had multiple cameras. They talked to a retired man who invited them in and showed them a glass case full of quartz-crystal watches in the living room, all synchronized to the second. Other than that, he had nothing.

An elderly woman had a thousand pounds of yarn in a bedroom, which she showed them with pride. She offered to knit them sweaters or scarves, but Lucas explained that as police officers, they couldn't accept gifts; and no, she had no idea what had happened to Sikes.

"She was a real pain in the posterior," the woman said cheerfully. "In the summertime, she used to tear around in that red car of hers. Sounded like a tornado was coming. I'm not surprised she was murdered. The world has only so much room for people like her, and occasionally, one of them has to go. Sort of like these Five people say."

She was correct, but Lucas didn't tell her so.

As they walked away from the house, Corian asked, "Why do you think the FBI is so hot about this? I mean, okay, there's a conspiracy that crosses state lines, but . . . they seemed completely skizzed out. For dead assholes."

"Nobody cares that assholes are being killed," Lucas said. "Dozens of people are murdered every day in the U.S., a lot of them good innocent people. What's intolerable to the FBI is the direct challenge to their authority. The media's been playing with that, and the feds can't take it."

"You're probably right," Corian said, in a glum voice. "Gotta take care of Number One, or the politicians might cut your salary."

FIFTEEN HOUSES DOWN the street, they got to Charlotte Roe, who lived in an ultramodern three- or four-story home that looked like a collection of intersecting cubes, lots of glass, exposed steel beams. During the course of the interview, Roe told them that she was a master gardener, yoga instructor, licensed aroma therapist, certified sommelier, and published poet.

Lucas and Corian were not quite hypothermic when she came to the door, eleven o'clock in the morning, already exercising her wine enthusiasm. She invited them in, sat too close to Lucas while ignoring Corian, and told him in the first fifteen seconds that she was a widow.

Her house was overheated and smelled faintly of cats, one of which, a red tabby, showed up to stare at Lucas, but not Corian. Roe offered them a delicious California chardonnay, which they declined, and then she said, "It's probably nothing."

"I'll take anything," Lucas said, parked on a wine-dark sofa.

"Well. You know this is an affluent neighborhood. Quite affluent. And also, quite contained. We don't have random sightseers going through."

"I could see that," Lucas said. He took off his gloves and flexed his fingers. They were white with the cold. Behind Roe's head was a painting that looked expensive and probably French, since America hadn't had picturesque peasants, until recently.

She said, "Yes. Quite affluent. My late husband was a *very* successful commercial real estate dealer. He did *very* well . . . until he died in a tragic mountain bike accident."

"Here in Minnesota?" Lucas asked.

"Right here in this house," Roe said. "He had a home bicycle repair shop down in the basement. His hobby. He was doing something with a drill-thingy, and he electrocuted himself."

"Really."

"Yes." She sniffed. "He never cried out. Nothing. The first I knew he was gone was when . . ." Another sniff. ". . . I smelled burning hair."

"That must have been awful," Lucas said, stifling a yawn.

"That's the most tragic story I've ever heard," Corian said, wide-eyed and sincere. "I wasn't on duty, but I remember that. Three or four years back, right at the end of summer."

Roe's attention drifted toward the uniform. "Yes, that was it. I often think of that day . . . actually, I published a poem . . ."

Lucas: "About the thing that's probably nothing?"

"Oh. Well, as I was saying, this is an affluent neighborhood," Roe said. "If you have only one million, liquid, you're considered trailer trash. So, everybody has household help. The thing about household help is, they get out of here between three and five, unless they're live-in. Hillary had a live-in. The people in this neighborhood know the live-ins, too. See them all the time."

"All right."

"In the last week or so, I've seen this car," Roe said. "In the evenings, after dark. It's not the kind of car the residents here drive. It's not one of the live-ins, unless it's a new one, and I haven't heard of any new ones. But it's something the help would drive. I mean, around here, it's Mercedes, Porsche, Land Rover. The Sikes have a Ferrari and a 911. I personally have a Mini and a Cadillac. This car I noticed . . . I first saw it when I was coming back from the Nez d'Vin. I don't know the kind, but I *think* it was one of those lesbian cars."

Lucas: "Lesbian cars?"

"You know . . . lesbian cars," she said.

Lucas had to think about it, then Corian asked, "You mean . . . a Subaru?"

"That's it," she said, nodding. "One of those. Green. I'd see this car after dark, six o'clock or even later, after the help is gone. I saw it coming both ways on the street, moving slowly. It occurred to me that the driver might have been a burglar, casing the neighborhood. But, you know . . . I didn't really take the idea seriously."

"Why not? Take it seriously?" Lucas asked.

"Well . . . everybody has guns. A burglar comes to this neighborhood, he's dead meat. I personally have a Mossberg 500 and I know how to use it. That baby'd blow a hole in a burglar the size of a picture window."

"That's true," Corian said.

Lucas: "Okay. A green Subaru, acting somewhat suspiciously."

"I wouldn't say *acting* suspiciously—being what it was, was somewhat suspicious," Roe said.

That was about all Roe had. Since it had been dark, she hadn't seen the Subaru's driver; nor had she paid any attention to the license plates.

Lucas was on his feet, about to leave, when Virgil called with a second possible break. Lucas answered, said, "Hold on a minute . . ." and said goodbye to Roe. He and Corian went out on the porch, where a breeze had sprung up, a wintry insult just short of intolerable.

Virgil said, "I got exactly one thing. There's a guy here who has a heated wildlife pond out on his front lawn. You know, fake pond, well lit, running on a pump that cycles the water through a heater and then out into the pond . . . Gets bobcats, coyotes, raccoons, and so on. Birds."

"I believe you," Lucas said. "So what?"

"He has a camera looking at the pond. It catches passing cars. Not at a good angle, but . . . his camera sees cars. A bunch of them last night. Several of them about the time Sikes must have been getting home from work."

"Porsches, Land Rovers, Mercedes . . ."

"Yeah, like that," Virgil said.

"How about a green Subaru?" Lucas asked.

"No . . . not last night. Should we look more?" Virgil asked.

"Yes, roll back a few nights," Lucas said. "See what you get."

"I'll call you. Where are you?"

"Standing on a porch about halfway out," Lucas said.

"That's where I am, about halfway up the road and my ass is a block of ice," Virgil said. "I'll call after we roll the video."

VIRGIL CALLED TWENTY minutes later. "Green Subaru. Four nights in a row, but not last night. About the time Sikes would have been getting home. Can't see the numbers on the plate and the memory card recycles after ten nights, so we don't have anything before then. If you think it might be something, we should talk to Sikes' assistant, find out what time she left her office on those four nights. The Subaru would usually go by between six and six-thirty—we've got the exact times on the camera—which would be right in Sikes' slot. If it turns out that she left later on one night, and the Subaru showed up later, and earlier on another night, and the Subaru showed up earlier . . . then we might have something."

"I'll call St. Vincent, have somebody talk to the assistant," Lucas said. "Give me the times from the camera."

Virgil gave him the times for the four sightings of the Subaru, and said, "If it looks like something, we can get a bunch of the locals and swarm the whole route out to 494. Lots more cameras out there, if we know what we're looking for."

Lucas called St. Vincent, told him about the Subaru, and gave him the times from the camera. "If this works out, I'll sponsor three Masses at the St. Paul Cathedral," St. Vincent said. "What are you guys doing next?"

"Same thing, knocking on doors," Lucas said.

"Well, stay warm."

When they'd done about two-thirds of the street out to the intersection, Virgil called Lucas and said that he and the cop with him were freezing to death.

"So are we," Lucas said. "We're talking about going back in for a while." Lucas suggested that he drive up the street and pick them up.

Virgil, who'd walked, said, "I would have offered you a hundred dollars to do that, if you hadn't offered to do it for free."

Lucas picked them up; he had the Porsche's seat heaters on high. Virgil said, "This sucks. We live in fuckin' Siberia."

When they got back to the Sikes house, St. Vincent wasn't hopping up and down, because FBI agents in charge don't hop, but if they *did* hop, he would have been. The Subaru's appearance times seemed to sync with the times Sikes would be arriving home from her office. Virgil had brought back a thumb drive with ten days of video and they spent an hour watching it on an FBI laptop.

"We have no idea if this is the killer," Virgil said. "Could be a delivery guy with a route . . ."

"Nope, nope, nope, this is the killer," St. Vincent said, as he peered at the computer screen.

"How do you know that?" Virgil asked.

"Because it's gotta be," St. Vincent said. "If it isn't, we're suckin' wind. And besides, the delivery boy theory . . ."

"Yeah?"

"Let me freeze the Thursday tape . . ." He did that and tapped the computer screen. "Can't read the plate numbers, but I'll tell you what—that's not a Minnesota plate."

Lucas crouched to get a closer look. "Huh. You know what? That looks like a Wisconsin plate. White with big numbers. Is that a smear of red in the upper corner? It's a smear of something and that's where Wisconsin puts the state name."

"How do you know all that?" St. Vincent asked.

"I've got a cabin near Hayward. I'm over there all the time, pushing Wisconsin farmers down the highway at fourteen miles an hour."

"Pennsylvania plates got a lot of white," Virgil said. "So does Texas."

"But it's a lead," St. Vincent crowed. He looked at his Apple Watch. "I gotta call Washington."

"All of it?" Virgil asked.

WHEN ST. VINCENT stepped into the kitchen to make the call, Virgil, in the living room with Lucas, muttered, "Fuckin' idiot."

"Not really," Lucas said. "Sometimes, God wants you to catch a break. I think we did. Has that feel about it. St. Vincent feels it, too."

"I'm talking about calling Washington, to get the suits involved."

An FBI agent on the couch said, "Hey. I'm wearing a suit."

Lucas shrugged. "See. They're already involved."

"Are you going to stick with this, or are you going to try to weasel your way out?" Virgil asked Lucas.

"Dunno . . ." Lucas said. "It's better than the other stuff I'm doing right now. Then, there was the call from Smalls. Those guys get me interesting work, so I want to stay on their good side. And Smalls was spooked. Politicians can smell trouble coming. If only it weren't so goddamned cold . . ."

"When I was coming out of downtown this morning," the FBI

agent said, "it was so cold the hookers were blowing on their fingers."

Virgil rubbed his forehead: "Jesus, maybe you ought to try stand-up instead of criminal investigation."

"I *am* pretty funny," the agent said. "You know the one about the blonde and the redhead walking through downtown Tifton, Georgia?"

Virgil: "Please, don't tell us."

St. Vincent came back. "Okay. We created some enthusiasm in DC. They want the video for the lab. They think they can bring up the tag numbers." He frowned. "Though our profilers are saying that whoever is writing these notes, these press releases, is certainly a college graduate and if he has the leisure to spend days or weeks scouting his victims, and then donating a Bitcoin for each killing . . . then a Subaru is an unlikely ride. They had already proposed that we look for a car in the hundred-thousand-dollar class."

"Could be a stolen car for this one thing, scouting Sikes and her house," Virgil said. "Could be stolen plates, too."

"Could be," Lucas said. "But if we find the car, we maybe get prints and DNA."

When Lucas and Virgil were thoroughly warm, they rounded up their door-knocking partners and went back out, found nothing new, but got cold all over again.

"Here's a moneymaking idea for you," Corian said, as he and Lucas drove back to the Sikes house. "How about inventing a heated vest that runs off a battery pack. Even if it only . . ."

"You're too late. They're out there. I know a hunter who swears by them," Lucas said. "The only drawback is, some guys don't wear warm-enough coats. Then, the battery runs down when they're three miles out from the cabin and they freeze to death on the walk back."

"Damn. I thought for a minute, there, that I was gonna get rich." Corian thought for a minute, then said, "You know what we really need for days like these? Something like space suits. Totally enclosed, heater in a backpack. Breathing tube like a snorkel to warm up incoming air."

"Maybe you *will* get rich," Lucas said.

When they got back to the house, they found Virgil talking to St. Vincent. St. Vincent brightened when they walked in, and said, "You were right, Lucas. Wisconsin plate. It's a 2019 Subaru. I've jacked up every police department from here out to the interstate to look at security cameras and spot the car."

"Then what?" Lucas asked.

"We try to track him," St. Vincent said. "It's unlikely, but possible, that we'll be able to follow him from one camera to the next all the way back to Wisconsin, if that's where he's going."

"Then you don't really need me and Virgil," Lucas said. "This is now a research problem. It's not a door-knocker anymore."

"Probably not in this neighborhood, but we might need some more door-knocking downstream," St. Vincent said. "If you work through the logic, it'd make sense for these guys, these Five, to kill locally. You solve a lot of logistics problems that way. The guy ditches the car on a local street downtown, walks over to a parking ramp, drives home. He has an excuse for everywhere he goes, because . . . he lives there."

"You're right. But it's gonna be a huge clusterfuck and I hate those."

"A clusterfuck does have one fine and desirable characteristic," St. Vincent said.

Virgil: "What's that?"

"Spreads the blame around if you don't catch anyone," St. Vincent said.

Everyone within earshot looked over at St. Vincent and nodded.

FIVE

The FBI took over.

Teams of cops pulled in from around the metro area, each team headed by an FBI agent, tried to locate and review every video camera that might look at a road leading away from the murder scene.

There were a lot of Subarus and not much Lucas or Virgil could do to help. They both hung around Minnetonka until early afternoon, when Lucas suggested that they find a diner for lunch, and then go home. Virgil saw the wisdom in that, and called Duncan, who had gone to BCA headquarters in St. Paul.

Duncan had always been reasonable, and once upon a time, a competent investigator. He said, "Yeah, I been talking to St. Vincent. Go on home. I'll call if we need you again. I'm not sorry we dragged you up here, Virgil—you guys got the only thing anybody got."

Lucas and Virgil trundled out to the nearby town of Hopkins, Lucas leading the way, skating across patches of black ice. When Virgil got out of his truck at the restaurant, Lucas said, "I got a call."

"Uh-oh."

"Senator Smalls. He wants me to *liaise* with the FBI on the investigation, wherever it goes," Lucas said. "I asked if they thought it might be possible to put together a Marshals Service task force out of Minnesota to follow it . . . wherever it goes. Sort of like the task force down in Florida."

Virgil had been on the task force in Florida. When one of the bad guys had tried to escape in a small plane, Virgil had shot out one of the wheels as it taxied down a runway. A number of national media outlets had simplified the story by saying that he'd shot down the airplane.

"You're dragging me into it?" Virgil asked.

"Not unless you want to go. Could be interesting," Lucas said. "Make you even more famous. Maybe get a series on Netflix."

"Give me a few minutes to think about it," Virgil said.

THEY GOT A booth at the Perkins, a semi-tired chain restaurant with semi-tired food, took off their parkas, ordered cheeseburgers, fries, and Diet Cokes—they were culinarily compatible—and Lucas asked, "How's the novel going?"

Virgil: "It's in New York. Esther says she can sell it."

"Holy shit! You think she can?"

"I don't know. I think so," Virgil said. He picked up a napkin and started shredding it: nerves. "The longest conversation I've ever had with her lasted thirty-two seconds, so it's hard to tell. There probably won't be much of an advance."

"What's that mean? 'Not much' is how much?"

Virgil shrugged: "Twenty-five grand, maybe. Could be less. After you take the taxes out, it's half a small car."

"It's a start," Lucas said. "Are you the hero? I mean, is the hero a cop who works out in the sticks?"

"No. He's retired military, a former lieutenant colonel, got out after twenty, in his early forties. Gets pulled into stuff because, you know, he's that kind of guy. Years ago, there was a thriller hero named Travis McGee, author was John D. MacDonald. I'm modeling my guy off of Travis."

"I remember those," Lucas said. "It's a good model. At least you won't be stealing stuff from C. J. Box."

"I kinda worried about that. I mean, I do read the guy. In the practice novel, which was set up in the Northwoods, I heard echoes," Virgil said. "This way, not so much. And there's already a cop writer in the Cities."

"Mostly that one guy," Lucas said. "Whatshisname. But his cop never does any paperwork. Or uses the can."

"Paperwork is boring and nobody wants to read about a hero taking a dump," Virgil said. "I learned that much from Esther." The Cokes came, and they paused the talk. When the waitress had gone, Virgil asked, "So . . . a task force?"

"I've got a speech about that," Lucas said. "The FBI plays zone defense. They're all over the place, but nowhere in particular. The Marshals Service is man-to-man. Right now, we've got no place to go, so we have to rely on the FBI's research. When they actually find something . . ."

"*If* they find something. . . ."

"*If* they find something," Lucas corrected himself, "then they might want a couple of hunters on the trail. Man-to-man. That's us. I'd like you to go along. Not so much as a cop, but more like a good-luck charm. You're a lucky guy. I personally rely more on intelligence and good looks."

"About six hours ago, you weren't that interested," Virgil said. "What changed?"

Lucas shrugged. "I thought about it. Six hours ago, I could see us walking around the Cities in January, ringing doorbells. But now . . . I think this could take us anywhere. Rather than sitting around the Cities in January, getting our nuts numb, we could be hitting some of the Bigs. Who knows, San Francisco, Houston, New York? Last year at this time, we were in Miami, nice and warm."

"Huh. And I had the five weeks in Hawaii with the scuba train-ing. That wasn't bad, except now, the whole goddamn family is bug-ging me to take them back."

"Maybe if you sell the novel . . ."

They talked more about the novel and the case, then Virgil took a phone call from Duncan:

"The feds found a video camera that got a good shot of the car when it was going past a streetlight . . . what they think is the car," Duncan said. "Wilderness Green Metallic. They saw it twice head-ing out to 494. Looks like what Lucas said: Wisconsin plates, got the number, looking for the owner. Haven't spotted it further down the highway."

"That's more than San Francisco or Houston got," Virgil said.

"Yes, it is. Expect press releases from everyone involved. The feds are organizing a posse from all the local departments to check every hotel in the metro area for Wisconsin-based credit cards and green Outbacks."

"Anything for us to do?"

"Not really—I thought you'd like to know."

VIRGIL PASSED THE information to Lucas, and they finished their meals and headed to their separate homes. When Virgil was almost home, Duncan called again: "The Wisconsin plates were stolen. The owner is in the clear; older schoolteacher lady. The plates weren't just stolen, they were replaced with another set of stolen plates. The schoolteacher didn't even notice, but the owner of the car whose plates wound up on her car, did notice, and reported the theft to the Eau Claire cops. Plates probably stolen three or four days ago."

"So well thought-out. The whole car thing."

"Looks like it," Duncan said. "And really, what'd we expect with the Five?"

Virgil passed the word on to Lucas, who watched some pro basketball that night, while Virgil went back to work on what he hoped would be his second published novel.

The next morning, Lucas continued a desultory search for a woman named Virginia Clayton-Weasling, who hadn't shown up for a federal court trial on tax evasion.

The day before the trial was scheduled to take place, she'd sent an email to the judge informing him that (a) she wouldn't be showing up, and (b) that she'd done a tarot-card reading on his future, which strongly suggested that he'd be dying soon, though he was only forty-five and in good health.

The judge had taken that as a veiled threat and wanted her picked up. Lucas tried to be interested but wasn't.

VIRGIL, WORKING WHAT he now thought of as his day job, resumed his hunt for a man named Ellis Hamm, who robbed gas stations. He'd arrested Hamm six years earlier, for the same set of crimes—gas station robberies—which was Hamm's sole skill set.

He'd been released from Stillwater state prison the month before, and gas station robberies, which, until then, had been almost nonexistent in southern Minnesota and northern Iowa, had flared up again. The robber was carrying a .223 semi-automatic rifle into the gas stations and had fired a couple of shots into ceilings. Virgil worried that sooner or later, somebody was going to get killed—maybe a gas station attendant and maybe the robber. Rural gas station attendants tend to keep revolvers under the counter . . .

Virgil had talked to Hamm's wife, Edna, who said she didn't know where he was, though Virgil had noticed a CAT hat hanging from a hook in the mudroom off the kitchen, and Hamm liked to call himself a heavy-equipment operator.

Threats and warnings hadn't produced Hamm, so the hunt continued until 4:45 p.m., the day after Sikes' body was found, when Lucas called.

Virgil was in his truck. "Yeah?"

"You want to go to Eau Claire?"

"What's there? Other than an older schoolteacher?"

"The cops found a burned 2019 Subaru this morning. Color is right. No plates. They called the fire department, but the fire was mostly out. Didn't realize the feds were looking for a green 2019 Subaru until late this afternoon. Car's still in place. I'm going. Stay overnight, the Marshals Service picks up the tab. Already cleared through Duncan, and I already got permission from Frankie. She's packing your bag."

"Wait. You called Frankie?"

"Of course," Lucas said. "She's talking about cleavage and a morning talk show. I don't know about the talk show, but she's definitely got the cleavage under control."

"I'm thirty miles from home . . ."

"So? You got lights and a siren. I'll see you at my place at seven o'clock."

"If Frankie says okay . . ."

FRANKIE SAID OKAY.

Getting her permission wasn't a hypocritical nod to equality, but more like a concession to reality. She was caring for two infants and a raucous preteen son, which was an exhausting job. Virgil tried to take some of the load off her, when he could, but she never had much work in the winter, and they needed his full-time job and the benefits that came with it.

She said, "Go."

Lucas and Virgil drove through the early dark of January to Eau Claire, Wisconsin, past a half-dozen dead deer carcasses on the shoulders of the interstate highway.

"I was heading up to the cabin last fall and between here and Menomonie I saw twenty-two dead deer," Lucas said. "Must have been in late October or early November . . . That's my all-time record for dead deer."

"The rut," Virgil said. "The annual highway massacre."

At Eau Claire, they checked into a Hampton Inn. At eight o'clock the next morning, Lucas called an Eau Claire investigator named Dick Presston who suggested that they meet at a McDonald's across the street from the hotel and not far from the burned car.

They were standing in line at the McDonald's when Presston walked through the door, red-faced, pulling off his gloves. He was wearing old-fashioned rubber galoshes and a parka. He spotted them and Lucas raised a hand.

"Flowers and Davenport?"

Virgil: "That's us."

"Yeah, you look like cops," he said. He looked up at the menu behind the counter. "God help me, I could eat six of those Egg Mc-Muffins. Goes straight to my hips."

Presston was a hefty man, maybe in his mid-forties, who might be right to worry about his hips. He had a heavy face and small cut-scars under his eyes, as though he'd once spent time in a boxing ring. He had a woolen watch cap on his head and was carrying a thin yellow file folder.

Virgil said, "Nippy this morning."

"Had a guy froze to death three weeks ago, under a bridge, street guy who used to hang around the university," Presston said. He wasn't grim about it, he was matter-of-fact. Freezing to death was something that happened to street people, like the light of the moon falling upon the earth. Not much to be done about it, unless civilization should unexpectedly occur.

They got their breakfasts and moved to a booth and Presston pushed the yellow file folder across the table. "This is what we got, sad to say. We already sent it to the FBI. The way they were talking, I expected them to parachute a battalion in by dawn today."

Lucas: "They didn't?"

"Not yet. They got one guy down at the car. I expect more of them will be poking around after they finish their meetings."

"How far are we from the car?" Lucas asked. "I think I spotted the location on a Google map . . ."

"A few blocks, I guess. You got a ride?"

"Yeah."

"You can follow me over. If this is the car you're looking for, there's not much left. Looks like somebody sprayed a couple cans of gas inside it, touched it off. Burned it right down to the tires."

"And stolen plates," Lucas said.

"Yep. Stolen plates."

THEY ATE AND talked about recent cases and goofy street shit and salaries and benefits and the weather. Outside, they saw a woman nearly slip and fall in the driveway, doing what looked like a Russian sword dance to keep her feet beneath her.

"One thing," Presston said, dragging the talk back to the burned car. "Two nights ago, we had thundersnow. Four inches of snow in an hour and a half. Lightning knocked out the power on the south side. Whoever burned the car left all four doors and the back hatch open, maybe to make sure it burned better. The fire combined with the snow made a real mess. On the passenger side you can still see some fabric on the bottom of the seats, both front and back. The passenger-side carpet got soaked with meltwater, both front and back, not all of it burned, so you can still see some of that."

"Will that be any help?" Virgil asked.

"Mmm, no."

"Your crime scene people over there now?" Lucas asked.

"Since daylight. Yesterday there was some confusion, but we threw a tarp over it in case it snowed again. Crime scene was swamped, we had four people stabbed in a bar fight and crime scene had to cover the situation in case somebody died. Nobody did, but . . . you know how it goes. They didn't make it out until this morning. The VIN plate had been pulled off the door panel and the dash, but the number is stamped into the firewall, and they got a partial from that, sent it to the feds. There might be a couple more VINs on it somewhere, we're checking on that with a Subaru dealer. If we can get a full number, we'll have the owner. If you're looking for blood or DNA, you're not going to get it—everything inside is soggy toast."

THEY FOLLOWED PRESSTON down a hill on the highway they came in on, then up a street through a business park, onto a narrow lane between a couple of industrial buildings, then onto a patch of dirt, partly covered with snow, partly cut up by truck tracks. A couple of dump trucks were parked on the edge of the open space, along with three pieces of heavy excavation equipment, unused orange road signs, and piles of dirt and heaps of broken asphalt.

The Subaru hulk was sitting between fifteen-foot piles of dirt. Two cop vans and a Toyota sedan were parked a few yards away, as the Eau Claire crime scene techs worked over the hulk. Presston pulled over and they parked behind him and got out.

As Presston led the way down to the burned car, Lucas asked Virgil, "Anything occur to you?"

"Nothing except what you're thinking: whoever brought the car here, had scouted it," Virgil said. "He didn't find this spot by driving around looking out a window."

Presston: "Especially not that night. Dark as the inside of a coal sack. He knew where he was going and knew what he was doing."

THE CRIME SCENE crew was excavating the interior of the car. A tall man in corduroy slacks, which showed a flash of white long underwear at the cuffs, and a puffy blue ski jacket, walked over and said, "Richard Gomez, FBI."

Lucas and Virgil introduced themselves and Gomez said, "I heard you were coming. I was sent over to monitor the crime scene work."

Presston introduced the lead crime scene investigator as Sandra Oakes, a heavyset woman in a white coverall. "We're mostly getting sludge from the burned interior," she said. "It appears the car was cleaned before it was burned. We did take two plastic gas cans out of it, but I'm not sure anyone will even be able to identify the manufacturer or where they're sold. They're melted, standard red with yellow spouts."

Gomez added, "We're packing them up and sending them to the lab. If we can find a chain store where they're sold, and somebody who bought two at the same time . . ."

The interior of the car was a bucket of muck, remnants of burned fabric soaked by the storm.

"Nothing else at all?" Virgil asked.

"One thing, only one," Oakes said. "Let me go get it. Some kind of plastic thing."

Oakes came back with a transparent plastic bag and held it up high, so Virgil and Lucas could look at it. "Burned, melted . . . Under the right side of the driver's seat, like it fell out of somebody's pocket. Not a bottle cap, or anything like that. I dunno. I kinda think it might be a button—you know, the kind with a loop on the back. Maybe the feds can identify it. Even if they do, it might just be a button."

"Might be able to use a button, if we can find a matching one," Virgil said.

The object was a plastic disk, originally white or beige, the size and thickness of a quarter, twisted, melted, charred by the fire. One face showed what might be tiny letters. It seemed to be something, rather than nothing—something peculiar to whatever it was. The other side of the disk showed a white melted lump, what Oakes had suggested might have been a button loop.

"You got a magnifying glass?" Lucas asked, his nose an inch from the bag.

"I do. Let me go get it," Oakes said. She went to get it, passing the bag to Virgil, who squinted at the disk.

Lucas called after her, "Bring some tweezers, so we can take it out of the bag, hold it up to the sun."

"Sure." Oakes got a magnifying glass and the tweezers, opened the bag, took out the disk. Lucas took the magnifying glass from her as she held the disk up to the hazy sun, turning it back and forth. "The letters . . . Looks like an uppercase W. Or, an uppercase M, if I'm holding it upside down. But I think a W. A W and a lowercase a and there's a little tail down, like a small g or j."

"You look like Sherlock fuckin' Holmes with that magnifying glass," Presston said.

Virgil said, "Gimme the glass . . . let me look." He looked and said, "I see that little tail . . . could say Wag? I dunno . . . Wag the Dog?"

Gomez. "What? Wag the Dog?"

"Could be a brand name," Lucas said.

"This is ringing a bell with me," Virgil said. "But I don't know why."

Lucas: "Well, think."

"I'm trying . . . it's something. Something I should recognize. Something I've seen in the Cities."

THEY PUT THE disk back in the bag and Lucas stepped away from the burned Subaru and surveyed it. "Tell you what, Virgie. St. Vincent said that first day that this is the car, and by God, he was right. This was a good car and somebody torched it and not because it was stolen. It was torched to get rid of the evidence. DNA, prints. Torched by a smart guy. This is the killer's car."

Virgil: "St. Vincent also said that the killer was probably local, because it would simplify the logistics of the murder. If he's right, then maybe the killer lives here, instead of the Cities."

Gomez took out his phone: "I'm calling it in. Maybe that button is something. They'll probably want me to ship it to our lab," he said.

He made the call as Lucas, Virgil, and Presston watched the crime scene crew and when Gomez came back, he asked, "You guys got computers with you?"

"Yeah, back in our rooms," Lucas said.

"Give me your emails. I'll send you Zoom links. Big Zoom conference at noon, eastern time. Eleven o'clock here. They want you on it."

SIX

Virgil took his computer to Lucas' room and at eleven o'clock they both clicked through the Zoom links sent by Gomez. With Presston looking over their shoulders, they found themselves talking with Louis Mallard, a deputy director of the FBI, along with a checkerboard of other FBI agents and cops they didn't know.

Mallard knew Lucas well, and Virgil somewhat. He opened the conference by saying, "One of our agents and a marshal and a Minnesota investigator are looking at a burned Subaru in Eau Claire, Wisconsin. It's the right year, the right color, and it seems to have been burned for no legitimate reason anyone can figure out, so we think the Eau Claire car was probably the one used by the Minnesota killer. Eau Claire crime scene investigators found that whoever drove the car tried to conceal its origin by stripping the VIN numbers off the door panel and the dashboard, but didn't realize that there are other VINs concealed on Subarus, including on the firewall."

He continued: "The Eau Claire police sent us a partial VIN number from the firewall, which we managed to reconstruct and trace to a Richard and Lorna Hogan of Elk River, Minnesota. Minneapolis. Agents visited the Hogans an hour ago and were told that the car had been sold in early December, for cash. The description of the buyer was unexpected—he was short, not very well dressed, and spoke with a Spanish accent. He told them that he'd been born in Mexico but had lived in the U.S. for twenty years and was now a citizen."

FBI analysts did not think the car buyer was the Minnesota killer, Mallard said. "If the Eau Claire car is the one used by the killer, then the car buyer was obviously cooperating with the killer and could most likely identify him, so finding this man has become a top priority."

A cop in the upper-left corner of the screen asked, "Why don't you think he's the killer?"

Mallard said, "Because of his dress and the physical indicators. The Sikes killer lay in the snow, on his stomach, at several spots as he made his way across the Sikes yard. Minnesota crime scene specialists believe he is between six feet and six feet, two inches tall. The Hogans estimated the car buyer's height at five feet, eight inches. Mr. Hogan is not tall himself, at five feet ten inches, but said he was taller than the buyer. Also, the killer was wearing a coat of a distinctive design. In two separate places, he actually melted that design into the snow outside the Sikes house, with body heat. One of our FBI researchers identified it as a Givenchy down parka that, among other outlets, was sold at the Neiman Marcus and Nordstrom stores for two thousand, nine hundred and ninety dollars. There is a Nordstrom store at the

Mall of America in the Twin Cities. Judging from the Hogans' description of the buyer's clothing and demeanor, he could not have afforded that coat."

Virgil looked at Lucas and said, "Slight unsupported assumption there."

"I heard that, Virgil," Mallard said. "Anyway, I'm right. We are now going through sales records at Nordstrom to see if we can determine who sold the parka, when it was sold, and hopefully, the credit card that was used to buy it."

A white-haired man chipped in: "So the earlier guesses were probably correct. These guys, or this guy, have the big bucks."

Mallard: "Yes. If we can identify the precise coat he bought, we'll know more about his height and weight. Hopefully, the salesclerk will remember him, given the price of the coat. A credit card would, of course, be perfect. Unfortunately, the coat was sold two years ago."

Lucas: "That much for a parka would tend to confirm that he's local and needs it for our weather. Either that, or he travels in cold weather places that rich people go. Like ski resorts."

Mallard: "I suppose that is correct. For those of you who don't know, Lucas Davenport is a U.S. Marshal from Minnesota, and Virgil Flowers is his partner. They're now in Eau Claire. We're going to ask Davenport and Flowers to go back to Minneapolis to join our FBI agents in tracing both the Subaru buyer and the parka . . ."

Virgil: "There must have been some papers connected to the Subaru sale."

"Yes, there are," Mallard said. "They are indecipherable. The Hogans didn't pay much attention to that part, they were too eager to get the cash. And they were paid in cash—hundred-dollar bills. It's possible that the last name on the buyer's signature is 'Anderson,' but that seems unlikely to be a real name. The hundred-dollar bills, by the way, are gone—deposited in the bank the same day the Hogans got them."

Lucas mentioned the discovery of the disk and that Gomez, the FBI agent, had it and would be overnighting it to the FBI lab. He added that Virgil thought he might have encountered the disk somewhere but couldn't remember where.

"It would be nice if you could remember," Mallard said, drily.

"I'm trying," Virgil said. "Maybe I'll remember when I get back to town, but we still have a few more things to do here . . ."

Mallard: "If you could be more specific . . ."

"The car was burned in a depression in an Eau Claire work yard . . . heavy equipment yard," Lucas said. "There was a serious snowstorm going on, and the fire wasn't seen at the time. A local worker discovered it the next morning. After he burned the car, the killer would have had to leave the scene on foot. The storm dumped several inches of snow in a couple of hours, as I understand it, but you could still see the tracks made by a single car in the snow. There were no other tracks. We think the killer either walked out of the quarry and was picked up on the street, or he had some other way to get out of there. We hope to figure that out, maybe find some witnesses who saw him leaving the scene."

Mallard: "Okay. Check what you can but be quick about it. I want you working in the Twin Cities by this evening."

The conference continued for another half hour, mostly to do with scheduling, with no additional salient information. When they signed off, Lucas scratched an ear and said, "Well . . . I think we're walkin' and knockin'. Again."

"One reason I'm getting tired of this shit," Virgil said. "Writing novels . . . you sit in a chair, write a couple hundred words, kick back, maybe have a latte, maybe fool around with the old lady, take the boat out . . . no walkin', no knockin'."

"With no knockin', you never find out what's behind Door Number Three, which can be pretty goddamn interesting," Lucas said.

"The difference between you and me," Virgil said, "is that I'm beginning to think that I don't need to know anymore."

THEY WALKED AND knocked and knocked and walked, with the help of Presston and three other Eau Claire cops, stepping high through snowdrifts, getting cold again. They talked to residents, passersby, to a snowplow driver. Nobody saw anything. Virgil suggested that the killer's accomplice, the man who'd purchased the car, might not have known what the killer intended to do with it, and might not have picked him up.

"Say you had a guy, a rich guy, with a couple of cars, or even three or four cars. He wanted to get rid of the Subaru after the killing and he wants to get it across a state line to confuse the investigation," Virgil said, as they high-stepped down a snow-covered sidewalk. "He doesn't think it'll be spotted around Sikes' house, but he's super-careful. He decides to dump it and burn it some distance away, without involving the accomplice. How does he do that?"

He would scout a place, Virgil argued, but it would have to be a place where he could pre-position a getaway car after he burned the Subaru. Where could he leave the second car where nobody would notice?

"We're close by the university here," Presston said. "And the technical college. They got big parking lots and some of them allow overnight parking . . . I think maybe you have to have a permit, but I'm not sure about that . . . But there's lots of parking."

"But after he pre-positions his own car, the getaway car, how does he get back to Minneapolis?" Virgil asked. "Without using a credit card? Without anybody seeing his face or an ID?"

They all thought about that and then Presston said, "You know, I believe there's a daily Jefferson Lines bus that runs from the university here, to Minneapolis. He could leave the car in one of the lots over there, catch the bus . . . he's all bundled up against the cold, wearing a hat and scarf and sunglasses, he pays cash for a ticket . . ."

"Be nice if we could find somebody who rode the bus," Virgil said. "But we don't know what day that would have been. And we don't know who the riders would have been."

"Could try to find the driver," Presston said.

"That's gonna be . . . sketchy," Virgil said. "Maybe a driver would remember some guy all bundled up in a super-parka, but if he couldn't see a face . . . we'd be out of luck."

"Gotta give it a try," Presston said. "But there are a hell of a lot of possibilities."

Lucas and Virgil agreed. They also agreed that the Eau Claire cops would have to take care of it, because they were making no progress at all, and Mallard wanted them back in the Cities. They said goodbye to Presston, checked out of the hotel. Lucas invited Virgil to stay in his guest room in Minneapolis, but Virgil declined.

"Duncan got me a room at the Radisson Blu at Mall of America. Frankie'll run up for a couple of nights—my mom is at the house now. She'll stay with the kids. She loves that. And me'n Frankie will have a nice little mini-vacation courtesy of the taxpayers."

"You won't have time for a vacation. When Mallard gets involved in something like this, it can get intense," Lucas said. "Anyway, let's stop at my place and get something to eat. I can call Ellen and get sandwiches."

THE RIDE BACK was as unscenic as the ride over had been, except that there were fewer deer carcasses on the westbound lanes, for reasons known only to the deer. They crossed the St. Croix River back into Minnesota, got off I-94 at Cretin Avenue, heading south toward Lucas' house. On their right, they passed the snowy open fairways of a golf course. Virgil, driving, scooted his butt around in the seat a bit, which helped him think, and then said, "I got it."

"What?"

"That disk. That's not a button—it's a ball marker. You know, a golf ball marker, for marking your ball on a green. The lump on the back was a little pin, for pushing down into the turf."

"I don't play golf, so . . . You're sure?"

"Yeah. Want to know where it was from?" Virgil asked.

"The famous Wag the Dog golf club?"

"No, the famous Wayzata Country Club," Virgil said. "That wasn't the tail of a lowercase g hanging down, it was the tail of a y."

"Ah, shit," Lucas said.

"What, we . . ."

"I'm hungrier than hell and now we got to drive across town to Wayzata? There's hardly any place further away from here that's still in the Cities . . ."

"That's a huge sacrifice, all right," Virgil said. "Probably take us more than half an hour to get there, you fuckin' slug."

"Tell you what—let's grab the sandwiches at my place and then go. Won't set us back much."

"What about the FBI, sweating bullets, hoping against hope that we'll come up with something . . ."

"Fuck 'em. Chicken sandwiches."

Lucas lived on Mississippi River Boulevard in St. Paul and, like Hillary Sikes, had a live-in housekeeper, Ellen Jansen, with her own apartment. She'd made them sandwiches and a cold pasta salad, which she left in the refrigerator before she went out shopping.

They ate, drank root beer, decided that Virgil had done enough driving, left his Tahoe in Lucas' garage, and took Lucas' Cayenne. They went straight across the Cities and out the west side, past the I-494 loop and into what in the summer looked like a bucolic countryside, but in the winter was revealed by leafless trees as an upper-middle-class suburb.

"Never been here in the winter," Virgil said, watching the passing landscape. "I was here in the fall once, when the color was good. One of the prettiest places in the state. Lake's a little dirty, though."

"After you're a rich author, you could move here," Lucas said.

"I'll keep it in mind," Virgil said. "Though as naturally humble as I am, I'll probably stay on the farm."

"Rich guy, have your own dock, put a Ranger 622 on it . . ."

"Okay, fuck the farm," Virgil said.

THE WAYZATA COUNTRY CLUB was set in a vaguely Tudor-style clubhouse perched up a hill. The driveway was nicely plowed and melted, and they bypassed the parking lot to park under the portico outside the front door.

A man popped out and said, "You can't actually park—"

Lucas said, "Federal marshals. Take us to the manager."

Bernice Atwood, the general manager, turned out to be a congenial enough woman. They found her in the dining room, talking to another staff member. Lucas explained the situation and she said, "We've got a number of Hispanic men around, both members and employees, but from your description . . ."

"Yeah?"

"I don't think it's any of the members or the inside staff. There are three men on the grounds crew that fit. Seasonal people. Let me get their information for you . . ."

She gave them three names, with addresses and cell phone numbers. Two of the addresses were the same, the third was in St. Paul, in the Frogtown neighborhood.

"Would you know if they all have driver's licenses?" Virgil asked.

"Oh, yes; that's a requirement. We won't hire illegals . . ."

In the car, Virgil got online with his iPad and into the state driver's license division and brought up the driver's licenses for the three men. He saved them to the iPad memory. Lucas called St. Vincent's office, was told that he was out of pocket and that St. Vincent or an agent would call back.

Sometime soon. Maybe.

"What now?" Virgil asked.

"Something's going on and they don't want to talk to us about it. Why don't we go back to St. Paul. That Frogtown address can't be more than a mile from my place. We'll hit that first, then get comfortable at home. Do some research on these guys."

"You think we've got something?"

"Maybe. Maybe fifty-fifty."

BACK ACROSS THE Cities, they went to the Frogtown address, a small, neatly kept house on a postage stamp lawn. A detached garage sat to one side, and there were tracks in the driveway, but no response when they knocked on the door.

"Feels empty," Virgil said.

"Yeah. We'll be back."

An agent named Woods called them as they pulled into Lucas' driveway and told them there'd been a major break in the case. "Agent St. Vincent ordered me to meet with you and brief you on it. Are you close by?"

She didn't sound happy about the assignment. Lucas suggested that she come to his house at three o'clock where he and Virgil would be working online. "We might have a break ourselves," he said. "We'll brief *you* on that."

Woods showed up promptly at three o'clock. She looked like a lot of young FBI agents, thin, nerdish, with overtones of workout queen. And she looked smart, with narrow black-rimmed spectacles under tightly coifed dark hair. Lorna Woods sat on a kitchen chair, took an iPad out of her briefcase, turned it on, and glanced at it from time to time.

"I don't know exactly what Director Mallard expects from you two, but we've had a major break in the case and we're moving on it. The Nordstrom lead produced a credit card purchase of the coat— they sold only one coat—and it went to a man named Howard Gates, who lives in Minneapolis," Woods said. "He fits the profile: well-educated, wealthy, six feet tall. Three cars registered in Minnesota: A BMW X5 SUV, a Mercedes Benz SL550, and a fifty-year-old

Rolls-Royce convertible. Twice divorced, now single. He inherited some of his money, apparently, but is known to have made more as an investor and bar owner."

"In Bitcoin?"

"Nothing about that. He does invest in technology," Woods said. "Other Nordstrom purchases show his foot size as a twelve or twelve and a half."

"Is he a risk-taker? Physical risks?" Lucas asked.

"Nothing like that has popped up. We've checked all the social media for background, as well as government records. He does have a presence on LinkedIn, but not much on any of the others. He doesn't tweet." She sounded disapproving.

"Alibi?" Virgil asked.

"Don't know. No credit card use outside the Twin Cities, except for some charges at Amazon. Nothing in the Eau Claire area or anywhere in Wisconsin."

Lucas: "Any servants?"

"We don't know. We only got the credit card charge from Nordstrom . . ." She looked at her watch. ". . . about four hours ago. We're looking at employment data, but if he hires illegals, and a lot of people do, then he'll be paying them in cash and we won't have employment records. When I left the office to come here, we hadn't found any employee records."

Lucas: "How old is he?"

"Fifty-six."

Lucas looked at Virgil, who raised his eyebrows and gave a short shake of the head.

Woods caught it, and asked, "What?"

"He's too old," Lucas said. "He drives conservative cars. From what you know, he doesn't seem to be a big risk-taker."

"You could argue that the killings are done by a person, or persons, who *aren't* big risk-takers," Woods said. "The killing itself is a risk, but they've taken every possible measure to eliminate the risk or limit it."

Lucas and Virgil both nodded, and Virgil said, "That seems right. But if you're smart, and these people seem to be, then limiting risk would be the logical thing to do, even though they're planning a high-risk crime. A guy could be a high-risk rock climber but insist on the best equipment."

"Our analysis is that he fits the primary parameters of the killer," Woods insisted. She brushed a lock of hair away from her forehead, where it had dropped a half inch. "So, we're moving."

"What does that mean?"

"He will be interviewed by a team this afternoon." She looked at her watch again. "Probably in an hour or so. I would like to be there, so if you're satisfied . . . I really don't have much more information for you."

"We'd like to be there, too," Virgil said.

"That would be up to Agent St. Vincent," Woods said. "You can contact him directly, he authorized me to give you his private number. But, he's really busy right now . . ."

"We'll give him a ring," Lucas said. "Thank you."

"What do you have for me? You were going to brief me?" She was skeptical.

Lucas said, "We may have a photo, name, and address for the man who bought the Subaru."

"What!"

Virgil explained, and said, "So it's a little thin at the moment. You could pass it along to Dave when you see him."

"Who?"

"St. Vincent."

"Nobody ever calls him Dave," Woods said. "Not even his wife."

"DIDN'T TAKE HER long to haul butt," Virgil observed, after the door closed behind Woods. "What do you think?"

"I believe the part about the parka, that whatshisname, Gates? That he bought it," Lucas said. "The feds better be polite until they find out whether he still has it, and if he doesn't, what happened to it."

"It's a good lead . . ."

"Yeah, it is," Lucas conceded. "Maybe they'll kick something loose. Maybe Gates will lock himself in the billiards room and blow his brains out. I wouldn't bet on it."

"You want to call St. Vincent and go watch the show?" Virgil asked. "Maybe they'll frog-walk the guy out of his mansion. If he has a mansion."

"I like that. I'll call them, get wherever they let us get."

SEVEN

They called St. Vincent and were politely disinvited from the initial confrontation with Gates. "We already have too many people pushing to go," St. Vincent said, in what wasn't quite an apology. "It would be best if we kept this contained within the FBI for the time being. Your efforts are appreciated but we've already laid down a careful plan about confronting Gates."

He did reluctantly give up Gates' address and told them that they were welcome to stand by, in case something unexpected should crop up, where their help or information might be needed. He added that Woods had told him about the possible identification of the man who'd bought the car used in the murder of Sikes, though she hadn't really sold the concept.

"We'll get to it today," St. Vincent said.

"The goddamn FBI," Virgil said, after St. Vincent rang off. "They'll get to it today? In the meantime, the entire Bureau is over-sweating this Gates guy."

"Yeah, but we still oughta go over there—check out the neighborhood, if nothing else," Lucas said.

THEY DID THAT. Virgil threw his gear bag in the back of Lucas' Cayenne, and they cruised the Minneapolis lake district, looking at houses, contemplating a few ice fisherman out with their bourbon flasks and buckets and tip-ups in the subzero temperatures; and as they went, listening to Raul Malo singing "Gentle on My Mind."

Virgil's iPad told them that Gates lived on Lake of the Isles. The house was built of a pale blue stone with a red tile roof. It had turrets and dark windows that looked out over the lake, and a wrought iron fence set into chest-high pillars of the blue stone with a wrought iron gate that looked like it should front a German chalet.

Lucas and Virgil rolled past. Three dark SUVs were parked in the driveway and a man in a dark overcoat and a tie, and Lorna Woods, who wore a dark overcoat, were pacing behind the gate, hands in their pockets, shoulders hunched against the cold.

"The feds are inside already," Virgil said. "Lorna didn't get to go in. She's like a parking attendant."

"Yeah. And here we are, driving in circles, can't even park," Lucas said.

At that moment, Lucas' phone rang: St. Vincent: "Where are you two?"

"Just cruised the house. Saw that you've got a couple of agents on the gate," Lucas said.

"Yes, we do. I'll call them and tell him to let you in," St. Vincent said.

"I thought we were disinvited because you didn't want a crowd," Lucas said.

"We've had a change of heart. Actually, we've had our heart changed by your friend in Washington, which pisses me off, but it is what it is."

"Is Gates the guy?"

"We're still talking," St. Vincent said.

"Five minutes," Lucas said. He was smiling as St. Vincent clicked off.

"He could hear you smiling," Virgil said. "Must be nice to have that kind of pull in high places."

"I can understand why he's pissed," Lucas said. "In St. Vincent's shoes, I'd be pissed, too."

"But you wouldn't have kept us out," Virgil said, as Lucas made a U-turn to head back to Gates' house.

"Not us, but there are people at the BCA—and the Marshals Service, for that matter—who I would've told to take a hike. But: Gates is not the Three killer. If he was, we'd still be disinvited."

Woods waved them through the front gate; she looked like she was trying not to look unhappy.

The three federal SUVs were parked in the driveway as it led toward a porte cochere; from there, the feds had a short march to the front door. Virgil drove under the arch that separated the main house from the coach house, which served as a four-car garage with a loft above it. On the other side of the arch was a stone block courtyard occupied by another federal SUV, this one with an agent still inside. Another agent stood by an elaborate rear entry.

"At least eight guys," Virgil said. "They weren't taking any chances."

They parked, got out, and walked to the rear door, which the agent pushed open for them. He grinned and said, "Just in time to save the day."

"It needs to be saved?" Virgil asked.

"I'll agree with anything my betters say about that," the agent said. And quietly, "Welcome to the jungle."

"Guns, but no roses, huh?" Virgil said.

"Taste the pain, brother," the agent said.

Inside the door, Lucas asked, "What was that all about?"

"You're a generation too old to understand," Virgil said, walking on.

"I'm going to annoy the shit out of you if you don't tell me what that was about," Lucas said, catching up. "I'll hum 'It's a Small World' when we get back in the car."

"Jesus, not that," Virgil said, appalled.

"So . . ."

"He said, 'Welcome to the jungle,' which is a Guns N' Roses song. So I said, 'Guns, but no roses, huh?' because the FBI has guns but isn't coming up roses. So then he said, 'Taste the pain,' which is a Chili Peppers song appropriate to a problem the feds may be having with Gates . . ."

"I just pissed away ten seconds of my life listening to that and I'll never get it back," Lucas said, as he led the way toward the sound of voices. "Though it amazes me that an FBI agent would know all that shit. With you, it doesn't amaze me."

Gates was a portly man, thinning dark hair combed straight back and glistening under a chandelier. His face was red from too much drink for too long, and it showed in a rough, oversized nose. He wore his hair long, tied back in a ratty ponytail because, Virgil suspected, he thought he looked like Jack Nicholson in *The Witches of Eastwick*. That image was enhanced by a red velour robe worn over green cotton parachute pants and ruby-red velvet slippers.

He and four FBI agents were sitting in a great room conversation pit that featured an overhead dome painted gold, with the crystal chandelier dropping from the center of the dome. The FBI agents sat in a semicircle facing away from Lucas and Virgil.

Virgil mumbled, "The Sikes killer climbed over a six-foot wall."

"You snatched that right out of my brain," Lucas said quietly. "That guy would have trouble climbing his back porch in the summer and it only has two steps."

Gates spotted them and asked, in a loud, angry voice, "Who are these asshats and why are they wandering around my house?"

The FBI agents turned to look and Lucas said, "Davenport and Flowers. Here to help."

"I didn't have a fuckin' thing to do with any murder," Gates shouted.

"Yeah, we know," Virgil said.

Gates: "What?"

"We haven't made that determination yet," St. Vincent said.

"I suppose he could be an accomplice," Lucas said.

Virgil: "Seems unlikely."

"It does," Lucas said.

The front door, located down a long hallway, opened, throwing a shaft of light toward the great room, and a chunky man in a suit, carrying a briefcase, stepped inside and looked around. Gates shouted, "It's about fuckin' time, Herb. I'm up to my ass in federal agents. They think I killed that broad out at Minnetonka."

To the agents, and Virgil and Lucas, he said, "My attorney."

Herb, the attorney, walked down the hall and into the great room and said, "All I can tell you, Howie, is don't talk to them until we get an actual criminal attorney here. I called Marv Fingerhut, he's on his way. You haven't talked to them, have you?"

"I said a few things," Gates said.

"Well, shut up, you idiot."

The attorney, Virgil thought, didn't seem intimidated by his client.

Gates pointed at Lucas and Virgil and said, "These guys don't think I did it."

Herb looked at Lucas and Virgil. "It could be they're playing good cop/bad cop."

Virgil said, "That's mostly on TV. In real life, it's bad cop/bad cop."

Gates asked Herb, "When's Marv getting here?"

"He's over in St. Paul at his curling club. He wanted to finish up a game, or whatever they call them. A match."

"That motherfucker," Gates shouted. "I'm dying here, Herb."

Herb said to the feds, "I'm not here to formally represent Mr. Gates, I'm here as his friend. I'm civil, not criminal."

"Get on your fuckin' phone and call that fuckin' Marv and find out when he's gonna fuckin' get here," Gates shouted.

Herb went off to corner, saying, "Don't talk," but Gates shouted at Lucas and Virgil, asking, "Why don't you think I did it?"

"The FBI is actually conducting this interview . . ." Virgil began.

St. Vincent: "Go ahead and tell him. I'm interested myself."

Virgil shrugged and looked at Lucas, who said, "The killer crawled over a six-foot-high wall with snow on top of it. No sign that he used a ladder."

All the feds turned and looked at Gates, who burst out laughing, and then said, "There you go, Agent St. Vincent. I couldn't get over a wall like that if I had a fuckin' catapult."

Herb, from the corner, shouted, "Don't talk."

Gates: "Fuck it, I'm talking." To Lucas and Virgil: "Sorry about that 'asshats' comment."

Herb called, "He has to change his shoes, he's on his way." And to the feds, "It's close. Less than twenty minutes."

"We've already decided I'm innocent," Gates called back. To the feds: "Haven't we?"

"We have some additional avenues to explore," St. Vincent said. St. Vincent turned to Lucas and Virgil and said, "Why don't you guys sit down. Mr. Gates told us that the coat was stolen, he believes during a charity event he held here last month."

"Middle of December," Gates said. "Reported to the cops, though they didn't do anything about it. I don't think they even tried. The next week, I was going to Aspen. I know movie people. We hang out."

Virgil said, "Uh-huh."

"So, I went to the back closet, off the kitchen, where I'd hung up the coat, like two days before, and it wasn't there. Tore the house apart. Gone," Gates continued. "Could have been stolen by one of the staff, but I'm ninety-nine percent sure that it wasn't. When they steal something from me, it's either money or something they think I wouldn't notice. You know, batteries, laundry detergent pods, that kind of stuff. Stuff they can use."

Virgil asked, "How many people were at the event?"

"I don't know the final count. It was for the Sandhill Crane Rescue League. I let them use the house and fed them. You know, cheese dip with fuckin' leaves in it. Maybe . . . a hundred people? Hundred and twenty? The Sandhill people should be able to tell you, their PR chick, Mary Ann, mmm, Slattery, I think is her last name. Got some nice tatas on her if I do say so myself. Carries them right out high. First time I saw them in a low-cut blouse, I thought it was a tray of oysters and I almost ate one."

St. Vincent took off his glasses and pinched his nose. "Jesus Christ."

"He ain't here," Gates said.

Virgil and Lucas took seats in the conversation pit and Lucas asked, "What do you do for a living?"

"I own bars," Gates said. "Eight of them. High end. No hookers, nothing like that."

Virgil: "So you're kind of a gangster?"

Gates: "Hey!"

Virgil: "I mean, if you'd wanted to off Sikes, you would've had some other guy do it, instead of doing it yourself."

"I don't know no people like that," Gates said, looking away.

"Do you belong to the Wayzata Country Club?" Lucas asked.

"What? No. I'm at Minikahda."

Lucas: "Do you think Mary Ann Tatas would have a list of people at the party?"

Gates shrugged: "Probably. I mean, it's all the same people, every time. Come to the party, write a check for five hundred bucks, write it off, everybody calls you a . . ." He hesitated. "Whatchacallit. Philanderer?"

Lucas: "Philanthropist."

"That's it," Gates said. "And you get your picture in the paper. If there's still a paper. I haven't checked recently."

Virgil turned to St. Vincent and said, "You've got the personnel. You need to get the list and start talking to people."

"I could give you the list right now," Gates volunteered. "It was invitation only. You had to give up your invitation when you got here, and if you brought a friend, you had to write who it was on the invite."

"And you've still got . . ."

"The invitations? Sure. Documentation for the feds. I can write off the food and booze as a charitable contribution. But, I've had some conversations with the IRS a time or two, and now I make sure I can document everything."

"Could we see them?" Virgil asked.

"Sure." Gates turned and shouted, "Raoul? Raoul?"

A man came to a second-floor railing and called down, "What?"

"Where'd you put the invites from the Sandhill party?" Gates asked.

"IRS cabinet."

"Bring them down, would you?"

Raoul went to get the invitations and Lucas asked St. Vincent, "Could we get the list of rich Bitcoiners?"

"I'll have it emailed to you."

"Could you do it now? Send it to Virgil. He's got an iPad, makes it easy to read."

"I'm in the middle . . ." St. Vincent shook his head and shouted, "Moeller? Where are you?"

An FBI agent came in from the doorway, and St. Vincent told him to get the list from the office and send it to Virgil. Virgil gave Moeller his email address, and Moeller went away to do that. Raoul came down the stairs in stocking feet and handed a stack of white invitation cards, wrapped with a rubber band, to Gates, who tossed them to Lucas.

Lucas said, "We'll be in the kitchen."

Not yet convinced of Gates' innocence, St. Vincent wanted to spend more time with him.

IN THE KITCHEN, Lucas and Virgil spread a hundred and sixteen cards on a breakfast bar and extracted all those containing only a woman's name. They were left with forty-eight invitations. As they were doing that, Virgil's iPad chimed with an incoming email. He pulled it up and found an alphabetical list of 1,121 names of people believed to be investors in Bitcoin. The names had been taken from membership lists of Bitcoin-linked associations and businesses, as well as media reports.

They spent five minutes alphabetizing the names of people on the invitations, then began comparing them with names on the FBI's list. They were twenty-one names down the list when they got a match: Jamie McGruder.

"One hit, but it's something," Virgil said. He went back to the iPad. "Let me look him up."

St. Vincent, who was sitting fifty feet away, called Lucas on his cell about the names of the Hispanic men who worked at the country club. He was pissed off:

"I got a call. The goddamn Hogans, who should be sitting home on their goddamned couch so they could tell us who they sold their goddamned car to, are in Vegas. Nobody knows where."

"That's unfortunate," Lucas said.

"We're looking for them, but I'm told there are 150,000 hotel rooms on the Vegas strip," St. Vincent said. "The Vegas office will start looking, but it's late, and they probably won't get anywhere until tomorrow."

WHEN HE'D RUNG off, Virgil asked, "Think we should tell him about this McGruder guy?"

Lucas thought for a moment, then said, "Fuck him. We'll look up McGruder ourselves, and if it turns out to be something, and we need the help, we'll call him then."

They heard a commotion start in the living room, and after a moment, went that way, and found Gates' criminal attorney, Marvin Fingerhut, kicking the feds out of the house.

Fingerhut was tall, thin as a pencil, wearing a gray suit. He had a series of small scars on one side of his face that might have come from burns suffered a long time ago.

He looked at Lucas and Virgil and groaned, "Fuckin' Davenport. You might know it."

He and Lucas were opponents in a men's hockey league. Fingerhut said, "I don't want you sneaking questions on my client."

"Yeah, we won't," Lucas said. "The FBI may be interested, but Virgil and I are working on a different angle."

"You can't trust cops," Fingerhut said to Gates. "Also, if this killer they're hunting lives here in Minneapolis, I could wind up defending him."

"When we catch him, and we will, we'll be sure to mention your name," Virgil said.

"I would appreciate it. In the meantime, stay away from Howard," Fingerhut said.

"These are the guys who think I'm innocent," Gates said to Fingerhut.

Fingerhut: "Bullshit. They don't think anything like that. They might not think you murdered the Sikes woman, but they think you're guilty of something. 'Cause they're cops."

To Lucas, he said, "I understand that my client turned over some party invitations. We want them back, and right now . . ."

St. Vincent: "Forget it. He gave them to us voluntarily. We have them, and we'll keep them."

"What? You're a lawyer now? What do you . . ."

"Yeah, I'm a lawyer," St. Vincent said. "Admitted to bar associations here and in Virginia. And I know more about this kind of thing than you do, Mr. Fingerhut, because I do it all the time. We'll keep the invitations."

Fingerhut, momentarily nonplussed, said, "We'll see about that."

"See all you want. Take us to court," St. Vincent said. "Though if you do, you'll just embarrass yourself and waste your client's money. The invitations will be returned if they're not material evidence."

Lucas smiled at Fingerhut, said, "High-sticked in a Lake of the Isles mansion, you fuckin' bender."

"Bender my ass," Fingerhut said. "You caught your breath from landing up in the bleachers last week?"

Lucas waved goodbye to St. Vincent and told him that if anything turned up from the invitations, they'd let him know.

Out in the truck, Virgil punched McGruder's name into Google. When he landed on the right McGruder, which took several minutes, he read the entry and then said, "I don't believe it."

"What?"

"Hang on a second."

Virgil went to Google Maps, typed in an address, got a map up and switched to a satellite view. Went to a saved page, found another address, typed it into the mapping program, and again switched to a satellite view.

He tipped the iPad toward Lucas. "You see the little red pointer things on the addresses?"

"Yeah. Hey, they're . . ."

"Exactly. McGruder lives on Minnetonka. He could see Sikes's dock from his back porch. What are the chances he knew her?"

"High. We gotta talk to St. Vincent now . . ."

"Why? I thought we were gonna . . ."

"Now we need his help," Lucas said.

St. Vincent was gobsmacked that the invitations had provided a hit. "Okay. What do you need from me?"

"We need a cop. Even a fed. But it's gotta be somebody with lights and siren and a cell phone. We'll get you an address as soon as we can."

"Why?"

Lucas told him.

EIGHT

They would meet the cop car, or the federal agent's car, at the corner of Shoreline Drive and Ferndale Road, in the town of Orono. Virgil was looking at a satellite image of McGruder's house, a sprawling mansion across a bay from the Sikes house.

"McGruder lives inside a wall, or a hedge . . . looks more like a wall," Virgil said. He tapped a bare spot on the satellite image and added, "We should be able to sit up here with a pair of binoculars and see everybody coming and going."

St. Vincent called and said a federal SUV would be coming, lights and siren attached.

Lucas drove. Virgil, still working the iPad, read a canned biography of McGruder—college education, Bitcoin, charitable works, a story about flying sailplanes—and found a sale for McGruder's house on a Realtor site: the sale was six years old, for eight-point-four million dollars.

"No more recent sale, so it was probably him. Can't see much of the house, they removed the real-estate photos. Fourteen thousand square feet, if you can believe that. Going to Google Earth . . . No way out the back, it's all lakefront. Except the lake is frozen right now."

"All for one guy."

"We don't know that. There could be eight maids-a-milking and nine ladies dancing, inside." Virgil sang a snatch of "The Twelve Days of Christmas."

"Now I'll have that fuckin' song inside my head," Lucas said. "But, the bigger the house, the better chance that he's got lots of help."

"Here's another idea," Virgil said. He called St. Vincent back and asked if he had a contact number for Hillary Sikes' husband, Anson Sikes. He did, and Virgil took the number and called it, putting the phone on speaker. After identifying himself, he asked, "Do you know a man named Jamie McGruder?"

"Sure. Not well. Got a boatload of money, I'm told. Lives across the water from us."

"Has he ever been in your house?"

"Yes. At the Christmas party. That was . . . December seventeenth. You think he was involved somehow? He's a slippery little weasel."

"We're just checking a lot of possibilities, all that we can think of," Virgil told him. "Anyway, thanks—we'll get back to you if we find anything."

"MCGRUDER SCOUTED THE cameras," Lucas said, when Virgil had hung up. "From inside the house, no less. Might have seen a video monitor."

They found a spot on Shoreline Drive and Virgil dug a pair of image-stabilized Canon binoculars out of his gear bag, rolled his window down and looked at McGruder's house.

"Can't see much. I do think there's a wall behind that hedge. Maybe . . . six feet tall? Big steel gate. If he's got household help, they must park around back. There's a parking pad back there, you can see it on the satellite photo."

"If you see a Bentley coming out, that probably won't be household help," Lucas suggested. "Wonder where that fed is?"

THE FED ARRIVED ten minutes later. Lucas and Virgil walked over and got in the back seat, behind a male FBI agent and Lorna Woods, who curled a lip at them. The male agent, who was driving, seemed amiable enough, and introduced himself as Jim Lambert.

"What are we doing?" Woods asked.

"We're looking for the cars of household help coming out of that guy's driveway over there," Lucas said, pointing down the road. "We don't know when anybody will come out, or even if. I don't have lights or a siren on this car, that's why we need you. If we do see somebody coming out, we'll call you and tell you whether or not to stop it."

"How are you going to decide?" Lambert asked.

"We're looking for older, rougher-looking vehicles. Something that would be driven by household help."

"Hope we don't have to wait long," Lambert said. "These houses, I'm starting to get Richie Rich poisoning."

"I've got to tell you," Woods said to Lucas. "This all seems crazy to me. Too random. Too loose."

"Not crazy," Lucas said. "Maybe a little loose."

IN THE FIRST hour, not a single vehicle entered or left the Mc-Gruder house. Virgil had cheese and cracker snacks in his equipment bag and shared them with Lucas. Then at three o'clock, two vehicles left, five minutes apart. The first was a single woman in an older Camry and Lucas sicced the feds on her.

They used their lights to pull her over a block from McGruder's and Lucas stopped behind the FBI truck. He and Virgil got out and were joined a moment later by Woods. A frightened-looking Hispanic woman rolled down her car window and asked, "What did I do?"

"Probably nothing," Virgil said, smiling. "We're stopping people at random in this neighborhood, looking for a man who may have worked in this area. We want to know if you recognize him."

He had the three driver's license photos ready, and he thrust the iPad at her. As she was checking the photos, a pickup appeared at the McGruder gate, stopped briefly, then turned the other way.

Lucas said, "I got it," ran back to the FBI truck, climbed inside, and he and Lambert went after the fast-receding pickup.

The woman in the car, still looking frightened, said, "You should ask Paul."

"Do you know him?" Lucas said, pressing.

She said, "Ask Paul. Paul might know."

"Who's Paul?" Virgil asked.

"The man in that pickup. He might know this man. He's that pickup that came out."

Woods said, "Ma'am, we need to see your driver's license."

The woman fumbled her license out of her purse and Woods asked her if the name and address were correct, and the woman said they were—Alejandra Escobar, from Minneapolis. Woods took a photo of the license with her iPhone and Virgil did the same. Woods warned the woman not to talk to McGruder about being stopped and told her that she could go. She and Virgil jogged back to Lucas' Cayenne, and on the way, Woods said, "It's hard to believe, but she knew him."

"I think so," Virgil said. "She was scared. Maybe illegal. We can always go back to her."

Virgil turned the Cayenne around and they drove a half mile up Shoreline, to where Lucas and Lambert were talking to the driver of the pickup. They got out of the truck and walked to the pickup, where Lucas told them, "This is Paul Riley. He just delivered a cord of fireplace wood. He's happy to cooperate."

Virgil showed him the photos. Riley squinted at them, then said, "Sure." He tapped one of the photos. "Dom Velez. He works for Mr. McGruder part-time in winter. He plows the road, blows off the driveway and the patios. What'd he do?"

"We need to talk to him about an investigation we're working on. You know where he lives?"

"St. Paul, somewhere, when he's here. I don't know where, exactly. Mr. McGruder would have a phone number for him. And an address. Dom's, you know, a Mexican, but he's an American citizen, he's legal, and so I think Mr. McGruder might have him on the payroll and have an address."

"You said, 'when he's here.' Where else would he be?" Virgil asked.

"Sometimes he goes to Worthington," Riley said. "I think he's got a wife down there."

"He just plows roads?"

"In the winter. He's on a golf course grounds crew the rest of the year, I think."

Lucas: "Wayzata Country Club?"

"Yeah, that's it."

"Does Mr. McGruder belong to Wayzata?" Lucas asked.

"Mmm, maybe. I know he plays golf sometimes," Riley said. "He has some nice clubs."

Woods said to Lambert: "Oh my God. I was here for it."

"We were both here for it," Lambert said. "I pulled him over."

Woods said, "Let's call St. Vincent . . . we can use my phone."

Lambert: "I got mine right here, let me punch him up . . ."

Riley frowned, asked, "What did he do? Dom?"

Lambert and Woods walked off a few steps to make the call to St. Vincent, arguing as they went. Lucas took a cell phone photo of Riley's driver's license, got a business card from him, warned him not to talk about being stopped by the FBI, and sent him on his way.

Virgil was watching the two excited FBI agents, and told Lucas, "They were arguing about whose phone they should use to call St. Vincent. They each wanted to use their own phone, so their name would pop up on St. Vincent's phone . . ."

"As somebody said—I think it was you—the credit gets sliced exceedingly thin," Lucas said. He looked back down the street toward McGruder's mansion. "But we've got Jamie McGruder. Yes, we do."

———————

ANOTHER ZOOM CALL with FBI deputy director Mallard, this time with only four faces in the checkerboard: Virgil, Lucas, St. Vincent, and Mallard.

St. Vincent emphasized the role of the Minneapolis agents in doing the interviews with McGruder's household help, which Mallard didn't quite ignore.

"That's good, David, that's great." Mallard's eyes tilted down on the screen. "Now we have a name for the man who bought the car. This Velez, and he's apparently right there in Minneapolis, so David . . . get on that. Get your people pounding it."

"I will. Now," St. Vincent said. "All night, if we need it."

"Let's all understand this: we won't get a conviction based on the evidence we now have against McGruder—his being at the party where the coat was stolen, his involvement with Bitcoin, the fact that he seems to be the right height . . . all that circumstantial detail," Mallard said. "Getting this Dom Velez guy on the stand might get us to sixty-forty. I appreciate everything you guys have done, and the speed you did it with, but . . . dig deeper."

Virgil and Lucas had done the Zoom call from the Cayenne, while St. Vincent did it from Minneapolis FBI headquarters. He called them immediately after the Zoom call ended and said, "We'll nail down every piece of paper we can find on McGruder, all internet references, all social media, all legal documents. Same with this Velez. Dom, is that Dominic, or Domingo? We'll find out. That'll be coming in heavily by tomorrow, if you want to come over and sort through it."

"We may do that," Lucas answered. "We'll see if we can figure out any other approaches. One thing you big brains should start thinking about—if we develop evidence linking to McGruder, but not enough for a conviction, will you offer him a deal if he points us at the other members of the Five? Stop the killing?"

"My personal feeling is, there's not a chance in hell of that happening," St. Vincent said. "But, I'll talk to Washington and get some people mulling it over."

When he'd rung off, Virgil said, "Well, the FBI are now filling up a big box with paper. The box we've got to be thinking outside of."

"Cliché. 'Thinking outside the box,'" Lucas said. "Did you put that kind of shit in your novel?"

"Fuck you."

"WE'VE BEEN LUCKY," Lucas said, as they drove back toward the Cities. "We look at those press releases and we kinda laugh, because they are kinda funny, and the dead people really are assholes. But McGruder and his pals are psychos. I'm thinking about when I was looking down at Hillary Sikes. Nothing funny about that. Nothing."

Virgil nodded. "I'm with you. We've both seen people get hurt or killed and we think that . . . how it happened was funny. Remember Del and the whole pinking shears thing?"

"A classic," Lucas said, grinning.

Virgil: "But I don't think I've ever dealt with someone who thought killing was *fun*. Who was doing it for entertainment. I mean, God help us, that's the feeling I'm getting from the press releases. That they're really having a good time."

"They say that they're all rich and I'm beginning to believe them, when I look at McGruder," Lucas said. "We'll see how hard they're laughing when we bring the pressure. These are not people who are used to getting squeezed."

Virgil picked up his Tahoe at Lucas' house. Frankie was waiting at the Mall of America, currently in a Barnes & Noble bookstore.

"See you tomorrow," Lucas said, as Virgil got in the truck. "We'll nail down this Velez guy first thing."

NINE

Jamie McGruder was sitting at a kitchen bar eating a late snack of red raspberries, blueberries, and strawberries soaked in cold unwhipped cream, when Paul Riley called. McGruder almost ignored the call, because he was deep into a streaming series on Netflix, which played on a television set into the kitchen wall, but Riley had never called before, so . . .

He picked up.

Riley said, "Mr. McGruder. I have a heads-up for you. Dom Velez might be in trouble with the federal government. I don't know why—they wouldn't tell me. They did ask me not to talk to anyone about it, but I thought you oughta know."

Like an ice-cold fist gripping his heart: "What happened?"

Riley told him how he'd been stopped as he left McGruder's an hour earlier and asked if he recognized a bad driver's license photo of Velez and two others.

"Where's Dom? You know?"

"He went home to Worthington, I think," Riley said.

McGruder knew exactly what Velez might have been involved in, but he asked, "You think he might have been haulin' drugs?"

"Could be. I know he liked his weed," Riley said.

"Okay. That's probably it. Keep me up on this if the federal agents come back to you," McGruder said.

"Sure. I never mentioned you, by the way."

"Thanks. There'll be a little extra appreciation in your next pay envelope," McGruder said.

MCGRUDER SAT STILL as a rock for more than a minute, the streaming video now unheard and unseen. Analysis: if they'd stopped Riley outside his house, with photographs, then they'd found the car and linked it to the sellers. How they'd gotten to him, he didn't know, but they'd somehow linked him to Velez. They'd only made the link an hour earlier, so they probably hadn't gotten to Velez himself, if he was in Worthington.

Not yet.

This, he thought, was why he'd taken all the ninja training. He finished the last of the fruit, rinsed the bowl, put it in the kitchen sink, got a flashlight, and walked down to his garage. He had four vehicles, but only regularly drove three of them. The fourth, a top-of-the-line Dodge Ram 1500 EcoDiesel, hadn't been out for a month.

Nevertheless, he took his creeper off the garage wall—he had some of everything he'd need if the SHTF—and slid under the truck, looking for any kind of electrical box that shouldn't be there. He didn't think he'd find anything, because the feds would need a warrant to enter the house and bug him, and if they were just that afternoon linking him to Velez, they wouldn't have had time.

He didn't find anything. Satisfied, but scared, with his heart thumping, he took the elevator to the top floor, walked to his bedroom and past the bed into a dressing room. The last of four ceiling-to-floor dressing mirrors doubled as a door into his safe room. He went inside the safe room and found the 9mm ghost gun he'd taken to Sikes' house as a last-resort backup. He put the gun in a pack along with two loaded magazines of Speer Gold Dots.

He pulled out a concealed drawer, removed a bottle of amphetamines and shook out two tabs, stuck them in his shirt pocket, and retrieved an unused burner phone. Out of the safe room, down the elevator to the first floor, to the kitchen. Two packs of Oreos, one chocolate and one vanilla, both with Double Stuf, went in the pack.

To the home office: he got on the computer, pulled up Dom Velez's legal home address in Worthington. Dom lived alone, when he was in Worthington, although sometimes his ex-wife stayed over. She could be a problem, he thought. Or, he could be a problem for her.

Back in the garage, he put the pack in the Dodge Ram and checked the fuel gauge: it was nearly full, and the computer said he had more than eight hundred miles of range. He rolled the garage door up and looked outside. There was a bare hint of sunlight on the western horizon. He went back to the garage, looked at the cars, decided on the Benz, retrieved the keys from a lockbox in the kitchen, got in the car and backed it out.

More ninja stuff: thank God he'd taken the training. He ran a twenty-mile counter-surveillance route, into town, around dark corners and down long alleys. He saw nothing suspicious. Which didn't mean that they didn't have a chopper up there, spotting him, but . . . you have to take some chances, and again, he didn't think they'd have had time to organize that.

Ninety percent satisfied that he was not being watched, he drove to a downtown club called the @&X, a big dark place known for the price of its drinks, which was high, and the softness of its hip-hop music, which was disgusting, and might have been taken from an elevator. He was known there; he climbed on a barstool and the bartender said, "Usual?"

McGruder said, "Let's go with a Manhattan tonight. I need something sweet." A woman he knew slightly was sitting down the bar with a friend, and he added, "Speaking of sweet, I'm gonna go see how friendly Annie is feeling tonight. Bring it down there."

The bartender said, "Good luck," and went to make a drink.

Down the bar, he asked the woman, Annie, "This seat taken?"

"Jamie," she said. Her blond bangs came down to her eyebrows, which were brown; she was wearing a tight gold choker. "You're buying."

"Of course. As long as it doesn't have umbrellas in it."

She introduced her friend as Gwyneth and McGruder said, "Really? Gwyneth? How'd that happen?"

"My mom watched the *Emma* movie about a hundred times, so . . ."

The women had two drinks as McGruder carefully nursed his Manhattan, and he bought them a third, and then said, "Whoops. Gotta go see the candyman."

RIGHTEOUS PREY

He nodded toward a drug dealer who'd just come in from the back door.

"Bring back something good," Gwyneth said.

He talked to the dealer, bought two hundred dollars' worth of cocaine in a small plastic baggie, put it in his pocket, drifted toward the back door, went out and around the building, got back in his car and drove home. The cocaine went down the kitchen sink. Coke frightened him—he worried about heart attacks and strokes. He burned the baggie and put the melted lump in his pocket, to be thrown out when he was on the highway south.

Sober, drug-free, and armed, he put two Cokes of the bottled kind in a cooler and climbed in the truck. Rested his head against the steering wheel for a moment and thought, *Do I really want to do this?*

No, he didn't, but he had no choice. Out of the garage, over to I-494, south to I-35, past the ski slope and into the Minnesota countryside. Remembered to throw the melted cocaine baggie out the window. He got off at a back road sixty miles south of the Cities, did another counter-surveillance run, stopped the truck and scanned the skies for lights of a chopper or airplane, saw nothing.

Maybe the ninja stuff had made him paranoid? So many ways to die . . . But as one of his many trainers told him, if you're paranoid, use it.

He made the turn onto I-90 at Albert Lea a little more than an hour and a half after leaving the house, made it into Worthington an hour and forty-five minutes after that. Velez lived on Tenth Avenue, a neighborhood of small postwar houses redone with molded plastic or aluminum siding, all looking much alike.

Guided by the Google Maps app in the burner phone, McGruder spotted Velez's place, a low yellow house showing the flickering light of a television set through a side window. He eased to the curb, turned off the headlights, killed the engine and sat, not so much thinking as sweating. If the cops had found the car and linked it to Velez and Velez to him . . . Velez, who had the morals of a wolverine, would sell him out in one second.

He watched as he sat, saw no movement outside any of the houses along the street. Not a common hour to be out, in the winter in Minnesota. As he came into town, the truck's exterior thermometer told him it was two below zero. He took the pistol from the pack, slapped a magazine into it, racked the slide, clicked off the safety. Sat for another minute, watching the rainbow colors of a television flickering off the curtain in Velez's house.

Still had time to go back to Minneapolis . . .

And be lynched.

McGruder climbed out of the truck, sniffed the air: somebody nearby had cooked something greasy and meaty: barbeque ribs, he thought. The walkway leading to the front door hadn't been shoveled, but had been walked in. A concrete stoop led up to the door. He knocked on the outer door, a glass storm door, that rattled in its frame. A moment later, he heard Velez's voice through the unopened door: "Who is there?"

"Dom—it's me. Jamie."

The inside door had small pieces of window glass inset into it, too small for a hand, but big enough to peek through. Velez peeked through, and a bolt unsnapped and the door opened a few inches.

"Mr. McGruder?"

"We may have trouble. You may have to disappear for a while. I've brought money."

The door now opened wide. "Trouble? Come in."

Velez was a heavyset mustachioed man with ample tats on both arms, memorializing a Navy ship on one, and La Virgen de Guadalupe on the other. He was wearing a white tee-shirt, dark cotton slacks, and a worried frown. Behind him, in the living room, a woman was sitting at the far end of a couch, two beer cans on a table beside the couch. Three more empty cans sat on a table at the near end, where Velez had apparently been sitting.

McGruder stepped inside: the room smelled like old fried chicken and bacon grease and tobacco smoke. He pushed the door shut with a foot and took the gun from his pocket. The woman asked, in a dry Plains accent, "Who the hell are you?"

Velez turned to her and began, "This is Mr. . . ."

He stopped talking when McGruder shot him in the back, right through the heart. The muzzle blast was ferocious but contained.

The woman on the couch tensed, said, "Oh, hell no," started to push herself up and McGruder shot her in the forehead. He listened and the house was still as . . . death.

He stood there, waiting.

Analysis: no alarms. Two shots, inside a closed house in winter, which was surrounded by other closed houses. He spotted both ejected shells, picked them up, put them in his pocket. He hadn't touched anything coming inside, except the door, and that with his shoe. He bent over each victim: they were dead, no question, Velez on his back with a bloody splotch over the exit wound, right over his heart. The woman had kicked back on the couch, from which she looked sightlessly at the television.

They'd been watching the streaming video *Yellowstone*, and as McGruder watched, a rancher and a woman were shot and killed with a machine gun.

He couldn't help but smile: lots of gunshots coming out of the Velez house on this winter night . . .

The woman had been using a paper towel as a napkin and he carefully lifted the towel and used it to open the door. Out in the street, everything dark, no eyes that he could see.

He left the lights off in the truck as he rolled out to the end of the block.

So far, so good: but he still had four hours to go, to get back to Orono. Might be ice on the highway he hadn't encountered on the way out. He took one of the amphetamine tabs out of his pocket and a Coke from the cooler. Between the speed and the caffeine, he should be wide awake.

Still in the danger zone, couldn't be caught . . .

Back on I-90, he slipped into the thin stream of traffic, moved into the slow lane, and stayed there, remembering to throw the paper towel out the window. That was part of the whole Five tactical discussion: if you throw anything perishable out a car window, that'll be the last anyone knows of it.

Another ten miles, and he pulled on gloves and began disassembling the ghost gun. He threw the pieces out the passenger-side window and into the roadside ditch, one piece every couple of miles. He followed with the remaining cartridges and then the magazine.

THE SUN DIDN'T come up in Worthington until almost eight o'clock. Shortly after it poked itself over the horizon, two young FBI agents knocked on Velez's door. They'd been rousted out of bed by St. Vincent and sent to the address found on property tax records registered to a Dom Velez.

Velez couldn't be linked to McGruder through any employment records they found, but he did have a Worthington address registered at the Wayzata Country Club, where he'd worked on the grounds crew. A researcher's midnight call to a neighbor confirmed that the Worthington Velez was the man who worked at the Wayzata Country Club, and that he was at home.

Nobody answered the agents' knock in Worthington. One of the agents walked around to the side of the house, where a Toyota pickup and an aging Corolla were parked in the two-track driveway.

"Got two vehicles . . ."

"What do you want to do?" asked the agent at the door.

"Open the storm door and knock on the inside door . . ."

The agent opened the screen and knocked on the inside door, which opened a few inches under his knock.

"The door's open," he said. "Unlocked."

The agent who'd gone around to the side joined him on the porch, used a knuckle to push the door open a few more inches, and called, "Hello? Anybody awake?"

The agent gave the door another nudge, then peered inside. The light was dim, but he knew a dead body when he saw one. "Oh my God . . ."

AS THEY DID that, McGruder was sitting in a chain restaurant, eating huevos rancheros and home fries with copious ketchup, staring—wide-eyed and semi-stoned on the speed—at a ceiling-mounted television. A security camera peered down from the corner. McGruder ate there two or three times a month. A known customer.

Good tipper. The waitress called him "honey" and "sweetheart" and kept his coffee cup filled.

Not so much a waitress anymore, McGruder thought. She'd assumed a far more important role.

She was a witness, like the women at the @&X.

Bookended alibis.

TEN

Virgil and Frankie had shopped at the mall, had eaten steaks at the hotel restaurant, and watched a distinctly not-family-friendly zombie comedy called *Zombieland: Double Tap*, which cracked them up.

At eight o'clock the next morning, with Frankie planning to sleep until the shopping started at ten o'clock, Virgil called Lucas' cell phone. Lucas answered with a groan and said, "It can't be morning."

Virgil said, "Yes, and reasonably warm for January, sunny, one above zero, could go to eight by noon. I've finished my morning yoga exercises, done some push-ups and sit-ups, shit, showered, and shaved, and I'm heading down to Cecil's. I thought you might want to come along, since it's not far from your house, and I know you like to chat up the waitresses."

Lucas hung up without a word and Virgil smiled at the phone. Mission accomplished: Lucas was not an early riser.

And Virgil had been telling the truth. He was set to go, except for his boots, which he pulled on and tied. He got his parka, kissed the sleeping Frankie on her forehead, caught an elevator, and fifteen minutes later was looking at the café's menu, trying to decide between pancakes with bacon or waffles with bacon.

He went with the waffles, which didn't have nearly the calories of the pancakes, so he could with a clear conscience supplement the waffles with a husky cinnamon roll with pecans and white frosting.

He'd finished the waffles and was working on the cinnamon roll when Lucas wandered in. He was wearing jeans and what appeared to be yesterday's shirt with no tie and a puffy down jacket. He carried his Walther in front of his left hip and had made no effort to conceal it. He slid into the booth across from Virgil, pointed an impolite finger at the waitress and then at Virgil's cup of coffee. Virgil had stopped eating and asked, "What?"

"St. Vincent called. The feds found Velez," Lucas said.

Virgil nodded: "That was enough to get you out of bed?"

"No. What got me out of bed is that somebody got to Velez before the feds did and shot him dead, along with a woman who may have been his wife or girlfriend. Blood is still tacky this morning, so they were killed last night, probably around midnight."

Virgil rubbed his forehead, spoke down into his cinnamon roll: "Ahhh . . . fuck me. We set it in motion by talking with McGruder's help."

The waitress came over with a cup of coffee and asked Lucas, "Is the gun absolutely necessary, Lucas?"

Lucas tried to smile at her and said, "I'm sorry, Caroline, I got some really, really bad news. I needed to share it with my suspect here."

She looked at Virgil and asked, "What are you suspected of?"

"Getting up too early in the morning," Virgil said.

Lucas put both hands to his face and rubbed. The waitress said, "You don't look so good, Marshal."

"I don't feel so good," Lucas said. He checked Virgil's empty plate and the half-eaten cinnamon roll, and asked, "Gimme . . . pancakes? With butter and lots of syrup. And bacon."

"Of course. Your suspect had about the same thing."

VIRGIL: "LET ME guess. They're not finding a lot of clues."

Lucas shook his head. "You know what happened?"

"I can guess. One of those household helpers told McGruder that we were looking for Dom Velez. He drove down there last night and killed him. The dead woman is collateral damage."

"Before he did that, he established an alibi up here, McGruder did," Lucas said. He knew that; he didn't yet know what the alibi would be. "He probably established another one this morning."

Virgil nodded: "Probably. We're SOL."

Lucas explained that with Velez's driver's license in hand, the feds had contacted his neighbors and had confirmed that he was probably in Worthington—a neighbor said his truck was parked outside the house. By that time, late in the evening, they decided to roll two agents out in the early hours of the next day, instead of the middle of the night. That was a mistake, which was now being buried.

After listening to the story, Virgil said, "We're gonna have to bullshit McGruder."

"We can't do it directly," Lucas said. The pancakes and bacon arrived, and he began to wake up. "If we go right at him, he'll get a lawyer and the lawyer will gag him. If we don't go right at him, he'd have no excuse to lawyer up—that'd be like recognizing the fact that he's a suspect in a murder, while not having any reason to think that."

"Will St. Vincent and Mallard let us get away with bullshitting him?"

"They won't have much choice. Not with Velez dead," Lucas said. "When I talked to St. Vincent, he wasn't just unhappy. He was crazy angry. He sounded desperate. I mean, we had McGruder in the bag and he unbagged himself. St. Vincent won't be blamed, but there'll be talk about how the local FBI people could have acted more quickly . . ."

"You know what they say," Virgil said. "Oh, well."

"Yeah. St. Vincent wants us to take part in another Zoom call with Mallard at ten o'clock."

"Better come up with some ideas then," Virgil said.

They talked about various flavors of bullshittery and drank coffee for forty-five minutes, then headed over to Lucas' house, a half mile away. At ten o'clock, with Lucas in the kitchen and Virgil in the living room, they signed onto the Zoom link, the four-square checkerboard again, Mallard and St. Vincent in the top two squares, Lucas and Virgil in the bottom two.

St. Vincent: "As you can imagine, there are some unhappy people out here. Nobody's pointing any fingers, it wasn't anybody's fault, we didn't move too slow, it was just that . . . McGruder moved fast. How could we know he had the guts for it? Or would even have any idea he should do that?"

"I doubt that CNN will take that attitude," Lucas said.

"Don't worry about CNN," Mallard said. "We can handle CNN. The question is, what do we do with McGruder? He's not only a lead, he's the actual killer."

Virgil: "Gonna have to bullshit him."

St. Vincent: "If we can't find something solid, I'd agree. I'm hoping Lucas and Virgil can come up with something . . . since they seem to be good at that kind of thing. I'm putting my whole team here on background research. We're already on McGruder's cell phone records and it appears his phone was turned on, plugged in, at his house all night. Earlier in the evening, we traced it to a nightclub. We're looking for any trace of him driving down to Worthington last night . . . if he did."

"He must've," Mallard said.

"Unless he had assistance. With his kind of money, he could buy some. We don't even know that Velez's murder was spontaneous," St. Vincent said. "He might have decided weeks ago to get rid of the only witness who could hang him, and the fact that it happened last night was a coincidence. I mean . . . I hate to use the word 'hit,' but the hit looks professional. Two shots, two dead. No shells, no witnesses as far as we know . . . None of the neighbors saw or heard anything."

Mallard: "Virgil, you want to manipulate him. What'd you have in mind?"

"That we seem to be building a case without needing Velez. That we maybe create a news story, that we leak that story onto the Five page on Facebook, where he's sure to see it, and hint that we're closing in," Virgil said. "He already knows we're around, looking at him, but we need to pull a reaction out of him."

"We can't let him stand pat," Lucas added. "We have to make him move."

"You're talking about manipulating the media as well as Mc-Gruder," Mallard said.

"We have to," Lucas said. "We have to get the worm in his ear from some other source than us. We can't talk to him directly or he'll know it's bullshit."

Mallard nodded. "But the media . . . we wouldn't want it to get out of hand," he said. "Keep in mind that not all the media is as gullible as it sometimes seems. You need to seem credible."

"We're thinking that we might suggest to a selected media outlet that the Velez murder in Worthington is connected to the Five. That'll get people scrambling around looking at Velez. Maybe we can get the Minneapolis TV news to send somebody over to knock on McGruder's door . . . you know, based on police rumors that he knew Velez."

St. Vincent: "Sounds . . . tenuous."

Mallard to St. Vincent: "Okay, David, what are your other options?"

"Well, better bullshit, for one. I haven't had the time to develop any ideas along those lines . . ."

"Then let's get these started," Mallard said. "Lucas, how are you going to feed the media?"

"You know I'm friends with Elmer Henderson . . . Senator Henderson."

"I do, somewhat to my past discomfort," Mallard said.

"He owes me one at the moment . . . and he talks to the Twin Cities media on an hourly basis," Lucas said. "I'll get him to feed a story to a woman at Channel Three who happens to have my phone number. When I refuse to confirm or even discuss Henderson's tip, she'll take that as *being* a confirmation. Since it is television news, they'll go with it. Then we'll feed that story to the Facebook page . . . McGruder's got to be looking at that."

"I hate this kind of shit," St. Vincent said. "Feeding lies to the media. They're already unreliable enough."

None of the other three cops responded and into the silence, St. Vincent began to tap-dance. "But I guess if that's what we gotta do, that's what we gotta do."

Mallard: "Lucas, neither I nor Agent St. Vincent want to hear anything more about this. The media connections. I expect you to do whatever you need to in your investigative capacity to stop these people, the Five, but the media . . . we don't want to hear about it."

"So when the shit hits the fan . . ."

"The FBI will remain shit-free," Mallard said.

When the call was finished, Virgil walked into the kitchen and said, "We're on our own, big guy."

"Not entirely. We'll still have FBI research and surveillance," Lucas said. "Let's figure out what we have to give to Henderson."

"Are you going to tell him it's bullshit?" Virgil asked.

"I have to. We . . . operate on the basis of trust and we've done some . . . hmm, what would you call them?"

"Felonies?" Virgil suggested.

"No, more like . . . things that unsophisticated people might feel are questionable," Lucas said.

"As I said, felonies," Virgil said. "Whatever you do, gotta be quick with it."

"If Elmer goes along, it'll be quick," Lucas said. "We'll be on the air tonight. I'll talk to a guy who can feed the Channel Three story to the Facebook page in an untraceable way."

"You're talking about your friend Kidd?"

Lucas' eyes narrowed: "How do you know about Kidd?"

"I spent some time talking to him up at your cabin, remember?"

"Oh . . . yeah."

Kidd was a painter and a computer genius, who'd been operating in the online swamps well before Google raised its head. He was married to a successful jewel thief, which Virgil didn't know, but Lucas did. Lucas had no way to prove that Lauren Kidd was a jewel thief, but he knew. Kidd was another University of Minnesota ex-jock, a wrestler.

"I was impressed," Virgil said. "One other thing, though. We should probably check on Paul Riley. I doubt the woman we stopped would have tipped off McGruder—she was too scared. Riley might have. While keeping the FBI shit-free, we ought to try to keep Riley bullet-free."

Lucas pointed a finger at his own skull and said, "Duh. I'll get my parka. We should hurry."

THEY GOT GOOGLE directions to Riley's business, and as they drove, Virgil pulled up a website on his iPad. The website was primitive but did have a photo of Riley standing in the center of a semicircle of employees, all smiling for the camera. On the way, Lucas called Senator Elmer Henderson's office in Washington and asked for an urgent call-back.

Riley operated out of a concrete-block building with a shiny metal roof, the place surrounded by hard-used pieces of landscaping equipment, plastic-wrapped lumber, burlap-wrapped dormant trees, and three older pickups.

They found Riley in his office, which was an unpainted plywood box at the back of the building, with a plastic window looking out at the rest of the shop, which was clogged with newer tools and machinery. He looked up when they came through the door, pushed away from his desk with a placating grin.

"He knows what he did," Lucas muttered.

"But does he know about Velez?"

"Why don't we ask him?"

Riley had come to the office door. He said, "Marshals . . . something happen?"

Lucas: "Yes. You told McGruder about our visit, didn't you?"

Riley said nothing, held out his hands. Virgil shook his head and said, "Don't lie to us, Paul. You know what happened, right?"

Riley took a half step back, confused. "What happened?"

"Somebody went to Worthington last night and murdered Dom Velez and his ex-wife in their home. Shot them to death," Virgil said. "You lie to us, you're an accomplice to first-degree murder. Otherwise, you're just a witness."

Riley crossed himself: "Dom?"

"Shot in the back," Lucas said. "His wife was shot in the forehead, right above her eyes. Saw it coming, never had a chance to stop it."

"Jesus, Mary, and Joseph . . . I . . ."

"Told McGruder . . ."

"I thought . . . should I get a lawyer?"

"You don't need one yet," Lucas said. "Unless you knew McGruder was going to Worthington to kill the Velezes."

"I did not. *I did not.* How do you know Mr. McGruder . . . ?"

"We're investigating him. He's a suspect in another murder," Lucas said. "If you tell him that he's a suspect, you *will* be an accessory and we'll put your ass in prison for a very long time."

Riley held out his hands again, palms up: "But . . . why would Mr. McGruder kill anyone? He's a billionaire. He doesn't have to kill anybody for any reason."

"He kills because he's nuts and he's bored and looking for something exciting to do," Lucas said. "Now: when did you talk to him, and what did you tell him?"

Riley didn't have much to say about that—that he'd made the phone call because he thought Lucas and Virgil were investigating Velez, not McGruder. Velez had worked directly for McGruder, and if he was a threat, he thought McGruder should know.

"Why was Velez living in Worthington if he's working for McGruder and at the country club?" Virgil asked. "He couldn't be commuting . . ."

"He has, had, two wives," Riley said. "Everybody knew that. One in Worthington and one here. He went back and forth. He was here, mostly. I don't know why he went back to Worthington this time. Keep that wife happy, I guess. I didn't know him that well."

The FBI hadn't found an address for Velez in Minneapolis, so Lucas asked, "Was the house in the Twin Cities in his wife's name? Do you know?"

Riley closed one eye, thinking or trying to remember, then said, "You know, it might have been. I remember he said something about how she had a nice house, which I guess means it was hers, not his. Besides, he didn't have enough money for two houses. I'm surprised he had enough money for one."

"You don't know her name?"

"No . . . but I think they met, mmm, I'm thinking she works at a Starbucks up in Highland Park. In St. Paul. He brought me a free Frap, one time."

When they'd wrung him out, Lucas warned Riley not to be alone with McGruder. "He knows you told us about Velez. He might be worried that you'll tell us about the phone call you made. He may want to shut you up. So . . . find a reason not to see him. Don't do any work at his place."

Riley said, "You think he might kill me? I mean, he is a little goofy."

Lucas: "How?"

"He would take all these classes. Jumping out of airplanes. Gun classes. Scuba. Driving like a spy. He has a wooden target in his basement that he throws knives at, and when he's tired of that, he throws tomahawks. He got a pilot license, but I think he quit that."

"Thrill seeker?" Virgil asked.

Riley scratched an ear. "Maybe. He had a rock band for a while, he paid all the members. He played guitar and sang. I watched them rehearse one time, and he was not a very good singer. I don't know if he's a thrill seeker—I think he just wants to be a cool guy and doesn't know how to be that."

Virgil: "When Lucas said he's nuts, he wasn't joking. Don't be his next victim."

Riley crossed himself again. "I have family in Janesville. Maybe I'll go for a visit."

"Good idea, but don't disappear on us," Lucas warned. "When we call, you answer. You're on a narrow ledge here—you're a witness, for sure. You don't want to make yourself into an accomplice."

After poking him a few more times without getting anything,

they gave him a final warning and left. On the walk back to the car, Virgil said, "The other wife. The one that's still alive."

"Yes."

THE HIGHLAND PARK Starbucks wasn't far from Lucas' house, and on some warm spring Sundays he'd walk there with Weather. The counter woman recognized Lucas, and told them that the manager wasn't in, but the assistant manager was available.

Amber was fetched. Lucas told her what Riley had said, and she said, "I think . . . I'm pretty sure that's Helen Socek. She has a live-in boyfriend. She calls him Dom. She's due in at three o'clock."

"Do you have an address for her?"

"I do, but she works mornings at a childcare center at her church. It's a Catholic church near her house . . ."

Amber got Socek's employment data off a computer. Virgil went to his iPad maps again, found her address. "She's in Frogtown," he said. "That's the house we made a pass at—nobody home."

A Francis Xavier Church was nearby. The church's website featured their daycare facility in what had once been an elementary school.

"Ten minutes," Virgil said.

THE DAYCARE CENTER was a plain one-level tan brick building. A yellowed notice on the entrance door said it was kept locked for security reasons, and that visitors were required to call the office for entry. Lucas tried the door, found it locked, as advertised, made the call and identified himself.

A plainclothes nun came to meet them at the entrance, introduced herself as Rose Ryan. Lucas showed her his badge and she asked, "Why do you need to see Helen?"

Virgil said, "There's been a tragedy, I'm afraid. Her . . . fiancé . . . was killed last night, in Worthington. She hasn't been informed yet."

Ryan put her hand to her mouth and said, "Oh, no . . ." She looked back into the building, then back at them, then took another step out on the stoop and pointed toward the end of the building. "If you go around the corner there, you'll find another entrance. There's a break room there, I'll get Helen and meet you there."

They walked around to the back entrance, saw another nun hurrying down the hall toward the door, and were let in and shown the break room. After a short wait, Ryan and a third grim-faced nun escorted Helen Socek into the room. They hadn't told her the reason that the marshal wanted to see her, but when she saw their faces, she blurted, "Did something happen to Dominic?"

Lucas looked at Virgil, who said, "I'm afraid so, Miz Socek. Would you like to sit down?"

She was a lumpy woman, probably fifty, gray hair cut in a way that would have been fashionable in 1940. "Just tell me. I bet Silvia was involved, wasn't she?"

Her face was clutched in fear and what might have been anticipatory loneliness. She began to cry, and Lucas, who'd done fewer notifications than Virgil, stepped away, and Virgil moved closer, looking in her eyes, and said, "Dominic was murdered. Silvia, we think it was Silvia, we don't have a positive identification yet, was killed at the same time by the same person. We're trying to find who did it."

Socek made a long wailing sound, groped toward a battered overstuffed chair, and the nuns helped her to sit. Lucas backed another step away, while Virgil squatted next to the chair and let her weep.

He remained that way for two minutes as she cried herself out, patted her shoulder; one of the nuns wrapped an arm around her, and Ryan asked if she wanted a glass of water or lemonade. Socek shook her head, no.

When Socek looked at Virgil again, he asked, "Did Dominic say anything, anything at all, about feeling threatened by anyone?"

"No, he didn't say anything like that . . . Was this at his house?"

Virgil nodded. "Yes. He and his friend were killed in the living room while they were watching television."

"Better than the bedroom, anyway," she said, with a hint of bitterness.

Virgil: "Do you think that might be a consideration? His love life . . ."

She shook her head. "No, no . . ." Then she looked up. "Are you going to ask me where I was last night?"

"Should we?"

"You can. I was at Starbucks until nine o'clock, I have a job at Starbucks in the afternoons and evenings. Then I went home and went to sleep, alone, then I got up at six o'clock and came here at seven o'clock for the first kids being dropped . . ."

Virgil: "Sounds like a very long day."

"Fourteen hours," one of the nuns said. "I didn't know that, Helen. We shouldn't ask so much."

Socek began to cry again and Virgil stood up, got a folding chair, and carried it close to Socek. When she subsided again, he said, "We need to get as much information about Dom's recent activities as we can, and as quickly as we can. We understand that he worked for a Mr. McGruder. Did he have any trouble with Mr. McGruder? Was there a conflict of any kind? Or with other people who worked for Mr. McGruder?"

She was looking down in her lap, sniffed, and Ryan said to another nun, "Go get some Kleenex," and Socek said, "There was no trouble at work. Mr. McGruder just gave him a bonus for his good work. We bought a new television with it so he could watch the Wolves."

A nun, with a querulous note: "Is that a nature show?"

Virgil gave her a look to warn her away from interruptions, but the look bounced off, so he said to her, "Basketball . . . Now, Miz Socek, when did he get the bonus? And you bought a television? Must have been a big bonus."

"I think so. Dom didn't tell me exactly how much. He was private about money. When he was asleep, I looked in the bank envelope and there were a lot of hundred-dollar bills. A lot."

"He got the bonus in cash?"

"He was always paid in cash, so . . ." She made a helpless gesture, a flap of the hands, a shrug. "You know . . . taxes. Dom didn't think taxes were fair."

"Okay," Virgil said. "When did he—"

Lucas' telephone buzzed and he looked at it, said, "I've got to take this. I'll do it outside."

He heard Virgil repeat the question to Socek and she answered, "Oh, I don't know exactly. Maybe two weeks ago? Somewhere in there."

OUTSIDE, LUCAS TOOK the call from Elmer Henderson. "I need a favor," Lucas said. "Your pal Porter hustled me into the Hillary Sikes investigation."

"I heard, and I wouldn't have. It was a well-deserved killing, a comment that I will deny if you tell anyone I said that. She was, without any question, the asshole these assholes said she is. Her husband thinks about two things: money and pussy. Hillary was worse, in my opinion, because she didn't even have the human dimension. All she thought about was money and how to get more. You couldn't even think why she wanted more—she had enough for about six Lake Minnetonka lives. Even worse, she donated to Republicans. She wouldn't give a nickel to save the whales, but if you were a tax-cutting Republican, she'd be right there with her checkbook."

"Yeah, okay, that's a wonderful word portrait, Senator, Your Excellency. I'm working a lead to her killer and I need you to leak some stuff to Channel Three, and specifically to Jennifer Carey, without telling her it came from me."

"I know Jennifer quite well. Isn't she the mother of your first kid?" Henderson asked.

"Yes, she is . . . but I don't trust her. She's way too honest. I need you to tell her that the feds are about to break the case and mention, kind of casually, that I'm on the case and I'm the fed who might break it," Lucas said. "I want her to call me, so I can decline to comment."

Henderson chuckled. "You're a sneaky rascal. I've always admired that in you. Maybe you should run for office, as long as it's not mine."

"Yeah, yeah. Here's what I would like you to do . . ."

Henderson listened, then said, "I can do that. I'll want a complete report later on—after you close out the killers."

"Thank you. We'll talk then."

VIRGIL WAS COMING out the door when Lucas rang off the call. "Not much more," Virgil said. "But, Velez's bonus is something. Maybe a big thing."

"We'll get St. Vincent's guys to look at McGruder's bank withdrawals. That's something they can handle. And you're right. That could be big."

Virgil took a pair of sunglasses out of his pocket, put them on, prompting Lucas to do the same thing. "That phone call was from Henderson," Lucas said. "He's in. He'll make the call right away."

"Excellent," Virgil said. "We can get the bullshit going."

Ryan came out on the steps, and said, "This is terribly sad. Helen is a wonderful woman."

"Are you telling us that she isn't involved in her cheating boyfriend's death?" Lucas asked.

"Absolutely. That she might deliberately hurt somebody is . . . unimaginable. If I were you two, I'd forget about Helen and follow the money."

"You must watch cop shows," Virgil said.

"I don't watch them, but I used to be one," she said. "Thirty years with the Golden Valley PD. Don't have much faith in federal cops."

"Really? An ex-cop? Anyway, I have to agree with you," Virgil said. "I'm a Minnesota cop myself, BCA, temporarily on this federal task force."

"Then you might get somewhere," Ryan said. "I liked the way you handled yourself in there, Virgil." She looked over her shoulder and said, "I gotta get back."

IN THE CAR, Virgil said, as he removed his shoes to warm up his toes, "Didn't see that coming—that Sister Rose was a cop. Maybe she's doing penance?"

"Nah. Fits right in. You'd know that if you'd gone to a Catholic school," Lucas said. "I've still got a groove down the center of my skull from getting hit by those hickory pointer sticks that the nuns carried. Some of the sisters had a deep affection for unnecessary violence."

"You even knew the sticks were hickory?"

"Sure. They had 'Louisville Slugger' branded right on the side."

"I didn't have to deal with that," Virgil said, pushing his seat back, the better to get his stocking feet on the dashboard. "Plain vanilla public school. The education sucked, but you didn't get hit."

"Honestly? I'm happy I went to a Catholic school," Lucas said, as he did a U-turn in traffic, looking over his shoulder. "Got a decent education and developed a dirty mind, which is one of the unstated benefits of a Catholic education. My women friends have greatly appreciated that."

"I struggled with it, developing a dirty mind, you know, as a Lutheran," Virgil said. "Though I feel I succeeded in the end."

"So I've heard," Lucas said. "Call St. Vincent and get him working on McGruder's bank records. And get your fuckin' feet off my dashboard."

ELEVEN

St. Vincent already had a researcher working on McGruder's bank records: "We need to get Socek down here on camera," he said. "McGruder moves a lot of money around and we were looking for that car purchase. We couldn't find the exact amount paid, but we found one for five thousand over the purchase price. That sounds like it might fit the Velez payoff, the envelope full of hundreds."

"You guys take that, the car payment," Lucas said. "It's pretty much research from this point on. Virgil and I are going to see if we can dig up some more pressure . . . Have you talked to ATF about gun purchases?"

"Yeah, and he's made some. Quite a few, actually, and spent some good money on them. I'd be surprised if he used one of his legal guns to kill . . . He's too smart for that."

"Still something to look into," Lucas said.

Virgil had been listening to the call, his stocking feet still up on the dashboard, his sunglasses down his nose, his eyes closed. When Lucas got off the phone, he turned to Virgil and asked, "How would you feel about black-bagging McGruder's place?"

"With or without a warrant?" Virgil asked.

"Without. I don't think we could get a warrant—not yet," Lucas said.

"The guy's a zillionaire, he's got to be heavily protected," Virgil said. "I wouldn't be surprised by full-time camera monitoring separate from an alarm."

"Is that a 'no'?"

"I'll bag a place if I'm reasonably sure I won't get caught and if the problem is serious enough," Virgil said.

"This is serious enough," Lucas said. "Five dead—three that he did himself."

"Yeah." Virgil turned and looked out the window for a moment, where an elderly woman was pushing a walker up the street, a bag of groceries in a front bin. Then, "How would you do it?"

"I don't know yet," Lucas admitted. "I have the feeling that we might kick something loose, if we could get inside."

Virgil: "The possibility of bagging the place had already occurred to me, of course. That woman we pulled over at McGruder's house, Alejandra Escobar, we've got her driver's license . . ."

"Oh, yeah."

"She was scared. Scared of us. She could be an illegal. If she's a housekeeper, she's got an alarm code."

"There you go," Lucas said.

"Now I've got another question," Virgil said. "How do you feel about terrorizing some poor woman who's just trying to scrape though life?"

"Not great," Lucas said. "Maybe we won't terrorize her, we could try to go a little gentle. Ask her help. Something . . ."

"Bullshit. We're gonna terrorize the shit out of her," Virgil said.

"Yeah, probably. To catch a serial killer."

"What about the cameras in McGruder's house? He's a billionaire, there're gonna be some."

"We talked about getting my friend Kidd to anonymously feed a Minneapolis news report to the Five page on Facebook . . . that would be child's play for him. I think he could fuck with McGruder's cameras, if he wanted to, and if they're connected to the internet, or a security service."

Virgil nodded: "So talk to him."

ALEJANDRA ESCOBAR, McGruder's housekeeper, lived in the Near North neighborhood of Minneapolis. She might be at McGruder's, but Lucas had a hunch that she wouldn't be—McGruder had been betrayed by one employee, he might have told the other one to take the day off.

As they drove to her address from St. Paul, Jennifer Carey called. Right on schedule. Lucas picked up, put the call on speaker, and said, "Yeah, Jen. What's up?"

"I understand you're running hot on the Sikes murder and have a solid lead on the Three killer," she said. She had a voice with some grit in it, and a decade and a half after their relationship had ended, Lucas still felt a tingle when he spoke with her. "We're going with that much of the story. I wanted to see how much more you're willing to tell me."

"You sound tired, babe. Maybe you should get some sleep."

"I'm wide awake. Give it up," Carey said.

"Jesus, Jen, I can't talk about an active investigation," Lucas said, not quite whining.

". . . Unless you decide that it'll help you out," she interrupted. "I mean, like, you've done it so often you've got a plumber on speed-dial just to fix your leaks."

Made Virgil smile. "That's unkind," Lucas said.

"But not untrue," Carey said. "So: you say it's okay to use your name . . ."

"I didn't say that . . ."

". . . But I would like the name of the other marshal you're working with so I can give equal credit if I hear a marshal's been shot and it's not you," she said.

"There's no other marshal working the case. I got pulled in personally because I work in the Twin Cities and was at the Three scene . . ."

"And because Porter Smalls and Elmer Henderson wanted you on it," Carey said. "I got called by one of them, and he kept saying 'them' instead of 'him,' so I know there's another marshal."

"Henderson never could keep his mouth shut."

"Hey! Did you take that fuckin' Flowers with you again?" she demanded.

Virgil called, "How you doin', Jen?"

"Much better than a minute ago. Now I can recount the whole buddy-act you two did down in Florida last year, the scuba diving and all that. I can promise our viewers that with two quality cops like you guys, you'll have Three in handcuffs by the end of the week. How about this: 'Davenport and Flowers, known for their sometimes unusual and occasionally grossly illegal, not to say fascistic, tactics . . .'"

Lucas: "Jen, don't do that. Be nice, and I'll give you a couple of things."

"Give," she said again.

"We do have a solid suspect," Lucas said. "Here's a fact that nobody else has, but you have to attribute it to another source . . ."

"I can do that."

He told her about the murder of Dom Velez and the belief that the Three killer did it in an effort to cover up. He sketched in the tracing of the killer's car from Minneapolis to Eau Claire and then to Velez.

She said, "Hot damn! So your suspect has killed at least three people, and the numbers gang have killed at least a total of five."

"You can use that, but you've got to attribute it to a source in the FBI," Lucas said.

"That would be wrong," Carey said.

Lucas: "Yeah? So what?"

"Okay, got me there," Carey said. "You know, I'm starting to feel the slippery finger of a Davenport manipulation in all this, the Henderson call, th—"

Virgil jumped in: "When will you put this up? On the air?"

"Five, six, and ten," Carey said. "I've got makeup standing here, ready to powder my nose. You think the Worthington cops will talk to me about Velez?"

"Use your feminine wiles," Virgil said.

"I did that with Davenport, once, and he knocked me up," Carey said.

LUCAS RANG OFF a moment later—she never said "thank you"—
and he and Virgil continued to the Near North, a neighborhood of
small crumbling houses, each one a different weathered color than
the next, with rough blacktopped streets, cars stored in driveways,
some covered with plastic wrappers. Escobar's house was painted a
rust-red with a driveway that ended at glass windows that had once
been a garage door, the garage having been converted into a room.
A Camry sat in the driveway, facing the windows.

"That's the car she was driving, so she's probably there," Virgil
said. "Want me around back in case she books?"

"Not a bad idea. Did she look like a runner?"

"She looked like somebody's overweight grandma," Virgil said.

"If she's not going to run, but other people do . . . you'd just be in
their way, and you might get run over. If somebody runs, but she
doesn't, it just lowers the pressure inside. Nobody gets hurt."

They went together to the front door, knocked. A face appeared
at a window to the left, then disappeared. Virgil said, "Maybe I should
have been around back . . ."

They knocked again, tried the doorbell, which didn't seem to
work. Virgil went sideways, to look toward the back of the house,
didn't see anyone running, but did see untracked snow. He walked
back to the porch as Lucas pounded on the door and then the door
opened a crack and a pair of dark eyes peered out. *"Que?"*

Virgil said, "We need to talk to Alejandra Escobar."

"She not here," the dark eyes said. They seemed to belong to a
young girl, maybe a teenager.

"Her car is here. We only want to talk," Virgil said. "We're police, but we don't want to arrest her or send her away. Talk only. We're not ICE."

The dark eyes pulled back, and seconds later were replaced by a slightly different set of dark eyes, older, but not as old as Escobar's. Their owner spoke good but accented English: "Why do you want Alejandra? She's asleep. She's done nothing."

"We don't think she has," Virgil said. "You need to wake her up. This is very important. Very important and you don't want to be on the wrong side."

"One moment," the woman said.

The door closed most of the way, they heard women talking, then it opened again, wider this time, and Escobar stood behind it. She looked at Virgil and said, "You're the policeman who stopped me."

Virgil nodded: "We need to talk to you about Mr. McGruder. We will not tell him we spoke to you."

She hesitated, reluctant, then let the door swing further open. "What has he done?"

"Maybe nothing, maybe something. You've heard about Mr. Velez . . ."

"I heard this. I am sorry."

Lucas: "Could we come in? It would be easier to talk inside."

Escobar let the door open all the way, and Virgil stepped through. There were six women and three children in the living room, looking at him. The room contained three old but full-sized couches arranged in a semicircle, so all three could see the same television, which sat on a table in the center of the room, with an extension cord winding off to an outlet. All three couches had blankets and pillows and were apparently used as beds. The house smelled of beans and rice, tacos, stewed tomatoes.

Lucas crowded up from behind and Virgil stepped deeper into the room. The walls were nicotine yellow-brown, bare, with one exception, a framed picture of the Sacred Heart of Jesus.

Lucas nodded at the picture. "My mother had that picture," he said to Escobar.

"*Catolico?*" she asked.

Lucas nodded. "Yes. Uh . . . we should talk privately . . . by ourselves?"

Escobar nodded.

Lucas had wanted to get inside, but once inside, there was no place to talk privately: there were a dozen people living in the house. They wound up sitting in the Porsche, Virgil in the back seat with Escobar, Lucas in the passenger seat, where he could turn to look at the woman. She was short, heavy, sallow-faced, weary. Not, Lucas thought, weary from the day, but weary from the life.

Virgil said, "We are investigating Mr. McGruder. We think he may be involved in the death of Mr. Velez."

"I know nothing of that. I clean the house," Escobar said. "Every day, I clean, wash the clothes, iron the clothes, make the beds, I vacuum . . ."

Lucas nodded and asked, "Have you ever known Mr. McGruder to do anything . . . evil? Very bad?"

She didn't want to answer: He could see it in her eyes. He pushed: "Miz Escobar, we don't want to cause you any trouble . . ."

She picked up the implication: that they could cause her trouble if they wanted to. She said, "One time he slept late with this woman and he hit her. She had blood in her nose."

"Do you know if she called the police?" Lucas asked.

She shook her head. "I don't think so. I think she scratched him. Maybe before he hit. He had blood on his shirt, I think he had scratches here." She made an X on her chest.

Other than the one incident, there was not much. She'd heard McGruder lose his temper on two other occasions, shouting into a telephone. He'd also gotten harsh with her once when she'd washed a silk shirt and ruined it.

"I told him, my fault, I pay. But, he said no, I don't pay, but I have to be more careful. He's not bad with me. He pays good."

Virgil asked, "What time do you go to work?"

"Seven o'clock in the morning. I stop at three o'clock or when I finish."

"Is Mr. McGruder awake when you get there?" Lucas asked.

She shook her head. "Never. Okay, maybe one or two times. He sleeps to ten o'clock, he tells me he works very late."

"If he doesn't wake up early, then you must be able to turn off the alarm?" Virgil asked.

"Yes, I have code."

"What's the code?" Virgil asked.

They got the code, they got the location of the alarm panel inside a door that opened on the back parking pad. Virgil asked to borrow her key, which she reluctantly gave him. "We need to make a Xerox copy of the key, but we'll bring it back in half an hour," Virgil said.

Lucas asked, "How long have you been in the United States?"

Escobar looked down at her folded hands, as if expecting a blow: "Fourteen years."

"Fourteen years, a long time," Lucas said. Then he added, "We are investigating Mr. McGruder. We don't want to warn him. You are not to tell him that we talked to you. Do you understand? You are to work like you do every day, but do not tell him that we talked to you."

She bobbed her head but didn't look at either of them.

Virgil, "I hope you understand. You can't talk to him."

"I understand very well," she said, peering at Virgil. *I understand you will send ICE to get me, if I talk.*

"THAT WASN'T SO bad," Lucas said, as they drove away from Escobar's house. Virgil had used his iPad to spot a Home Depot not far away, where they could get the key copied.

"Bull. We scared the shit out of her," Virgil said.

"You think she'll talk to McGruder?"

"No. Or, not for a while," Virgil said. "She's caught between him and us. He pays well. We don't pay jack shit."

"But we got ICE on our side."

"Fuck those assholes," Virgil said. "But you're right. That's the way she'll see it."

"So?" Lucas had a question mark in his voice.

"Bag the motherfucker. Call Kidd, see what he can do about the cameras."

LUCAS CALLED KIDD, who cross-examined Lucas on the importance of the proposed hack, and when Lucas finished explaining, Kidd made a crunching sound and then said, "Sorry. I'm eating a stick of celery."

"How about it?" Lucas asked.

"Five dead. Three assholes and two innocent people. Or at least one innocent person. Give me a few hours—I'll look into it."

"The faster the better," Lucas said. "We'd want to go when it's dark. He's a nightclubber, so . . ."

"It'll take what it takes. I'll concentrate on it," Kidd said. "You wouldn't happen to know what security service he uses?"

Lucas hadn't told Kidd that Virgil was listening in, so Virgil stayed quiet but held up a finger, and went to his phone. He called up the camera, flicked through a couple of photos, then showed Lucas the foot-square security service sign that sat next to McGruder's driveway.

To Kidd, Lucas had said, "I'm checking my phone, I took a picture . . . Okay, It's Bass-Antrim Security, Armed Response."

"That's great, an armed response, shoot first, ask questions later," Kidd said. "Glad I'm safe in St. Paul, instead of sneaking around the affluenzia."

Virgil, looking at Lucas, mouthed "camera lens" and pointed at three concentric circles on the security service sign.

"I thought the sign had a circle on it, but looking at it, I think the circle is supposed to be a lens," Lucas said to Kidd. "They may run the cameras."

"I'll get back to you," Kidd said. There was a final celeric crunch, and he hung up.

THEY GOT TWO copies of Escobar's key at Home Depot, no questions asked. They drove back to Escobar's house and returned her original key, and Virgil said once again, "We needed to document the key, so we know if it is changed."

She nodded her head, her face down again, not believing a word of it.

"Really," Virgil said, feeling ashamed of himself. "That's what we did."

TWELVE

McGruder was lying on a yoga pad doing stretches and watching television when the fortyish blonde came up over a caption that read, "Channel Three Investigates: Jennifer Carey."

Carey said, "Channel Three has learned exclusively that two well-known Minnesota law-enforcement veterans, working with the FBI, are closing in on one of the infamous Five killers. A source with the Justice Department confirmed that U.S. Marshal Lucas Davenport and Minnesota Bureau of Criminal Apprehension agent Virgil Flowers have determined that the Three killer also murdered two people in Worthington, Minnesota, yesterday, apparently in an attempt to cover up . . ."

McGruder thought, *No, no, no . . .*

Carey's report lasted three minutes—forever, in television terms—and ended with a brisk, "The FBI refused to comment."

He lay back on the yoga mat: had they dead-ended at Velez? Maybe. But they'd stopped Riley outside his gate, so they were obviously looking at him. He had a momentary fantasy about appearing in court, looking tough but elegant, a team of smart-looking lawyers at his elbow . . .

But what if they lost? And he thought: the shoes. He had to get rid of the shoes.

And these two cops. He couldn't remember the name of the marshal, but the other one, the state agent, had a weird name. Flowers. Virgil Flowers. Sounded almost fictional, like the guy changed his name from Bob Jones or something.

On his way to retrieve Hillary Sikes' shoes, he paused to jot the name down on a sticky note. Virgil Flowers . . .

THE SUNLIGHT WAS dying fast, going a sulky orange, when Lucas and Virgil returned to McGruder's house, which was showing lights on all three floors. They cruised the front of the house and Virgil finally said, "I'm getting cold feet. That wall and gate look like they were modeled off Stillwater prison."

"Gonna be dark, though," Lucas said. "We've got that going for us. Not much traffic."

"That wall is old—old walls sometimes have glass shards embedded on the top cap. It used to be a thing."

Lucas said, "I hadn't thought of that. I'm thinking, 'Not in this neighborhood'—the glass thing. I'm willing to take the chance. We're not going to do anything until we hear from Kidd."

THEY'D PASSED A grill that called itself The Grille, a sure sign of mediocre food, but it was close by, so they went there. The place was crowded with prosperous-looking Minnesotans, a sprinkling of diamonds and pearls among the women. They waited ten minutes for a booth and ordered steaks and crinkle fries and beer, and Lucas called St. Vincent and asked where McGruder was.

"At home," St. Vincent said. "We're tracking his phone and we've got four cars on the ground. If he moves, we'll be on him like a coat of paint."

"Don't chase him back home, for Christ's sakes," Lucas said. "We need to see where he goes when he's out and about. Who he talks to."

"He won't see us. By the way, I saw this Jennifer Carey report on Channel Three. What, you guys hire her as a publicity agent?"

"I haven't seen it," Lucas said. "She is known for overcooking her investigations."

"Well, she's now gone national—CNN and Fox have picked up her story. She did mention the FBI as an afterthought. Implied that we were assisting your investigation. Thanks for that."

"Sorry, boss," Lucas said, grinning at Virgil.

"Yeah, right," St. Vincent said. "What are you two doing?"

Virgil said, "We talked to another one of McGruder's household workers, no help there. Did you get with Helen Socek?"

"Yes. No exact count on the cash that Velez got, but she can testify that it was a lot. She estimates a half-inch-thick stack of hundreds."

"Good. Listen, I'd like to talk directly with your surveillance guy, if that's possible," Lucas said. "We want to know everywhere

McGruder goes tonight, if he goes anywhere. If he's clubbing. We may go in on top of him, see who he talks to."

St. Vincent: "Okay, but keep me in the loop. Don't make any big moves . . ."

"We'll take care of you," Lucas said. "No more of the Channel Three stuff."

St. Vincent gave them the phone number of the lead surveillance agent, and Lucas called him. The agent took Lucas' phone number and said he'd call the moment McGruder left the house, if he did, and where he went after leaving. Lucas thanked him, and the steaks arrived.

"We'll park on that side street, a block down from McGruder's," Lucas told Virgil, as they ate. "We'll walk along next to the wall, check out possible neighborhood watchers. When we get most of the way down the wall, you give me a stirrup with your hands and boost me up, and I'll go over. After I'm over, you keep walking around the block, back to the car and watch for anyone who might be coming. We'll keep our phones on so we'll always be in touch."

"How will you get back over the wall when you're done?"

"Getting back over won't be as bad as getting over in the first place," Lucas said. "It'll be darker inside the yard, we won't have to worry that somebody might be watching. Six feet. If there's no glass up there, I could pull myself high enough to get over, even without anything to stand on. And if those vines go over the wall, onto the back side, I can use those to pull myself up."

"Still risky."

"Be okay," Lucas said. "But getting across the wall, we gotta be quick."

"At least there's nothing close by that looks right at the house—no old lady in her bedroom," Virgil said.

Lucas nodded and settled back, satisfied. "Wave at that waiter. See if we can get some ketchup or 57 Sauce. I think this steak came off the bottom of a shoe."

When the waiter had dropped off a bottle of ketchup, Virgil took out his phone and asked, "Wonder if there's a Walmart around here?"

"What are you looking for?" Lucas asked, as he smacked the bottom of the bottle.

"Burners."

"Of course." An ounce of ketchup exploded onto his steak.

There were Walmarts all over the place, including one five minutes from The Grille. As they were on the way there, Kidd called. "You oughta drive over to that security service and slap the owner in the face."

"You got in?" Lucas asked.

"I could hardly avoid getting in. I own the place. You give me a time, and if the house is empty, I can freeze the video feed—I doubt they have anybody looking at it anyway. I think it's just scrolled to the 'net so somebody can look at it later, if there's a reason to. Also, when you're out, I can erase the computer record of the maid's entry code."

"Excellent," Lucas said. "When you say freeze the video . . ."

"The cameras are fixed—they don't pan. If there's nobody moving around the house, the camera views don't change. I can freeze the video, so if anyone looks at it, they'll see what they expect."

"How many?"

"Cameras? Fifteen. They're in every hallway, every stairway. There's one that appears to be in a small room on the third floor. I think it might be a safe room. I'd try to find that, if I were you—there are a lot of small cupboards and drawers. Some of the drawers look like they might be file cabinets."

"Good," Lucas said. "How much warning do you need to freeze the cameras?"

"Minute or so," Kidd said. "And listen, I fed that Channel Three report to the Five Facebook page. It's already gotten three thousand comments."

"I'll call you when I'm ready to go in," Lucas said. "I owe you."

"Yes, you do," Kidd said.

They got their burners at Walmart, and Lucas bought a pair of vinyl kitchen gloves, a fibrous door mat designed to soak up snow before it could be tracked into the house, and a three-pack of boys'- sized Jockey shorts. He paid cash for it all. At one point, as they waited in a checkout line, Virgil said, "Maybe it'd be better if I just bent over and you walked up my back?"

"Stirrup will be fine," Lucas said. "I just hope the damned shorts fit on my head."

A woman in the next line over gave them an odd look: she must have ears like radar domes, Virgil thought.

He looked at Lucas, tipped his head toward the woman and said, quietly, "Shhh."

When they walked out of the Walmart, Lucas said, "I don't want to sit in the car and wait, we can't go back to McGruder's because the surveillance guys would spot us. Let's find a bar, get a beer . . ."

They did that, a place called Fantastiks, a fake dive bar inhabited by silver-haired patrons wearing cashmere turtlenecks, while the waitresses flashed tattoos. A piano man was playing flowery arrange- ments of Beatles songs, which Lucas suspected might well bring on premature dementia. The piano player had moved on to an elevator version of the Stones' "Brown Sugar" when the lead surveillance agent called: "McGruder's moving, out of his house, heading east. We're on him."

"Don't let him see you," Lucas said.

"He won't."

To Virgil: "We gotta get the fuck outa here before the music kills us."

MCGRUDER HAD DRESSED himself all in black. He'd had one ear pierced a couple of years earlier, after checking which ear was supposed to designate homosexuality so he could avoid that problem, and had snapped a 5.5-carat diamond on it. All black with a diamond the size of a dime, and he was good to go. He had a Minnesota carry permit and considered taking a nine with him but decided not to: if a confrontation with cops was coming, he didn't want to give them an excuse to blow him up.

He'd planned to hit a club or two: he was an innocent man, doing what he usually did. Keep the routine going. He left the house, couldn't help running a brief counter-surveillance route, determined that there was nobody following, and headed for downtown Minneapolis.

AS HE AND Virgil walked out into the brutally cold night, Lucas asked, "You still worried?"

"Sure. But I'm up for it. If I tell you to get out . . ."

"I'll go. Out the back, around the house and down to the far end of the wall and over. I'll talk you through it, I'd want the car right there when I come over."

"You're getting puckered," Virgil suggested.

"A little."

"Me too. Not as bad as you, though. Think how embarrassed you'd be to get caught burglarizing a house with your head inside a pair of boys' underpants."

"That'd be bad," Lucas admitted. "And listen, if I can't get to the parking lot, I'll head out onto the lake. I'll run over to the hockey rink the kids have scraped out."

THEY DID A couple more runs in the car along the wall, saw nothing new. The houses were rich and widely spaced with heavy landscaping.

"No traffic," Lucas said. "Let's do it."

He called Kidd and told him to freeze the cameras inside McGruder's house. Kidd said, "Hang on . . . Okay, they're frozen. The house is empty."

VIRGIL WAS DRIVING. He parked down the block and he and Lucas walked back toward McGruder's, on the opposite side of the street, then crossed when they got there. "All the way to the end of the wall," Lucas muttered.

"I feel like a burglar," Virgil said. "A bad one."

"Yeah, well . . ."

There was little sound, except a distant snowmobile. The night was cold, windows and doors were closed. McGruder's house was showing multiple lights, but no sign of motion behind the curtains and shades.

Lucas called the surveillance team lead: "Where is he?"

"Downtown. He's going somewhere. He actually ran a little counter-surveillance pattern on us, which is kind of interesting."

"He didn't see you?"

"Of course not."

"Keep talking to us," Lucas said. He signed off, handed his phone to Virgil with his password. "If anybody looks at our track, it's in the car, where we were doing surveillance."

"Check."

A car rolled by, showing no evidence of curiosity about them, if they'd been seen at all. They walked past McGruder's gate and continued another hundred feet, where McGruder's masonry wall connected with a fence from the next house.

"Car, let it pass," Virgil said.

They slowed, let another car pass. When it was a hundred feet down the road, Lucas pulled on the kitchen gloves, took a pair of underpants from his jacket pocket and pulled them over his head, arranged so he could look through a leg hole. He looked around a last time, flipped the door mat atop the wall and said, "Stirrup."

Virgil made a stirrup out of his clasped hands and Lucas put one foot in the stirrup and stood up as Virgil boosted him up the wall. Lucas flopped on top of the door mat, lay there for a moment then called quietly, "No glass . . . I'll be coming down on a shoveled driveway, no footprints inside."

Then he was gone, over the wall.

Virgil pulled the mat down, tucked it under his arm, and ambled on. He felt like a guilty cartoon character, like he should have his hands in his pockets and maybe should whistle a happy tune. He didn't do either. Instead, he walked down the block to the car, got in, threw the mat in the back, and started driving in circles around the dark streets. He wanted to keep moving, rather than attract a curious eye by sitting in the dark in one place, but he had to hang close to McGruder's.

He'd driven the first loop when Lucas called on his burner: "I'm at the back door. No sign of life. Can't hear anything inside. I'm going in."

"I'm here, keeping the phone on."

AT THE BACK door, Lucas found the key went into the lock smoothly enough, but the lock wouldn't turn. Escobar's morose face popped up in his mind's eye, and he muttered, "Goddamn her," and he jiggled the key and moved it slightly back and forth in the lock and then it turned.

He pushed the door open with a gloved hand, listened, stepped inside and listened again, then pushed the door closed. It had a turn-lock, and he locked it. The house smelled like cleaning products and floor wax. There were lights here and there throughout the house, so he could see where he was going—and he was going up a short two steps to a hallway, where a backlit alarm box was making a beeping sound. He pulled down the cover, entered Escobar's maid code, and the beeping stopped.

He made himself relax as he stood there, listening. The house buzzed with electronics, and twitched with age, but he sensed nothing human inside. He walked down the hallway past a laundry room lit by the colored LED lights on a washer and dryer, which were silent, turned a corner and nearly had a heart attack when a man loomed up in front of him—the man was himself, reflected in an antique mirror.

"Jesus!"

He caught his breath and continued down a short hall and found himself looking at an expansive living room; a full-sized Steinway concert grand piano stood in one corner, something he knew because he had a smaller grand piano of the same brand in his own living room. To his right, a short hall ended in a dead end but with an opening to the left. He hurried down it and checked: kitchen.

He went back to the living room. At the far end, across two enormous Persian carpets, a curving set of stairs went up two flights. He waited for another thirty seconds, listening again—ears were as important as eyes in a nighttime burglary. Nothing. He crossed the carpet, soft and silent underfoot, and began climbing the carpeted stairs.

Kidd had said that the safe room was on the third floor, off the master bedroom. There were two elevators in the house, but elevators aren't for burglars. On the second-floor landing, he paused by the top newel and slipped the burner from his pocket and whispered, "In. Second floor. Clear."

Virgil came back instantly: "Nothing moving here."

Lucas clicked the phone twice to acknowledge, then continued up the twisting staircase to the third floor. The house was enormous. Lucas lived in a large house in St. Paul, six thousand square feet. Standing at the top of the staircase on the third floor, he thought that floor alone would be as large as his entire house.

The layout was complicated. The house, from the outside, appeared to be a cube, but the interior was complicated, each of the floors a square laid out with two long intersecting hallways forming a cross. More hallways and doors branched off the cross. The floors were covered with carpets, small spaces of dark wood floors showing between them.

He hurried down one hall, looking in open doors. No master bedroom. He went the other way, jogging; no master bedroom. He returned to the intersection and from there hurried toward the back of the house. Halfway back, he found a pair of elaborately carved wooden doors, pushed through them, and found himself in what must have been a fifteen-hundred-square-foot bedroom. The bedroom featured a super-king four-poster bed featuring a dozen pillows and a red satin coverlet. A television projection screen hung from one wall, the projector itself on the wall above the bed.

There were four lights on, pale pink vertical multiple-bulb lamps set flush into the room's corners. They were on a dimmer switch, Lucas thought, because they allowed you to see around the room, but few details. They would, he thought, make anyone's skin look good, just enough pink light for a pleasant romp.

Two doors led farther into the interior of the bedroom: one to a huge bathroom with a pool-sized tub that Lucas imagined you might literally swim in; the other to an expansive dressing room, twenty feet long, and the same width, clothing arrayed on both sides. At least a dozen suits, probably another dozen sport coats with slacks, perhaps eighty to a hundred shirts of varying levels of formality, from ruffled-front formal shirts to short-sleeved pastel polos.

Below the racks for suits and shirts, along two long walls, were rows of wood-faced drawers. The center of the room was dominated by a dressing table, with racks of shoes beneath the rosewood tabletop.

The room had no windows, so he closed the door and turned on the lights and began opening drawers. Socks, underwear, dozens of tee-shirts, empty leather wallets in different styles and colors. He opened one drawer to find a watch-winding machine, its gears tipping ten Rolex watches back and forth, keeping them perpetually wound. Another contained men's bracelets, silver, gold, some set with gemstones.

One cupboard held at least a hundred neckties. He opened the next cupboard, and found even more, and more in the next. *Three hundred neckties*, he thought. He looked at labels: Charvet, Zegna, Ferragamo, Tom Ford, Hermès—probably none cost less than two hundred dollars.

The end of the room featured four mirrors—two were fixed, two others folded on one of the fixed mirrors to give a good all-around view. The fourth mirror was fixed and seemed useless.

Interesting. He pushed and pried on one edge, then another, and the mirror popped open and he was looking at a heavy door covered with a sheet of painted steel. He pulled open the door and it was as heavy as it looked. A safe room.

The room was carpeted, with one chair, which sat next to a table that held a hardwired phone and a cell phone. He pulled open a cabinet door and found three guns: a .44 Magnum revolver, a twelve-gauge shotgun, and an AR-10 semi-automatic rifle with two magazines of .308 ammunition. If a war came to McGruder, he had a solid chance of winning it.

He opened another cabinet and found a safe, shoulder high with an electronic lock. No possibility of opening it. A narrow cupboard held a steel shield on wheels; another revealed a fifty-inch television divided into squares, each square devoted to a security camera. Nothing moved in any of the squares.

Another cabinet showed a bulletproof vest, a helmet, and a long, dark coat that had been rolled into a cylinder. He unrolled it and found a parka with a funny breast pocket—the parka that had been stolen from Gates. Lucas got on the phone: "Found the parka."

Virgil: "Then get out."

"Five more minutes. There are some filing cabinets here . . ."

He started pulling filing cabinet drawers, found reams of financial, tax, and medical records, deeds to property in the U.S. and in Mexico, the Virgin Islands, and France. One of the file cabinets was locked and the lock was a good one.

He hurriedly pulled out all the other drawers, looking for keys, found nothing.

Where do men hide important stuff like keys? Sock drawers. Beneath underwear. He hurried back into the dressing room and pulled open a sock drawer and quickly searched it, found nothing, and was about to open another when Virgil called.

"Lucas! Lucas!"

"I'm here."

"A woman just came up to the gate and used a key to let herself into the yard. I think she's coming into the house. I'm not sure about this, but it looked like she was wearing a ski mask."

"Shit."

Lucas closed the sock drawer, looked around, saw nothing else disturbed—he'd been careful—and hurried out to the bedroom door. He stepped out in the hall and heard what had to be an exterior door opening, then quietly being closed. Sneaking quiet, he thought.

No lights came on—until a flashlight did, and then the light began splashing off the stairwell walls as somebody started climbing the stairs. He retreated to the bedroom, then to the dressing room, and then to the safe room, where he saw the parka unfurled on the floor. He grabbed it, with a hanger, and hung the parka on a mirror in the dressing room. At he did that, he could hear somebody jogging down the hall, footfalls muffled by the carpets. Whoever it was, was in a hurry. He retreated again to the safe room, where he pulled the mirror closed, but left the safe room door open an inch.

He went to the video screen that showed views from security cameras, but nothing was moving, because Kidd had frozen them.

He went back to the safe room door and listened: nothing at first—all those carpets. Then somebody turned on the lights in the dressing room, the light filtering around the edges of the mirror. Lucas closed the safe room door, as silently as he could, then carefully locked it.

Hidden for the moment, he sat on the floor and listened, and heard absolutely nothing. His phone clicked—Virgil—and he clicked back: *Can't talk.*

Ten minutes passed. Nobody tried the safe room door. He let it go another five minutes, then carefully unlocked the door and eased it open. No more light around the edges: the dressing room had gone dark again.

He shut the safe room door and locked it and called Virgil, speaking as quietly as he could. "Whoever was up here has gone, I think."

"I haven't seen her come out."

Lucas looked at his watch, planning to give it another five minutes. One minute into the wait, Virgil called: "She's out. She's carrying a shopping bag."

"Stay with her," Lucas said. "You gotta stay with her. We need her."

"Why?"

"She saw the parka," Lucas said. "It was right in front of her eyes. She couldn't miss it."

"Ah. What about you?" Virgil asked.

"I'll get out and hide until you can get back."

"I'm going."

LUCAS UNLOCKED THE safe room door, listened, pushed the mirror open. Listened some more, closed the dressing room door and turned on the lights.

The place had been looted. The Rolex watches were gone, as well as all the neckties and the extensive collection of belts and belt buckles. The parka still hung in place. He called Virgil: "Where are you?"

"Behind her. She parked one street over from us. One of those Mazda ragtops. She hasn't seen me."

"She stole a bunch of stuff—watches and neckties and belts and so on."

"Neckties?"

"Hundreds of them, maybe fifty grand worth," Lucas said. "She knew what she was going for, and where to get them—girlfriend, I bet. Or ex."

"I'll get her plate . . ."

THE MAZDA WASN'T moving. Virgil drove by it, catching the license plate in his headlights. Muttering the plate number to himself, he turned a corner, stopped, and wrote it down. He pulled into a driveway, backed out, turned around, and as he did, saw the Mazda go by, left to right.

Virgil gave her a hundred yards, then followed, memorizing her taillight pattern. He got on the burner: "I got her plate. I'm a hundred yards back."

"Stay with her. She's the key that'll get us a warrant," Lucas said.

"Going."

"Use my phone and call the surveillance team and find out where McGruder is now."

Virgil did that and was told that McGruder had gone into the @&X club, and one of the team was inside watching him. He called Lucas to relay the information.

The woman in the Mazda drove east toward downtown Minneapolis for twenty minutes, turned south into the Uptown neighborhood. She made two turns on narrow, dark streets in Uptown, then pulled into a parking space outside an old house with a neon sign in a window that read "Line Gallery."

Virgil waited until she got out, then cruised slowly by her. She turned to look at him—pretty, oval face, brown hair to her shoulders. He would know her if he saw her again.

He spotted an empty space down the block, pulled into it, got on the phone to Lucas. "I tracked her to a house, she's going inside," Virgil said, looking out the back window of the truck.

"Pick me up?"

"Twenty minutes."

Lucas: "Call me when you're a minute out. I'm freezing my ass off."

Virgil drove back to Orono, and when he was a minute away from McGruder's, made the call.

Lucas said, "I'm squatting on top of the wall. Right at the very end of it, where I went in. Pull over there and I'll drop down."

Virgil did, Lucas did, and a second later, they were rolling away.

"Nothing to it," Lucas said, although he was out of breath.

"The parka," Virgil prompted.

"It's the right parka. Now, we nail down the chick you followed because guess what? I hung that thing right in front of her face," Lucas said. "If she tells us that, if she identifies it . . ."

"We got him. Well, maybe."

THIRTEEN

Virgil drove them back to the Line Gallery, where the mysterious woman had gone with her shopping bag.

Lucas: "You can identify her for sure?"

Virgil: "Yes. Caught her in my headlights. She looked right at me."

Lucas got on the phone to St. Vincent, who was at home. "We were watching the house, hoping to catch more employees . . ."

As they were watching, they spotted the woman going in, Lucas said, and she appeared to be wearing a ski mask. They caught glimpses of what appeared to be a flashlight on the upper floors. When she came out, they followed her to what might be her home. Her car was still parked outside.

St. Vincent: "She was burglarizing McGruder?"

"That's what it looked like. What I'd suggest is, we put all this in the mouth of a Hennepin County deputy we can trust . . . if we can find one. Have him call McGruder and ask him to check to see if he'd been burglarized. You know, the deputy says the woman was spotted by a routine patrol car, and they noted the license tag. If McGruder tells the cops he's been hit, we pick up the woman and squeeze her about their relationship, if they have one, and what she might know about the Five."

"What could she give us?"

"Don't know, but if we caught her with burglarized stuff, we'd have her ass in a crack. She'd talk to us about the guy."

St. Vincent thought about that for a moment, then said, "I'll check with the Hennepin sheriff. We can work out something."

"We're sitting outside the woman's place, watching. Call us."

As they sat watching, Lucas told Virgil about his trip through McGruder's house. "I was kinda disappointed. The guy claims to be a billionaire, but I didn't see anything you and I don't own, just more of it. You've got one suit from Penney's, he has a couple of dozen from a tailor. You have two shirts, he has a hundred . . ."

"Why don't we compare his stuff to yours?" Virgil asked.

"Okay. He has a Steinway concert grand in his living room, I have an O model, which is like fifty thousand bucks cheaper. He has three hundred neckties, I've probably got . . ."

". . . One hundred."

"No, no . . . Okay, maybe. He has these huge Persian carpets and Persian runners down the hallways. He has real paintings on all the walls, and I don't know anything about paintings, but they looked good. The frames did, anyway. All gold and so on."

"You've got paintings."

"Sure. By Joe Blow. I do have one original Kidd, which Weather bought years ago, and which we could sell for about a nine hundred percent profit but she won't even talk to me about it . . . We could use the money to buy a really nice Boston Whaler center console and not touch our investments."

"And she won't do it? That's fuckin' crazy," Virgil said.

ST. VINCENT CALLED back a half hour after they'd asked for his help. "Here's the deal. A Hennepin County sheriff's car will come to your location. There'll be one guy in it, a carefully chosen senior sergeant. He will call McGruder's security company, who will get in touch with McGruder. The sergeant will leave his phone number with the security company and ask that McGruder get back in touch with him. If McGruder calls back and if he's been burglarized, you grab the woman. Since you actually witnessed the crime being committed, we can get you a warrant in about five minutes, if McGruder says he's been hit."

"We're here," Lucas said. "I'd like to get this done . . ."

"The patrol car is on the way. He needs to know your exact location . . ."

THE CAREFULLY CHOSEN police sergeant turned out to be a compact black woman who wore an attitude of skepticism like a cloak. She parked behind them—they'd rolled a block back from the mystery woman's house—and climbed into the back seat of the Tahoe, introduced herself as Sergeant Jasmine Green. "You saw her go in and then you followed her? Why didn't you stop her?"

Virgil and Lucas looked at each other, and then back at her, and Virgil asked, "We were told you were carefully chosen. Why are you carefully chosen?"

"'Cause I can keep my mouth shut if I need to," she said.

Lucas said to Virgil, "We should tell her."

Virgil told her the story that concluded with the probability that McGruder was one of the Five who'd also murdered two people in Worthington. "We were watching his place when she came along and . . ."

"You mean . . . she just came along?" The skepticism was thick in her voice. "She's not one of your assets?"

"No. We never saw her before," Lucas said. "And yeah, she just came along."

"And you're gonna jack her up . . ."

". . . To see if she can help us hang McGruder."

She studied them, her head bobbing, then said, "Okay. I've heard stranger shit than that, I guess. Who do I call, and then what do I do?"

THEY LIED TO her a little—didn't mention that Lucas had been in-side the house—and showed her the photo of the security service sign. She knew the service, got a twenty-four-hour phone number from the police dispatcher, and called.

"There was just something funky about her," she told the woman who answered at the security service. "I didn't have reason to stop her, but I got her tag number and I wonder if you could call the home-owners and ask them if they had a female guest, or if this is some-thing we should look into?"

They could do that and would pass the question on to the home-owner. McGruder called Green two minutes later. He wasn't quite shouting:

"I'm the homeowner you were calling about . . . Jamie McGruder . . . I didn't authorize anyone to be in the house at that time. It was all locked up . . ."

"When I saw her, she looked like she was locking up that gate, so she has a key," Green said. "Like I told your security lady, she looked kinda funky."

"I am thirty minutes away. I'm on my way to my car right now," McGruder said. "I think I know who it might have been, that miserable bitch . . ."

"What's her name? If you got it wrong, she won't get hurt by you mentioning it."

"I don't care about that—Nicole Walker. I can get you her phone number, but I don't have her address. She always came over to my place. She lives in some kind of art gallery."

"We can find her," Green said. "You call me when you know. If she ripped you off, I'll go grab her right now. Maybe get your stuff back, if she took something."

"On my way, on my way . . ."

They heard a car lock beep, and then McGruder rang off.

Green said to Lucas and Virgil, "When we ran the plates you gave us, that's the name we came back with: Nicole Walker, twenty-four, nothing on her record but traffic offenses, all fines paid on time."

"Okay. Now: we'd like you to go over there, to McGruder's house," Lucas said. "It's about twenty minutes from here. If he thinks cops might be coming to look at a burglary scene, he might try to get rid of any evidence from his murders. If you could just hang out around his place, see if he tries to sneak back out, maybe hit a dumpster somewhere . . ."

"I can do that . . ."

"You *are* carefully chosen," Virgil said.

"That is correct," Green said, as she climbed out of the Tahoe. She walked back to her patrol car, pulled away. Lucas and Virgil went back to waiting.

St. Vincent called: "Anything yet?"

"Not yet," Lucas told him. "We'll call."

When he'd rung off, Virgil said, "St. Vincent wants to be somewhat in the loop, but only somewhat. He wants to be able to back away if we fuck it up, but get in the middle of it, if we happen to break it."

"So true. That kind of duplicity makes me sad to think about," Lucas said.

"I'm not sure 'duplicity' is the word you wanted," Virgil said. "Maybe 'deviousness.'"

"Thank you, famous author."

They waited some more. Fifteen minutes in, Virgil asked, "How many hours of our lives have we spent waiting with nothing happening?"

"Jesus, Virgil, buck the fuck up," Lucas said. "You heard anything more about your novel?"

"No, and I'm getting nervous."

"You mean, 'more nervous.' You were already nervous."

"Okay. More nervous."

"Why don't you call your agent? I mean, right now."

"Because it's an hour later in New York and I don't want her to think I'm nervous."

A stakeout conversation about nothing.

GREEN CALLED BACK forty-five minutes after she left them: "He's been ripped off. Says he's down at least a hundred and twenty grand in Rolex watches, another fifty in neckties, if you can believe that shit, and maybe ten more in belts. Plus, she took a one-of-a-kind signed vibrating dildo molded in vinyl from the manly works of a famous porn star, which he says is another grand."

Lucas: "You got a detailed description on that last item, Jasmine?"

"Look in your underpants and then multiply by ten," she said.

"Hey!" They started laughing.

"Just sayin'," she said, laughing along. "I'll be here to keep an eye on him."

THEY CALLED ST. VINCENT. "I've got a judge sitting in his home office ready to go with the warrant. I'll drop it to Virgil's iPad if somebody wants to see it. You'll have it in five. I'm sending a car over there."

"Man, don't do that," Lucas said. "Your people might not want to . . . mmm . . . get cross-examined about what gets said to this woman. If you catch my meaning."

"Okay, I didn't hear that and I won't be sending a car. But we'll have one handy if you need it. Watch the iPad for the warrant."

The warrant came in as scheduled and they drove down the block, parked behind Nicole Walker's car, got up and walked to the front door. "Line Gallery," Virgil said. "I wonder if they specialize in drawings . . . Line Gallery. Like pen-and-ink lines."

"I'd be willing to bet that the owner's name is Line," Lucas said.

"I've known Liens, Lanes, and Loans, but never heard of anyone named Line," Virgil said. He knocked on the door, pushed a doorbell, then knocked again.

After the second round of that, a man came to the door wearing a sleeveless undershirt and gray sweatpants. He was barefoot, bearded, and possibly stoned: when he opened the door, the sweet scent of weed floated out to them. The door was on a heavy security chain. He said, over it, "It's after nine o'clock, what . . ."

Lucas held up his badge and said, "U.S. Marshal. We have a warrant to find and arrest Nicole Walker, who was seen entering the building less than an hour ago."

The man scratched an ear, then looked over his shoulder. "Nicole?"

"Nicole Walker. Open the door, sir, we're coming in, and we'd rather not damage your doors as we do that."

The man took a step back, and Lucas saw that he had a pistol in his hand. "Put the gun on the floor, put the gun on the floor . . ."

Lucas had his Walther out and Virgil stepped back, but the man pointed the gun toward the ceiling and said, "It's a rubber gun. It's a fake. See?"

He bent the barrel of the gun sideways, like a piece of licorice. Then he reached out and touched a light switch, and the lights came on in the room behind him. "Let me . . . the chain. Don't hurt my door."

He pushed the door mostly closed, removed the chain, then said, "Nicole is upstairs. Listen, I don't know what she's been up to. I don't know her all that well . . ."

"Is this your place?" Lucas asked.

"Yes."

"You're lucky I didn't shoot your ass with that rubber gun trick."

"You gotta have something, living around here, and I don't believe in guns," the man said.

Virgil: "This address is on Nicole's driver's license, so you must know her fairly well."

"Not necessarily . . ."

"Upstairs?"

The man pointed, and Virgil led the way to a set of narrow stairs that went to a narrow landing and then continued in their narrow upward climb, smelling of old flaking paint and new weed. At the top of the stairs, a door opened on a bathroom and Nicole Walker stepped out, wearing nothing but a thong, and said, "Who was that . . . Hey! Hey!"

She stepped back into the bathroom and slammed the door. The man came up, trailed by Lucas, and Virgil said to Lucas, "She was naked, but this guy doesn't know her?"

From inside the bathroom, the woman shouted, "I'm calling the cops."

Virgil called back, "We are the cops."

"What?"

"Put on some clothes and come out of there," Lucas shouted.

"How do I know you're cops?"

"Because we've got badges and guns and we've got a warrant for your arrest for burglarizing Jamie McGruder and stealing his neckties, belts, watches, and a dildo."

The man frowned and said, "She stole a dildo? Why would she do that?"

Virgil: "I wouldn't want to make a comment that could be construed as awkward."

Long silence, then Lucas asked the man, "Is there a window in there, that she might be crawling out of?"

"There's a window in there," he said, "But she couldn't get through it. It's too small and it's painted shut."

Virgil: "Did she take a shopping bag in there with her?"

"Not as far as I know. She had a shopping bag when she got here, it's in . . ." He pointed to a bedroom, where they could see a large denim shopping bag laying on the floor. Virgil stepped over to it, pulled it open, looked inside and said, "Belts . . . ties . . . watches . . . dildo. This is it."

"Come out of there," Lucas shouted at the bathroom door, "or we'll kick the door."

The man said, "The lock doesn't work."

"What?" Lucas tried the bathroom doorknob. The knob turned, and he pushed the door open. Walker was standing in a claw-foot bathtub, now fully dressed except for bare feet.

"I did not steal a single thing," she shouted at them. She was dark-haired, dark-eyed, pretty, and scared. "He owed me that stuff."

"Let's talk about it," Lucas said. "As soon as we pat you down."

THEY TALKED ABOUT it, after telling the man, who said his name was Richard Line, to take a hike. The upstairs area had a single small room, formerly a bedroom, that had been arranged as a living room, in addition to the bedroom and bathroom. A two-cushion couch and two easy chairs were arranged around an IKEA table with a copy of *Architectural Digest* sitting on it. Lucas took the couch and Virgil and Walker the two chairs.

Virgil opened with, "You may or may not be charged in a rather serious burglary. We had the house under surveillance and saw you enter and leave, and we tracked you here. We've found the things you stole from McGruder, and McGruder has reported the theft to the Hennepin County Sheriff's Department."

"If you knew what Jamie did to me . . ." Walker began, twisting her hands as she talked.

Lucas: "Was violence involved?"

She hesitated, then said, "More like intimidation."

"Tell us."

She and McGruder had met during a reception at the Minneapolis Institute of Art. They had gone on two dates and then she'd invited him to another reception at an artist's studio in St. Paul's Lowertown.

"Anthony Coppella—he's very, very hot right now. Jamie pretended to be really interested in his art, which is bold, nonrepresentational stuff, very New York, post-Basquiat, unlike the stuff that Jamie has in his house. Anyway, if Jamie bought a piece that I introduced him to, I'd be in line for a commission . . . maybe five thousand dollars. I was interested in keeping him happy and he knew that, so he took me home and fucked me."

They'd slept together a number of times, not without some stress and a couple of arguments. About a month earlier, she began to suspect that McGruder had no intention of buying any of Coppella's art and that he'd almost certainly dump her when she figured that out.

She got out of bed earlier in the morning than he did, and one morning, while exploring the kitchen, she'd found a drawer that contained a wooden box full of keys. She'd tried several on the front door, and when one worked, she kept it—it happened that the same key opened the gate to the yard and the front walk.

"I didn't know what I was going to do with it, but then last week, he did it—he dumped me," Walker said. "Told me to get out, he was tired of me, he didn't want to see me anymore. He told me Coppella was a talentless hack and his work was junk."

"And you wanted your commission," Virgil suggested.

"Exactly. I wanted my commission. He was screwing me under false pretenses."

"He was never violent with you?"

"No. He'd get angry, but . . . he's very, very calculated. That's how he got rich. He calculated. You'd see him calculating all the time. He'd talk to somebody, and he'd calculate what he could get from that person. He calculated me and what he could get from me, which was sex."

"Why did you wait until tonight to go in?" Virgil asked.

She shrugged. "I saw him going into a club. He left his car with a valet, and I saw him, and I figured he'd be a while getting back. I'd have time to get in and out."

Lucas looked at Virgil and asked, "What do you think?"

"I think we should get Jasmine back over here to take possession of the loot and read Miz Walker her rights. And I think we should see if Miz Walker could give us any information about McGruder."

Lucas looked at Walker: "If you help us, the burglary problem could go away."

"What do you think he did? Jamie?" Walker asked.

"You've heard of the Five?" Virgil asked.

Her hand went to her mouth. "Oh. My. God. Jamie could so totally be a member of the Five. Totally. He's guns and knives and boxing and karate and high-speed driving. He totally wants to kill somebody."

"That's nice to know, but we've got no hard evidence of that— some, but not much," Virgil said. "There's one thing in particular we're interested in. The person who killed the woman in the Twin Cities wore a peculiar, very expensive parka. An imprint was left in the snow and we happen to know that it was stolen from a man here in Minneapolis, at a party that McGruder went to. Did you ever happen to see, during your relationship, a long, knee-length parka anywhere in the house?"

She gaped open-mouthed at Lucas and then Virgil before blurting, "Totally. Totally. It's hanging on a mirror, in his dressing room, the one I was in when, you know, I . . . possessed . . . the neckties and stuff. Let me think: okay, dark green. Like an Army green, but darker than that. Oily, kind of, like one of those British coats that old men think are cool. But not so stiff as them. Barbour coats."

"I've got a Barbour," Lucas said.

"Okay, mostly older men," she said, backtracking. "It's got this weird pocket on the front . . ." She tapped her chest where the pocket was.

Lucas again turned to Virgil: "Good enough?"

"Yes. I'll call St. Vincent. We'll hit him at midnight."

They called St. Vincent, who was at first flustered and then excited. He would get the warrant and an FBI entry team, and he wanted to move immediately. When they ended the call, Lucas called Jasmine Green, told her what had happened, and asked her to come collect the McGruder loot and arrange to take a statement from Walker.

"We need to see what her cooperation might get us," Lucas said, looking at Walker. "If she's a good girl . . ."

"I'll encourage her," Green said. "I'll get a couple more deputies over there to take a statement and so on and stay with her until after we hit McGruder. I would love to go on the raid. Really love it."

"Get a couple guys here, to take care of Miz Walker, and you're invited," Lucas said.

FOURTEEN

Three deputies showed up to take possession of Walker and her loot from McGruder's house. Walker began to cry—she'd never been arrested or put in jail—but that didn't bother any of the cops much, because a lot of women cried when they were arrested, and quite a few men as well. After a few years on the job, cops got accustomed to it.

"We got her," the lead deputy said. He didn't know exactly what was going on, but he knew something was. "You guys have a good time."

THE SWAT TEAM gathered at the FBI field office on the north side of Minneapolis at 11:30, along with a dozen federally deputized SWAT officers from the Minneapolis police force. They'd already been

briefed and were getting last-minute adjustments in their assignments when Virgil and Lucas arrived, followed by Jasmine Green.

"Love this stuff," Green said, and she did look like a happy cop as
they headed for the clunky gray building that housed the feds. SWAT
trucks and a couple of SUVs were idling in the parking lot, wasting
gasoline, but then, it was the FBI, and the temperatures had fallen
through zero again.

Lucas, Virgil, and Green were sent up to an oversized conference
room where St. Vincent was presiding over a gathering of key SWAT
members, just then breaking up.

"Quite a crowd," Lucas said, as they edged inside.

"We need a lot of guys because . . ." St. Vincent said, waving a roll
of paper, ". . . McGruder did a complete remodel of the house after he
bought it. We got the remodeling plans from the building department. It's a rabbit warren in there. There are three sets of stairs that
go from top to bottom and a mess of intersecting hallways. We know
he's been into all this prepper nonsense and he might try to run for
it. Or fight it out."

"We got something that'll help out, we think," Lucas said. "We
got a key to the front gate that also works in the front door. Got
them from his ex-girlfriend. And we got a key to the back door from
his housekeeper."

"Outstanding," St. Vincent said. "Looks like we'll need some more
adjustments."

"McGruder's ex said he's into guns and has had some training,"
Lucas said. "She said he has armor."

"Good to know," St. Vincent said. He looked around the room,
where a dozen agents were lingering to listen in. "Everybody got
that? Subject has gun training and may have armor. Pass that along.

Where'd Darnell go? Is he outside? We need to get those keys to him . . ."

After some more confusion, everybody had what they needed for the raid, including the keys.

"We want him uninjured, because he might be able to give us the other members of the Five . . . if there are other members," Virgil told the group. "Don't get yourself hurt, but go easy if you can. If he looks like he might resist, we need to talk him down."

St. Vincent: "Remember the parka that the subject's girlfriend says is hanging in a third-floor dressing room. If you make it to the dressing room and you spot it, don't touch it, but guard it tight. We don't want to contaminate it. Everybody ready? Then let's get going."

Jasmine Green, standing behind Virgil, muttered, "He didn't say, 'Let's roll.'"

"He wanted to," Virgil whispered back. "He did get to say, 'Outstanding.'"

"True."

The field office was twenty minutes from McGruder's place, down Highway 100 to I-394, and then west. The SWAT teams went out in five military-style trucks, led by St. Vincent in a dark Chevy Suburban and by a smaller SUV, with Green in her patrol car and Virgil and Lucas trailing.

Snow was spitting down as they ran along brightly lit highways and then onto dark exurban streets, where the falling snow and the occasional brightly lit plastic angel or crèche scene still lingered from Christmas, putting out a "Silent Night" vibe. They paused a quarter mile out while two SWAT members went ahead in a harmless-looking white Chevy Equinox to open the outer gate with the key.

Virgil and Lucas knew what was going on from the briefing but didn't know what was happening with the approach; it all went well, they decided, when the SWAT trucks started to move again. The trucks were not quiet, which would be noticeable in McGruder's neighborhood, but the team moved efficiently enough that the noise made no difference.

McGruder's house was brightly lit, looking like an advertisement for a rich family's Christmas. The four SWAT trucks stopped adjacent to the now-open gate and the team flowed out of the vehicles, some headed to the front door, others around to the sides and back, jogging silently through a dusting of new snow.

Lucas, Virgil, and Green waited by the gate. A half-dozen men were arrayed along the front of the house; they hovered there for a few seconds, then one of them moved to the door, used the key to open it.

When the door opened, they could hear an alarm buzzer go off, and then the team members swarmed through the door, shouting, "FBI, FBI . . ."

They occupied the bottom floor of the house in a minute or less; not enough time for McGruder to get out. The team from the back door pushed in, cleared the first floor, and began climbing the interior stairs after locking down the elevator.

Lucas, Virgil, and Green followed St. Vincent into the house, and could hear the team members calling back and forth as they cleared the three floors. McGruder was not to be found.

"He's here, somewhere," St. Vincent said. "The surveillance team saw him go inside, and he hasn't come back out."

Virgil, moving close to Lucas, said, quietly, "Safe room."

"I think so."

They went on to the third floor, where three SWAT team members had nailed down the bedroom and dressing room, after checking that the bathroom was empty. The parka, Lucas saw, was no longer hanging in the dressing room where he'd put it.

St. Vincent came up and Lucas pointed to the mirror and said, "That's where Walker said the parka was hanging. She described it exactly."

"We can't do without it," St. Vincent said. "Where's McGruder?"

Virgil and Lucas had adopted Green, and she'd followed them up the stairs. Now she piped up, "He's a rich motherfucker: I bet he's got a hidden safe room somewhere."

Lucas and Virgil glanced at each other: somebody else had said what needed to be said.

"Yes, that's good, that's good," St. Vincent said. He put a handset to his face: "We're looking for a safe room. Subject may have gone to a safe room."

"You look under the bed?" Green asked one of the SWATs, who said, "Yeah. Not even dust bunnies."

"Safe rooms are usually close to the bedroom, because rich people see themselves attacked at night when they're in bed," Green said. "Usually by extra-large black men, even in a neighborhood like this, where a black guy could get arrested for stopping at a red light. I know about this shit out here."

St. Vincent frowned at her and began, "I can assure you . . ."

Virgil interrupted. "Everybody shut up for a minute. Okay?" When they did, he cocked his head back and shouted, as loud as he could, "Hey! McGruder! FBI! We know you're in here! We'll tear down your walls if you don't come out! We got sledgehammers!"

Virgil stopped yelling and Green said, "Maybe the room is sound-proofed."

But then they heard a muffled "I'm coming out. Don't shoot me. I'm not armed. My lawyer's on the phone, listening in."

Virgil shouted, "Then come out! Keep your hands up! Where are you, anyway?"

Muffled again: "Behind the mirror. In the dressing room."

They'd been standing next to the oversized bed and now they all trooped to the entrance of the dressing room. One of the agents took out his gun.

The last of the four mirrors shuddered, once, twice, and then pushed open, and McGruder stepped out. He was fully dressed, pale, his hands open above his shoulders, one of them clutching a cell phone, the camera lens pointed toward them, recording.

"What are you doing?" he demanded. "I was robbed. I was robbed, I talked to a Hennepin sheriff's deputy."

St. Vincent: "You're under arrest for the murder of Mrs. Hillary Sikes. I need to tell you that you have certain rights . . ." With his eyes on the cell phone, St. Vincent then recited the full, technical Miranda warning that most cops learned during training, then mostly forgot; St. Vincent hadn't.

Lucas stepped past him, as that was going on, and looked into the safe room. The parka had been rolled up again but was laying on the floor under the television. Lucas tipped his head at it; Virgil looked, raised his eyebrows, and Lucas nodded.

When St. Vincent finished with the Miranda, Virgil turned and smiled at McGruder and said, "There seems to be a parka under your TV in there. Is that the parka you stole from Howard Gates and wore to Miz Sikes' house?"

Scratchy sounds came from the cell phone, and McGruder, who was looking at the parka, said, "I won't say anything without a lawyer."

"Give me that cell phone," St. Vincent said. He snatched it out of McGruder's hand, gave it to another agent and said, "Keep it turned on—there may be information in there that we can use."

There were more scratchy sounds from the phone, but they ignored them. The agent walked out of the room, looking at the phone's screen, tapping from one app to the next, keeping it running. Another agent said, "Go to settings, we need to change the passwords . . ."

With the phone gone—and McGruder's lawyer with it—Virgil said to McGruder, "You are one coldhearted creep. Murdering a neighbor? What's all that about?"

"I have no idea what you're talking about . . ."

"And then Velez and his wife? I mean, Jesus, you're a full-blown psycho. I know that being nuts is not a good way to go through life, but I think you'd be smart enough to tamp down those urges. With your money? And all the ninja training you had? Why didn't you go to Iraq and sign up to fight the Kurds? You could have killed all the people you wanted, and nobody would have said 'boo.' But a neighbor? Talk about stupid."

All the cops knew what he was doing—McGruder had his Miranda warning, and if he chose to talk to the cops after that, it was on him.

McGruder knew that, too: "Fuck you," he said. The feds cuffed him and hauled him away.

FBI CRIME SCENE technicians photographed and then bagged the parka to keep any loose evidentiary particles, like grass or twigs, from falling off. They would also be looking for Howard Gates' DNA, to link McGruder to the theft of the coat.

After McGruder was taken away, St. Vincent was on the phone to Washington, where it was after one o'clock in the morning. "Yes. Yes. Yes, we have . . . He called a lawyer while he was hiding in his house, we'll have to deal with that in the morning . . ."

Green had been walking around the third floor, looking but not touching. She marveled at the swimmable bathtub. Then she asked Lucas, "Now what?"

"Now we should go talk to Nicole Walker . . . though we can wait until tomorrow to do that. Give her an overnight in jail to scare her. Then the FBI will pull the house apart. We think McGruder took some trophies from Sikes—her shoes. Very identifiable. Could be back in that safe room or even in his safe."

"He's got a safe back there?"

"I'm sure he does," Lucas said. "Maybe they'll find something that'll take them to the other four. McGruder's got a lot of paper and at least a couple of computers. Gonna take a while to process."

"Not my thing," Green said. She poked Lucas in the navel with a sharp index finger. "Hey, it's been fun working with you two. If you're surveilling anyone else and you happen to see a burglary, give me a call."

"We'll do that," Lucas said.

When she was gone, Virgil said, "She knows something's fishy about the surveillance thing, but she doesn't know what."

"We should keep it that way," Lucas said.

THEY HUNG AROUND for two hours, watching the feds haul file cabinets, weapons, and laptops out of the house. That would continue for most of the night, and St. Vincent told them that an enhanced crime scene crew would be brought in from Washington.

"That's kind of surprising," Virgil said. "I'd have guessed an enhanced public relations crew."

"I resemble that remark," St. Vincent said; nothing was going to get him down.

"If I were guessing, I'd guess that the crime scene crew won't find anything new," Virgil said. "I'm surprised that he hung on to the parka. Wonder why?"

"Maybe he was planning to return it and was waiting for a chance," Lucas said. "That'd confuse everybody."

"I bet he wore it around the house," St. Vincent said. "Maybe with the shoes. I would have thought we'd find the shoes . . . that kinda worries me. Anyway, it's past my bedtime."

"It's past mine, too, but Frankie won't let me sleep until I tell her every last second of what happened." Virgil yawned. "Gonna be interesting, huh? See where this leads?"

ST. VINCENT, CHEERFUL but sounding beat-up, called at eight o'clock the next morning, and told Virgil that Lucas was sound asleep, but he wanted Virgil and Lucas to know that Nicole Walker had been transported from the Hennepin lockup to the FBI building for an interview. "We're taking her by her house to get a shower and a change of clothes. We hope that might loosen her up."

"She got a lawyer?"

"A pro-bono guy from one of the big law firms. I think he mostly sits in a basement and looks online for possible class action lawsuits, so he shouldn't be a problem."

"I'm dressed, my girlfriend's going to be heading home, so if it's okay with you, I'll run up there and listen in."

"Yeah, you're invited. Come on up."

Virgil went. St. Vincent was wrong about the lawyer. He was a problem. He didn't know much about criminal law except that it was best if the suspect kept her mouth shut.

After some argument about cooperation, a pissed-off state prosecutor said to Walker, "I've got no more questions, since you're not giving me any answers on advice of your fuckwit counsel. I do have a recommendation, though. I'd fire him and get an actual criminal attorney who'd understand that we're trying to deal. We can prosecute and you'd go to jail. That's not what we want, but jail is what you're gonna get, if you keep this lunkhead as your attorney."

The attorney said, "I . . ."

"Shut up."

The prosecutor left and Virgil said to St. Vincent—they'd been watching through a one-way window—"That went well. You gotta get her a real attorney, David."

"Somebody does, but the burglary is a state charge. I don't do that system . . ."

Virgil: "What about Marvin Fingerhut, the guy we met at Gates' house?"

St. Vincent shook his head. "Can't use Fingerhut."

"Why not?"

"Because McGruder hired him. That's who he had on his cell phone last night."

NICOLE WALKER GOT an experienced public defender and was released on her own recognizance. She'd done a deal that committed her to telling the feds everything she knew about McGruder. She'd do no jail time for the burglary.

LUCAS ROUSED HIMSELF early enough to get to federal magistrate's court, where he met Virgil in the hallway outside the courtroom. "Just in time," Virgil said. "They've gone to get him."

McGruder was marched into the courtroom by two marshals and by Marvin Fingerhut, who spotted Lucas and Virgil and nodded, as if to say "Thanks for the client."

The prosecutor argued that McGruder should be detained until an appropriate bail hearing could be held, since he would be charged with first-degree murder. The magistrate agreed, over Fingerhut's objections, but scheduled a full bail hearing for two days later.

As they walked out of the courthouse, Virgil asked, "You think McGruder will get bail? First-degree murder, lot of heat from the media . . ."

"Yeah, he'll get it, but it's gonna cost him. Ten million plus, I'd bet," Lucas said. "We need more stuff to nail him down . . . Fingerhut's gonna want to see the evidence and when he sees the size-twelve footprints from the crime scene report . . . Did you look at McGruder's feet?"

"Yes. Small for his size. Nine or ten," Virgil said.

"That's bail, right there," Lucas said. "Then there's going to be some confusion over where Walker saw the parka and where Mc-Gruder knows it was . . . not hanging from the mirror. Fingerhut could get into that. Are you going over to McGruder's? See what crime scene has come up with?"

"Can't imagine it'd be much," Virgil said. "Since you're going, I'll pass. If anything turns up, call me."

Lucas shrugged: "Okay. I have a feeling Jennifer will call and try to get me on camera, but that's not going to happen. If you're interested. . . ."

"Nope. If the Five stay on schedule, they may be killing somebody in a couple of days," Virgil said. "Maybe the day of the bail hearing. If they do, are we going to wherever it is?"

"That'll depend on what Mallard wants," Lucas said. "We might not be welcome in, say, Detroit. Or Miami. Or wherever."

"We weren't really all that welcome here," Virgil said. "But it seems like you're the senators' pet bloodhound, so I figure you'll be going."

"I'll invite you, if it's someplace warm," Lucas said.

"If it's warm, do that," Virgil said. "I'll see you at the bail hearing."

THEY SLAPPED GLOVED hands. Virgil headed home, and Lucas went to McGruder's where he spent the afternoon, poking around the house, trying to stay out of the way. McGruder's housekeeper, Esco-bar, whom he and Virgil had blackmailed out of the house key, was sitting on a couch by herself. When she saw Lucas, she turned away.

Lucas chatted with the federal crime scene people, and eventu-ally asked if the housekeeper had given up anything good. She had not, he was told. She'd done some routine cleaning but hadn't hauled anything out of the house except the recycling, the garbage, and a scuttle full of ashes from the big stone fireplace.

"We're going through it all," the crime scene supervisor said. "We're sifting the ashes. If what we think about the Velez murders is correct—that McGruder went there and killed Velez and his girlfriend—then the fire was set the same night. The housekeeper said she found the ash the morning Velez was found shot. Big fire, must have been a dozen logs. Lots of ash. She said McGruder hardly ever uses it, so maybe he was getting rid of something."

Lucas was still there when a crime scene tech came in with two steel pins taken from the garbage. They'd been bagged, both with some ash attached.

"What are they?" Lucas asked.

They looked like long thin drawer handles but weren't drawer handles. "If you put a gun to my head and threatened to shoot me if I didn't come up with the correct answer . . . I'd say they're the heel supports from a couple of high-heeled pumps."

Lucas smiled. "Ah. We need to x-ray some Manolo Blahniks."

"Yes, we do."

Lucas called Virgil to tell him about it, and at the end of the conversation, asked Virgil what was happening with his novel.

"I don't know. I finally called Esther and her secretary said she was out in the Hamptons with some publishing big shots. I don't even know if she was out there for my novel."

"Probably not. She's probably out there for one of those polar-bear things, you know, dipping her ass in the ocean at fifteen below. Or talking to people about Carl Hiaasen or somebody else important."

"Thanks for the thought."

BOTH LUCAS AND Virgil did some online paperwork involving the case, and filed individual reports, and spoke separately with a federal prosecutor who said she'd be back to them for depositions, but probably not for a few weeks.

On the second day after McGruder's initial appearance, they both returned to the magistrate's court, where, after some argument, McGruder was allowed to post a cash bail of fifteen million dollars and agreed to add his house as further security.

The paperwork had been done in advance, and McGruder was released. A car was waiting at the courthouse plaza's curb and he got inside with Fingerhut and disappeared down the street. Lucas knew the assistant U.S. attorney who would be leading the prosecution and caught her in the hallway: "What do you think?"

"It's about seventy-thirty," she said. "Those burned heel pins, from the Blahnik pumps, might do it for us . . . But Fingerhut is good. We need more if you can get it."

"Seventy-thirty . . . will you deal with him for information on the rest of the mob?"

"We're talking," the prosecutor said. "Fingerhut first told us to go fornicate with ourselves, but that was before the pumps. Now . . . We'll see. Fingerhut didn't hang up on us this morning."

"He can't walk. McGruder can't."

"No. But at his age, he could take twenty, get out at fifty and still have a lot of money ditched down in the Islands. If he gave us the rest of these killers . . ."

"The rest of the Five have probably made that same calculation," Lucas said. "You think they'd let him get away with talking?"

She thought about that, and said, "I don't know. But I do know, it's not my problem. It's your problem. Yours and the FBI's. I'd just like to say . . ."

"Yeah?"

She grinned and tapped his chest. "Good fuckin' luck, Lucas."

FIFTEEN

McGruder was both astonished and frightened when the FBI came through the front door. He'd been standing in the bathroom, looking at his teeth and wondering whether he should pay for dental whitening, sporadically flashing to the burglary that had torn up his dressing room, when he heard the first-floor door bang open and the intruders shouting: "FBI."

He reacted instinctively: he dropped his toothbrush and ran for the dressing room and then into the safe room, latching the mirror and door behind himself. He huddled there, stunned, then called an acquaintance who had once been arrested for income tax evasion and who recommended that he call Marvin Fingerhut.

He did that. Fingerhut had been asleep, but he had an overnight associate who got him out of bed to talk to McGruder.

When Fingerhut asked why the FBI was swarming his house, Mc-Gruder lied and said he didn't know. "I think I paid all my taxes . . ."

"That's not it," Fingerhut said. Fingerhut thought, but did not say, "This is the jackass who killed Sikes." He said instead, "Gotta be something bigger than taxes. Don't tell me what it is, or if you're guilty or not. I don't want that cluttering up my thought processes."

Fingerhut recommended that McGruder give himself up and to make it clear that he was unarmed and surrendering. "Are you talking to me on a cell phone?"

"Yeah, of course."

"Turn on the camera app, turn on the video, and hold it out in front of you, make movies of the arrest," Fingerhut said. "If there's something irregular about it, we can use the video."

At that moment, McGruder heard somebody, a man, shouting that he should give himself up or they'd knock down the house with sledgehammers.

"They know I'm hiding here," he told Fingerhut. "They're talking about knocking down the house."

"Be calm, be cool, don't talk to them. *Do not talk to them.* They'll try to get you to chat, and it's hard to resist, and they're good at doing that. Leave your phone on and make movies as you talk to them. I'll see you at the courthouse."

THE NEXT THREE days were a chaotic mess. When he wasn't in a cell, Fingerhut stuck to him like a tick, which made things a little more tolerable, but McGruder decided that a jail cell was not the way to spend your life. He spoke to an officer from Pre-Trial Services, who, with Fingerhut, tried to come up with a bail package that would be acceptable to both a magistrate's court judge and the media, as well as McGruder.

"What does the media have to do with it?" McGruder asked.

"The magistrate won't want the TV people peeing on his shoes, so he'll jack up the bail to an insane level. Fortunately, you have the resources to pay an insane bail," Fingerhut said, having inquired about how large those resources might be.

In his cell, McGruder had waking nightmares: he'd burned the red pumps he'd stupidly taken from Sikes, and he assumed Escobar had cleaned out the fireplace—she was meticulous that way—but if the feds found any remnants of the shoes, he could be screwed. Had the garbage been hauled away? He had no idea of what day that was done.

He was still thinking about the problem on the day before the bail hearing, when Fingerhut told him, "They say they've got some metal supports from a woman's shoes. Can you think of any reason a pair of women's shoes might have been burned in your fireplace? I need to know if they might have been planted by the cops. Don't answer right now—think about it. Let me know."

The bail package was agreed upon the night before the hearing, though Fingerhut warned him that the magistrate would do some posturing for the media, pretending to think about exactly what should be fair, before announcing the agreed-upon bail. McGruder would also be required to wear an ankle bracelet with a GPS locator to monitor his movements. The bracelet, Fingerhut warned him, would be the best the federal government had, and if he did anything, like cut it off, he'd be in jail in an hour.

"Do not talk to anyone on the way out of the courthouse," Fingerhut told him. "One of my investigators will have a car waiting for us right outside. I'll be with you and I'll take you straight to the car.

Don't fight me. Keep your chin up, don't look left or right, don't do anything dramatic, get in the car and we go."

"Should I say 'no comment' to reporters?" McGruder asked, sounding stupid in his own ears.

"No! Don't say anything. If something absolutely must be said, I'll say it. You keep your mouth shut. Do not smile. Do not frown. I'll take a look at your wardrobe tonight, pick out an ensemble for you. We want you looking like a rich but conservative accountant, not like a crazy playboy. Somebody who could never commit a crime like this. If you pay attention to me, that's how you'll look. I'll check your appearance before we go into the courtroom . . ."

McGruder began to feel more confident, and it had all worked out exactly as Fingerhut said it would. McGruder walked stoically out of the courthouse, looking good in a dark blue pinstripe suit, white shirt, and muted red necktie. He looked neither left nor right, though he flinched when somebody shouted—a woman from Channel Five, he thought—"Is it true you throw tomahawks at a target in your basement?"

In the car, Fingerhut looked at him and asked, "Tomahawks?"

It occurred to McGruder then that if some of his ninja training became public knowledge, that information might not work entirely to his benefit.

"It's a joke, yeah, a tomahawk, it's like throwing darts . . ."

Fingerhut spoke to the car's window. "No, Jamie, it's not like throwing darts. Not like that at all."

Fingerhut and an associate spent an hour at McGruder's house, talking about behavior issues. They didn't want him going to clubs, he wasn't to visit hookers, he wasn't to leave the seven-county Twin Cities region. "I would not be surprised if they did some on-the-ground surveillance," Fingerhut said. "They have the right to check on you any time between eight in the morning and midnight, without warning. If you go to Hudson, Wisconsin, for a drink, they'll pick you up and slap you back in a cell. Don't do that."

"Can they bug my house? Have they done that?"

Fingerhut shook his head. "I wouldn't put it past them except for one thing—we're having attorney–client discussions here. If we find a bug, we'll stick it so far up their asses it'll crawl out their nose. They won't take that risk."

AS A FINAL item, Fingerhut said, "The remnant of those shoes in the fireplace is going to be an important piece of evidence, if we can't find a way to defeat it."

Wink wink, nudge nudge.

When he was finally alone, McGruder spent an hour wandering through the shambles of his house: nothing was wrecked or ruined, but the search party had gone through the place inch by inch. In the kitchen he found a note from the housekeeper telling him that she couldn't work for him anymore.

"Bitch," he muttered into the silence.

He started putting the place back together, got bored after an hour of it, spent another forty-five minutes soaking in the spa pool in his bathroom, got dressed in clean, comfortable clothes, then went for a drive, just to be doing it. He drove around the lake, following some counter-surveillance routes, and saw nothing.

Not even media—they'd been all over the place at the magistrate's court, but now, for a while, he'd be yesterday's news. That would change, he thought, as he got closer to a trial.

If he went to trial.

Fingerhut had suggested that the prosecution might talk about a deal—a substantial prison sentence, but not an unsupportable sentence—in return for evidence against the other members of the Five, assuming, of course, that McGruder was a member.

"We don't need to think about that yet," Fingerhut said. "If the members of the Five keep killing, the pressure on the feds will keep increasing . . . right up to the point where they catch somebody else who agrees to deal. That means that you'll have an opportunity to get a better and better deal, right up to the point where they catch somebody else and you won't get any deal at all. Is that clear?"

"Yes. It's what I'd do if I were a prosecutor," McGruder said.

He drove back home, feeling the isolation. The housekeeper wouldn't be coming in, he didn't want to talk to Fingerhut anymore, at least not that day, but he did need to talk to someone. Bored, he shoveled the back deck, the parking patio, steps down to the lake level, and the stone path that in the summer would lead to the dock.

Then he took a nap; when he woke up, it was nearly dark, which surprised him. Of course, he hadn't been able to sleep in the cell and the stress had been all over him. He went down to the kitchen, ate some Cheerios, watched the six o'clock news on which he featured prominently.

He looked good coming out of the courthouse, he thought. Like a young businessman.

At ten o'clock, he killed all the lights in the house except the bedroom and bathroom. He put on an all-black winter ninja outfit—that's how he thought of it, black jeans, a black hoodie, black gloves and shoes—and slipped out the back door onto the deck, then down to the parking patio.

He was next to invisible, unless the cops had put an infrared camera on him. A chance he'd have to take. He walked down the stone steps he'd cleared earlier in the day. He lay on the bottom step, and felt over the edge, groping along the bottom of the stones until he felt the edge. He pulled on it, hard, and the stone reluctantly pulled out: his SHTF survival cache as recommended on all the better prepper sites.

Two thousand dollars in cash, which he didn't want, a .357 Magnum, which he didn't want, a bunch of other shit he didn't want—would he ever have needed a handheld GPS under any conditions? Now that he actually thought about it, he doubted it. The whole fantasy about surviving in the wilderness was bullshit.

But the burner phones and the chargers . . . those he needed. There were four of them, and he removed two, and pushed the cache rock back in place. Moving slowly, he climbed the stairs, crossed the parking patio and the deck, and went back into the house. In the basement, he opened a drawer on a workbench and put the phones inside, trailed the charging cords out the back of the workbench to an outlet and plugged them in.

Charging lights came on in both.

That done, he climbed the stairs to the bedroom, changed into pajamas, went to a window that faced the front yard, pulled back a curtain. If anyone was out there, they'd see him. He killed the lights in the bathroom and bedroom and lay down on the bed.

Couldn't sleep, turned on the television projector, went to Netflix and watched an Angelina Jolie movie called *Those Who Wish Me Dead*, which turned out to be pretty good.

When *Those Who Wish Me Dead* ended, he called up another movie, amped the sound a bit, then slipped down the stairs to the basement, dug out one of the burner phones, and called the disaster number.

Vivian Zhao answered on the second ring. She said, "You really hacked this up."

"I don't know how they tracked me," McGruder said. "Not yet. I'm going to need some help. Not much, but some."

"That's not part of the deal."

"It is now. What I want isn't much—and I really better get it," McGruder said. "My attorney is suggesting that if I cooperate with the FBI, I could get fifteen or twenty years instead of thirty to life without parole."

"Is that a threat?" Zhao asked.

"Take it any way you want. But. I don't want much. I just want a little bit."

"Suppose I agreed. What kind of help do you need?"

"I need you to find a red, a scarlet, Manolo Blahnik BB pump in size 8 and I need you to half-bury it in a roadside snowbank across the street from Hillary Sikes' house. I'm sure you can find her address . . ."

"And that would . . ."

"That would suggest that the steel heel supports that they found in the ashes from my fireplace were planted by the cops. No way Sikes was wearing three pumps."

After a moment of silence, Zhao said, "I can do that. I can be there the day after tomorrow, late."

"Can you get the pump that fast?"

"In LA? Yes. But—I'll want to talk face-to-face. Is your lake frozen?"

"It is, but why—"

"Because I'm going to ski across the lake and bring a cell phone with me. I'm going to do a video of you confessing to the Sikes and Velez murders. I've been talking to the others and we were all worried that you might begin to cooperate. I'm not sure the FBI could identify the others even with you cooperating, but they don't want to take a chance. If we even get a hint that you are cooperating, we'll send the video to the FBI and to CNN so you'll go down for the whole life-without-parole number."

"How do I know—"

"We wouldn't use it unless you were cooperating. We wouldn't dare. If we bombed you with it, then you'd cooperate simply out of revenge. When we get this video, we'll both have a gun and neither one of us would dare to use it."

McGruder thought about it and said, "What time will you get here?"

"Don't know. I'll call you."

"There are snowmobilers on the lake. They run over each other a couple times a year. If you're out there on skis . . ."

"A chance I'll take," Zhao said. "And you have to spend the next two days looking for bugs and hidden cameras."

"I've been looking. My lawyer says there won't be any and I haven't seen anything that looks suspicious. But: I'll go over the place inch-by-inch tomorrow."

"Then I'll see you in forty-eight hours. Give me a new number and get rid of the phone you're on."

McGruder hung up, satisfied. He should get rid of the phone, and he should have left the shoes with Sikes, as tempting a trophy as they were. And the parka! What the fuck was he thinking, to keep the parka? But the parka hadn't seemed to be any kind of a threat. He was still mystified by the fact that he found it hanging from the dressing room mirror. Had Walker done that? And why would she? And how did she find the safe room? Anyway, he should have burned it the night of the killing and scattered the ashes in the countryside. There just hadn't seemed to be any urgency about it. Was it possible that he actually was a dumbshit? How could he be? He was a billionaire.

LUCAS HAD INTERRUPTED his search for the woman named Virginia Clayton-Weasling, wanted for skipping out on a federal trial for tax evasion, to help hunt for the killer of Hillary Sikes. While he was working that case, another Minnesota deputy U.S. marshal had captured Clayton-Weasling, who was now in the federal lockup.

When the U.S. Marshal for Minnesota asked Lucas what he would do now that McGruder was in jail, Lucas replied, "Nothing, for the time being. Is nothing good for you?"

Virgil was owed some time off from the BCA, after working overtime during the McGruder hunt, and he used it to lay down the first chapter of what he hoped would be his second published novel. His agent had left the frozen wasteland of the outer Hamptons for the Bahamas, on a boat, reportedly with executives from Penguin Random House. Did she not, he wondered, have cell service? Something? Why hadn't she called?

FOR MCGRUDER, THE forty-eight hours crept by at a snail's pace. He could watch only so much television—mostly CNBC during the day, streaming movies at night. After some thought, he wrote a letter to Virgil Flowers, whose name he'd written on the sticky note. He put the Flowers letter in an envelope, sealed it, addressed the envelope to "Virgil Flowers—Eyes Only," put that envelope in another larger envelope with a letter to Fingerhut, and wrote Fingerhut's name on it. He gave the letter to Fingerhut and said, "Don't open it unless I'm dead."

Forty-six hours after he talked to Zhao, she called back.

"I planted the shoe. Soaked it in ice, buried it in the snow. It's gonna work—the snow mounds on the side of the road look like they probably have salt in them, road salt. We'll want that to get into the shoe for a while. I'll call on a burner two or three days from now, tell the cops I don't want to get involved, but I saw a shoe . . . I'll tell them they better report it, or I'll send a video to the media, and they'll all be fired."

"Where are you?"

"In my car across the lake from you. Tavern parking lot, there are other skiers here, they tell me there's a track that follows the perimeter of the lake. Haven't seen any snowmobile lights. I'll be coming. I've got a portable GPS, it'll lead me right into your dock, or where your dock should be. Checked it out on Google Earth."

"Should I meet you at the dock?"

"So we can make a video by shining a cell-phone light in your face so everybody can see it? No. Unlock the door that goes on your deck, meet me there, twenty minutes. We'll go to the quietest place in your house, the place where the cops wouldn't put cameras—inside a coat closet or something, I'll let you choose—and I'll make the video. All we need is the light."

McGruder turned off the first- and second-floor lights, one by one, as he'd done the first two nights after his arrest. He took off his shoes so he could move soundlessly and went down to the sliding doors that led out onto the deck.

McGruder had only met Zhao in person a few times. He didn't know her well, but he did know that she was a manipulative psychopath, like he was, faking her way through life with the normals.

Twenty minutes after she called, he saw movement against background lights, and she was there, by the glass door, dressed all in dark clothing. He pushed the door open, and she slipped inside and he pushed it shut.

She looked up at McGruder, who towered over her, and said, "We shouldn't be standing here together. I'm taking a huge risk."

"What about Four? Is he going ahead?" McGruder asked.

"Yes. But he's holding off for a day or two. We didn't want to make your problem worse during the bail hearing."

"And the shoe?"

"The shoe is in place. SFO cracked Sikes' American Express account and spotted the shoes she bought. We got an identical pair. They're not somewhat similar, they're exactly alike, and one is now half-buried across the street from the Sikes' house."

"Great," McGruder said. "Not only do I get off the hook, we fuck with the cops."

"I gotta get going and I need that video. Where can we shoot it?" Zhao asked.

"I thought about that," McGruder said. "The pantry. Plenty of light, doors close tight and it's small enough that I checked every freckle in the place: no cameras, no bugs."

"That will work," Zhao said. "Lead the way."

McGruder backed away from her, and said, "This way . . ." and he continued backing away.

She frowned and asked, "Why are you walking backward?"

"Because I trust you about as far as I could spit a rat," McGruder said. He reached behind his back and produced a large silver pistol.

Zhao: "Jesus, Jamie, I'm trying to help you. You want to shoot me?"

"No, of course not," McGruder said. "Maybe I'll need some more help from the group. But if you *did* shoot me, that'd solve a lot of problems for you and the rest of them, wouldn't it?"

"We're all in this together," Zhao said. "All together. We wouldn't do that. We wouldn't even think about it."

McGruder continued to back away from her, down a hallway, and into the pantry. There was already a light on, and he backed into the pantry, said, "Walk around me." His hand was still holding the gun, but it was pointed at the floor. When she'd walked around him, he reached back and shut the pantry door.

Zhao said, "I'm going to take a cell phone out of my pocket. Don't get twitchy."

"Okay."

Moving very slowly, she unzipped a pocket, and slowly slid a cell phone out. "I want you to say your name, say where we are, and then say that you killed Sikes and the Velezes. Doesn't have to be anything fancy, but it's gotta be clear and convincing."

"I can do that. I've had media training," McGruder said.

They made the video, McGruder admitting to the killings, Zhao holding the phone close enough that his face was clear, as well as some of the surroundings.

When they were done, he asked, "Good enough?"

"I think so," Zhao said. "Let me replay it."

She started to replay and stepped closer to him, and not thinking, he turned to open the pantry door. Quick as a grass snake, her hand went into her open pocket, the same pocket that she'd kept the cell phone in, and she pulled out her .22.

McGruder caught the sudden movement from the corner of his eye and jerked his head back around. Zhao had brought the gun up to shoot him in the temple, but with the sudden jerk of his head, she wound up shooting him in the cheekbone, penetrating up through his eye. He staggered, tried to bring his own gun up, but she shot him in the forehead, then shot him in the other eye, and he slumped against a cabinet, his feet slipping out from beneath him, and as he started to fall, she fired two more fast shots into his head.

The shots were loud, but as was the case with the Velez house, McGruder's was closed up for the winter and there was nobody to hear them.

As she stepped outside the pantry, she glanced back once: the fuckin' moron, she thought. He actually believed there was a shoe in a snowdrift. She collected her skis and disappeared into the dark.

THE NEXT MORNING, Fingerhut called, as he did each morning, to ask even more questions, but McGruder didn't answer. Nobody answered an hour later or two hours later and the lawyer said to his assistant, "That fucker better not be running."

"If he was running, wouldn't the L-Wop have called?"

L-Wop meant "life without parole," and was their code for the federal prosecutor who'd been assigned to the case. Fingerhut shrugged. "Don't know. Jamie has a billion dollars and he's not *too* stupid, so he's probably got a good chunk of it offshore. Maybe the Five have got a bail-out program if one of them gets in trouble . . . maybe he's on his way to Brazil."

"You think?"

Fingerhut touched his nose, thought about it, and said, "No. Go out there and bang on the door until he answers. If he doesn't, I got a guy, I can check on his bracelet, see if it's still on his leg."

The assistant drove out to McGruder's house, which looked terrific. There'd been flurries after midnight, and an inch of fresh snow dressed up the neighborhood. He noticed that there were no new tracks on the driveway. The front door was locked, and nobody answered the door. He walked around the house, saw tracks that he supposed were made either by squirrels or rats, but no human tracks anywhere.

He called Fingerhut, who said, "I called my guy and he says the bracelet hasn't been cut and it's in his house."

"What do you want me to do?"

"Give me a minute." His assistant gave him a minute, then Fingerhut came back on the phone and said, "I'm calling the cops."

VIRGIL WAS EATING a peanut-butter-and-grape-jelly sandwich when Lucas called.

Lucas said, "McGruder won't be cooperating."

Virgil said, "Basically, I don't like the way you said that. He shoot himself?"

"No. Somebody did it for him."

SIXTEEN

Virgil had an early morning talk with his boss, Jon Duncan, who told him that there wouldn't be much more for him and Lucas to do now that McGruder was dead.

"You guys were fantastic. Even the FBI admits it. But now . . . nobody really thinks that McGruder's killer is from around here. We had a killer in San Francisco who apparently knew his way around, another in Houston who apparently knew his way around—"

"Or her," Virgil interrupted. "The feds think it might have been a woman, or a very short man . . ."

"Or her," Duncan conceded. "There's no special reason to think he, or she, comes from here. The ball is now in the federal court."

An hour after talking to Duncan, Frankie called him in from the barn, where he'd been skating on horse urine. "Some guy," she said. "He says it's important and it's about McGruder."

Virgil had left his phone in the house so he wouldn't have to talk to anyone, and he only grudgingly took it from Frankie and said, "Hello?"

"Virgil Flowers? This is Marvin Fingerhut, Jamie McGruder's attorney. We met at Howard Gates' house."

"Oh, yeah. Lucas called you Gates' mouthpiece. What's up?"

"Mouthpiece my ass. Davenport can't get over the fact that last week, I took him into the boards so hard that his false teeth flew into the ninth row of seats."

"Good story," Virgil said. "I love hearing about old people slowly playing hockey, especially the stories that have nothing to do with me. If you're all finished, thanks for calling . . ."

"Hey! I've got a letter for you."

"What?"

"I know. But, I do," Fingerhut said. "Jamie McGruder gave me a letter, said that if anything should happen to him, meaning, you know, he was worried that somebody might bust a cap in his ass. He was right to worry."

"I heard," Virgil said. "Couldn't you just open the letter and read it to me?"

"Nope. Can't do that. You'd turn me in and I'd get disciplined. The bar dipshits already don't like me."

"How about if Davenport . . ."

"Nope. It's for you and only you," Fingerhut said. "I have to hand it to you personally. You have to sign for it."

"So I have to drive up there from Mankato?"

"Well, I guess I can't require you to. I could stick the letter in the office safe until we both forgot about it."

"I'll come up," Virgil said. "I might bring Davenport with me."

"Feel free. It's your letter," Fingerhut said. "We're out of the office for two hours around lunchtime, back at one-thirty or so. You'll have to sign a letter acknowledging delivery. After that, I don't care what you do with it."

Virgil called Lucas.

"This is really interesting," Lucas said. "Never heard anything like it. Why don't you come up for lunch? We can speculate."

"Should we call St. Vincent?"

"Hell no. This is us. Let's see what it is before the FBI sticks its nose in."

Virgil filled in Frankie and headed north in his Tahoe. He was early and met Lucas at a Baker's Square restaurant a few blocks from Lucas' house for pie and conversation. Neither one of them could figure out what McGruder might have to say to Virgil, but Lucas suggested that he'd gotten Virgil's name from Jennifer Carey's television broadcast.

"I can't think of any other way he could do it—not unless Fingerhut filled him in. And if he did, why would he choose you? Fingerhut knows *me*," Lucas said.

"Maybe he's trying to poke you in the eye?" Virgil suggested. "No, wait—this is a letter from McGruder, not Fingerhut. No reason McGruder would prefer me over you."

"We need to find out," Lucas said.

FINGERHUT HAD AN office in a brick, glass, and fern building on the edge of St. Paul's Lowertown. Virgil and Lucas walked in at five minutes after two. A bulky male receptionist, bracketed by potted palms, and whose right hand was covered by a desk that might conceal a firearm, passed them along to an efficient-looking secretary who said, "I saw your pictures on TV. Marv's waiting for you."

She pushed a button on a box on her desk and said, "Butch and Sundance are here."

"Which one am I?" Lucas asked.

She looked at him, then at Virgil, then back to Lucas and said, "Butch."

"Ah, poop."

"Go on in," she said.

FINGERHUT WAS SITTING behind a twelve-foot-long table that served as a desk, with computers at both ends and a wide sheet of plastic on the carpet so he could roll back and forth between them. He was wearing a wine-colored cashmere V-neck sweater over a white dress shirt.

He picked up a parchment-colored envelope from his desktop and said to Lucas, "You're lucky to be back on your feet after the way I took you into the boards last week."

"I let you take me," Lucas said. "I thought you might need the morale boost given the fact you guys were getting the shit kicked out of you."

Virgil said, "Yeah, yeah. You both can take the testosterone test later. Is that the letter?"

"This is the letter," Fingerhut said, holding up the parchment-colored envelope. "Sit down, sign here, and you can have it."

Virgil took a visitor's chair as Fingerhut pushed a sheet of paper across the desk along with a heavy black-enamel Montblanc pen. Virgil read the paper—a simple acknowledgment of delivery of a letter from Jamie McGruder. He signed and dated it, and Fingerhut pushed the McGruder letter across. "Why don't you open it here? I'm dying to know what's in it," Fingerhut said. He tossed a silver letter opener across the desk.

Virgil looked at Lucas, who shrugged, and he picked up the letter opener, slit open the envelope and took out a single sheet of paper. Lucas, still standing, bent to read the letter over his shoulder.

To Virgil Flowers:

I saw on a news program that you and your partner were leading the investigation into my case. I am sending this letter to you because I couldn't remember your partner's name. This letter was to be delivered to you only in the case of my death, so if you're reading it, I'm dead.

If I'm killed, my murderer would most likely be the member of the Five who we call "Six." She is the only one who knows the identity of all the members of the Five. She issues the press releases and maintains our web page, which, by the time you get this, will have changed. She has murdered a man herself, but not one of the five we've been going after. She murdered:

Josh Roper, a hedge fundie, in Los Angeles, Ca.

She's like our teacher. I do not know where she lives, except that I believe it is in Southern California, probably in the San Diego area. She may be involved with the University of California at San Diego. That is all speculation which I won't bother to explain. (All right, I will. I met her at Bitcoin conventions. The first time, when she walked up and identified herself, she was pulling a suitcase with an airline tag on it. She'd flown out of SAN, which I later

figured out was San Diego International. When I was talking to
her, she said something about getting a PhD.)

Her name is Vivian Zhao. You're welcome.

Jamie McGruder.

PS: If this is Fingerhut reading this, you're so fucking fired, you
asshole.

Lucas said, "Holy shit."

Fingerhut: "What is it?"

Lucas shook his head. "We can't tell you that. Or maybe we can
tell you a little?"

He looked at Virgil, who said to Fingerhut, "We may have another client for you." He stood up. "Keep watching your television
for updates."

"C'mon, guys," Fingerhut said.

"Took me into the boards, my ass," Lucas said, and Virgil followed
him out the door.

OUTSIDE, VIRGIL SAID, "We need to talk to St. Vincent."

"We need to talk to Mallard, is what we need to do. St. Vincent
isn't in San Diego. You might have noticed." He kicked a dirty hump
of snow between two parking meters, spraying it onto the trunk of a
Prius, if Priuses have trunks. "Let's go back to my place to make the
call. We can figure out what we want to do, on the way."

Virgil, in the car, observed that they'd just identified a serial killer.
"We solved the cases—I mean, not really, but nobody else did."

On the way, they agreed that it would be interesting to go to San Diego, if Mallard was interested in sending them. "Here's the thing: Mallard got a lot of internal credit inside the Justice Department for our whole deal down in Miami," Lucas said. "He got more credit for the work we did here. He's gonna get credit for this. I figure he's going to ask us to go. What do you think?"

"Give me a minute . . ." Virgil went into his iPhone and came back a moment later. "The high in San Diego today will be sixty-six degrees."

Lucas flicked his hand toward the outdoors: snowbanks and a sky with the color and warmth of concrete blocks.

AT LUCAS' HOUSE, they sat in the den and Lucas made the call. A secretary doubted that Mallard would have the time to talk, but she knew who Lucas was, so she'd ask. Mallard came up fifteen seconds later: "What?"

"We got a letter from McGruder. We thought you'd be interested, so we're willing to share it with you," Lucas said.

"When you say, 'we,' you actually mean . . ."

"Well, Virgil. It was addressed to Virgil. McGruder left it with his attorney to be given to Virgil if anything unkind happened to him. And it did."

"Read it."

Virgil read the letter. Mallard said, "Talk to my assistant—she'll tell you where to fax the letter . . ."

Virgil: "The FBI faxes?"

"Or, you can scan it and send it that way," Mallard said. "We'll want the letter itself, of course. We'll want to see if McGruder's fingerprints are on it. I assume you were careful when you were handling it?"

"Pretty much," Virgil said. "Maybe not entirely."

"Good. I'll have St. Vincent send somebody to pick it up from wherever you're at. I'll contact the San Diego office and get some research going. How soon can you two get out there?"

THEY COULD GET out on a nonstop Delta flight leaving at seven o'clock. On his way back to Mankato in his truck, Virgil called Frankie and told her to pack the bag for him, jeans and shirts and underwear and socks and the Dopp kit, along with a couple of sport coats. "And maybe a couple pairs of shorts."

"I can't believe you conned your way into another winter vacation," Frankie said.

"Hey. You want to go on a morning show and show off your cleavage, I gotta do this," Virgil said.

"You want me to pack your necktie?"

"It's California. I don't think I'll need it."

VIRGIL WAS AWARE that Lucas was a white-knuckle flier, so he didn't mention until they were in the air that the San Diego airport was considered one of the nation's scariest both for takeoffs and landings.

"You're so full of it," Lucas said.

"No, really," Virgil said. "We've got WiFi on this flight, you could look it up."

Later in the flight, Lucas did that, pretending to be casual about it, an afterthought to his real interest, which was national news. But when he did, Virgil said, "See?"

"Shut the fuck up."

THEY SURVIVED THE LANDING.

Mallard's assistant had gotten them a rental car—a blue Chevrolet Equinox—and rooms at the Residence Inn in La Jolla, north of San Diego itself but next to the University of California at San Diego and only about ten minutes from the FBI's San Diego field office.

Virgil drove while Lucas scrolled through messages from Mallard and from the San Diego feds. "We're meeting them tomorrow morning. Early, so we've got to get up. They found an address for Vivian Zhao but she no longer lives there, and they don't know where she went. Moved out two months ago, no forwarding address. She flew to Dallas, New York City, and Seattle two years back, but hasn't flown anywhere in the U.S. in the past year and a half. She has TSA clearance. She's a native American citizen with an American passport, born in San Francisco. She has a California driver's license and hasn't applied for a new driver's license in any other state. She's thirty-four years old, was a PhD candidate in economics at San Diego but never finished it, dropped out of school four years ago. Current thinking is that she may have moved somewhere else in California."

"Car?"

"Old Toyota pickup," Lucas said. "They're looking for it."

"Facebook, Twitter, LinkedIn . . ." Virgil suggested.

"Nothing on that—I gotta believe that they looked."

"Driver's license photo?"

"Got it." Lucas turned the iPad toward Virgil. Zhao was a plain-looking Chinese-American; either that, or the California driver's license division made her plain.

"I got a bad feeling about this," Virgil said.

"How's that?"

"I got a feeling we're walkin' and knockin'."

"Walkin' and knockin' in sixty-six degrees."

THEY MET THE next morning with Roger Callis, the San Diego agent in charge, a thin, white-haired, quiet-spoken man who wore a quiet off-the-rack blue suit. He got them cups of decent coffee and wanted to hear about their adventures in Miami. "Louis filled me in a little on that," he said, referring to Mallard. "Wish I'd been there."

"Didn't seem all that wonderful at the time, but, yeah, it worked out," Virgil said. "That took a lot of planning—you guys and the Marshal's Service spent three months setting it up. This time, it's more like we got lucky."

"You got lucky with this Zhao, too," Callis said. "First of all, we checked the murder that McGruder referenced. It's real. Multiple shots from a .22 pistol close enough to the victim's skull to burn hair. Exactly the same situation we see with McGruder. Shells were recovered from both locations, so the lab should be able to tell us if they were fired from the same weapon, and exactly what kind of gun that is. With nothing but McGruder's word for it, we couldn't arrest her until that gets back."

"You know where she is?"

"No. She's disappeared—and that makes me think McGruder was telling the truth. She had six thousand dollars in her savings account before she vanished and she took it all out. She was a manager at an In-N-Out Burger for three years while she was going to the university; that's a corporate-owned chain so she wasn't involved in a franchise or anything. She didn't have a financial interest. In-N-Out says she was competent, but not outstanding. Hasn't used a credit card since she went away. And that's tough: we live in a credit society. Some places don't even accept cash anymore. She can't fly, can't rent a car . . ."

Virgil: "Six thousand dollars? She's not one of these rich Bitcoin people? We understood she was."

"Doesn't look like it," Callis said. "Maybe she stashed some money offshore, but from what I'm seeing yesterday afternoon and this morning, she wasn't living like it. Her vehicle is a seven-year-old Toyota Tacoma pickup."

"Interesting," Lucas said. "Was there anything at all at her address?"

Callis shook his head. "She moved out right around the end of November. Left no forwarding address, maybe because her landlord said she never got mail."

"Then she split before the killings started . . ."

"Yup. Just before. Like she knew they were coming and she might be exposed," Callis said.

"McGruder said he met her at a Bitcoin convention. Maybe she was just hustling the rich guys," Lucas said. "She didn't look that great in her driver's license photo."

Callis shrugged: "In my driver's license photo, I look like somebody made a mistake and took a picture of my ass. I've got a better photo I can send you, from Zhao's college ID. She's kinda cute in that picture, but no raving beauty."

"We need to check out her neighborhood. Knock on some doors," Lucas said.

"We're doing that, but, go ahead," Callis said. "You might pick up on something we didn't see."

"Any sign of a boyfriend or girlfriend?" Virgil asked.

"I'm getting back word that she had a boyfriend when she was a PhD candidate at UCSD. We've got his name and address, he's apparently around, but we haven't been able to hook up with him yet. We'll find him."

"She dropped out of college years go," Virgil said.

Callis nodded: "But that's all we've got in terms of relationships."

"Political activity?" Lucas asked.

"Yeah, back in 2020 she was involved in anti-Trump demonstrations, but this is California, so that's not exactly uncommon," Callis said. "Haven't gotten a lot on that, yet, but we should have more by this afternoon."

"Sounds like you guys actually got quite a bit," Virgil said.

Callis shrugged. "Washington called, we jerked ten guys off their regular assignments and got them running. We've talked to several people who knew her when she was a grad student . . . So far, all we've got is background."

They talked for another few minutes, getting that background on Zhao. She was originally from San Francisco and agents from the San Francisco field office were interviewing her parents. Callis hadn't yet heard back on that.

"Bottom line is, we should know a lot more by this evening. If you want to stop by at five o'clock, we'll have a team meeting and summarize everything we've got."

"So if you've got her last address . . ." Lucas said.

"I do, but there's nothing there but a house with a back apartment that somebody else has been living in for a month. The landlord lives in the front."

"It's a place to start," Lucas said, standing up.

"I'll be slightly annoyed if you get something we didn't," Callis said.

ZHAO HAD LAST lived in the community of Mira Mesa, in a yellow box of a house whose most prominent architectural characteristic was the garage door, as it was on all the houses in the neighborhood. The small front yard featured a flagpole from which an American flag fluttered in a weak breeze.

They parked in the driveway and before they could get to the front door, it opened, and a man stepped out on the porch. He was in his late fifties or early sixties, bald, overweight, wearing khaki shorts, a long-sleeved shirt with pearl snap buttons that cradled his gut like a bowling-ball bag, and Nike cross-trainers with over-the-ankle white athletic socks. He looked harassed.

"More FBI?" he asked, as he met them halfway down the sidewalk to the house.

"U.S. Marshal," Lucas said, "Coordinating with the FBI."

"I told the agents everything I knew," he said.

"I doubt that," Virgil said, cheerfully. "You look like a guy who knows a lot. About a lot of stuff."

The man considered that for a moment, then said, "Well, I do. But, not about Vivian."

"Bet you know a lot more than you think," Virgil said. "The thing is, the FBI does interrogations. We bullshit. If you don't mind bullshitting for a while, maybe we can come up with a few things you didn't tell the feds."

The man's name was Dwight Bernard, called Ike—"My parents named me after Eisenhower"—and they wound up sitting in his living room drinking off-brand cola that he got cheap at Sam's Club. "I go in for the rotisserie chicken—a whole chicken for five bucks, I have chicken sandwiches for a week with one chicken, and then I wind up buying a bunch of other shit, like this," he said, holding up his soda can.

"It's not bad," Lucas said. "I might have to start drinking it."

"Let me ask you this about Vivian," Virgil said. "She ever get laid back there? You let her bring guys home?"

"I had no problem with it—and back when she first rented the place, she did. I mean, do either of you know about a singing group called Peter, Paul and Mary from the sixties?"

"Vaguely . . . sort of beatniks," Lucas said.

"That 'Puff the Dragon' song," Virgil said. "Magic Dragon."

"Yeah, that's right. Folkies. This guy she brought home, looked exactly like Peter. Or Paul. I never knew which was which. But, you know, tall, thin, going bald, got this beatnik kinda beard. You know?"

They did.

"She brought him home a few times, I couldn't hear anything going on, but he stayed the night. Drove a Volkswagen, of course. And they smoked some weed. I told them that if they wanted to smoke, I didn't care, but they had to do it in the yard," Bernard said. "I didn't want the apartment smelling like dope. Anyway, I don't know his name. To tell you the truth, I kinda think the last few years, she might have been singing on our side of the choir, if you know what I mean. Not that she brought any women home, that I know of."

Zhao had rented from him for six years, he said, both as a student and later as a manager at In-N-Out Burger. "She never brought me a freebee In-N-Out burger, not even one time."

They asked about places she might have hung out. "I think, mostly down at the university . . . even after she quit her program and went to work for the burger place."

Any personal peculiarities?

Bernard pursed his lips thinking about it, then his eyebrows went up. "She wore a lot of green," he said, "black jeans with long-sleeved green tops, because she had green eyes and green looked good on her—made her eyes seem to glow.

"I let her use my washer and dryer—I mean, why not, she never had much of a load, and only used it once a week. One time, though, the washer went out and I couldn't get a part for it right away. We both had to do our wash down at the Advantage. That's a coin-op place, and I ran into her there. She was wearing shorts and a sleeve-less pullover blouse because, you know, she was washing everything else. The only time I ever saw skin that wasn't on her face. And that girl had the ink!"

"Tattoos?" Virgil asked.

"From her neckline down as far as I could see. When she bent over to take some clothes out of the dryer, her shirt pulled up and I seen tats go down under her shorts. So I think she was tatted up from top to bottom."

Virgil: "You know who did the work?"

"Something she said made me think she got them local, and maybe not until she started living here. She said something about her mother wouldn't allow it, and she got them after she started college," Bernard said.

"Did they look like good work?" Virgil asked. "Or were they crude, like prison tats, or . . ."

"They were sort of Oriental, you know, tattooed tigers and gemstones with rays coming out of them, and such. What I could see."

"Did she drink?" Lucas asked.

"Wine, some. Not much. There'd be a bottle in the recycle every couple of weeks."

"She seemed nice enough, huh?" Virgil asked.

"No, she didn't. She acted like she was always pissed off," Bernard said. "Didn't take it out on me, though. She was quiet and paid the rent on time. We didn't talk so much—I don't think she was shy, I think she . . . maybe she was a little arrogant. I retired from the Air Force and got a job as a driver, an escort, with a real estate company. She thought I was like a cabbie—not in her social class."

"Never mentioned Bitcoin, or anything like that?"

Bernard frowned. "I don't even know for sure what that is. Some kind of funny money, or something?"

"Over in that direction," Lucas said.

"You know what? We didn't talk much, but money is one thing I know she was interested in. Where to get it, who had it, how to get it. I told her I bought this house right after I got out of the Air Force for one twenty-five. You know what it's worth now? Look on Zillow. Zillow says it's worth eight hundred and eighty thousand. She was always amazed by that. She'd talk about finding another place where you could still buy cheap and get rich. She'd talk about flipping houses and so on."

They talked about that for a few minutes and when they'd covered everything they could think of, Lucas asked if she had any hobbies. Bernard said, "Well, I know she did karate. I told the FBI about that and they said they'd send an agent over. The school's right down here in the shopping center . . ."

He gave them directions to the shopping center. There wasn't much more to talk about, so Virgil gave him a card, asked him to call if he thought of anything else that might be useful, and said goodbye. In the car, Lucas asked, "What do you think?"

"I think the karate place is about four blocks from here," Virgil said.

And it was. The karate studio was in a storefront. It wasn't open yet, but they could see somebody moving inside and they pounded on the door until a man came to open it a crack. He said, "We're not—"

Lucas: "U.S. Marshal. We need to chat."

The man opened the door wider. He was dressed in a white *gi* with a worn black belt; he was barefoot on a wooden floor. "The FBI was already here . . ."

They did the thing about bullshitting instead of being interrogated, and the man, whose name was Alec Smith, let them in. A woman was on her knees in a corner screwing a metal plate to the floor. Over her shoulder, she said, "We really couldn't tell the FBI much."

Zhao had worked out at the studio for two years and had reached the rank of purple belt, which was about halfway between nothing and black belt. "She would have made first *dan*, first-degree black belt, in a couple more years; she had some ability," Smith said.

Both he and the woman were in their late forties or early fifties and looked like they'd been carved from blocks of wood. The woman introduced herself as Shelby Smith, Alec's wife. Zhao, they said, was one of the angriest women they'd ever met.

Shelby Smith: "She was kind of a feminist—she believed that most of the rotten things in the world happened because of men, which is true, but she took it personally. We'd tell her that karate wasn't really a solution for the world's problems, but it might help her through some personal troubles. She disagreed. She said people had to take world troubles seriously, and if they needed to be solved one at a time, then we ought to start doing that."

"What did you say to that?" Virgil asked.

"We disagreed, but that was okay. I told her it would take time to get things straight, and she said that was what people always said. It would take time, but it would never get done. She said we had to solve the problems now. I think she was in a Biden campaign group for a while, even after the Trump-Biden election . . . but I don't think she'd agree with them too much, either."

Lucas: "Why not?"

"She liked rich people," Alec Smith said. "She wanted to be one. It seemed like every time we talked, we'd wind up talking about how to make money. I told her that we had our way—karate is our careers, Shelby and me. Our business. She sorta . . . dissed that idea. Working for your whole life. She wanted a trick that would make her rich right now."

Virgil: "Then she just went away?"

"Well, yeah. She was working hard on her karate, here every day, until one day last November, she didn't show up and never did again."

The studio had separate dressing rooms for men and women and Shelby Smith said that Zhao did, in fact, have collarbone-to-knee tattoos, but had kept her arms and her legs below the knees untouched. "She loved the tattoos, but she wanted to keep the visible parts of her arms and legs clean, in case she had to work in a corporate environment," Shelby Smith said. She added that Zhao's tattoos covered her buttocks and apparently all the way through what Smith called her "frontal thong area."

Lucas said, "Ouch."

Shelby Smith shrugged: "She didn't seem to react much to pain. We're non-contact here, but there's always some contact, by accident, and when she got hit, it'd make her smile."

Virgil: "You think . . . I don't exactly know how to ask this . . . she must have had a . . . mmm . . . trusting relationship with her tattoo artist?"

"I expect so," Shelby Smith said.

"You could ask her, the tattoo artist," Alec Smith said. "She got her tats from Cheryl Leung. She's over by the university. Great artist." Roger unwrapped his black belt, shrugged out a shoulder to show off a tattoo of a kata pose. "Got it from Cheryl."

Virgil: "Nice work."

"You talk to the FBI about her?" Lucas asked. "About this Leung?"

"No . . . the FBI never got to tattoos," Alec Smith said, as he re-wrapped his black belt.

They got rough directions from Smith for the Leung studio, found it on Virgil's iPad—Satori Ink in La Jolla—said goodbye to the Smiths, and headed west.

A mile into the trip, Virgil got a phone call, looked at his phone and said, "Holy cats. It's my agent."

"Maybe you should answer the phone," Lucas said.

Virgil answered it, said, "Hey, Esther," listened, then said, "San Diego, yeah, I'm working a case with my marshal friend. Yeah, the same guy . . . Who? Penguin Random? That's good, huh? Yeah, that's great, that's fine. Thank you. How long to get a contract? Man, this is great, Esther, thank you. Uh-huh. Uh-huh. About fifteen thousand words right now, I can have it in four months. Uh-huh. Okay. Email me everything. Thanks again."

He hung up the phone and Lucas said, "You should have thanked her at least one more time."

When Virgil didn't respond, Lucas asked, "What?"

"That's kinda private."

"If you don't tell me, I'll tell Frankie about that time you drank those Manhattans and started talking about her tits to those marshals in Miami."

"Two-book contract," Virgil said. "Two hundred grand. Thirty-three now, thirty-three on publication, thirty-three on paperback, which is a year after hardcover publication. Same for the second book."

"Jesus! Virgil! Man, congratulations, that's terrific," Lucas said.

"It's really fuckin' great," Virgil said. A smile slipped onto his face. "I never thought it'd be that much."

"Enough to quit?"

"Gotta think about that. Be pretty marginal. The money will actually come in over four years for the two books. That's only fifty grand a year. I make twice that now and I got medical and pension. With the kids . . ."

"Well, hell, it's a start. Damn! I know a fuckin' author." Lucas laughed out loud. "They got a country club in Mankato?"

"Yes, they do. Mankato Golf Club, here I come."

"Sounds primo, if you gotta play golf—which is a stupid fuckin' game if you spend one minute thinking about it. But still! Man!"

"I gotta call Frankie," Virgil said. "She's gonna freak out. This is, I mean, Esther said I can make a living at this."

THEY KNEW SATORI INK was open, because they saw a FedEx man walking inside, carrying a box. The tattoo parlor was in a strip mall, between a juice place and a closet-sized store that sold esoteric books and crystal necklaces. They parked at the edge of the parking lot and Lucas got out and walked around while Virgil made an excited call to Frankie.

A woman in the bookstore recommended that Lucas buy a moonstone ring that he should wear on the small finger of his right hand and said that it would increase his feminine energy and smooth out both his mind and body. She added, "Your body looks like it could use some smoothing out."

"I have a smoother back home," Lucas said.

Virgil and Frankie spoke for fifteen minutes and then Virgil got out of the car and said to Lucas, "Frankie says I definitely shouldn't quit until I've got five or six books under my belt and know for sure it's what I want to do. I dunno . . ."

"If you talk to the woman in the bookstore, she could sell you a ring that would smooth out your mind and your body."

Virgil looked at the store and said, "Ah, Jesus, you didn't buy a moonstone ring, did you? I mean, you could definitely use the Kundalini energy . . ."

"Sometimes, I don't know why I talk to you," Lucas said.

Virgil was explaining potential moonstone effects on law enforcement officers when they walked into Satori Ink.

SEVENTEEN

The interior of Satori Ink looked like a beauty parlor decorated by the Hells Angels: black walls, two black leather chair/tables with extensions and rests that would allow a customer to stretch out in almost any shape to get almost any part of his or her body inked up; three vases of enameled-metal flowers on steel stems, for sale; and a crazy-quilt-painted chrome Harley-Davidson in the center of the floor.

The black walls were mostly obscured by framed images of tattoo possibilities and examples of actual skin results, including ink over and around female breasts; all with piercing. In one corner, a stuffed antelope looked out at the customer chairs, its eyes replaced by blinking red LED lights; and on its back sat a teddy bear that was missing its head but was equipped with a fuzzy brown after-market penis. A coffee table showed magazines ranging from *The New Yorker* to *Iron Horse*.

There were no customers. A thirtyish Asian-American woman was leaning on a counter, next to a cash register with an attached credit-card reader. She was reading a *San Diego Union-Tribune* and had just blown a pink bubble gum bubble as they walked in, which, Virgil thought, proved she could read and chew gum at the same time.

She looked up as the bell over the door tinkled, let the bubble deflate, chewed a couple of times and said, "Hey, guys. Matching ink?"

Lucas said, "Uh, no. I'm . . ."

He was interrupted as a fire door that led into the back was banged open and a metal pushcart came through, followed by an Asian-American woman who looked at them and shouted, "No!"

She shoved the cart into the room then jumped back and pulled the door shut, as Virgil snapped, "That's Zhao!" and he and Lucas stampeded to the door and tried to pull it open, but it was locked from the other side and the woman at the counter shouted, "Wait, wait: who are you guys? Wait, I'm calling the police."

The door wasn't moving. Virgil kicked it, but it was solid. Lucas shouted at the woman, "Keys! Give us the keys."

The woman shouted back, "Fuck that! I'm calling the police."

Virgil kicked the door again, then gave up and followed Lucas as he ran out the front and looked both ways. Virgil said, "If she went out the back . . ."

They were in the middle of a block-long strip mall and Lucas said, "You go that way . . ."

"Gonna try the crystal shop," Virgil said. "If it's got a back door . . ."

He ran to the book and crystal shop and shouted at the clerk, "Do you have a back door?"

The clerk said, "No. We're a closet."

Lucas had run into the juice store, had come back out, looked at Virgil, and had then run into a tee-shirt shop two doors down. He didn't come back out right away, so Virgil ran that way and when he burst through the front door, the counter girl pointed toward the back and Virgil went down a hallway past a unisex bathroom and then out the back door, where he found Lucas in an alley.

"You see her?" Virgil asked, looking both ways.

"No, but I think that's her truck," Lucas said, nodding at a gray Toyota Tacoma parked next to a dumpster.

"Did you check the back room? The door's open."

They both jogged to the tattoo parlor's back door, looked inside. It was a small narrow space filled mostly with metal storage racks and a desk; there was nowhere to hide, and Zhao wasn't there, so they went back outside.

"She's gotta be on foot. You go that way," Lucas said, pointing. "I'll go this way. Be careful, she might be hiding behind one of the dumpsters and she might have that .22."

Virgil started running again. One side of the alley was contained by an eight-foot chain-link fence, spotted with wind-blown trash; the other side was a concrete back wall of the strip mall, with a dumpster between each two doors. Virgil realized as he ran that if Zhao had an intimate knowledge of the stores, she might know if one had an unlocked back door and she might have run through to the front. Nothing he could do about that, so he kept running.

He didn't see another living human until he got to the end of the alley and emerged on a street that defined one end of the strip mall. A man with a white dog on a leash was crossing the street; Virgil saw no one else in either direction. He ran up to the man with the dog, flashed his ID at him and shouted, "Police. Did a woman come running past here a minute ago?"

"Not that I saw," the man said.

He ran around the corner to the front of the mall, where several people were walking back and forth to their cars. No Zhao, but lots of cars, and she could be inside or behind one.

He ran back toward the tattoo shop, his head swiveling, looking for motion between or inside of cars. He saw Lucas come around the far end of the strip mall, just as a black-and-white San Diego police car turned into the parking lot and moved to block Lucas, who raised his hand and shouted something Virgil couldn't quite hear.

Four skater girls were lined up outside a smoothie shop, fruit smoothies in cups, wearing soccer jerseys and overshirts over sports bras, shorts, or sweatpants, their near-hip-high boards leaning against their legs, watching the action. Virgil, out of breath, called, "You see a woman come running by here?"

One of the skaters gave him the finger and Virgil could see they were all thinking the same thing: cop.

No time to argue about it. He ran toward Lucas.

LUCAS RAN DOWN the back of the strip mall in the opposite direction from Virgil, checking behind each dumpster. He turned the corner, didn't see anyone resembling Zhao. He ran back toward the front of the shopping center in time to see Virgil a block away, running in his direction, and then a San Diego cop car bumping over a street entrance into the parking lot.

The cop car stopped thirty feet from Lucas, blocking the line he was running on, and two cops popped out, both with guns drawn, and shouted something he couldn't make out. When he'd seen them coming, Lucas had taken his badge case out of his jacket pocket and he held it up and shouted, "U.S. Marshal! U.S. Marshal."

One of the cops shouted, "What?"

"U.S. Marshal!" Lucas was closing in on the cop car and he slowed to a walk, and he shouted, "We have a runner, we have a fugitive!"

"What?"

"A runner, a runner!" Lucas shouted, still with the badge case in his hand.

The cops said something to each other and put their guns away and the one closest to him said, "Let's see your ID."

Virgil was running toward them, and Lucas said, "He's with me. She's one of the Five killers. She's running. She was in the tattoo shop."

The cop handed back Lucas' ID and looked around and asked, "Where'd she go?"

"If I knew that, I wouldn't be standing here with my dick in my hand," Lucas said. "Short, skinny Asian-American named Zhao, on foot. She's probably armed, she's a killer who's murdered two people that we know of."

Virgil came up and they were joined by the second cop, who walked around the front of the car. He had sergeant's stripes and a name tag that read "Raymond" and asked, "What do you want us to do?"

"We need cars in this area to look for her. She was wearing jeans and a gray blouse, long sleeves, dark hair down to her shoulders . . ."

"White running shoes," Virgil said.

Lucas said to Virgil, "I gotta call Callis."

One of the cops asked, "Who—"

"FBI," Virgil said, as Lucas turned away. "Could you guys call in, get people looking for this woman? She is bad news. If she's panicked and got a gun, she could force her way into a house and shoot the people inside just to get a car."

"Right," the sergeant said, and he hustled around the patrol car and got back in.

LUCAS GOT CALLIS: "We spotted Zhao, but we lost her. She saw us at the same time."

"Sweet bleedin' Jesus, what . . ."

Lucas explained what had happened and Callis said, "I've got the San Diego chief on speed dial, I'll flood the zone."

"Do that," Lucas said. "While you do it, we're gonna sweat the woman in the tattoo parlor."

"I'll send some people over there to help out. Where exactly are you?"

"Tequila Sunrise Shopping Center, over by La Jolla," Lucas said, reading the name off the shopping center sign.

"You're not far from us. I'll have people there in fifteen minutes," Callis said. "I'm calling SDPD now." And he was gone.

AND SO WAS Zhao. San Diego flooded the zone, but never saw any sign of her.

CHERYL LEUNG HAD locked up, waiting for the police to arrive, but only reluctantly let them in when the uniformed cops knocked on her door.

"Do you know where Vivian Zhao lives?" Lucas demanded.

"In Mira Mesa . . . I have her address. What did she do?"

"Get her address!"

Leung, now worried, found an accountant's tax register and gave them the address of the house Lucas and Virgil visited earlier in the day. "She doesn't live there anymore," Lucas told Leung. "Hasn't she mentioned that?"

"No . . . What'd she do?"

Virgil jumped in: "We suspect her of murdering two people."

Leung scoffed at that. "Vivian? Vivian wouldn't hurt a flea."

"Maybe not a flea, but we think she shot two people," Virgil said. "Both of them execution style."

Leung said that Zhao had taken part-time work at the studio, cleaning, after leaving her job at a burger place. She drove the gray pickup parked behind the studio, and as far as Leung knew, had no nearby friends where she could have gone to hide. She'd taken time off the job a few weeks earlier, to fly to San Francisco to see her mother, who was sick.

"I drove her over to the airport and picked her up two days later. You know, to save parking money," Leung said.

Lucas: "Did you just drop her off? Did you see her go through security?"

"No, I just dropped her off."

"So you're not really positive she flew," Lucas suggested.

"Why wouldn't she? She checked her ID and her tickets, here in the store, to make sure she had them. She had the tickets on her phone."

Virgil said to Lucas: "She flew. She's got a good ID, is what she has. She was getting ready to run if she had to."

Leung had no idea about an alternative ID.

"Goddamnit. That's something for the FBI to do, find out where she got the ID and what it is," Lucas said.

"Lot of good IDs around, right out of the DMV," Raymond, the SDPD sergeant, said. "Comes with the whole illegal-immigration business. Want a working Social Security number? No problem."

Two FBI agents, both male, arrived a few minutes later, and Lucas suggested that they find out about the ID. "I'll call it in now," one of the agents said. "Flying with a fake ID is a federal crime."

Virgil turned toward Lucas and rolled his eyes.

The SDPD sergeant asked, "When you guys ran out the back door . . . how far behind her were you?"

"Maybe a minute or a minute and a half. No more than two," Lucas said. "Why?"

"Just . . . she got lost in a hurry if you were only a minute or two behind her. We didn't see anyone running down the street . . . We were two blocks away when Miss Leung's 9-1-1 call came in. I would have thought you'd have seen her if she went down that side street. Or we would have seen her on the main drag out there. I didn't see anybody running."

He looked at his partner, who shook his head: "I didn't either. And we're always looking for people running."

Virgil asked Leung. "Where do you live? Could she be there?"

"No way. I don't think she knows my actual address, that's never really come up."

"She ever borrow your car?"

"Never. I don't live here, I live up north, Ocean Beach. I drive, I park out back . . . it's the red Mazda right next to her truck."

Virgil said to Lucas, "There's no red Mazda out there."

Leung: "What? Oh . . . no. My purse . . . my keys are in the back."

Lucas: "She took your car. She was thinking."

Leung got a key from the cash register and unlocked the door to the back, a narrow extension of the front but with raw concrete walls, a steel rack for boxes of stuff, and a long table used as a desk, with a couple of filing cabinets beneath it. An antique-looking wooden box, open at the top, sat on the desk, and held Leung's green leather purse, which was also open at the top. "She got my keys," Leung groaned. "Okay, I'm starting to believe you."

"We'll find the car," Raymond said. "That's one thing we're really good at. I'll go make the call."

Virgil said to Lucas, "It's been half an hour since she left. If she stayed in the car, she could be fifteen miles from here and we don't know which way she went." He rolled his eyes up and did some math. "That'd be a circle of . . . more than seven hundred square miles."

Raymond said, over his shoulder, "Of course, a good part of that circle would be in the Pacific Ocean . . . but I get the point."

LUCAS, VIRGIL, AND the two FBI agents, Cooper and Snell, took Leung back into the front room and pushed her: hinted that she might be cooperating with a serial killer, which could earn her, Leung, a life sentence, if she'd done it deliberately.

"Give us anything, any hint you got that she wasn't living in Mira Mesa and where she might have be living now."

Leung, who was dressed in jeans and an ivory-colored blouse, had what looked like a raw emerald strung on a gold wire around her neck. She was sitting in one of her tattoo chairs and she shook her head and said, "I assumed she was in Mira Mesa. How often do you talk to your friends about where they live, if you already know where they live? If she moved out at the end of November . . . I don't think we talked at all about where she lived since then."

They talked that around and then Leung frowned. "You know, she did say one odd thing, but I don't know if it involved where she lived. This was right after Christmas. She said something about almost running over a pig. A pig in the road. I don't know if you can have a pig in Mira Mesa."

"I don't think so," the SDPD cop said. "You can have chickens, though. Unless maybe it was one of those potbellied pet pigs that ran away."

"Fuck a bunch of pigs," Lucas said, irritated by the idea of finding somebody by looking for a pig. He looked at the cop: "Go call the DMV. See if she got any tickets or anything that weren't in Mira Mesa. Anything after August."

"Got it," the cop said, and he left.

Lucas looked at the FBI agents and said, "Well? Come up with something."

"Utility bills, uh, her phone . . ."

"Got a new ID and I'd bet she's got a burner," Lucas said. He asked Leung: "You got a working phone number? Did you ever call her in her off hours since November, when she might be at home?"

"Well, yes, a few times."

Lucas said to the FBI agents: "There you go. Get the number, go to the phone company, see where she's been calling from. See if we can find a cluster."

Cooper, the junior agent, said, "I used to be the phone guy. We can get that in an hour."

"Then do it."

Lucas was pacing around the tattoo parlor, looking at pictures on the wall, peering at various bits of equipment. He stopped to ask, "Is Zhao an angry woman? We were told by somebody that she was the angriest woman they'd ever met. Is that right?"

Leung considered the question, and then said, "Yes, I'd say that's correct. I told her at one point that I couldn't have her around if she kept haranguing me about all the micro-oppressions she'd run into on a daily basis. Nothing was ever done right, by anybody. She thought my tattoos were okay, but I told her she couldn't talk to my customers after she told this Navy guy that his tattoo request sucked. Which was the word she used. Sucked. And she hadn't been asked for her opinion."

Lucas: "What was the tattoo?"

Leung: "Oh, you know, the name of the ship, USS Something, and the number. I do one of those a week. It's crap, but it pays the bills. Some of them, anyway."

Virgil: "Give us one thing more about her. Anything. Anything . . ."

Leung thought about it, then said, "She really, really wanted to be rich."

THEY GAVE UP. They told Leung not to leave town and she said she wouldn't, since the strip mall was a business condominium, and she owned the tattoo parlor and all the equipment inside of it.

Outside, in the parking lot, they saw the two feds, Cooper and Snell, sitting inside a black Tahoe, engine running. Snell saw them coming and ran the passenger-side window down. "We're working it. Nothing yet. You done with Leung?"

"Yeah, you can have her if you want," Lucas said.

"We're actually monitoring her phone right now, see if she calls anyone, and who that might be."

"Good thinking," Virgil said. He looked down the strip mall and said to Lucas, "There's a fake Chinese food place down the way. You want to get some fake sweet-and-sour pork?"

"Fuckin' pork," Lucas grumbled. He looked at his watch, then said, "Time for lunch. Okay. Sweet-and-sour pork."

"We're sitting here waiting for a return," Snell said. "If we get something significant, we'll let you know."

"Do that," Lucas said. "Keep in mind that one of my very, very best friends is a deputy director of the FBI. We talk hourly, and he's personally monitoring this investigation . . . Agents Cooper and Snell."

EIGHTEEN

They were halfway through their sweet-and-sour pork when Snell and Cooper came through the door, spotted them and hurried over. "Okay. We were able to jump from Leung's phone to Zhao's new burner and there was a cluster," Cooper said. "The cluster is in a neighborhood, or maybe a town, called Eucalyptus Hills. Or maybe a little east of there, on the other side of a highway. And get this: there are pigs out there."

"How far away?" Virgil asked.

"Half an hour east," Snell said.

"Anything since we spotted her?"

"She's been silent for the last hour and a half. The last call came out of the tattoo parlor and went to a pizza place. She might have been ordering lunch."

Lucas: "We're going to this Eucalyptus place. You're invited. Give us five minutes to finish. Get yourself something to go. Some fake fried rice or fake egg rolls. We'll mention your names in dispatches."

"We'd appreciate it," Cooper said.

Virgil: "Good job, guys."

THEY LEFT IN a two-car convoy five minutes later, Virgil driving, Lucas on the phone first to Callis, the San Diego AIC, and then to Mallard, who asked, after Lucas told him what had happened, "How in the hell did you miss her? You say she was fifteen feet away?"

"Hey, fuck you, Louis. She slammed a metal fire door on us," Lucas said. "We tried kicking it and it didn't even dent. Your guys would have been investigating for three weeks before you got the door slammed on you."

"Naw, I think instead of barging in, we would have done a little surveillance, and then grabbed her when she wasn't suspecting anything," Mallard said.

Lucas got hot: "Why in the hell would you have been doing surveillance on a place where you wouldn't even have any reason to think she'd be? And why in the . . ."

Virgil said, quietly, "He's pulling your weenie."

Lucas said to Mallard, "Okay, Louis, I'll just stay with my original 'Fuck you.' We've got two of your guys going out with us, and if you want to build even more cred inside the bureau, you could give them a call. They're Agents Cooper and Snell and they're in a car right behind us. They seem like okay guys."

"I will do that. And, as Virgil said, I was pulling your weenie, Lucas. You're on a roll. Keep it going."

———

THEY DROVE TO Eucalyptus Hills on the improbably bucolic Highway 52. There were densely populated housing developments on both
sides of the highway, most often hidden by artificial forests or dry
weedy hillsides. Snell called when they were approaching the end of
52. "Go north on 67, then east on Willow Road, and north again on
Moreno Avenue," he said. "The cluster, as we saw it, would have been
east of 67, probably along Moreno or just off it, maybe a half mile up
the road."

THEY GOT OFF the highway, followed Snell's directions until they
were driving up Moreno Avenue.

"This doesn't look like California," Virgil said. "This looks like
somebody kidnapped Oklahoma horse country and stuffed it into
suburbia."

The land was dry, sparse; instead of houses jammed elbow to elbow, the lots were big and often something other than rectangular.
There were fences and animals, brush along the highway, a few nice
houses and many that weren't, the occasional coconut palm. The sky
was dissected with power lines hung off big brown wooden poles.
Neatly kept yards and acreages were mixed with yards stacked with
what appeared to be abandoned cars and trailers. Horses ignored
them as they rolled by.

"Pig," Lucas said, looking out the driver's-side window. A black-
and-white pig was grazing by itself in a field. A few seconds later,
"Another pig."

They saw goats, sheep, and a llama grazing along the road, and chickens.

"Everything you need for fake Chinese food," Lucas said.

"Llama fried rice?"

"There's no place to eat here," Lucas said. "Where would she go to eat?"

They called Snell, who said, "We were thinking the same thing. We need to go back south, there's a whole cluster of fast-food places right off the highway. It's the closest place. She called that pizza place this morning, and there's a pizza place down there. Also the post office and some pharmacies and so on."

They turned around, got back on the highway and then back off, found themselves in a sprawling business district of low buildings and strip malls, auto-related businesses of all kinds, fast-food places, liquor stores, tanning and tobacco shops, dollar stores. They were on Woodside Avenue, followed it almost to the end, to a nice-looking post office with a sign that read, "United States Post Office Lakeside California 92040." They parked at the side of the building, and Lucas said to the two agents, "Let's break up. Cooper, you've got your iPad. Do you have Zhao's pictures on it, the ones from Leung?"

"Yup."

"Okay. Walkin' and knockin'. Right straight back up Woodside. You guys on the right, we'll take the left. We'll start with the post office. You don't have to hit every place, just places she might go often enough that they'd recognize her. Probably food."

The two agents locked their vehicle and marched off with what looked like enthusiasm. Lucas and Virgil went into the post office, asked for the boss, and were introduced to the assistant postmaster.

He didn't recognize Zhao, but took them through the post office, to where mail carriers were putting mail in pigeonhole boxes, so they could show Zhao's picture to everyone in the facility. Nobody remembered her.

Lucas told the postmaster that they were parked at the side of the building, and he said that was fine, and "Good luck, marshals."

Cooper called: he thought they might have got a sniff of her at a delicatessen that did takeout. The counter man was almost sure that she'd been in several times but had no other information. If he was remembering right, she paid cash, which he thought was odd; everybody else paid with credit cards.

"He's pretty sure," Cooper said. "So . . . we're on the right track."

"Keep moving," Lucas said.

They kept moving. The day was pleasant, but they were starting to sweat, their pores loosening up after the Minnesota winter. "Should have worn shorts," Virgil said. "Gotta be seventy degrees."

Lucas: "Look around. The locals are wearing parkas."

Virgil looked, and saw a tall woman who was wearing a parka, with the hood up, and sunglasses.

The deli was the last sniff of Zhao until they'd almost exhausted the food district. Virgil spotted a Starbucks and said, "I'll buy your coffee if they haven't seen her. That's one place she'd hit for sure."

"And I'll buy if they have: I don't trust your intuition."

Cooper called: "We're still across the street. Are you heading for that Starbucks?"

"Yeah, c'mon, we'll get a bagel or something."

"Great. Right behind you."

INSIDE THE STARBUCKS, an assistant manager looked at their pictures of Zhao and looked up at Lucas and asked, "What'd she do?"

"You've seen her?"

"She's come in." She turned and called to a barista: "Hey, Suze: C'mere."

Suze stopped steaming milk and came over to look, and said, "Yeah. She comes in with the crazy commie motherfucker." She looked unapologetically at the four cops, and said, "That's what everybody calls him. The crazy commie motherfucker."

Snell: "Who is he?"

The assistant manager shrugged, smiled, and said, "The crazy commie motherfucker. What'd they do?"

"You know where they live?" Lucas asked.

"Everybody knows where the crazy commie motherfucker lives. He's up on Moreno, maybe five minutes up past Willow . . . right side of the road. Kind of a low house with a dent in the roof and he's got a flag outside the house, one of those Antifa flags, everybody says. I take riding lessons up there, and it's like, this black flag with a circle in the middle, and there's a black flag and a red flag in the circle."

The four cops looked at one another, and Cooper said, "Bingo," like they do in cop movies, and Lucas said, "We'll have four coffees and bagels for everybody. I'm paying."

THEY WENT OUT to the agents' Tahoe and ate inside and talked about the approach to the crazy commie motherfucker. Cooper called Callis, who wanted to send out a SWAT team but Lucas argued against it.

"We're two hours behind her. She's smart and if she came here, we've gotta know right now—if she's here, we can either grab her, or we can freeze her. But if she already left, we need to know how, what she's driving, where she's going. Every hour that passes, she gets another sixty or seventy miles off in some direction."

"If this guy is really a crazy commie motherfucker . . ."

Lucas turned to Virgil. "Virgil: How many square miles in a circle with a radius of seventy miles?"

There was a moment of silence on the telephone speaker, and Virgil rolled his eyes up, doing the math, and he said, "Somewhere around . . . fifteen thousand square miles."

Callis: "What? That can't be right."

"It is," Virgil said. "And the area of the circle goes up fast. If we give her a ninety-minute lead, and she's traveling at highway speeds, the area's going to be around thirty thousand square miles."

Callis: "How do you know that?"

Virgil: "I work out in the countryside in Minnesota. If there's a killing, I need to know what the limits of the search area are. Because up there, there are back roads in every direction, so . . ."

Callis: "All right, I'll make the call. Go in. Be careful, for God's sakes. You guys got armor?"

Lucas told him that he and Virgil didn't, and Callis said that Cooper and Snell did, so they should approach Zhao's hideout, or whatever it was. "The crazy commie cocksucker's place."

"Motherfucker's," Snell said.

THEY WENT BACK up the highway, off at Willow, left on Moreno. Five minutes north, across from a horse farm, they saw a low rambling gray house partly fenced with chain link, partly with a horse-farm-style wood fence showing only traces of having once been painted white. The roof did have a distinct dent in the center of the spine.

The flag was there, hanging limply from the top of a twenty-foot pole. They couldn't tell if it had two flags in a circle, but they could tell it was mostly black, and they could see some patches of white and red.

Four cars and a pickup were parked on the side of the house. The pickup looked beat up but drivable, three were larger American sedans. One of the sedans was in decent shape, one was possibly operable, and the third looked like it was being disassembled for spare parts. The fourth was a red Mazda parked at the end of the line, but not quite hidden.

"Leung's car," Virgil said, and Lucas said, "Yeah."

The feds pulled up the dirt driveway, and Snell turned the Tahoe so it blocked the drive. The two agents got out, both wearing armor with the letters FBI on the front. They talked to each other, briefly, then started toward the house. Virgil stopped their Chevy in the middle of the entrance gate, fifty feet farther down the driveway from the feds' truck, and he and Lucas got out. "Spread," Virgil said, "Get wide and watch the back."

Lucas moved off to the right, Virgil off to the left. The two agents approached the front of the house, and when they were ten feet away, the aluminum front door opened and a man stuck his head out and shouted, "I give up. What the fuck?"

Snell and Cooper told him to come out into the yard, which he did: he was a tall man with long black hair and a heavy black beard, grossly overweight, wearing a tee-shirt that read, in small letters, "Mistakes Were Made."

Lucas and Virgil converged from the sides as Snell asked the man's name, and he said, "Larry Loma. What's going on?"

Snell: "Is Vivian Zhao still here?"

"No. She left an hour ago. Threw her shit in her car and took off. She has a truck but I—"

"What kind of car is she driving now?" Cooper asked.

"Toyota Corolla. Silver. Five or six years old, I guess. What'd she do?" He had no idea what the car's license plate number might be.

"You sure she's not inside the house?" Snell asked.

Loma said, "She's not here. You can come in and look, if you want."

Virgil: "Thanks. We better do that. We need to make sure she's not pointing a rifle at your back."

"A rifle? I don't have a gun."

Virgil: "You don't think you might need a little self-protection, with that flag and all?"

Loma said, "Ah, they call me a what, a miserable commie mother-fucker, but they don't really give me a hard time. I come from around here, my mom keeps them off."

Since he invited them, the four cops moved into the house, and very cautiously around it, until they were satisfied that Loma was the only occupant. The house was notably less messy than its occupant, who apparently spent a lot of time in front of a projector TV screen that must have been ten feet wide.

Cooper asked, "Watch a lot of porn?"

"Sure do," Loma said with some enthusiasm. "What's your favorite? Wait: Let me guess: girl on girl."

"I don't watch porn," Cooper snapped.

Loma shrugged. "Okay, it's a free country."

Lucas glanced at Virgil, who was glancing at him: Virgil lifted an eyebrow and Lucas nodded. They agreed. Cooper watched porn, and probably, Lucas thought, girl on girl. Shouldn't lie about it when you have professional lie detectors listening in.

While they continued prowling the house, they questioned Loma about Zhao, and told him that she was wanted for murder, that she might have been a member of the Five group of killers.

He seemed astonished at that and Lucas thought his astonishment was genuine. He said he didn't know much about the Five but had seen a story on his news feed that he hadn't read. "I thought it was just more sensationalistic media bullshit," he said. "But I mean, wow! Viv's a killer? Actually, she *can* be pretty harsh."

He and Zhao had met at an anti-Trump rally in 2020, and he said they were not a couple—"No sex, not that I wouldn't if she'd let me." He said that she'd been thrown out of her former apartment when the owner decided to sell the house, and she needed a place to stay, cheap, so he offered his back room.

"He didn't sell the house," Lucas said. "She was looking for a hide-out in case the cops came after her. Do you know what her alternate ID is?"

"What?" Mystified.

"You know where she was going?"

"San Francisco. That's what she said. And I think she is. When I asked, she said, 'San Francisco,' and then she looked like she'd fucked up by saying that. By telling me that. Anyway, I know she has family there, but really . . . I don't know," Loma said. "She lies to me, but I can never tell when until afterward."

They went over the back room inch by inch. She'd cleaned it out, but they found one significant item: a used .22 shell. Snell went out to his truck and got an evidence bag and put the shell into it.

"If this is the same as the shells they picked up at the McGruder house, that'd seal it," he said.

"It's already sealed in my mind," Virgil said. "You think it'd do any good to call the highway patrol to see if they could spot her?"

Cooper shrugged. "Maybe . . . if you only want to watch the free-ways. But she's a San Francisco native and has likely traveled between here and there quite a bit, so she might know the back roads, and she's running . . ."

"So probably not," Virgil said.

"And you gotta remember," Snell said, "that there's that big blob of Los Angeles just up north of here. She's probably already there and . . . a silver Corolla? I mean . . ."

They were still talking to Loma when three more feds arrived in a cloud of dust. Two did crime scene analysis; they'd be looking for Zhao's DNA and anything that Lucas, Virgil, Cooper, and Snell might have missed.

As they were about to leave, Snell got a call on his cell phone. "Washington," he muttered. "Hello?"

He listened, then looked at Lucas: "He says to turn the speaker on."

"Then you better do it," Lucas said.

He did, and Mallard said, "Good work, all four of you. Cooper and Snell, I'll have a word with your AIC, about your work on this. Good going. Lucas, Virgil, you need plane tickets."

NINETEEN

They survived the takeoff at San Diego. When they were in the air, a cabin attendant asked Lucas what he wanted to drink, and when he said, "Nothing right now," she said, quietly, "I'm not really asking you what you want to drink, I'm thinking you might *need* something."

Virgil, sitting on the window side, ostentatiously jammed the knuckle of his right index finger into his mouth, as if biting down on it to keep from laughing.

Lucas said, "Fuck you," and to the cabin attendant, more politely, "You may be right. How about a double gin and tonic?"

"At least," she said, and hustled off to get the drink.

"She didn't even bother to ask you what *you* wanted," Lucas said to Virgil.

"Because she realized she had an emergency situation on her

hands and wanted to get a drink into you before you went screaming down the aisle," Virgil said. And, "Does this plane seem tippy
to you?"

"THE BIG PROBLEM here is, what do we do when we get to San
Francisco? Wander around all the Starbucks until we find her?" Lucas said, sipping on the gin and tonic.

"We put her on TV," Virgil said. "We've got four photos of her,
let's get them out there. Might provoke a response from her if nothing else."

"I'll send a note to Mallard," Lucas said. "If he makes a big enough
fuss about it, the TV stations will bite. Especially since that homeless
guy got strangled in one of their alleys."

Lucas went online with his laptop and sent the note to Mallard. Virgil got on his iPad and found an email from Frankie:
"There's a guy who's been calling you from North Carolina who
thinks he might have information about one of the Five killers. He
says he wants to talk to you directly. He doesn't want to talk to
the FBI."

Virgil sent back a note: "Why me?"

As they were approaching San Francisco, Frankie sent back, "He
told me that he doesn't trust the FBI. He heard about you and Lucas
on a news program and thought you sounded more approachable.
He sent me a contact phone number and wants you to call him right
away. He says if he doesn't hear from you today, he's going to throw
the phone away."

Virgil had shown both the first and then the second email to Lucas, who said, "We'll call as soon as we're on the ground. You seem

to have a magnetic attraction that works over a TV connection. First McGruder and now this guy."

"This guy could be a lunatic," Virgil said. "I guess we'll see."

"I don't think he is," Lucas said. "He mentioned throwing away a phone. That means he's got a burner. That means he's probably thought about this."

They survived the landing at San Francisco and as they were walking out of the jet bridge into the terminal, they spotted a cop and flagged him down. The cop got them to an empty conference room, where they called the North Carolina number.

A man answered, his voice cautious: "Who is this?"

"Virgil Flowers. I understand you called me."

"Is anyone else listening?" The man's voice was a middle tenor, cultivated, fluent, each word carefully articulated. There was an almost subliminal foreign accent behind it, perhaps from eastern Europe.

Virgil hesitated, then said, "A U.S. Marshal. My partner. If you're real, I need a witness."

"All right. I heard about him, too. I'd rather not talk to the federal government, but I guess a marshal is better than the FBI."

"You had some information about the Five?"

"Maybe. Listen, I go to Bitcoin conventions. There have been news stories about how McGruder was a Bitcoin billionaire and how these people, these killers, are offering Bitcoins to do-gooder groups after they kill an asshole. I went to an ABC convention—American Bitcoin Council—last year, well, not last year, but a little more than a year ago, in November, and there were rumors of a group of people who were talking about killing assholes. I didn't want to have anything to do with a group like that, but I know a guy who did, and I think he might be one of the Five. Black man, lives in Cleveland. Made beaucoup bucks in Bitcoin. I don't know if he's a billionaire, but he might be."

"Why do you think he might be one of them?" Lucas asked.

Virgil said, "That was Lucas."

"Okay. I was at this council meeting and there were four or five of us talking about whatever, and somebody brought up this rumor about killing assholes. I laughed it off, but this guy, Bill Osborne, he didn't laugh. He defended the idea, and pretty . . . vigorously. So did his girlfriend. I mean, so much so, that I remembered it for a year."

"His name is Bill Osborne? Spell that."

The man spelled it, then added, "His full name is William D. Osborne. I saved a program and looked at it this morning. It says he's from Cleveland and his work is listed as 'investments,' so that could be anything."

"This girlfriend. You know her name?"

"I do, because she was in the program as a speaker. She's an economist from California named Vivian Zhao, Z-H-A-O. Kind of a cute Asian-American woman."

Lucas poked Virgil with his elbow.

Virgil: "We're gonna need your name . . ."

"No chance," the man said. "I don't want to be involved in this, I don't want any contact with you guys and especially not the FBI. I know you're tracing this call and are recording it so you can do voice recognition later on. I hesitated to call, but I don't want anyone to get murdered. Not even assholes."

"I'm in a conference room at the San Francisco airport. I got here from San Diego about five minutes ago," Virgil said. "We're not tracing anything. We really do need your name."

"Not going to happen," the man said, using the correct American idiom, but without the correct *gonna*. "These people are killers and we don't even know how many of them are out there. You know about the murder down in Jacksonville this morning? The city councilman?"

"No, we—"

"He was shot in a parking garage when he was getting in his car. He's got a number on his forehead. A six. What does that mean? What happened to Four and Five? My feeling is, if I cooperated, they'd hunt me down and kill me, like they killed McGruder. If these people are who I think they are, from the Bitcoin convention, they are smart. You're not going to catch them unless somebody like me helps you out. But if it gets on TV that I talked to you, the next thing I know, I've got a box of .22s in my cerebellum, like McGruder."

"Did you know McGruder?"

"Yes. To chat with, but he wasn't a friend or anything. Bill Osborne knew him, too. I saw them talking several times."

"We really—"

"I've got to go. I know you're trying to keep me on the phone, so I've got to go. Goodbye."

Click.

THEY CALLED MALLARD, who said, "This could be the break we were waiting for. I'll get Cleveland on it immediately and we'll review all the people who went to that convention. You two stay on Zhao for the time being—our media people are talking to every outlet in San Francisco. Her face will be all over town tonight. We were pushing the stations to break into regular programming to put her face out there, but they decided to go with the insurance commercials. She will be on all the news programs."

"Are you covering her parents?" Lucas asked.

"Of course. And her brothers. We're covering everybody we can connect to her."

Virgil: "What's this about a so-called six getting killed in Florida?"

"We're on it, we're almost sure it's a copycat," Mallard said. "Looks like a spontaneous killing. The killer's on video, we don't see the kind of care the Five are taking. Could be a personal feud, although I'm told the dead man was a spectacular asshole."

"Let me ask: what are we doing here?" Lucas asked.

"You're being available. And vigilant. Doing what you did in San Diego. She'll pop up."

"No, she won't," Lucas said. "She's already gone."

TWENTY

Zhao got to Palo Alto after dark. She was exhausted from tension, from sitting humped over the steering wheel. With the car's crappy suspension, she felt every expansion joint in the freeway and her back was a knot of cramped muscle. She made two stops on the way, to get gas and to buy junk food and Pepsi Cola. A few miles out, she called Sonnewell on his burner: he picked up after a dozen rings, when she was about to give up.

"What?" Terse, gravelly voice.

"I'm on the run. We need to talk," Zhao said.

"Are they on you?"

"They know who I am, but I've slipped them for the time being," Zhao said.

"You're sure?" Sonnewell asked. He seemed controlled, if not calm.

"Yes. They'll grab me as soon as they spot me. They haven't done that yet."

Sonnewell: "Unless they're tracking you to see who you contact . . ."

"George! I'm clean! I'm sure of that!" Zhao said.

Sonnewell: "Okay. Your burner has a mapping app, right?"

"Of course."

"Put in the Palo Alto Costco store. There's a big parking lot, with a McDonald's down in one corner of it. Park in the lot, somewhere around the middle. I'll call you when I get to the McDonald's. Do you have a bag?"

"A backpack," Zhao said.

"Bring it. Leave your car. Lock it. Walk over to the McDonald's, I'll see you coming," Sonnewell said. "I'll be in a dark blue Mercedes Sprinter van. I'll open a side door. Throw the pack in, then get in with it. I don't want any of my neighbors to see a woman with me, so I want you in the back."

"Won't Costco have the car towed when they close for the day?"

"I don't think so. There are always a couple of dozen cars in that parking lot. Overnight employees or some such. They won't tow it right away, and you're not going back to it. I assume it's registered under an alternate identity?"

"Yes, but not my main one," Zhao said. "They won't find me through the car."

"Great. How far away are you?"

"I'll have to look at the mapping app, but probably not more than a few miles."

"I'll be there in an hour," Sonnewell said. "Dark blue Mercedes Sprinter."

ZHAO FOUND THE Costco store without trouble, parked in a cluster of vehicles a hundred yards from the McDonald's. She slid low in
the car seat, eyes barely above the steering wheel, watching people
come and go. A cop car went by on the street, running hot, flashers
screaming for attention. An hour passed, and several minutes more,
and she saw a dark van-like vehicle pull into a parking space at the
McDonald's.

Sonnewell called: "You see me?"

"Just pulled in, looks like a big black van, a high van," Zhao said.

"That's me. Lock your car and come over."

Zhao got her pack, checked the car for anything that might identify her, then locked it and hurried across the parking lot. The pack
was heavy, and she wasn't a large woman; she was panting when she
got to the van. The side door slid back as she approached and she
threw her pack in and climbed onto a leather seat.

She was facing a panel of painted aluminum or fiberglass, and a
locked door, that separated the front of the van from the back. There
was a window in the middle of it, with a sliding cover that had been
pulled open. Sonnewell said, "I'm feeling stupid about doing this,
picking you up. You're apparently not as smart as we all thought you
were."

"I think that fucking McGruder gave me up," Zhao said. "Maybe
he told his lawyer who I was, and the lawyer tipped off the FBI. Couple of agents walked right in on me at my job: I was lucky to get
away."

"I hope you *did* get away," Sonnewell said. "If somebody spotted
me picking you up, we're both finished."

"George . . . I'm clean. I'm sure of it."

Sonnewell said, "We're twenty minutes from my house. Sit back and take it easy. There's a Pepsi in the refrigerator."

One side of the van was lined with aluminum cabinets, as well as a sink and a compact refrigerator. She opened it, and a single bottle of Pepsi sat there. She took it out, icy cold, and twisted off the top. The other side of the van had a long worktable, with a pull-out bench beneath the table. Above the table was what appeared to be a pull-down bunk.

"What's this van for?" she asked.

Sonnewell said, over this shoulder, "I'm a landscape photographer. I travel around the west. The best times to shoot are dawn and sunset and the best spots are usually not that close to a motel. I camp out in the van."

"Really." That sounded odd to her: why be a billionaire if you're going to camp out?

"Yeah. Really," Sonnewell said.

During the twenty-minute trip, Zhao told the story of how the FBI agents—she assumed they were FBI—had walked into the tattoo parlor and apparently hadn't expected to find her there. She managed to escape in her boss's car, but only by the skin of her teeth. She'd traded that car for a getaway car she'd kept at the house where she'd been living.

"It's not a great car, but I hate to give it up," she said.

"I've got a better car for you. My secondary alternative ID will sell it to your primary alternative ID, so you'll have some paper for it. It was going to be my getaway car if I needed it."

"Ah, George, that's great. I can sell it for cash if I need to . . . I'm hoping the others will help out financially. I'll get to New York, then fly to

Hawaii. I'm going to stay in Hawaii if I can—forty percent of the population is Asian and I should be able to slip right into the community."

"That's a plan," Sonnewell said.

They stopped outside Sonnewell's house, waited for a gate to open, and then Sonnewell drove behind the house and into an enormous garage. There were at least eight cars inside, and one—she thought it might be a Ferrari—was disassembled and apparently being worked on. The van's side door slid back, and Zhao climbed out, pulling her backpack. She looked around: the disassembled car was sitting in a semicircle of red tool chests, tools sitting both on the car and atop the chests.

Sonnewell walked around the nose of the garage. He had a shotgun, and it was pointing at her.

"George . . ."

"Take your clothes off," Sonnewell said.

"What?"

"Take your clothes off. You don't have to take your underpants off, but everything else."

"What?"

"I have a bad feeling about you, Vivian. You went to Minneapolis and killed McGruder and I'm wondering why," Sonnewell said. "I know you said that he was going to give us up, but he wasn't, really—he was going to give *you* up, not us. Now I'm thinking you might be planning to go around the country cleaning us up."

"George, I would not do that," she said, her voice going shrill. The shotgun never moved from the center of her chest.

"We've got two ways to go here, Vivian. Take off your clothes or God help me, I'll kill you right here. That would solve *my* problem. Which is, that you know me."

Zhao stared at him, then nodded: "Okay. You won't be the first man to see me naked."

And it really didn't bother her. She'd seen her share of naked men, and a number of men had seen her naked. They were all animals, after all, the basic parts well known by most adults. She took off her clothes, and after removing her blouse, pulled the .22 pistol out of the back of her jeans and carefully laid it on the floor.

"That's what I'm talking about," Sonnewell said. The muzzle of the shotgun held steady on her chest. "Take the jeans off."

When Zhao had taken off every piece of clothing but her semi-transparent underpants, Sonnewell ordered her to walk to the side of a Mercedes SUV and stand there, hands on the car, her back to him.

"You're crazy paranoid," she said. The garage was cold, and she had goose bumps the size of oranges on her arms, legs, and back.

"And not on the run," Sonnewell snapped.

While keeping an eye on her, Sonnewell picked up the .22 and put it in his pants pocket. Then he felt through the remaining clothes on the floor, and when he was satisfied that they held no weapons, he balled them up and threw them to her.

As she dressed, he opened the backpack and dumped it on the floor, removed a switchblade and a long kitchen knife. When he was done, he put the pistol, the two knives, and his shotgun on the passenger seat of the Sprinter and closed and locked the door. Watched as she pulled on her jacket.

"What's with all the tattoos?" he asked.

She shrugged. "I like them. And I like the pain when I get them."

"Okay." He shook his head. She liked the pain? "Put your stuff back in the pack."

When she'd done that, he said, "This way. You've talked in the chat room about that karate you were studying. I'll tell you, karate or not, I was a farm kid and I'm in great shape and have been beat up since I was a toddler. You try to fuck with me, I'll strangle you and throw your body in a canyon where nobody will ever find it. I ought to do that anyway, but I won't."

She followed him around the nose of the Sprinter and into the house. She hadn't been able to see much of it from the van, but it appeared to be two stories high and ultramodern in style. He led the way to the kitchen, where two sheets of paper were lying on a stone countertop with a pen.

From the kitchen, she could see past a stone fireplace to the living room, where she saw what looked like a Calder mobile hanging above a sprawling walnut coffee table, like metal teardrops. A Calder—worth more than all the money she'd made in her life, and more than she'd make in the rest of it.

"Papers for the car," Sonnewell said, nodding at the two sheets lying on the countertop. "It's a four-year-old Toyota 4Runner. It's a little grimy on the outside, on purpose, but it's in perfect mechanical condition and has a full tank of gas. You can read the papers when you get out of here."

He pulled open a kitchen cupboard and took out a brown paper bag. "My bug-out cash—fifty thousand dollars in small bills up to fifties. Nothing larger."

"George, I . . ."

"Don't bullshit me, Viv. Like I said, I'm afraid of you," Sonnewell said. "That you might have or find a weapon. I want you to take the money and the car keys and get out of my life. And one more thing."

A silver kitchen pot was sitting on a gas stove. He took off the lid, reached into the pot, and came out with a small black pistol.

"Works exactly the same way as your .22, but it's a nine-millimeter and a lot more powerful. Not a friendly gun to shoot, but it gets the job done and you can put it in your pants pocket," Sonnewell said. "If you can find a lonely place wherever you're going, stop and shoot at some cans. I'm giving you two magazines, man-killers, fourteen shots in all, and a half box of extra rounds."

"You want me to leave right now? I'm so tired I'm seeing double."

"I want you out . . ."

"Goddamnit, George, you've got my gun locked up, you can hide your gun where I can't find it. I need sleep."

Sonnewell frowned, shook his head, considered, and changed his mind. "A few hours. Okay. I guess I can risk that."

"There's no risk, George."

"Of course there is. You're radioactive. I'll give you three hours, then I want you to drive over to the airport, find a spot in the parking garage, climb in the back of the truck. There's an air mattress back there, and the back right seat folds flat. I'll show you before you leave. I'll give you some food and some bottles of water, you can sleep there overnight in the parking structure. I don't want to know where you're going."

"I already told you, I'm going to—"

"What you do is up to you. Stay away from me."

SONNEWELL GAVE HER a sheet and a bed pillow, put her on the expansive couch in his home theater, showed her how to use the television remote. She wrapped herself in the sheet and turned on the television.

"Want to catch the news," she told him. "I can't believe they'd have anything on me, though I expect they will have gotten to my parents by now."

Channel Five, the CBS affiliate, came up, and after an inane story about a sailboat collision in the bay, and as Sonnewell was turning to leave, her face popped up.

"Oh, Lord," Sonnewell blurted.

The newsreader identified her as the leader of the Five gang, a self-described economist and part-time employee at a tattoo parlor. She'd fled early in the day from San Diego, the newsreader said. That she might be headed for the San Francisco area. That she was armed and should not be approached. If seen, call 9-1-1 immediately . . .

"Am I fucked?" Zhao asked, wide-eyed.

"Probably," Sonnewell said. He chewed on his lower lip, then said, "Here's my analysis. There are always a few state patrolmen out on the highways late at night and after a certain point, they don't have much to do. They start pulling people over for the entertainment value. You know, changing lanes without signaling, when there's nobody else on the highway. I guess I won't kick you out tonight, after all, but if I were you, I'd get out about six in the morning when the traffic is starting to build and the cops are at the end of their shifts. Get across the Nevada state line as quickly as you can without speeding. Go up I-80 and keep going. The farther you are from California, the better off you'll be."

"I'll set my phone alarm for five-thirty," she said.

"Do that."

She did that; and she slept after a while, and it seemed like only minutes had passed when the alarm went off. Sonnewell came down wearing workout pants and a tee-shirt, showed her to a bathroom where she could shower.

When she was dressed, he gave her a fast breakfast of instant oat-meal and a glass of green juice, then showed her how the back seat folded flat in the 4Runner, so she could sleep in it. He gave her back the .22, the nine-millimeter, and the two knives, told her she should get rid of the .22 as soon as she could, if it was the gun she'd used on McGruder.

When she was ready, with car keys and money, he said, "Sun comes up a little before seven-thirty. It'll be light for a while before then. Still dark now, get on the freeway and get gone. Good luck to you."

"I'm gone," she said. A minute later, she was.

SHE'D SET HER travel app for Reno, Nevada, and it faithfully guided her out to I-80 and then northeast out of the Bay Area. She was feeling better, rested and clear-eyed. She stayed in the slow lane, driving carefully, only a few miles over the speed limit, like every-body else in the slow lane, and barely flinched as two state patrol cars passed her.

Four and a half hours after leaving Sonnewell, she reached Reno, and felt safer as she crossed the state line. She stopped at a McDon-ald's, got online, went to the dark web chat room and left a message for the remaining members of the Five: "I'm on the run. The FBI has identified me. I need cash. SFO has generously chipped in. I need to stop and pick up additional funds from MSY, CLE, and JFK. I'm driv-ing, I've got a good ID and papers for the car. I can pull this off, but whatever cash you can give me, I'd appreciate."

From Reno, she stayed on I-80, and at eight o'clock that night, ar-rived in Salt Lake City. She'd stopped at a highway rest stop and had seen a sign that forbade overnight camping. She suspected that the prohibition was rarely if ever enforced, but she didn't want to take a chance. Using her travel app, she found a downtown parking garage, parked in a cluster of cars, crawled into the back of the 4Runner, pushed down the passenger seat, unrolled an air mattress and a sleeping bag, and went to sleep.

The next morning, needing to pee, she found a Starbucks, used the bathroom to pee and wash her face and hands, got coffee and two bagels with cream cheese. With a ski cap pulled low, and a coat collar turned up, she took the risk of sitting inside to go online; she'd had four answers to her chat room message.

SFO (Sonnewell) wrote: "I think we all need to help her out. I did. Be careful. She's armed, and she might be tempted to get rid of witnesses against her."

MSY (Carter) sent, "I'll get you cash, soon as I can, but I'm in Miami right now and won't be back home until tomorrow night. We can either meet, or you can message me where I can send a FedEx . . . if you think you can trust a FedEx with a box full of cash."

CLE (Osborne) said, "I'm good for a cash donation. When you get here, call me on my burner. I don't want to meet at my house. I'm listening to what SFO said, so we'll meet somewhere public."

JFK (Meyer): "What CLE said. Same terms."

CLE: "For everybody's information, I'm moving on Klink tonight. I'm in too deep to change the timing now, and I want to get this done."

Zhao left an answer of her own: "CLE: That's great. Call on your burner when it's done. I'll do a press release, as usual. All of you, thank you. Will call, will see you soon."

She got back in the car and pointed it east.

TWENTY-ONE

Lucas and Virgil didn't get to downtown San Francisco until after nine o'clock in the evening. Despite the hour, they went to FBI headquarters where a Five task force was meeting. After checking through two layers of security, they were escorted to a conference room where a dozen agents were sitting around a table littered with laptops and coffee cups.

Martin Quayle, the agent in charge, came to the office door to shake hands and to point them at chairs.

"Happy to have you," he said, "though I don't know exactly what you're doing here."

"We talked about that on the plane from San Diego. We don't know what we're doing, either," Lucas said. "I'd guess you have her parents nailed down?"

"Yes. We put them through the wringer, and honestly? We don't believe they know anything. Neither do her brothers. They seem genuinely appalled by what we've told them."

"But you're watching them anyway."

"Of course. It's the only thing we've got," Quayle said. "Other than she's driving a silver Toyota Corolla, which is like saying she's wearing Nike cross-trainers. Not exactly an identifying characteristic."

Lucas told him about the tip on the potential killer in Cleveland, Bill Osborne, and Quayle shook his head. "So do we try to find a needle in a haystack here, or look at a suspect in a much smaller haystack in Cleveland?"

"Let's call Mallard again," Virgil said to Lucas. "We won't do any good here."

Quayle said, "It's midnight in Washington."

Lucas took his phone from his pocket. "Not only that, we talked to him an hour ago and he was already in bed. He does like his sleep. On the other hand, he keeps his personal phone on his nightstand, right next to his ear."

Lucas found Mallard's personal phone number and clicked on it. Quayle said, "Don't mention my presence." He turned to one of the other agents. "If he mentions my presence, shoot him."

The agent nodded: "Will do."

Mallard came up and said, "You better have caught Zhao, calling me at midnight."

"Not even a sniff of her," Lucas said, cheerfully. "We've checked into the St. Regis, but we got the FBI rate of four hundred and fifty dollars a night, and the rooms are really nice."

"What do you want, Lucas?"

"We want to fly to Cleveland tomorrow. Not too early. I like to sleep in."

"Why go to Cleveland?"

"The only reason we're here is that crazy commie motherfucker thought she was coming here, maybe to see her parents. But that's the last place she'd go—she's gotta believe that your FBI guys are stacked up three deep around her parents' place. But I do think she came here. She came to see the San Francisco killer. She knows we've identified her. I think she came here to get money. I think she'll probably tap the others for money, too. Cleveland and Houston and one we don't know about. As far as she knows, we're all over Houston looking for that killer, but she has no idea that we might have identified Osborne. I think she'll go there. I-80 runs out of San Francisco and right past Cleveland. She could be there in three days and a long way from the heat in California."

"Give me a minute," Mallard said. "I'm still asleep."

Lucas pressed: "Here in San Francisco and all we can do is stand on a street corner and wait for Zhao to walk by. That's all we've got. If anyone is going to catch her here, it's your guys, with your full-court press. My belief is, she's gone."

"Have you talked to the AIC out there?"

"Yes, we have." Lucas raised his eyebrows at Quayle. "He seems to be incredibly competent and, like I said, if anybody catches Zhao in San Francisco, it'll be his team."

"Martin's listening to this, isn't he?"

"Of course not," Lucas said. "He totally isn't."

"I'll talk to you in the morning, Martin," Mallard said. Then, after a moment of dead air, Mallard said, "All right. I'll make a phone call. You'll get a text with the flight details. I expect that fuckin' Flowers will be going with you?"

"As always," Lucas said.

When Mallard rang off, Virgil said, "You realize we just had a Mallard talking to a Quayle?"

Quayle ignored that and asked, "You're not really staying at the St. Regis?"

Virgil shook his head: "Hilton. And lucky to get it."

AT FIVE O'CLOCK the next morning, with Lucas in a deep stage 4 sleep, the phone on his nightstand buzzed. The first two buzzes didn't wake him, the second two brought him up to stage 1, and the third two buzzes brought him briefly awake, and then the phone cut over to voice mail. Whoever was calling didn't leave a message, but called back again.

With his frontal lobes barely functioning, Lucas picked up the phone and rasped, "What?"

"Louis Mallard, here, and good morning. It's eight o'clock here in D.C., a beautiful January morning, brisk and sunny. We've begun our surveillance on Bill Osborne."

"Is this revenge for the call last night?"

"No, no. This is to tell you Four got hit last night. Ghost gun manufacturer shot while standing in his backyard fifteen miles from Osborne's house. A racially unconscious neighbor said he saw an n-word lurking in the neighborhood, thought he might have been casing houses for a burglary. Called the police, but nothing came out of it."

"Goddamnit!"

"Exactly. He must have been waiting for Klink—the dead man's name was Roland Klink. According to Mrs. Klink, Klink went out back to smoke a cigarette, which she doesn't allow in the house since they got the new couch, and when he didn't come back in, she went out, and found him dead with the numeral '4' on his forehead."

"Goddamnit!"

"Still want to go to Cleveland?" Mallard asked.

"Yes. Maybe . . . I dunno. Louis, will there be anything for us to do? We're a day late and a dollar short."

"You should go anyway. You guys see things. And you need to get up, and get going. San Francisco can be a tough airport to get through."

When Mallard had rung off, Lucas called Virgil, who asked, the sleep thick in his voice, "Who's dead?"

"Number Four. A guy named Klink. In Cleveland."

"Goddamnit!"

"What I said. We got a press release. I'll have somebody email you the text."

LUCAS AND VIRGIL were at the San Francisco airport at eight o'clock, and despite Virgil's embarrassment, Lucas cornered a TSA supervisor and got him to cut them in to the front of the long security line.

They had breakfast at an airport café, watched dozens of attractive young women with briefcases walking by, all looking gym-fit and upbeat, ready to unload more crap on tech enthusiasts. At nine-fifteen they were on the plane for the five-hour flight to Cleveland, arriving at five o'clock in the evening.

On the way, Lucas went online with his laptop, got his email, and brought up the press release from the Five.

THE FIVE

We suffered a tragedy last week with the death of our friend Jamie McGruder, a good man. We believe he was killed by Twin Cities police, well known for their violent tendencies. We hope the good people of America who are tired of living under the thumbs of our nation's assholes will pause for a moment during the day and say a prayer for our Jamie.

On the good-news front, we are pleased to announce the death of Roland Klink, manufacturer of ghost guns, in Cleveland. We shot him in his backyard as he was smoking a cigarette, a plague that's killed even more people than ghost guns. Maybe we'll get to tobacco companies later in this journey. In any case, Klink's passing is a benefit for all of us, and eliminates not only a dangerous asshole, but one who insisted on dumping untraceable weapons into the hands of street gangs.

Klink was most notably quoted as saying, "Freedom comes from the barrel of a gun," and "Black Guns Matter." He forgot to mention that the deaths of countless children come from the same place, the barrel of a gun, every year.

So, begone, Klink.

In another piece of news, a "6" was killed in Jacksonville, Florida, and from everything we've read, the dead man was a true asshole and deserved everything that happened to him. But: that wasn't us. That's you people, the righteous, joining in the fun. Let's keep that snowball rolling downhill, folks!

The Five

P.S. One of our number was murdered last week, as we said. Up to this point, each of the Five have donated an anonymous Bitcoin to a wallet sent to a charity working against the assholes we've killed. With Jamie murdered, we're upping the donations: each of the remaining Four will donate two Bitcoins to Americans Against Gun Murder. The eight coins are worth, at this writing, $353,264.

Next up: Ah, we won't tell you anything except that YOU KNOW HIS FACE. That's right, you do. Please be proud of us when that asshole goes down next week.

Lucas and Virgil were met at the gate in Cleveland by an FBI agent who said he had a car waiting.

"We've got a ride for you; we've got a briefing set up at a Travelodge motel near Osborne's place," the agent said.

The agent's name was Lawrence Toms, he was taller than either Virgil or Lucas, was thin as a knife blade, and wore a gray pinstriped suit that made him look even taller and thinner.

"We got the alert about Osborne just about the time Klink was murdered," Toms said. "By the time we had a surveillance team on station, Osborne was already home playing the piano. If we'd moved an hour earlier . . ."

"Nothing to be done about it," Lucas said. "Spilt milk."

"Osborne lives right on Lake Erie," Toms said. "He's home, but he's not moving around at all. It's a tough place to watch. We can't see him from the lake side. We're thinking of putting somebody out on the lake in a boat, down the lake front where it won't be so noticeable. Our AIC has a friend with a yacht and if we anchor it a few hundred yards away . . ."

"On the lake? I thought the lake froze over," Virgil said.

"It does, most of the time," Toms said. "Not this year. Could start in a week or two, if we get another cold front like this last one, but so far, it's mostly open."

"Then the yacht could work," Lucas said.

"It could," Toms said. "Don't usually see FBI agents driving yachts. Don't usually see yachts out on the lake when the water temperature is thirty-four degrees, either. So we have to think a little more about the yacht."

"Is Osborne known to be a shooter?" Lucas asked. "From what we heard from Mallard, sounds like the shooter used a suppressed weapon, if Klink's wife didn't hear any shots inside the house."

"Klink's ghost guns are threaded for suppressors—and a lot of ghost guns picked up in the Cleveland area have suppressors and we think Klink was running an underground suppressor business to go with his ghost guns. It's possible that Osborne bought one of Klink's guns to shoot him with. Osborne is known to have a sharp sense of humor."

"Our tipster says he was a Bitcoin investor," Virgil said.

"Definitely. He really fits the whole Five profile. Bitcoin-rich and angry. Smart. Tough. That Bitcoin conference your tipster was talking about was in Atlanta and the conference organizers hired a pro photographer to do standard event coverage. We whispered softly in his shell-like ear and he sent us his online portfolio from the event. One of the things he did was take pictures during a social hour, groups of people holding drinks and smiling at the camera. One of the groups has Osborne talking to McGruder and . . . guess who?"

Virgil: "Zhao?"

"Got it in one," Toms said. "There were five of them in that group. We've identified the other two, we'll be interviewing them this evening . . . about now . . . in Miami and Charlotte."

The fed's Tahoe was parked in a no-parking zone outside the terminal, under the watchful eye of a cop. "I told him the trunk was full of machine guns, so we needed some extra security," Toms said.

Virgil: "Is it?"

"I hope not," Toms said. "It'd make me all self-conscious."

THE FEDS HAD two connecting rooms at the Travelodge, the beds pushed against the walls, folding chairs set up in the new open spaces. Eight agents were scattered around the two rooms, drinking coffee and soft drinks; a tray of vegan bagels with vegan non–cream cheese sat on a sideboard. Two of the agents, male and female, had a small chessboard set up on the corner of a bed and were playing chess. They looked up briefly when Lucas and Virgil came in with Toms, then went back to their game.

The senior agent at the site, Donald Clark, told them that they might be more interested in the discussions at the FBI headquarters in downtown Cleveland, that the Travelodge location was more of a convenience for the agents watching Osborne.

"He's less than a mile from here," Clark said. "We've got people on him full time, but we're rotating through here, so he and his neighbors won't see anyone's face more than once or twice. We're doing two-hour shifts right now."

"We'll want to cruise the place ourselves, to get a feel for it," Lucas said.

The crime scene crew had recovered a shell from the shooting site, Clark said, and had sent it to an FBI lab to be examined for prints and DNA.

Virgil shook his head: "Bet you won't find anything. The killers seem to be careful about DNA. Nobody's gotten anything, as far as we know."

"Did Klink move around after he was shot?" Lucas asked.

"Nope. Looks like he dropped in his tracks," Clark said. "One shot to the head."

"No signs of a struggle, nothing at all?"

"No."

Virgil: "Did Osborne have any history of being involved in radical civil rights actions?"

Clark scratched an ear. "That gets complicated. He was one of the rare politically involved black Republicans around here. A fiscal conservative, against high taxes, that whole thing. Conservative about most things. Came out strong against gay marriage, has something of a reputation as a homophobe. Until 2016, he was the head of the local Republican Party committee. That ended when he came out against Trump and even told the newspaper that he'd vote for Hillary Clinton. When he was the head of the committee, he was considered a big hope for Republicans recruiting black voters. He was strong on racism and street guns and ways that conservatives could deal with those things through private nongovernment initiatives. That went out the door with Trump. In 2020 there was a Black Lives Matter action here, but he never got close to it, as far as we can tell. He's a very rich guy, was never a radical anything, but he was seriously concerned about guns. And racism."

Virgil: "And he's a homophobe."

"Yes."

Lucas: "What are the chances that he's innocent? That we were sicced on him as some kind of misdirection by the actual killers?"

Toms held up his hands, ticking off fingers. "He's a Bitcoin rich

guy. Hangs out with Zhao. Knows McGruder. Anti-gun. Gun manufacturer shot. Neighbors see what they describe as a black guy cruising houses in Klink's very white neighborhood, days before the
crime."

Virgil: "And a credible tip comes in from North Carolina, pointing us at him."

"Pretty strong," Lucas said.

Clark asked, "So are you two heading downtown?"

Lucas looked at Virgil, and then they both shook their heads.
"You guys have all that FBI stuff handled. We're more of the hang-
out types," Virgil said. "We'll cruise the house, look for people who
might help us out . . . When will you know about the DNA?"

"Another day," Clark said.

"We'll at least hang around until then, see if we can develop anything, or we can do anything useful," Lucas said. "We won't try to
get too physically close—we'll leave that to you and your surveillance team. We'd like to know when he comes and goes and where
he goes to."

"We can do that," Clark said. "If you want to hang out, they've
got empty rooms here."

TWENTY-TWO

Bill Osborne was a tall man, beefy, with heavy cheeks around a small nose, deep-set dark eyes, pro-football shoulders though he'd never played sports, and a deep, resonant voice with which he sang Broadway show tunes while accompanying himself on a grand piano.

He'd left the Republican Party when Donald Trump was elected president, but had become neither a Democrat nor a liberal; he simply couldn't tolerate the proliferation of handguns that was killing his hometown.

He had a whole rap about Democrats: "Way back in the sixties, the Democrats wanted us black folks to be all equal, so they built thousands of playgrounds in the inner cities so that slow, short, poorly coordinated black kids could spend six hours a night shooting baskets and hoping to get in the NBA, when they would have been

perfectly good doctors, lawyers, and businessmen if they'd had decent schools and had spent their evenings reading. The Democrats
didn't build decent schools. Not their thing. Don't believe me, look at
Cleveland."

And, he'd once told the Cleveland *Plain Dealer*, "You had to love
those liberal jobs programs. They taught my mother to be a hairdresser and my father to be a janitor. In fact, they taught all the black
men and women to be janitors and hairdressers. That was the first
step on the way up to what? Becoming Super-Janitor? Flies through
the air with his mop?"

AS VIRGIL AND Lucas were working the freezing streets around the
Sikes' house, the Five were meeting in their chat room to congratu-
late MSP on what looked like a clean kill.

And to urge on CLE, who was next up.

Osborne's designated asshole was a manufacturer of ghost gun
kits—parts kits that could be assembled into fully operational semi-
automatic pistols, lacking only the serial number required for ordinary pistol sales.

Roland Klink was delivering a hundred kits a week around the
East Cleveland area, where Osborne had grown up. A group of bicycle messengers—Klink called them "gun runners"—would deliver
the kits, along with the extra-cost tools required to assemble them.
The gun runners would also pick up the payment. Cash only. Nothing illegal about any of it.

The guns had turned East Cleveland into an even darker dystopia
than had existed previously, when it was only drugs and poverty that
were killing the town.

Klink had the unfortunate habit—for him—of stepping out on his back stoop at night to smoke, because his wife wouldn't let him smoke in the house. The thin snow around the stoop was littered with cigarette filters, which his wife would pick up before the spring barbeque, because, as she said, "They look like shit."

Osborne didn't like guns, but after joining the Five, he'd made himself familiar with them, shooting at a range an hour and a half from his home, in the countryside south of Akron. He also became familiar with the gun culture, and a fashion for suppressors, which some people still called silencers, but which weren't very silent. He eventually bought, in the parking lot behind a gun show, one of Klink's ghost guns, completely assembled, along with a screw-on suppressor, for $1,750.

Perfect for going into a 7-Eleven, the redneck salesman told him, making an assumption that Osborne, a black man, almost found funny, he being a billionaire.

As he'd been told, the suppressed nine-millimeter wasn't very quiet, but was it quiet enough?

A little more than a week after McGruder killed Sikes, he found out.

AS LUCAS AND Virgil were flying into Cleveland, Osborne went to the Five's dark web site to take a calculated risk. He'd been checking the site hourly, for posts by Zhao and other members of the Five. He thought the others would be doing the same.

Zhao had checked in late the night before, saying that she'd pushed all the way to Salt Lake City, and in the morning, wrote that she expected to make Omaha, Nebraska, that night. She'd sleep in another parking garage, and then make the final push to Cleveland, she said.

"I need to rest. When I get to Cleveland, I'd like to bag out at CLE's place for a couple of days. I did that with SFO, no problem."

Sonnewell had replied, "SFO here. We didn't have a problem, but if I were CLE, I wouldn't let you in the house, and if I were you, I wouldn't want to go there. We've become a cause célèbre, we're getting close to two million followers on Facebook and the FBI is freaking out. They'll be all over rich Bitcoin investors in Cleveland since the killing of Klink. I'm not sure, but from what he's written, I suspect CLE is black, and he killed a gun manufacturer, so what goes for white Bitcoin investors goes triple for him (if he's black)."

Osborne had replied, "CLE here. I agree with SFO. I don't want you in my house. I want you gone. I don't know how much SFO gave you, but I'll match it or better. I am black and I agree with SFO's analysis on that aspect, as well. I knew that would happen, so I'm prepared for it. I haven't seen any obvious signs that the FBI is watching me, but then, I probably wouldn't. Your arrival is an unanticipated danger point for me."

Zhao wrote, "Meet here again late tonight. I'll get into Omaha at ten o'clock or so, if I can keep this up. We'll figure out a final plan then."

At midmorning, Osborne went back to the site, identified himself with the CLE code, and left a phone number for one of his burners. "Call me."

Andi Carter called him ten minutes later. "How do I know this is CLE and not a police trap?"

"You don't have to talk much," Osborne said. "I'll make an

observation—some people might get away from the FBI, but not many. We've all learned some things about Vivian through this whole process. One of them is, she's a manipulator and a dealer. I have to think her chances of getting away are low, at best. If she's caught, she'll deal. She'll have three killers to give up, you, me, and SFO, and if JFK gets his man next week, four of us. The FBI might let her walk if they could bag the four of us in trade."

"What are you suggesting?"

"I'm suggesting that we need to lose Zhao," Osborne said. "Permanently."

"Can you do that?"

"I can. You don't know me, but I'll tell you, I live on Lake Erie, and I have two dark kayaks down by the lake. I'll offer to meet Vivian at a local park, in the middle of the night. I can paddle there from my house, and if the FBI is watching, there's not a chance in hell they'll see me. I'll ambush her, like I did with Klink, put her in the kayak, paddle a mile or so out into the lake, wrap an anchor chain around her and drop her over the side. She'll be gone for good."

"I kind of like her," Carter said.

"So do I," Osborne said. "But that's not the point. The point is, keeping your ass and mine out of a federal prison."

"A strong point, since I like my ass right where it is," Carter said. "What do you want from me?"

"Your thoughts, your analysis," Osborne said. "She's a danger to us all, but I think we could also take the chance that she *will* get away and help her do that. I can give her a hundred K that I've got stashed at the house and send her on to the last two of the Five."

Long silence, and Osborne said, finally, "You still there?"

"Yes . . . Thinking. If you can dispose of her, I think that would be best. Yes. That would be best. Are you going to check with the other three?"

"If they call me. I'm taking down this phone number in an hour. I think Vivian's driving steadily across Wyoming and Nebraska and probably won't see it. If she does, and she calls me, I'll make some excuse about how much money we should all donate."

"All right. You've got my vote. Makes me sad, though."

"I'll keep this phone in my pocket until tonight," Osborne said. "If you change your mind, or have some more thoughts, I'll still be here. I'll listen to what you have to say."

JFK CALLED A few minutes later, and SFO an hour after that. They agreed that they'd be better off if Zhao were dead.

"I should have taken her when I could have," SFO said. "I didn't have enough time to think about it or get my head ready to do it. Damnit. Listen, if you can do it without endangering yourself, I say, go ahead. Remember that the FBI may be watching you. I've been reading about their surveillance teams, and they're supposed to be the best in the world."

"Then it's unanimous," Osborne said. "I'll take her out tonight."

Osborne had a live-in girlfriend. If he'd had a live-in wife, his preparations might have been more troublesome. With his girlfriend Elaine, all he had to say was, "Go visit your mother tomorrow. Take her to SouthPark Mall or something. Stay over at her place tomorrow night. I've got some things to do. I need serious privacy."

This had happened before, and she said, "Okay," and accepted the envelope he handed her. Inside she found five thousand dollars, with which she and her mother would have quite the good time. Between the two of them, they could spend a thousand at Sephora alone.

"You're not doing anything illegal?"

He smiled and said, "Of course not. The people who will be visiting me would rather not have somebody see them who could place them in northern Ohio. I mean, I know you can keep your mouth shut, but they don't."

"Arabs?" she said.

He said, "Let's not go there," and let her think he'd be visited by Arabs from Detroit. Then, while she was puttering around in the kitchen waiting for the cook to arrive, he went down into his basement to handle his pistol, to make sure everything was working.

He lifted the unloaded pistol up to eye level, aimed it at a light, and squeezed the trigger.

The gun went *klink* . . .

TWENTY-THREE

Clark, the senior FBI agent, gave Lucas and Virgil the keys to a dark blue Nissan Rogue, a car so inconspicuous that it was functionally invisible, and in-ear radio pickups with coat-jacket transceivers so they could listen to, and talk to, the surveillance team. When they'd finished discussing the FBI setup, Virgil and Lucas walked down to the motel office and checked in. They agreed to sleep late and meet at nine o'clock to find breakfast somewhere.

The next morning, they wound up in a Detroit Avenue café eating blueberry pancakes and sausages with a Greek flavor. "What are we going to do?" Lucas asked, over the first of his three cans of Diet Coke.

"Hope like hell that Zhao shows up here," Virgil said. "Houston would be closer to San Francisco, but if she's gathering money, her route would depend on where the *next* pickup would be . . . the one after this one. If it's East Coast, she comes here. If it's south, she probably went to Houston."

"If she's picking up money at all."

"That's a good bet, in my opinion," Virgil said. "On the other hand, maybe she got everything she'd need from the San Francisco killer. If she did, she could be on her way to Vancouver or Hawaii. Thousands of Asian-Americans in both places, she'd be hard to spot."

"Yeah. Thank you for that."

"You don't sound all that inspired."

"I'm not," Lucas said. "But. We're the only two cops who have seen Zhao in person, so I think we need to hang here for a while. If she's coming here, and plans to contact Osborne, she won't arrive until tomorrow night. I can't believe she'll drive up to his front door: he'd be nuts to let her do that. If he goes out to meet her, we need to be there."

"So we come back to the basic question. What are we going to do right now?"

They pondered the question for a moment, then Lucas forked up a piece of sausage, wagged it at Virgil: "Have you ever been to the Rock & Roll Hall of Fame?"

"Nope."

"It's here in Cleveland," Lucas said. "I have a few opinions I'd like to share with them on the galactic suckedness of the Beatles."

"Then let's go. Maybe Zhao will turn up there."

OSBORNE WENT OUT to a gym, worked out, got lunch, browsed watches at a high-end jewelry store but didn't buy anything, and went back home. The surveillance crew didn't see him touch anyone, or leave anything in a drop.

When Clark asked Lucas and Virgil what they'd done all day, they didn't mention the Rock & Roll Hall of Fame—which they gave a C+ as a tourist attraction—or shopping.

Virgil said, "We scouted the place out. If Zhao is coming here, and she's driving, she won't get here until tomorrow at the earliest. We wanted to understand the contours of the territory."

"Good for you," Clark said. "By the way, we've pretty much identified that shooter in Jacksonville who claims to be Six. Nothing he did resembles the Five's killings. He's a copycat. He was feuding with the victim over a real estate deal."

"Was the victim an asshole?" Lucas asked.

"Yeah, he was. As is the guy we're looking at," Clark said.

"So if you bust him for murder, we've got an asshole twofer," Virgil said.

"I guess you could look at it that way," Clark said, his tone implying that he didn't look at it that way.

WHEN THEY'D LEFT the FBI agents staring at their laptops, Lucas said, "You lie well."

"So do you. We got skills," Virgil said.

"What next?"

"Dinner?"

"I guess. I'm so fucking bored I'm tempted to chew my arm off. Dinner, then we stare at the TV, maybe actually scout the place out tomorrow."

"I saw an ad for *Venom: Let There Be Carnage* at a theater around here somewhere. I never saw it and can't believe it's still in theaters."

Lucas was skeptical: "Is it sort of realistic?"

"Oh, yeah. Your basic crime-fighter movie. Serial killer thing," Virgil said, lying well.

"I'll go. I like realistic movies. Is the hero a cop?"

"Not exactly," Virgil said.

THE NEXT DAY, they scouted the neighborhood, looked at Osborne's place on Google Earth, spotted a marina west of Osborne's, up an unfrozen river. They went there to talk to the marina manager, who hooked them up with a tour-boat operator who had nothing to do in January, since the temperatures were in the low thirties.

He couldn't take his tour boat out, but he had access to a cabin cruiser, and they rented it, and killed two hours cruising past Osborne's place, without telling the tour boat operator what they were looking at, then cruised back to the marina. Osborne's house was a modernistic hulk on a low bluff. Steps had been cut in the bluff and there was some access to the water, although the shore was iced in.

"You fall in the lake, we got about a minute to pull you out before the cold penetrates and your heart blows up," the tour-boat operator said. "Another degree colder and it's ice."

Osborne didn't have a boathouse. There was no sign of watercraft nearby, or even an accessible dock.

When they got back to the marina, the sun was on the horizon. They thanked the tour-boat operator, paid him, got a receipt and started back to the Travelodge. Then Clark called: "Zhao could be here if she drove hard and Osborne's moving."

"Where's he going?" Lucas asked.

"We don't know, but we're tracking him," Clark said. "Where are you?"

"Leaving the marina," Lucas said.

"Then he's coming your way," Clark said. "He's on I-90 heading west. We got him, but we don't know where he's going."

He was going to an Orvis store.

Lucas and Virgil arrived in the Nissan five minutes after Osborne walked into the place. A short, bespectacled FBI agent, part of the surveillance crew, followed him in, browsed the post-Christmas sales table, and called the watchers when Osborne left with a sack.

"Nothing going on here," the agent reported. Virgil and Lucas listened in on the in-ear monitors. "Walked in, told a clerk that he'd ordered a winter jacket and had an email that it'd come in. The clerk got it for him, he tried it on and paid for it. He looked at some fishing stuff, didn't buy anything, and walked back out."

"He's not going home," another agent said. "He's on local streets . . ."

They followed him to a Whole Foods store, where the lead sur-veillance agent said, "Okay, guys, be on your toes, that's gonna be complicated in there."

Lucas touched the transmit button on his transceiver and called, "This is Lucas. We're going in. We'll try to stay away from Os-borne, but we'll be looking for Zhao. This would be a great place to hook up."

"You two look a lot like cops . . ."

"We'll stay away from Osborne," Lucas said. To Virgil, he said, "Could have gone to Orvis to see if he could spot a tail. He didn't, so now he comes here."

They parked, walked into the store, Virgil got a shopping basket, handed it to Lucas, took another for himself. Inside they walked behind the checkout counters to the bread/bakery/deli section. No sign of Osborne. No Zhao.

Virgil put a loaf of bread in his basket, passed two baguettes to Lucas. They continued past the deli to the back of the store, walked along the dairy case. Still no Osborne, no Zhao.

One of the surveillance agents, a woman, said, speaking into their ears, "Lucas, Virgil, I see you, Osborne is in the frozen food aisle, he appears to be looking for ice cream. I haven't seen anyone that might be Zhao."

"We'll skip that aisle, walk down to produce," Lucas said. As they passed the back end of the frozen food aisle, they saw Osborne at the front end, standing by an open glass door, peering into a freezer. They moved quickly past, checked five more aisles, saw nobody who'd concealed their faces with the winter clothing, saw no one who looked at all Chinese.

The produce department was at the far side of the store from their original entry point. No Chinese women. Lucas touched his transmit button and said, "Nobody obvious, we're going back out to the car."

They were almost out of the produce department when the woman called, the words tumbling out of her, "Lucas, Virgil, he's got his ice cream and he's walking toward you, fast. You're gonna bump right into him."

"Split up, head toward the back," Lucas said to Virgil.

Virgil said, "No time and he'll pick us out if we run." He shifted his basket to his other side, and said, "Hold my hand."

"What?"

"C'mon, hold my hand. He's a 'phobe. Lean your head a little sideways into me, look me in the eyes, and we walk toward the front of the store, taking our time . . ."

Lucas said, "Ah, shit," and took Virgil's hand.

One of the FBI agents said, watching them, "Oh my God."

Osborne went past them and as he did, he looked away. They continued to the front of the store, put their baskets behind a display of fresh flowers, and went out.

The woman called, "What'd you do? Did he see you?"

A male agent, also inside the store, who'd been looking at tomatoes, said, "They walked by him holding hands. Osborne wouldn't look at them. He's a homophobe and thought they were gay."

Lucas, not transmitting, said to Virgil, "I won't live this down. You will, of course, being an ambisexual hippie."

The woman agent said, "That's so cool. That's really *so* cool."

Lucas: "Ah, Jesus."

Back in the Nissan, Lucas said, "Makes me think Zhao's not coming this way. He's out drifting around. He's cool, not hot. I think he'd be hot if she was coming in."

Virgil: "Like you said, he might be scouting for a tail. We almost blew it in there."

Osborne was out of Whole Foods five minutes later. He went straight home, carrying a small brown bag containing a quart of raspberry delight and three ripe bananas.

TWENTY-FOUR

Clark called from the motel: "His girlfriend is moving. We're putting four people on her. She's headed south, same route she took the first day we were watching her—we think she's probably headed toward her mother's apartment."

"I like that," Lucas said. "Could be Osborne clearing the deck for a meeting."

"Or she's making a delivery to Zhao," Clark replied.

Lucas and Virgil talked about it, and decided to stake out Osborne's house, staying well back from the first layer of surveillance cars. "Wish we'd gotten some sandwiches at Whole Foods," Virgil said. "The crap we've been eating is getting me down."

"We could risk a fast bite at that café," Lucas said. "That wasn't too bad."

"We could," Virgil said. "If she left San Francisco when we think she did, she wouldn't quite be here yet. Maybe. If she had some speed on her, she could have cut a few hours off."

They called out to the leader of the surveillance team who told them that Osborne's head could be seen through a window in his house; he was apparently playing a piano and singing to himself. His girlfriend was at a shopping mall called SouthPark with her mother.

"Let's take the chance," Lucas said, and they did.

WHEN HE'D SUNG his voice out, Osborne spent a couple hours watching an old Denzel Washington movie called *Déjà Vu* that he'd missed when it came out years earlier. He liked it, thought it was one of Denzel's better movies, though *American Gangster* was still his favorite. That scene where Denzel shoots a rival in the forehead and the entire neighborhood runs for it . . . Wow!

How did that mesh with his distaste for handguns? It didn't. It was just a good movie.

LUCAS AND VIRGIL had spent hundreds of hours on stakeouts. They were fundamentally boring, but you did see unusual things, especially when you were staked out in an unusual part of town.

On this evening, they saw a man cycling down the street with a sleek, streamlined dog running beside him on a leash. Nothing unusual about that, except that the man was on a unicycle.

"Not something you see every day," Lucas said.

"Maybe you do in this neighborhood," Virgil said. "He's gotta be a local, riding around on that thing."

"I'm amazed that his dog isn't embarrassed," Lucas said.

An hour after that, a long blue car that Lucas identified as a 7 Series BMW ran a stop sign, barely made the ninety-degree turn, ran over an opposite curb, a sidewalk and a piece of hedge, swerved back onto the street and accelerated past them.

"Blond woman, maybe fifty," Virgil said.

"Yeah. Hope she doesn't kill anybody."

"Drunk or pissed off?"

"Could be either, but I'd guess she was pissed about something," Lucas said. "Most drunks drive slow. Her reflexes were pretty good, getting off that curb."

"Mmm."

"Quiet out here."

"Yeah, but . . . here comes that unicycle guy again."

OSBORNE GOT THE call on his cell phone at 11:05. "How are we going to do this?" Zhao asked.

"Okay. Where are you?"

"At a gas station off I-80, right straight south of you. It'll take me forty-five minutes to get to you."

"I've got a hundred thousand for you. I put it in a book bag. I'll meet you at Lakewood Park. If you look at a map on your phone, there's a place right in the northeast corner called Lookout Point."

"Hang on . . . okay, I see it. Why that deep in the park? Why not at the basketball courts, it'd be easier for me to get to, from the street."

"Because I've got to deal with a kayak. I'll be climbing up there with the kayak tied to a rock down below. I can't take a chance that it'll blow off. If the FBI is watching me, I'd be fucked."

"All right. I should be there by midnight," Zhao said. "If I can even find a place to park."

"I might be later than that—the lake's a bit rough tonight. Watch for me, I'll be coming up from below."

They talked about where she could park, and when they'd rung off, Osborne, already dressed in a waterproof paddling suit, turned off two lights on the bottom floor, turned on one light on the second floor. He walked back down the stairs, and farther down another flight to the basement, then out a back door onto steps leading up to the lakeside lawn.

The yard was heavily landscaped, naked maples and a string of cone-shaped evergreens. He moved slowly, watchfully, through the trees to the flight of stone steps leading down to the lake. The steps were set into a cut in the bluff above the water, and he'd left a kayak in the cut where it couldn't be seen.

He shouldered the kayak with its bungee'd-on paddle and moved awkwardly in the dark down the rest of the way to the lake. He set the kayak on the lakeside rocks and turned to check his surroundings. He could see almost nothing and was moving as much by familiar feel as by sight.

After a minute, he went back and recovered his pack of chain. The pack went in the front hatch of the kayak. He moved the boat into the water, working by feel, and settled into it.

His target was a ten-minute paddle. Once out on the lake, he could see better, because he could see the lights in the top floors of the lakeside homes. When the bluff went dark again, he knew he was at the park.

He beached the boat—the beach was a jumble of rocks—risked a penlight, and made his way up a rocky grade, across a street, up a steep heavily treed slope onto the frozen turf of the park.

He was breathing hard, but now there was more ambient light. He was at the center of the park's northern edge, above the lake. He'd told Zhao to meet him at the northeast corner, at Lookout Point. He made his way diagonally through the park, nearly bumping into a tree as he went, until he was in a group of bare bushes where he could set up an ambush.

He would be behind her as she walked in. If she stayed on a side-walk, as he hoped she would, it'd be an easy shot.

He was carrying the pistol in a shoulder holster, under his pad-dling jacket. He unzipped the jacket, took the pistol out, jacked a shell into the chamber and settled down to wait; the night was mostly quiet, but he could hear passing cars and a small plane off to the west, marked by a red taillight. A bit nervous now, he imagined he heard footsteps coming up from behind, but when he turned his head . . . nothing.

Clicked on his Apple Watch: eleven-thirty.

Maybe twenty minutes to wait.

ZHAO HAD BEEN nowhere near I-80, which ran south of Cleveland, when she called Osborne. She had, in fact, already been sitting in her car a block from the park. As soon as she got off the phone, she opened her car door, and in the overhead light, checked the 9mm pistol that Sonnewell had given her.

She was wearing a black down jacket and black tactical pants with oversized slash pockets, and a black ski mask that she'd rolled up into a watch cap. She'd bought the new clothing at a Cabela's store in Sidney, Nebraska, off I-80. She'd taken a risk in making the stop, but not, she thought, a huge one, and nobody in the store had given her a second look.

She'd stopped once, on a back road, to load and fire the gun. She knew about pistols, mostly from research she'd done on the run-up to the Five murders, and from shooting her .22. Sonnewell's nine-millimeter kicked considerably harder than her .22, and when she'd looked at it closely, she found it had no serial number: it was a ghost gun.

And though a ghost gun, it worked as efficiently as the Ruger American it mimicked, the only difference being the lack of a serial number.

The gun was compact, but heavy in her hands; she chambered a round, made sure the safety was on, and slipped it into her pocket. The gun could be a problem if she ran into a cop: Ohio required concealed carry permits. If she were stopped, and arrested, she'd have cops looking at her closely. Her primary alternative ID was very good, but her face had been all over the news, and posted to the Five Facebook page.

On the other hand, her experience with Sonnewell in San Francisco had been a warning: he'd been close to killing her, she thought. All the people she was dealing with were proven killers, except, so far, JFK in New York, and she had no doubt that he'd be pulling a trigger next week; she'd realized that she represented a risk to them all.

So she took care.

Out of the car, she walked fast along the sidewalk, shoulders hunched, head swiveling, like a lone woman might do in the middle of the night. There was virtually no traffic. As she approached the park, she heard what sounded like running feet, and she stepped into the front walk to a house, then over onto the lawn, where she was concealed by a hedge.

She'd been correct in thinking she heard footsteps, but they weren't human footsteps, rather those of a running dog, accompanied by a loony-tunes on a unicycle. The dog and the cyclist continued down the street, although the dog, she thought, had sensed her presence, and turned to look at the place where she was concealed. When they were gone, she hurried on to the park.

A nearly full moon was rising overhead, casting intricate moon shadows from the mature trees. There was snow on the lawn, trampled down by walkers, and she stayed on it, away from the sidewalks. Lookout Point would be to her right as she approached the water. She walked all the way to the slope down to the lake, then backed up, and huddled behind the trunk of a barren tree.

She didn't have to wait long. Osborne said he might be late; in fact, he was fifteen or twenty minutes early. She heard his kayak scraping over rock—didn't know exactly what it was when she first heard it, but figured it out quickly enough from the hollow sound when he dragged it ashore. He was west of her, down the lake; she heard him climbing the bank, then saw him, not clearly. He was dressed in dark clothing, from head to foot, but that only made sense, she thought.

Instead of moving toward Lookout Point, she watched as he walked diagonally across the park, behind her, nearly stumbling into a tree, and eventually settling in some landscaping bushes near the sidewalk that ran between Lookout Point and the street.

She thought he was looking toward the street, and away from her. She stood, and moved cautiously toward him, her approach muffled by the snow. When she was thirty feet away, she stopped, and knelt next to a tree. He was doing something she couldn't make out, but she heard a zipper being pulled, and then saw him handling something that appeared to be mechanical.

Then she heard a familiar ratcheting sound: he'd just chambered a round in a handgun. He'd killed Klink with a handgun. He was set up to ambush her.

She closed her eyes and felt the anger clutching at her throat. He was planning to kill her. There was no hundred thousand. She'd risked her freedom to get here, and he was set to kill her.

She watched him for a minute, confirming his plan by watching his movements. If she'd come up the sidewalk, he would have shot her in the back. Probably dumped her body in the lake.

The motherfucker!

She'd pulled the ski mask down as soon as she'd gotten into the park, and nothing showed of her face except her eyes and the bridge of her nose. She eased the pistol out of her pocket, stood up and moved closer. At fifteen feet she spoke softly, but with an edge of authority.

"Were you going to shoot me in the back?"

She was close enough to see him in some detail now and saw him stiffen. He turned his head without moving his body and said, "I wanted to make sure you weren't going to kill me. I was going to keep you far enough away that I could show you the cash and then back away from it."

"Yeah? Dump the money out on the ground."

"Here," he said, and for a moment she almost believed him. But not quite, and she kept the gun centered on his body when he suddenly pivoted with his right hand coming up . . .

She shot him: *bam bam bam bam*, just like with the .22, but with more recoil, more impact, snarling as she fired and Osborne toppled over in the snow. She stepped closer and fired one more time, *bam*, directly into his head.

He wasn't carrying a pack: there was no money.

She stood there, looking down at him for two seconds, five seconds, then broke into a panicked run, heading for the car. It was a hundred yards away, maybe twenty or thirty seconds in the dark. She stumbled twice and fell down once, her hip impacting on a piece of icy concrete, got up, twisted, ran, got to her car, piled inside.

In the movies, the car wouldn't have started. The 4Runner started instantly, and she was rolling away, less than a minute after Osborne died in the snow.

She didn't care where she was going or what streets she was taking. She only wanted to go one place.

Away.

TWENTY-FIVE

Virgil was considering a witty reply, stakeout conversation being what it was—desultory bordering on stupid—when they heard the gunshots. Instead of his witty reply, he stated the obvious. "Gun!"

Lucas sat up, turned: "Yeah. Where was it?"

They twisted in the car seats, looking for any kind of movement, any light, but from where they were parked, they could see nothing at all except the surrounding houses. Virgil started the car and said, "I think it came from behind us."

"Yeah! Yeah! Go!" Lucas pressed the transmit button on the transceiver: "You guys hear that? Gunshots?"

The head of the surveillance crew came back: "We heard something. Sounded pretty far away."

"Sounded close to us," Lucas said. "Maybe from that park? Have you seen Osborne?"

"No, but the top floor is all lit up, must be his bedroom."

Virgil: "That was Zhao. The gun was Zhao. She just killed Osborne. Five shots . . ."

Lucas repeated that to the FBI listeners. "Virgil says she just killed Osborne. Somewhere close by."

Clark came up: "Why? Why do you think . . . ?"

"Because we heard four or five fast shots, and that's how she killed that guy in California, the hedge fund guy, and how she killed McGruder, same thing, five fast shots," Virgil said.

Lucas repeated that to the surveillance crew, and added, "This wasn't a .22, this was bigger. We're going to the park, we're going to the park . . ."

The park was two minutes away, taking into account both their reaction time and their standing start, including the U-turn.

On the way, Clark came up: "Is it possible the shots sounded muffled to us, because they were inside Osborne's house?"

Lucas: "No. I don't think so, because they sounded clear to us, but muffled to the people who were closer to the house."

At the park, Virgil did another U-turn and pulled to the curb and killed the engine and said, "Guns."

"Yeah." They checked their guns and got out. The park was dark, but there was enough moon, and ambient light from the houses along the street, that they could see distinct shapes.

"Wish I had my shotgun," Virgil said over the hood of the car as they headed into the park.

"So do I," Lucas said. "Get your gun up, get your gun up . . ."

Virgil brought his gun up and they moved side by side down a sidewalk past a basketball court and then a big unlit building.

"I'm going left," Virgil said. "I'll hang on the corner of the building until you clear around it. Yell when you're clear."

Lucas moved quickly down the side of the building until he was looking into the back of the park, and yelled, and Virgil came around and Lucas said, "Ten yards apart. Let's go straight down the middle . . ."

Their eyes weren't yet fully adjusted to the dark, and Clark was shouting at the surveillance crew to get close to the front of Osborne's house, without giving themselves up, and Virgil and Lucas simultaneously took the earbuds out and put them in their coat pockets, the better to hear movement around them.

Two-thirds of the way to the water, Lucas said, "I maybe got something. Over to my right. Looks like a lump, not a tree. Not a stump. Solid-looking, could be a boulder."

Virgil walked in an arc around Lucas, still ten yards away, and they edged toward the east side of the park, pistols up. As they got closer, Virgil said, "Yeah. I see it. Is that what you're talking about?"

"Body. I think."

"Osborne?"

Lucas got close and said, "It's a body, I can't see his face, he's rolled on it . . . what . . . If she shot him, she's gone. I'm going to use my phone flash."

Lucas turned on his iPhone flashlight and shined it at the lump.

"Gun by his hand," Virgil said. "Hand is black. Gotta be Osborne."

Lucas went to the radio: "Clark. Clark. We've got a body in the park, we think it's Osborne. Zhao might still be here, it's pretty dark.

We got here in two or three minutes and didn't see anyone leaving . . . We need some of the team to cover the street-side exits . . ."

Clark came back: "You're sure it's Osborne?"

"It's a big guy, he's facedown. We can see a hand, and a gun, and the hand looks like it's black. I don't want to touch him, I don't want to mess up the scene."

"Ah, that's him . . . We'll have four guys there in one minute, maybe less. I'm thinking if she didn't get out on the streets, she'd have to go over some walls or go down to the water and walk out. That doesn't seem likely."

"She had a car parked close by," Lucas said. "Hang on."

Virgil was on his knees, looking out toward the street. He pulled his cell phone out and turned on the flashlight, pointing at a line of small footprints in the snow, including one with red droplets, stepped on after the blood sprayed onto the surface of the snow.

"Woman's footprints," he said. "She ran to the street. She's gone."

FIVE MINUTES LATER, a line of FBI agents, including Clark, were working through the park. The senior agent kept everybody away from the body, while sending agents through the park with powerful LED flashlights. A kayak was spotted, pulled up on rocks at the edge of the lake, which explained how Osborne could have gotten out of his house without being seen. When the park was cleared, Clark sent his agents down the street to pound on doors, waking people up, to ask if anyone had noticed a strange car near the entrance to the park.

One man had. He lived a block from the park, and said he'd been cycling late with his dog, and had seen a dark SUV parked in front of a neighbor's house. He said he hadn't seen it before on his nightly rides. He hadn't heard the gunshots—he and his dog were watching a movie—but it had been late. He didn't know the make of the car, nor had he noticed its license plates. When the FBI talked to the neighbor he'd mentioned, the agents were told that she knew nothing of a car parked in front of her house.

"Zhao's in a dark SUV," Clark told Virgil and Lucas. "There are almost three hundred million cars registered in the U.S. Do you think there are less than, say, twenty million dark SUVs?"

"Probably not," Virgil said.

They were sure the dead man was Osborne, but not technically sure—Lucas and Virgil hadn't touched the body once they'd seen the massive wound to the victim's head, and Clark was reluctant to roll it until he was cleared to do so by the crime scene technicians. He was sure enough about the dead man's identity that he sent an agent to pound on Osborne's door. If Osborne answered, the agent was to ask him about nearby gunshots.

"He must've known we were out here. If he'd killed Zhao, we would have been his alibi," Clark said.

They rolled the body at four o'clock in the morning and confirmed Osborne's identity. He was wearing what one of the agents said was a winter paddling suit, a sweatshirt, and jeans. He had a wallet in his jeans with an Ohio driver's license issued to William Osborne.

By that time, more senior Cleveland agents, including the AIC, had been roused and had come to the park. When Osborne's identity was confirmed, the FBI entered his house with a warrant, Lucas and Virgil trailing behind. A full search would be done beginning later in the morning, and the agents sealed Osborne's office and found a safe concealed in the music room. That room was sealed as well, with agents assigned to make sure nobody went in or out until the search began.

Lucas and Virgil got Clark aside and Lucas said, "We want to observe the search."

"I'm sure you can. Let me check with Henry." Henry Moore was the AIC. "We're fully aware of your friend in Washington."

"Good," Lucas said. "This is the second time we've missed Zhao by a minute or two, and I'm getting tired of it. I'm hoping we can find something that'll tell us where she's headed. I'm gonna kill that bitch."

Clark flinched at the word and looked around; there were no female agents close enough to have overhead.

"Well, I hope it doesn't come to that," Clark said. "If we can get her alive . . ."

"What? She'll give up the other members of the Five? She's already murdered two of them," Lucas said. "I've got a feeling that she'll either kill them, or one of them will kill her, or she'll just disappear."

Virgil: "She'd be crazy to keep talking to other members of the Five—they've got to believe that she's coming for them. They've got to be looking for her, especially when the news breaks about Osborne. If she collected cash and a different car in California, which we think she did—she's probably driving that SUV now—maybe she'll give up on them, at least for the time being, and head for a hideout."

Lucas nodded. "We know she's smart. If she really has thought about it, and has cash from San Francisco and buries herself, finding her will be close to impossible."

"We'll tear the house apart, and if there's anything to find, we'll find it," Clark said. "Be there."

TWENTY-SIX

Zhao at first paid no attention to where she was as long as she was away from the park. She fled east, then south on a major street, without any sign of pursuit. Ten minutes after leaving the park, she spotted an all-night Walgreens pharmacy with several cars in the parking lot, and pulled in.

She sat in the parking lot unmoving, calming herself, trying to think. She'd planned to continue driving east out of Cleveland, to the man they called JFK, but now thought better of the idea. JFK hadn't yet acted, and now might decide not to—at this point, he hadn't committed a provable crime, and the heat on the Five was getting intense. He could afford to wait, to keep his head down, and simply stay away from her, and not act at all.

She had nothing to blackmail him with, except a shaky charge of conspiracy. A threat to burn JFK could backfire with her other available resource, Andi Carter, in New Orleans.

She had fifty thousand dollars in cash, in a shopping bag, in the car. A lot of money . . . but not enough. Basically, it was a year's shelter and food, which could be stretched if she got a low-level off-the-books job somewhere, but not enough to get comfortable. Living in a shithole somewhere, doing the kind of menial janitorial stuff like she'd been doing at the tattoo parlor, was not her idea of an inviting future.

And the surviving members of the Five had *so much* . . .

She'd been turning it over in her mind since she left San Francisco and had considered the possibility of checking out with the fifty thousand, and then returning in six months or a year to tap into Andi Carter and Meyer, and maybe asking Sonnewell for another shot of cash.

They all, she thought, should be seriously interested in providing a permanent hideout for her. If she were caught, she would represent a serious threat, as she was sure they all understood. Sonnewell had, and Osborne, too, or they wouldn't have threatened to kill her.

Another thing had persistently tapped at the back of her mind as she drove across the country. She'd met Andi Carter on four different occasions and felt some kinship with the other woman. Maybe Carter would still be willing to help her, even though she'd now killed two of the Five.

But she hadn't wanted to do it!

McGruder had brought it on himself with a threat to expose them all, and she'd killed him to protect the others. Osborne had come to the park to kill her, and she'd killed him in self-defense. Carter would understand that.

She thought more about it, slumped down a bit when two police cars, a hundred feet apart, went past in a hurry, sirens and flashers blowing up the quiet night. They were headed in the general direction of the park, and she felt an impulse to get farther away, and quickly.

She quelled it, and still thinking about Carter, got out of the 4Runner and went into the Walgreens, bought three boxes of Good & Plenty licorice candy, two bags of potato chips, and a half dozen bottles of Pepsi. She would kill, she thought, for a pizza. The thought amused her: the *kill* part.

Back in her car, she picked up her burner and called Carter. Carter didn't answer. She thought about calling again, decided against, started the engine, and was about to back out of her parking place, when the phone rang.

"Yes?"

"This is me," Carter said. "I was asleep."

"I killed CLE," Zhao said. No point in dressing it up.

"What!"

"Bill Osborne. I think you knew him. He tried to ambush me in a park. He told me he had money for me, but he brought a gun and tried to shoot me with it. SFO gave me a gun and I shot Bill with it. Before he could shoot *me*."

"Oh my God, Vivian! That's awful. I mean, awful for you!" Carter said. "He tried to shoot you like he did that ghost gun guy?"

"Exactly like that. I got to the meeting place early and he came sneaking in, all dressed in black and he hid in some bushes that he thought I'd walk past. He was going to shoot me in the back. I actually talked to him, asked him if he was trying to shoot me, and he spun around . . ." She started lying a little. ". . . and he shot at me but missed because he was off-balance . . . I don't think he missed me by an inch, I felt the bullet go through my hair."

"Oh my God!" Carter said again. "What are you going to do?"

"Same as I was planning before I came to this place—I want to disappear," Zhao said. "I don't want to hurt anyone else . . . I only did McGruder because . . ."

"I know why," Carter said. "Where are you now?"

"Sitting outside a Walgreens in Cleveland. I got that money from George, but it wasn't all that much. I really need cash from the rest of you guys. Bill had no intention of giving it to me . . ."

"Well, I will. How about JFK?"

"He hasn't done anything yet. He's still in the clear and this whole . . . program . . . seems to be coming apart. I decided you'd be my best chance for more cash . . . if you're still willing."

"Of course I am! What was Bill thinking about? Christ, all he had to do was give you a little money. JFK and I are willing to contribute . . . A hundred thousand dollars? Bill wouldn't even have noticed that it was gone. Neither will I. As a matter of fact, I'm willing to up the amount. Considerably. Where can we meet?"

"I dunno. I haven't thought through it that far. We can work that out tomorrow. I'm going to head south, get out of here, find a place to sleep. I'll call you tomorrow on this same phone. I'll call you in the morning."

"Good. Do that. This is fuckin' horrible! Horrible! I can't believe Bill would do that . . ."

They talked for another minute, then rang off. Carter had sounded genuine, Zhao thought, but then, as a psychopath, Carter was probably a well-practiced liar. She'd have to be careful. Their meeting would be in a crowd somewhere; somewhere she wouldn't be recognized, but where Carter wouldn't be able to pull any crazy shit.

She called up a map of the U.S. on her cell phone, narrowed it to the center of the country. She could drive to either Columbus or Cincinnati, both on the road to New Orleans, find a parking garage, get some sleep.

She fired up the car and pulled out of the Walgreens.

ZHAO NEVER THOUGHT that she might have erred, but she had. She'd referred to Sonnewell as "George" instead of by his airport code and Andi Carter only knew of one George who lived in the SFO area and was also a Bitcoin richie. She went online to a private American Bitcoin Council website, found his name, an email, and a phone number. She looked at her watch: eleven o'clock in in California.

She made the call. The phone rang for a while, then went to a voice mail. She said, "This is MSY. If you're SFO, call me back at this number."

Five minutes later, her phone rang and Sonnewell said, "What's up, Andi?"

Carter laughed and said, "You knew I was MSY?"

"I thought it was likely," Sonnewell said. "How did you figure me out?"

"I just talked to Vivian and she slipped up and referred to you as 'George.' I thought, hmm, who do I know named George in the San Francisco area who's got a lot of Bitcoin cash and has muscles big enough to strangle that piece of shit Duck Wiggins?"

"I'm not admitting anything on a phone call, but okay. Something bad happened?"

"Vivian killed CLE. She saw him coming; she's smart, and we didn't give her enough credit for that. She's running my way now. Still looking for money."

"Goddamnit. What do you think?"

"I think you and I have to work something out. She's wary now. I don't think it's something I can do on my own."

Sonnewell looked at his bedside clock. "I go to bed early, so I can get out of here at six tomorrow morning, be in New Orleans before noon. If she's in Cleveland and driving, she won't make it before then."

"She'll want to meet someplace public," Carter said. "She said you threatened to kill her and so she's . . . you know."

"I'm willing to do her, if you can set her up," Sonnewell said. "But I won't, if I think I might get caught."

"I was hoping you'd say that. We do have to be very careful, but I'll figure out something that'll work for you."

They traded ideas, and eventually agreed that Carter would pick up Sonnewell at Lakefront Airport in New Orleans the next morning. When they rang off, Sonnewell called his charter service and made arrangements to fly out at six o'clock.

He crawled back into bed, stared at the ceiling for a while. He thought, *Andi Carter.* He'd never spent any time talking to her at the ABC meetings, but she'd definitely caught his eye.

Before Sonnewell got rich, when he was just another big lunk, he'd never done well with the best of women, because he was . . . a lunk. And perhaps a little nerdish. Then when he was rich, he'd had the impression that the women who approached him were much more interested in his money than in him, which was purely offensive.

He'd always been a bit shy with women, and after his experiences with the grifter culture, he'd become more so. Andi Carter didn't fit any of the categories that bothered him: she was possibly richer than he was. She was tough, not soft. She was smart.

He'd thought of her at odd moments over the years, and now . . . She'd called him and he'd made her laugh.

Maybe?

Andi Carter?

TWENTY-SEVEN

Virgil and Lucas got back to Osborne's house the next day at ten o'clock, and found the long driveway jammed with dark SUVs, local cop cars, and anonymous sedans with Hertz vibrations. A rank of television mobile units was parked on the street, with thoroughly chilled reporters and cameramen standing in clusters around the trucks.

"This is a big deal, I guess," Virgil said, as they pulled into the driveway. "We don't kill billionaires all that often and now we've got two of them dead in the last week." He parked off the driveway, on the lawn, so he could escape the crowd if he needed to.

That annoyed an FBI functionary, who jogged over to them, swinging his hand back, telling him to get off the lawn. Virgil dropped the window and asked, "What?"

"What do you think you're doing? You're parking on a flower bed."

"I'm parking so I can get out of here if I need to and won't be jammed up by a bunch of circus cars. Like you dummies," Virgil said. "Got a problem with that, talk to Henry."

Henry Moore was the agent in charge. That backed the functionary off, and he said, "I will," and he jogged away. Lucas asked, "You think Henry will have any idea of what he's talking about?"

"Who cares?" Virgil asked.

"Attaboy," Lucas said. "Let's see what they're doing in there. They're gonna need advice."

The last billionaire's house they'd been in was McGruder's and it had been a disappointment. As Lucas mentioned at the time, the stuff McGruder had inside wasn't much different than what Virgil and Lucas had inside their homes, except that it was more expensive, and there was more of it—three hundred neckties, instead of a dozen. A concert grand Steinway, instead of Lucas' smaller model.

That, Virgil told Lucas, as they walked through Osborne's house, had been the result of McGruder's poor imagination and lack of taste.

Which didn't apply to Osborne.

In addition to all the usual crap that billionaires piled up—rare mid-century furniture, custom-made lighting fixtures produced in studios instead of factories, carpets woven from the pubic hair of Tibetan virgins instead of rugs from Crate & Barrel—Osborne had dedicated several rooms to things that apparently appealed to his personality.

He had a formal library, but instead of books that seemed to have been purchased by a decorator, the shelves were stuffed with books that appeared to have been read, on currency markets, economics, history, and art.

He had a music room with a piano identical to the one in Lucas' house, apparently good enough for him, with a thick clump of sheet music on the paper rack, instead of the E-Z Play piano books that had decorated McGruder's. The room had odd-shaped fabric panels in the corners, to improve the acoustics, and a pretty Arts and Crafts carpet over a hardwood floor.

He wasn't, Virgil told Lucas, a dilettante.

"No shit," Lucas said.

Most of the action in the house was taking place in the home office, where Osborne had a set of computers on a conference table, and in the music room, where a floor-standing safe had been found behind paneling under a line of cabinets filled with stereo equipment, vinyl records, and CDs.

Clark was there, watching an FBI technician fiddle with an electronic lock. To Lucas and Virgil, he said, "The girlfriend, Elaine West, was here an hour ago. Pretty torn up. She wanted to get some of her personal stuff out of the bedroom, clothes and such. She knew about the safe but says she didn't know the combination. The tech is talking to the manufacturer, he should be able to get it open."

"Anything else worth looking at?" Virgil asked.

"One of the computer guys found a website that Osborne went to five times yesterday, that doesn't have anything in it. Nothing. We think it might have been used to communicate with the other members of the Five, but they've now moved to a new site."

"Be nice if Osborne had written down the new website's name," Lucas said.

"He probably did—those sites have names so long and garbled you couldn't remember them. He most likely stuck it in an encrypted file that our computer guy says the NSA could break open if given enough time. He said enough time would be about two billion years after the sun goes dark," Clark said.

There were twelve members of FBI evidence response teams working through the house, searching everything. Each piece of clothing was removed from the closets, each pocket turned out, each piece of paper examined for anything that might be significant.

When the safe technician, working with the manufacturer, got the safe open, Clark had to push people away while an emergency response team specialist wearing white Tyvek coveralls and surgeon's gloves removed the contents and placed them in plastic evidence boxes.

There was money: fifty or sixty thousand dollars, that would be counted before the evidence box was sealed. They found gold and silver coins, exotic watches, men's gold bracelets, a loaded Smith & Wesson .357 Magnum, a notarized will and other estate-related papers that ran to seventy pages, and a notebook with codes that one tech said appeared to be Bitcoin account codes.

Nothing about the Five.

Then, unexpectedly, one of the specialists who was working through the office called, "I've got something here."

Clark, several agents, Virgil, and Lucas trooped out of the music room and into the adjacent office. The specialist had a yellow scratch pad that resembled a legal pad but was only about four by six inches in size. Taken from a collection of similar used scratch pads the specialist had found in a desk drawer, he'd found two dozen random notes, and a scribbled list.

SFO: DW
MSY: JD

MSP: HS
JFK: WOR

There were some further scribbled words around the note, but they weren't immediately decipherable.

"The first letters are airport codes," the specialist said. "SFO is San Francisco, I don't know what MSY is . . ."

Somebody said, "New Orleans."

The specialist continued: "MSP is Minneapolis–St. Paul, CLE is here, Cleveland, and JFK is . . . JFK. The second letters are the victims. Duck Wiggins, Jack Daniels, Hillary Sikes, and WOR, who hasn't been killed yet, but will be, by JFK, whoever that is. He doesn't list his own victim because he didn't need help to remember it."

The specialist pinned the pad down with his gloved hands so Clark and his senior agents could see it. Virgil crowded in as Clark said, "This is important. The next killing will be in New York. We need to get it to Henry and he needs to get it to Washington ASAP."

Virgil looked back through the cluster of agents, to Lucas, who hadn't tried to push through. Lucas raised his eyebrows, and Virgil nodded: "It's real."

And to Clark: "Let me get a shot with my cell phone."

Clark seemed reluctant but couldn't think of a reason not to let Virgil take a shot, and Virgil did, backed out of the group, and showed it to Lucas.

"WOR?"

One of the agents said, "It's a conservative talk radio station in New York. Lot of big names in talk radio are on it."

Clark turned to the agent, whose name was Barnes: "Are you sure?"

"Yes, I'm sure," Barnes said. "I come from there. My dad listens to it all the time."

"Remember what Osborne's press release said?" Lucas asked Virgil. "You'll know his face, or something like that?"

"A radio station doesn't have a face," Virgil said. "People on radio stations don't have faces. They're not on TV."

"Some of them are, the famous ones," one of the milling agents said.

The scratch pad was placed in an evidence bag after Clark had taken a careful photo with his cell phone. He stepped away to send it to Henry Moore, the Cleveland agent in charge. When he got Moore, he explained what had been found. "I'm told it's a right-wing talk station in New York."

"Conspiracy theories," Barnes said to him. "Right up the Five's alley."

Clark repeated that to the AIC. "John Barnes says it's a well-known station, does conspiracy theories."

He listened and then said, "Yes. Yes. Yes. I'm going to send you a text message with an image of the scratch pad . . ."

THE SCRATCH PAD was the find of the day. Lucas and Virgil hung around until late afternoon, talking to agents and ERT specialists, without being much help. Other than the gun they found in the safe, and the one under Osborne's body, they found no other weapons.

"Didn't keep evidence around, is what he didn't do," the specialist said. "If he hadn't been killed by Zhao, or whoever, we wouldn't have had anything here to pin him with."

The feds had brought in food from a catering service, and Virgil and Lucas pecked at it during the course of the afternoon, but when nothing else significant came up, after the scratch pad, Lucas suggested they get something real to eat and figure out their next move.

"We can stop by tomorrow morning and see if there's anything more. I want to get online and research this WOR," Lucas told Clark. "You can't kill a radio station—we need to know who the target is. The guy. The specific guy."

An agent who'd been listening in said, "Maybe he goes into the station with an automatic weapon. Kills a bunch of people."

"Not really the Five's style," Virgil said. "I suppose it's possible, but it would be a suicide run and the other members of the Five have been very careful. And most stations have security now . . . I dunno. It's a head-scratcher."

They left Osborne's as it was getting dark, went back to their rooms at the Travelodge, called home, took showers, went out on the Internet to read about WOR. At six-thirty, as they were eating at the Greek-flavored café, Mallard called.

"I heard about the WOR thing. This can't happen. We have to get to the JFK guy before he kills whoever it is he's targeting."

Lucas: "You want us to go to New York?"

"I want you to stop an attack on WOR and I want you to catch Zhao and I think New York is the best bet. She seems to be contacting the various Five members. She's already done SFO, she killed MSP and CLE, the next closest place is JFK. Cleveland is less than a day's drive from Manhattan. A lot closer than New Orleans."

"They haven't had any coordinated, two-person killings as far as we know," Virgil said. "If she's going there, it's for money, or maybe to eliminate the JFK guy so he can't testify against her, but it won't be connected to an attack on WOR."

"Still, it's all converging on New York," Mallard said. "I've talked to the assistant director there, who I believe you both know . . ."

"Yeah, he doesn't like us," Lucas said.

"A little rain must fall in everyone's life, although you two guys are more like a shitstorm, but that's neither here nor there," Mallard said. "I want you up there. Go to the radio station, stir things up, see what comes out of it. I'll have tickets for you tomorrow and a car will meet you at LaGuardia."

"Not too early in the morning," Lucas said.

Mallard rang off and they finished dinner, talking about the problems New York might pose, including the fact that the Manhattan assistant FBI director *really* didn't like them. By eight, they were back in their rooms. Lucas watched a movie and Virgil got out his laptop and worked on an outline for the next chapter in his second novel. At eleven they were both in bed, Virgil asleep, Lucas not quite.

In that not-quite state, his eyes opened and he said, aloud, "Uh-oh."

He called Virgil, who answered, groggily, "What happened?"

"I had a thought," Lucas said.

"Any chance it could have waited until tomorrow?"

Lucas ignored the comment. "Remember when the Osborne press release said, 'You'll know his face'? And you said, 'Radio stations don't have faces'?"

"Yeah, I remember all that clearly. Can I go back to sleep now?"

"You were right," Lucas said. "I was lying here in the dark trying to think of a radio face that I know. There's Soucheray in the Twin Cities, but that's about it, and I mostly remember his face because of his columns in the newspaper. And maybe a billboard."

"Okay . . . So what?"

"So I started thinking, WOR. And I thought, Woody Rap. Or, as he sometimes refers to himself, Woodrow Orion Rap."

Woody Rap had a ten o'clock cable television talk show out of New York City; his florid, jowl-wagging face was known across the country.

Virgil sat up in bed: "Sonofabitch. WOR. You think?"

"He's got a face. He's in New York. He's a fruitcake. He's the guy who told us COVID was seeded in the U.S. by Democrats trying to pull down Trump. That the Joint Chiefs of Staff were all communists and that's why the military didn't intervene to stop the election from being stolen by Biden."

"Lucas, I gotta think he's about a hundred times more likely to be a target than some fuckin' radio station," Virgil said.

"We'll talk to Mallard in the morning. But *think* about this. I don't know that Rap's ever called himself WOR. And the radio station would be a hell of a target."

"But Rap does use all three names, and Osborne used the initials of the other victims, too. You nailed it. It's not a fuckin' radio station. It's just not. It's Woodrow Orion Rap."

TWENTY-EIGHT

Mallard's assistants got Lucas and Virgil a flight out of Cleveland to LaGuardia airport in New York City at one o'clock in the afternoon, but Clark, who was the Osborne on-site supervisor, knocked on their doors at eight o'clock to invite them to a nine o'clock briefing at the FBI field office in downtown Cleveland.

They made it, not by much, parked in front of the brick and concrete FBI lump on Lakeside Avenue and crossed through a black steel picket fence and into the building.

Henry Moore, the AIC, had turned the briefing over to an assistant who summarized all the evidence so far turned up in all the Five killings, which amounted to nothing in San Francisco and Houston, closed cases in the Twin Cities and Cleveland, and the open possibility in New York.

When the assistant was finished, Moore stood up to say, "The

New York office is already coordinating closely with WOR. This is a delicate situation because we would prefer that the killer approach the station without attacking it: we want to catch him in the act, but before he does any damage. The WOR people, of course, are interested in eliminating any possibility of damage or injuries, but we have pointed out to them that if there is an obvious increase in security, then the killer may simply back away and attack later. It's not a situation where we can provide a security blanket forever, although the WOR executives don't seem to appreciate that."

An agent raised a hand and asked, "Will any of us be going to New York to supplement their security effort?"

Moore shook his head: "No. New York is confident that they have it under control."

Another agent: "What about Zhao? We were talking about it yesterday afternoon with the marshals . . ." He waved a hand at Lucas and Virgil ". . . and we agreed that there wasn't any necessary connection between her and an attack on WOR. So . . . what are we doing about that?"

Moore said, "There's no reason to think she stuck around here, with Osborne dead. She's on the road, somewhere, and where that is, your guess is as good as mine."

Another agent: "If she gets to New York City . . . I looked it up on Google last night and there are more than a million ethnic Asians in New York, most of them in the city. Half a million ethnic Asian women . . ."

"That's certainly a serious problem," Moore said, with a hint in his voice suggesting that while it *was* a serious problem, it wasn't *their* serious problem. "Anyone else?"

Virgil looked at Lucas, and Lucas raised his hand. Moore pointed at him. "Marshal?"

"Woody Rap," Lucas said.

Moore frowned. "What about him?"

"He lives in New York City, or around there, I believe. When he's feeling extra pompous, which he is about once a night, he likes to proclaim himself to be Woodrow Orion Rap. WOR."

A smattering of conversation sprang up around the room, like a winter breeze, and Moore put a hand to his lips, then said, "Oh . . . that's . . . interesting."

Virgil: "The press release from the Five said we'd recognize the next victim's face. I don't recognize anyone from the radio station, even though they're famous, but I do know Woody Rap's face."

Moore: "I will talk to Washington as soon as we get out of here. Actually, I'll talk to them right now. I believe Deputy Director Mallard is keeping a close eye on developments . . ."

"He is," Lucas said. "But we haven't spoken to him about this. We haven't talked to him since last night."

"I will see if I can get through to him now," Moore said. He turned to his assistant: "You've got it, Jack. I'll be in my office."

The briefing went on for another fifteen minutes, mostly repetitive questions and speculations about Woody Rap, with several agents using laptops to go out to Google or Bing or to the FBI's own information system. When they broke up, Lucas and Virgil walked out to the elevators and were waiting there when Mallard called.

"I'm told you two had a finger in the whole Woodrow Orion Rap pie, and may have baked it yourselves," he said.

"That was Lucas," Virgil said. "He's right."

"It's a distinct possibility and we'll be discussing it with the assistant director in New York. You guys figure out what you want to do, but whatever that is, stay in touch, because we'll have agents doing the same thing. We'll be watching over both Rap and the radio station."

Lucas: "It's Rap."

"I lean that way," Mallard said. "But hypothetically, if the attack is on Rap, and we screw up and he's killed, that's one man. If it's on the radio station, and we screw up, then it could be a massacre. We have to juggle those priorities."

"When you talk to New York, you might do well to keep our names out of it," Virgil suggested.

"Can't do that," Mallard said. "You'll have to coordinate with our people there. If you don't, and you start hanging around Rap, and you're spotted, there could be some confusion about who is who . . . I don't want you accidentally shooting one of my agents. Or vice versa."

"We'll check in with them," Lucas said. "I can tell you right now, we'll be covering Rap, not the station."

THEY FLEW TO New York that afternoon, shouldering their way through the jammed-up corridors of LaGuardia, stopping only to take a leak in a bathroom that resembled that of a Shell station in the 1930s, the floor so wet that they splashed going in and out. They found the agent waiting for them in the baggage claim area, and he drove them, without much in the way of conversation, to the Manhattan FBI headquarters at Federal Plaza. After passing through a few functionaries, they met with the FBI assistant director, Ransom Kelly, in an office decorated with framed law degrees and a basketball signed by Kareem Abdul-Jabbar.

Ransom was a slender man in a good blue pinstriped suit who looked like he got slender by diet, rather than by exercise; he wore round steel-rimmed glasses that gave him a professorial air, and he knew it. When he opened his mouth to speak, he seemed to have two thousand small pearly teeth. He didn't like Lucas and Virgil, and they didn't like him, a stress point that went back to the year before, and a case involving heroin distribution, murder, and the Mafia.

"You know you guys piss me off," Kelly said, as Virgil and Lucas took guest chairs. "I never particularly cared for the Marshals Service and I have no idea what some backwoods Minnesota deputy is doing roaming around with you, Marshal Davenport . . ."

"We got you on TV with a big pile of heroin. You never thanked us for that, though you seemed to enjoy taking all the credit for the arrests," Virgil snapped. "Lucas has handled more murders than all the FBI agents in this building put together, and I probably have, too, so don't give us that superior FBI shit. Every real cop we know thinks you guys are a joke."

"Picking up a bunch of fuckin' dummies who shot a bunch of other fuckin' dummies with street guns over a five-dollar bag of crack, and then ran home to their mommies, that doesn't interest me," Kelly said.

Lucas opened his mouth and stood and Kelly pointed at him and said, "Shut up. I know what I gotta do and I don't like it. Deputy Director Mallard says you guys want to cover Woody Rap and I gotta send some of my own people out there with you. I don't like that, either, but I'll do it."

"And while you surround some fuckin' radio station with as many agents as you can, we'll probably save your bacon by saving Woody Rap's bacon," Virgil said.

Kelly held up both hands: "So we've established that we don't like each other. Good enough. Now . . ."

He had an intercom and pushed a button and said, "Is Orish out there?"

A mechanical voice said, "Yes."

"Send her in."

Kate Orish pushed through the door so quickly that she must have been waiting right outside. A tall woman with reddish hair, she was wearing a muted gray-green suit that set off her eyes. She looked at Lucas and Virgil and said, to Kelly, "Sir," and to Lucas, "Marshal Davenport." She and Lucas knew each other fairly well, and she'd met Virgil briefly during a series of narcotics and murder trials in South Florida and nodded to him, as though she didn't remember his name.

Kelly said, "Okay, Orish, you've been briefed, you know these two . . . officers . . . so, take them in hand and stay in touch. I understand you'll be working out on Long Island, so keep Susan Thomas informed about what you're doing."

"I will do that," Orish said.

She turned to Lucas and Virgil, but before she could speak, Kelly said, "Then go," and he swiveled to a desktop computer and poked a key.

Orish led the way out; Lucas got to the door and turned and said, "So, Assistant Director Kelly, I just wanted to say on behalf of Virgil and myself, go fuck yourself."

He pulled the door shut and Orish stood there for a moment, eyes closed. When she opened them, she said, "I can't believe I heard that."

"Well, you did," Lucas said. "How have you been, Kate?"

"Up until a couple of minutes ago, I was feeling good," she said. "I don't mind that you said that, I just didn't want to be known to have heard it. We need to talk. How have you been, Virgil?"

"Until a couple of minutes ago, I was feeling good," Virgil said. To Lucas: "We've got to get her promoted to a Washington job so she can kick some Kelly ass."

Orish held a finger up in front of Virgil's nose: "Do not let anyone hear you say that. Not in this building. Or anywhere else."

Virgil: "Yes, ma'am. I will do everything I can to show some respect for that prick."

Orish said, "Okay. Susan Thomas runs the Long Island district office. We'll be calling on some of her agents, as well as some from here and Connecticut."

Lucas asked, "What's this about Long Island? Woody Rap has a house in Manhattan, right?"

"And a place in Suffolk County, which he doesn't talk about on TV," Orish said. "He's supposed to be a man of the people. If the people found out he has a twenty-room mansion in the Hamptons, surrounded by several square miles of incredibly rich liberals, he might lose some of his credibility with the nutjobs. He's got a studio out there, along with the one here in the city, but he calls the Hamptons site his 'bunker.' On TV it looks like a bunker. None of the viewers get to see the rest of the house."

Orish took them to her office, a bland cubicle decorated, like Kelly's, with framed law degrees, but without the basketball. She sat behind her desk and pointed them at her two guest chairs, turned to her computer, clicked on something she'd already found, and swiveled the computer screen so they could see it.

"He lives here," she said, tapping the screen with the eraser end of a yellow pencil. The screen showed a satellite photo of a piece of

eastern Long Island not far from the shore, and a house with a mul-
tilevel roof. "It's in an area called Sagaponack. He has, according to
the Suffolk County assessor's office, two-point-two acres, on which
he has the aforesaid mansion, a large swimming pool, a tennis court,
and a studio, which you can see here."

"Holy cats, he's draggin' in the big bucks," Virgil said, peering
at the photo.

"Yes, he does, but he also has a big mortgage. Though, with a
three percent interest rate, it's like getting a free house. I looked
up the sales price of his place, when he bought it six years ago, and it's
about doubled in value, so there's that."

"All for selling bullshit on TV," Virgil marveled.

"He's not only selling bullshit, he's selling some dangerous over-
the-counter medications that he supposedly takes himself, but
doesn't," Orish said. "Because if he did, he'd be dead."

"Have you talked to him yet?" Lucas asked.

"We have. He's worried. He's venal but not stupid. He has a town
house here in Manhattan and we wanted to keep him there, because
we thought we'd have the best chance of grabbing JFK, whoever he
is. He disagreed, with, I have to admit, some justification. He lives
on a narrow street here in the city without much traffic at all, and
our protection people would have to be inside of something. Inside
vans, inside apartments . . . He's afraid some casual passerby would
gun him down before we could react."

"But we would catch that guy," Virgil said.

"And he'd be dead. He'd prefer he not be dead," Orish said.

"New York people are so entitled," Lucas said.

"I can't see that he'd be much better off in Saga-whatsis," Virgil
said. "The place looks tough, fences, hedges, all kinds of obstructions

like those pools and the tennis courts . . . I see a few walls . . . lots of trees . . . parts of it are almost like a forest. Guy could go sliding through there like grease through a goose. I think Osborne could have done it. Even McGruder, with those ninja lessons he was taking . . ."

"It's not a forest . . . there's lots of grass and other stuff out there . . . certainly not the Northwoods," Orish said. "It's one of the most groomed, wired-up places in the country. Those are very rich people, with overlapping security systems, cameras everywhere, anti-intrusion radar . . . everything you can think of. A killer, a stalker, wouldn't have to worry only about the target's property, he'd have to worry about every property he crossed. Every step he took."

She reached out and fiddled with the keyboard and brought up street-view photos. "This is right outside his driveway. You can see he has a hedge around the house. So do most of the houses in the neighborhood. You don't want to be in a gunfight in there, especially not after dark. A shooter could hide anywhere, you wouldn't see him if he was six feet away."

Virgil: "Maybe we need dogs . . ."

Orish snapped her fingers: "Good thought. We've got dogs, somewhere, but I don't know if they could warn us about somebody approaching you . . . maybe a search and rescue dog could. Most of our dogs are for detecting explosives and so on. I'll check."

"How many people will we be working with?" Lucas asked.

"Twelve agents. Three shifts of four agents each, covering him around the clock, plus you two, whenever you want to be on-site. Rap has also ordered up a private armed security service, ex–New York City cops. There'll be two ex-cops for two shifts a day, from early morning to late evening, seven to eleven. He can lock down his house overnight—if somebody comes for him then, it'd be a smash and shoot."

"Will we get to meet him?" Virgil asked.

"Yes. Tomorrow morning. If the Five killer is on schedule, he won't make an attempt for another day or two," Orish said. "With the McGruder and Osborne killings, JFK might go early. Or he might call it off, for now, anyway. We'd prefer he didn't do that. We don't need Rap to get shot six months from now."

"All right. We got us a trap," Lucas said, sitting back in his chair. "And JFK shouldn't know we're even out there."

They arranged to ride out to the Long Island FBI offices the next morning with Orish, where they would get an unmarked surveillance car to work from. Lucas had arranged to get rooms at a Holiday Inn in the financial district, where Orish would pick them up.

When they'd said goodbye to her, and were walking to the elevators, Lucas said, "Steak house . . ."

"Mmm, I, uh, have a dinner date," Virgil said.

"What?"

"I called my agent from the Cleveland airport. We're going to get together at some place on the Upper East Side."

"Maybe I should come along as your advisor," Lucas said.

"I don't think so," Virgil said. "All I need is some Davenport bullshit to knock me out of the book business. I don't know how late I'll be, but I'd recommend that you go to bed early. We got that stuff coming from the Marshals Service, and Orish is coming for us at eight."

"That *is* an unnaturally early hour," Lucas said. "All right. And hey: watch your mouth. You don't want any of that Flowers' hick-wit on display. Show her the straight-up Midwestern work ethic: you're good for twenty books, maybe more, you're humble, intelligent, and you wash your hands every time you pee. You've already got it in the bag, don't lose it now."

"Ah, Jesus, I did have it under control, and now you're freaking me out," Virgil said. "Tie or no tie? Wait, I don't have a tie . . ."

"I've got several with me," Lucas said. "We'll find one that goes with your eyes."

TWENTY-NINE

The ride the next morning, to Melville, where the Long Island branch of the New York City FBI was located, was tedious, not without some contention, and way too early, in Lucas' opinion.

Even earlier that morning, Lucas had taken delivery of a tan canvas bag from the New York Marshals Service office. The bag clanked when he dropped it in the back of Orish's Tahoe.

"What's in there?" Orish asked.

"You know, protective equipment, vests, night-vision stuff, helmets in case we need them . . ."

"That didn't sound like Kevlar to me. That sounded like guns," Orish said.

"Maybe some guns," Lucas said.

"Ah, boy. What kind of guns?"

"Maybe some . . . shotguns?"

"Ah, boy."

When they got past the discussion of the contents of the equipment bag, Lucas asked about Virgil's date with the literary agent and Virgil said they'd gotten along well enough.

"She told me that I had to push now. I've got a start, and now I've got to push hard. More books, better books. She says I need to develop a shelf—you know, a bookstore shelf of paperbacks that'll catch the eye of browsers and will keep selling for years. That's apparently a moneymaker for publishers. Christ, I have trouble thinking about what I'm doing next week, much less thinking about getting six or eight books out . . ."

"You sit in a chair and type, so what's the problem?" Lucas said. "You got all kinds of actual stories you can throw in around your plot, to give it a real-life feel, even if the main story is complete horseshit, which it probably is."

"Yeah, yeah, she even mentioned that," Virgil said. "She liked the true-crime kinda characters, street characters. She said it gave the novel a certain tactility."

"Don't make your hero into superman," Orish said, from the driver's seat. "I hate that. You know, they're in thirty-two gunfights in three days against a hundred terrorists and get a flesh wound in the shoulder. They ought to be getting blisters on their trigger fingers. And, I'd like to point out, no hero ever gets shot in the balls."

"Yeah, I'm not doing that," Virgil said. "My big problem now is that I'm supposed to be thinking about WOR and all the possibilities around him and all I can really think about is *Blood Moon Rising*."

Lucas: "What?"

"The second book," Virgil said.

"That's a stupid title," Lucas said. "Who thought of that?"

"I did," Virgil said.

"I think it's a fine title," Orish said, unconvincingly.

Virgil pressed a palm against his forehead: "Oh, Jesus, the first two people I tell the title to, they think it sucks."

"It doesn't suck," Orish said. "But yesterday I was listening to that James Taylor song, 'Fire and Rain,' and I was thinking, that'd be a good name for a novel."

"What, I steal 'Fire and Rain' for a title, and James Taylor cries himself to sleep at night, knowing I stole it? How would I live with myself?" Virgil asked.

"Goes on the bestseller list, you'd probably manage," Lucas said. "And it's a lot better than *Bloody Moon Rising*."

"'Blood Moon,'" Virgil said.

"See? I already forgot the title."

THEY WORE OUT that topic, and Lucas, paging through a stack of Wikipedia printouts that Orish had given him, about Rap, said, "I don't want to read all this shit. Just tell me."

"I've talked to him twice, in person. He's possibly the most cynical person I've ever met—he knows that medical stuff he sells on his show is junk, but he does it anyway, because he wants the money. He laughs all the time, especially on his TV show, but he's not funny, he only thinks he is. What he is . . . he won't deny it, if you accuse him of it—is a fascist. I'm not overstating that: he believes in a system of government that has a strongman at the top, ruling the place. He sees himself as a latter-day Goebbels, ready to follow the leader into the storm . . ."

She went on a while, and when she finished, Virgil muttered, just loud enough, "Fuckin' deep-state libtard."

"I'm *so* not a libtard that I usually don't even vote," Orish said. "Though, I'm embarrassed to admit that, I guess."

THE FBI HEADQUARTERS in Melville were in the most modern FBI building that Lucas had ever seen, like an enormous white calcium pill. They met with Susan Thomas, the agent in charge of the office, in what looked like a classroom, with the other agents assigned to the WOR problem. They discussed the work shifts at Rap's house and physical areas of responsibility. A video projector put large-scale high-resolution satellite photos of Rap's house on a pull-down screen.

"The problem with the photos is that they don't show what's hidden by the tree canopies," Thomas said, using a red laser pointer to tap key points in the photo. "If Rap is the target, we would like JFK to come in on him, so we can intercept him. That means we can't do a lot of last-minute reconnaissance, because if JFK is doing the same thing, he could spot us. So, we sneak in, hide our cars, and when we're in position, we stay in position. We assume if JFK attacks Rap, he'll do it at night, because an attacker would be too obvious in daylight. So, we're looking for movement, at night, closing on Rap's house."

"What if he comes in at two o'clock in the afternoon disguised as a FedEx guy?" somebody asked.

"Then he'll probably kill Rap," Orish said, "because anybody who could get a FedEx truck is too smart for us."

Virgil and Lucas looked at each other, then Orish added, "He has bodyguards who answer the door. With guns."

"Will us night guys have access to night-vision equipment?" one of the agents asked.

"Yes. We don't have enough sets for everybody, so you'll have to hand off your goggles to your relief agent at the end of your shift," Thomas said.

She looked at Lucas and Virgil: "Do the marshals have experience with night-vision goggles?"

Lucas and Virgil both nodded and said, "Yes," and Lucas said, "We have our own. We have quite a bit of gear from the Marshals Service, including vests and the night-vision stuff."

"And shotguns," Orish said.

"Shotguns may not be optimal," Thomas said.

Lucas: "Will your guys have rifles? Or are you going with shotguns and sidearms?"

"Sidearms," Thomas said. "The distances will be short—you can't see very far if you're on the ground out there—so pistols should be sufficient. I hope you have been trained . . ."

"I mostly work with shotguns, when I need a weapon," Virgil said. "So yeah, I'm good."

"So am I," Lucas said.

Thomas shook her head and then said, "Okay. I hope you're right. I'm aware that you're both extremely experienced. Remember, we will have a lot of people out there . . . and we would prefer to effect an arrest without gunfire, of course. When you're out there you mostly see trees, bushes, and hedges, but it's densely populated, as you can see from the satellite views. You might not be able to see a house because it's screened by all the foliage, but it's there. Rifles would be a serious problem."

"Especially if you don't want to kill a rich guy while he's drinking his martini six blocks away," someone chipped in.

"That's exactly right," Thomas said. "Now, let's make sure everybody is up to date on our radio protocols . . ."

LUCAS AND VIRGIL were given a blue Camry to drive to Rap's house. Orish rode along in the back seat, leaving the ponderous Tahoe at the FBI headquarters. The car smelled of pizza, cheeseburgers, and tortilla chips, which was to be expected in a surveillance car, but was missing the normally required Ding Dong or Hostess Snoball wrappers.

"Smells like real cops were in here," Lucas said to Virgil.

From the back seat, Orish said, "Fuck you."

Virgil: "She's loosening up."

Orish said, "Virgil, try not to be too much of a wiseass with Rap. He's an easy target, I know, but we don't need him pissed off. We want him cooperative."

"I can do that, be nice," Virgil said.

THEY SPENT TWENTY minutes rolling around the neighborhood, pointing out tactical considerations.

Virgil: "You notice the streetlights?"

Lucas: "Yeah. There aren't any."

Virgil had said he could be polite to Rap, but a half hour later, he wasn't sure of that. Rap was a tall, fat, bald man wearing cutoff jeans that could have been used as a hot-air balloon, under a tent-like white dress shirt that fell nearly to his knees. He was wearing a leather thong around his neck with a turquoise dodad on it and a turquoise bracelet on one hairy forearm.

He never stopped talking.

"What you guys don't realize is that I'm on the same side as the Five. We need to kill assholes: that's what I'm talking about. Killing assholes. Not that I'd do it myself because I'm a live-and-let-live kind of guy, but honest to sweet Jesus Christ if you were gonna shoot assholes, New York would be the happy hunting grounds. You could open fire in Times Square and start mowing people down and nine out of ten would be assholes blah blah blah blahblahblahblah . . ."

Orish slowed him down when she said, "We're asking you not to go out on that front balcony. If the killer is really out there, he could have a .50-caliber with 300-grain expanding bullets that if it hit you in the chest would leave nothing but a few scraps of bacon out in the backyard . . ."

Rap: "Say what?"

She took the break to introduce the three supervising agents on the three shifts that would be watching the house, plus Virgil and Lucas. Rap introduced his two beefy bodyguards on the seven-to-three shift, battered-looking ex–New York City cops, who, he said, had been hired "to make a point that you don't fuck with Woodrow Orion Rap."

"Does that mean that they're going to kill this JFK if they have a chance?" Orish asked.

"Only to save innocent life," one of the ex-cops said, who said it in the odd New York way, with half-hooded eyes that meant he was lying and he knew you knew it and they would empty their seventeen-shot mags into any motherfucker who tried to get close to the client.

Lucas nodded at him and said, "Glad to have you."

The other beefy ex-cop said to Virgil, "We looked you up. You done okay, that thing last year. Shooting down an airplane; made me laugh."

They spent an hour figuring out who would be where, and for how long. The two ex-cops would be inside the house, blocking access to Rap wherever he might go inside. Four agents would be at key points around the lawn, concealed in landscape shrubbery, wearing night-vision goggles. Orish would be inside the house, in the parlor, monitoring radios and feeding information to the agents outside. Lucas suggested that they might be too static and might do better with a couple of people wandering around.

"We have infrared armbands that you could wear that would identify you for any of our agents wearing night-vision goggles, if you want to wander," Orish said. "Of course, if JFK has night-vision goggles, you'd jump out like neon signs."

"I don't want them—there'll be enough light around with the moon and all the houses that it'll never be completely dark," Virgil said. "We'll work it so Lucas and I stay at least a couple of backyards away from Mr. Rap's house. If we see somebody coming in, we can call you, then let him through, and have him boxed."

"It can get real fuckin' dark out there," Rap said. "I was out a couple weeks ago at night and walked into a tree branch that goddamn near scalped me. Bleedin' like a stuck pig. Poured half a bottle of Strane Ultra Uncut on my head to sterilize the wound."

One of the ex-cops, eyeballs sucked back in his skull: "You poured gin on your head?"

"Goddamn right. Eighty-two percent alcohol. Three drinks a day stops Covid in its tracks."

At the end, Orish said to Rap, "At night, if you simply sit and watch your television until you go to bed, or go down to your gym, or get an escort to your studio, or sit in the living room and talk on your phone, you'll be perfectly safe. Don't show yourself. There's only a small chance that JFK is even after you, but there's a chance, and you should be careful."

"My middle name is 'careful,'" Rap said. He did a spit-take and said, "Oh, wait. My middle name is Orion." He thought that was hilarious, and proved it by strolling through the house, issuing bursts of laughter, trailed by his cops.

LUCAS, VIRGIL, AND Orish were staying at a motel called the Royce. On the way there, Orish looked at her phone and muttered, "We didn't get the drone. The drone's up in Boston, they've got something going on and they wouldn't let us have it. I don't think we'll get the dogs, either. They're over at WOR—the radio station."

"The FBI has drones?" Virgil asked.

"Of course. Why wouldn't we?"

"I don't know," Virgil said. "It just . . . I don't know."

"What are you guys planning to do until dark?" Orish asked.

Lucas said he planned to watch movies, talk to his wife and kids, and take a nap since they'd be up all night. Virgil said he would break out his laptop and lay down some words on the newly renamed *Fire and Rain*, and talk to Frankie and the kids and maybe take a nap.

"What kind of authentic stories will you tell?" Orish asked. "Since

I'm one of those people that real cops think are a joke, I'd like to know what I'm missing."

"I wasn't talking about you, Kate," Lucas said.

"Yes, you were."

Virgil: "I've been thinking about that, the stories. And I'm thinking one might be, the dog shock collars on toddlers."

"That would be a good one," Lucas agreed. To Orish: "I've heard this story."

"I'm not sure I want to," Orish said. "But go ahead."

There was an asshole in a small town in southwest Minnesota, Virgil said, who reasoned that he could best discipline his three children by equipping them with shock collars meant for training dogs. He had the power turned all the way up so the kids would get a serious jolt, enough to leave burn scars on their necks.

"How old were they?" Orish asked.

"Mmm, this was a few years back, but it seems to me they were three, four, and five at the time."

Orish: "Oh my God. You busted him and he's in prison . . ."

"No, I never met him," Virgil said. "I didn't hear about it until the problem had been solved . . . maybe a year later, or a little more than that."

"If you didn't . . ."

"The older kid was sent away to kindergarten and the teacher spotted the burns. This was in a do-it-yourself part of southwestern Minnesota. Instead of calling the cops, she told the hockey coach, and as I got the story, the coach and a bunch of his players got a bunch of Taser stun batons—possibly from the local sheriff's department, though the sheriff denies it. They put on ski masks and went over to the guy's house and had a Taser party. These weren't the shooting kind of guns, but the ones that look like flashlights and you press them against somebody's body. I'm told they pressed them against some pretty shocking parts of the guy's body. He left town shortly thereafter, to parts unknown, which is why I never got involved."

"I just spotted a reason you shouldn't tell that story in a novel," Lucas said. "It takes too long. It'd break up the flow of the book."

"You know what really breaks up a book?" Orish asked. "Sex. I mean I like a good shower scene as much as anyone, but not in a thriller. You're galloping along at a hundred miles an hour and then you slow down to a crawl for the in-and-out. If you're going to put sex in a book, make it a slow read to begin with, not a fast one. Something sultry."

"I will take that under advisement," Virgil said.

Orish said, "Well, if you plan to ignore my advice, my further advice would be to make the sex really kinky."

ALL THREE OF them spent the rest of the daylight hours at the Royce, trying unsuccessfully to get some decent sleep, but dozing at least part of the time, eating junk food from a machine, swilling diet sodas, watching CNN, CNBC, Fox, and MSNBC. Virgil put down a thousand words on *Fire and Rain*, while Orish spent the day talking on the telephone to anxious FBI bureaucrats who found themselves in an unwanted line of fire. She took a half-dozen calls from Assistant Director Kelly, who told her things that she already knew.

Lucas caught a romantic comedy on HBO Max that sucked, he

said, "because I saw the whole thing coming after the first two minutes. How in the hell can you have a romantic comedy when the two main characters are totally unlikable?"

"Maybe they were likable to everyone else, but not to you," Virgil suggested.

"No, they were unlikable. Period," Lucas said. "And you know what? The sex scenes slowed down the story."

"Told you," Orish said.

Virgil said he'd seen a movie called *We're the Millers* and enjoyed it.

"Romantic comedy?" Lucas asked.

"Sorta. About a group of unrelated people forming a family," Virgil said, his voice suspiciously flat.

"Sounds dull," Lucas said.

"Well, you'll probably want to get your kids and Weather and check it out," Virgil said. "There aren't that many movies entire families can enjoy."

RAP HAD A four-car garage, but only two cars, so they put the Camry in one of the empty stalls, where it would be out of sight; the other stall would be used by the senior agent on each shift, who'd bring three more agents with him. The New York cops came in a single car, which could be effectively hidden in a courtyard, not visible from the street.

When they'd all gathered at nightfall, they re-rehearsed exactly what everybody would be doing. The senior agent, whose name was Cothran, warned them all against falling asleep: "It's gonna be boring, you're not going to be able to move much, everybody's got sweaters and heavy coats, so you'll probably be warm. That can make you sleepy, but you can't fall asleep. I'll be beeping you every so often and I want you to beep back instantly . . ."

They had agreed that the attack, if there were one, would most likely come from the back of the house, rather than the front or the sides, because the cover was thicker in the back, and escape routes easier to lay out. The sides and front of the house would be well covered by the agents in the corners of the yard and would be protected from longer shots by the adjacent houses. From the back, a shooter could be three or four hundred yards away, if he climbed a high enough tree, or got on a rooftop, and could still see the back windows of Rap's house, which included the master bedroom.

"We'll keep the blinds down in the bedroom, avoid silhouettes," Orish said.

Before they went out, Cothran distributed fleece-covered cushions meant for deer stand seats, to put on the ground beneath them; the air temperature was expected to fall to twenty degrees and the ground was frozen solid. The cushions had belts so the agents could secure them around their waists, leaving their hands free when walking, but still have the cushion when they stopped walking and took up a new stand.

"The big brains in DC think if JFK comes after WOR, it'll be in the deep dark, two to four a.m.," Orish said, pronouncing Rap's name as *War*. "Keep that in mind . . . don't let your guard down early."

The shift would change at midnight; Orish would work both nighttime shifts, as would Virgil and Lucas.

At six-thirty, the four agents who would post themselves at the corners of Rap's yard went out through a side door into the court-yard where the cops' car was parked and disappeared into the dark. Rap came down to watch, and said, "Get him, boys."

Lucas and Virgil followed ten minutes later, night-vision goggles clamped uncomfortably over watch caps. The images coming through the sensors were different than the goggles they'd used in Minnesota and were white rather than green, but easily un-derstandable. They were equipped with eye cups to eliminate side-glow. Both Lucas and Virgil carried Remington 870 twelve-gauge shotguns with optical reflex sights, and two six-round maga-zines each, the shells loaded with #00 buckshot, as well as their sidearms.

As previously agreed, Orish warned the agents in the yard that Lucas and Virgil would be coming through. They walked together to the back of the yard, marked by a hedge but no fence, pushed through the hedge at a thin spot, crossed a neighbor's backyard, walked through a marshy area that had frozen solid, pushed through another hedge, across a tennis court to the end of that yard, and through the next hedge, where they sat down.

There was not much to see. The sky was partly cloudy, so stars appeared only intermittently. A waning moon was up and threw moon shadows, when it wasn't behind a cloud; the shadows some-times seemed to be moving shapes. Orish would talk to them occa-sionally, through their earbuds, and Cothran would beep them and they'd beep back.

Virgil was behind what he thought might be a lilac bush, dense and leafless. He sat cross-legged part of the time, stretched out from time to time, his shotgun across his lap. He had a shell in the chamber.

There'd be no TV-style shotgun ratcheting noise before he was ready to fire.

Lucas had no idea of what kind of bush he was in, just that it was short and had a spray of delicate limbs that nearly surrounded him. There was little wind, and both he and Virgil had wrapped their necks in woolen scarves and were warm enough.

From their spots next to the hedge, they could see lights going on and off in the surrounding houses, slowly migrating from lower floors to upper floors as people moved upstairs into bedrooms. At least two of the houses were probably empty, as they showed lights going on and off at predictable intervals, as though on timers.

At eight o'clock, they could hear some banging around from a few hundred feet farther ahead of where they were, and then the odor of steaks being cooked on a charcoal grill. Cars went quietly by on streets on the other sides of the houses they were behind.

The streets were in nothing like a grid, but wandered between houses on odd-shaped lots, and some that looked like streets weren't streets at all, but long private driveways, everything bordered by hedges. That geography would make the job harder for the agents at the sides of Rap's yard because an intruder might not be coming in at a predictable angle.

And so they sat, impatient, yawning, looking at their watches, dozing between beeps. A shift changed at midnight, which occasioned some talk about movement, but Lucas and Virgil stayed where they were. As in Northwoods deer hunting, they frequently imagined that the sun was coming up—that it was getting lighter in the east, when it wasn't.

Until finally, it was.

Traffic picked up, and then bigger shapes became visible, and lights began going on in the houses around them, and detailed shapes appeared.

That was the first night.

Nothing happened.

THIRTY

Sonnewell arrived at Lakefront Airport in New Orleans at 11:30 in the morning, where Carter picked him up.

"That your plane? The jet?" she asked, as Sonnewell wheeled a midsized Tumi suitcase across the tarmac toward her.

"No. Owning a plane is stupid. That's my analysis," Sonnewell said. "If you own a plane, you're more likely to die in a plane crash. You want a service that has newer planes and that flies a lot. Flies all the time. I've got a deal where I give them six hours' notice and they get me a plane that'll take me anywhere in the U.S. Europe is second-day."

"Sounds like a deal," Carter said, sizing him up as they went out to her car. She'd met him a few times at ABC conventions but never before had seen him when he wasn't wearing a suit and tie, with carefully styled hair. He was a big guy, rugged, tanned, brown hair now worn too long for a businessman. He had a faint accent that she would have identified as "farm." She knew he'd grown up on one; and he sounded a bit like the country singer Merle Haggard, who she liked.

Sonnewell was smart and rich and at an ABC convention, she'd heard him discussing modern European painting with some other art enthusiasts, and he seemed to know a lot about it. And those muscles . . . He was wearing a blue tee-shirt under a canvas overshirt, worn unbuttoned, jeans, boots, and a Raiders ball cap.

When they got to her car, a blue-gray Porsche Panamera, he threw his bag on the back seat and inside the car, said, "One of the good things about flying private is they don't ask if you've got silenced pistols in your bag."

"You do?"

"One. A .22, like Vivian used on Jamie McGruder. I did give her a compact nine-millimeter, which she probably used on Osborne. I shouldn't have done that, in retrospect. I should have settled her when I had the chance, but I didn't want to do it in my house."

"Afraid of ghosts?" Carter asked, with a smile.

"Blood spatter," Sonnewell said, returning the smile. "I hear it's hell to get out of real plaster walls."

Carter: "If you're ready, right now, I'd like to leave from here, instead of going back to my condo." She didn't want to say that she preferred that he not see exactly where she lived.

"I'm ready, let's go." As they were rolling out of the parking lot, Sonnewell asked, "I guess you've figured out how we'll do this?"

"Yes. For your approval—you can veto it if you want," Carter said. "When was the last time you were in a Macy's store?"

Sonnewell shrugged. "I don't know . . . maybe years ago? Anything I'd buy at a Macy's, I'd go online for."

"Okay. Well, I do go into Macy's every once in a long while. I can tell you, you could shoot a cannon off in those stores and not hit a clerk. Vivian is afraid of me and I'm a little afraid of her, but she wants money, and I've told her that I'm ready to supply it. And I've got it with me. In a buckskin backpack. Sort of elegant, to fit her mental scenario. I'll carry it over my shoulder when we meet, that's just in case killing her doesn't work out. And by the way, I don't want to do it here in New Orleans."

"I can understand that. Where do you want to do it?"

"Vivian and I agreed that the exchange should take place in public, where a gunfight would get noticed," she continued. "There's a Macy's store in a shopping center called Riverchase Galleria in Birmingham, Alabama. Birmingham is a five-hour drive from here and the mall is off I-65, which she'll be driving down from Cleveland. I'll call her and suggest that we meet there, in neutral territory, to deliver the money."

"You think we can kill somebody in a Macy's store and get away with it?" Sonnewell sounded amused.

"If we do it right," she said, her voice cool and serious. "We'll have to pick the spot, get her to go to it. I can cut her if I get the chance, or you could come up behind with a rope. Or if it's really vacant, we could risk a shot, if the .22 is quiet enough."

"It's not quiet, even with the suppressor on it, but it might be quiet enough," Sonnewell said. "I'll tell you, though, probably the best thing would be a hammer or a club, something heavy. A crowbar. Something where I could come up from behind and hit her. Quick and quiet and final. When she's down, you could use your razor as a backup."

"Huh. That'd work," Carter said. "I happen to know where there's a Home Depot in Slidell, we could stop there on the way out of town. They'd have what we need. I don't have a razor anymore, so I'd have to pick up a knife. I'm sure they have some."

"We'll need something to hide our faces. I've got a Tilley hat that will cover mine. If we won't look too weird, a Covid mask . . ."

"We're thinking along the same lines," Carter said. "I've got a brown felt cowboy hat. I don't like it, so I could burn it. And I've got Covid masks in two different colors."

"Great."

"I'll give her a call from Slidell," Carter said. "She'll be going through Birmingham this evening. She told me she needed some sleep, but then she'd drive the rest of the way straight down."

"What if she doesn't want you to pick the spot? What if she wants to go to one of those cinnamon roll places, if they got one there . . . or wherever?"

"I'll be willing to bet that she'll bite on Macy's," Carter said. "I mean, it sounds so big and public and out there . . . like the Macy's Christmas parade."

"Give her a call. See what she says," Sonnewell said. He'd slipped on a pair of aviator sunglasses, the better to look her over without giving too much away. She was seriously attractive, he thought. He hadn't paid too much attention to her appearance at the ABC conventions, which were overrun with attractive, hard-hustling women.

At this distance, with that southern comfort voice, he now thought she might be the most attractive, desirable, alluring woman he'd ever met. A striking raven-haired psychopath who could crack walnuts between the cheeks of her ass . . . the complete package.

She said, "That's an old Raiders hat you're wearing. I'd have thought you'd have burned it after they split for Vegas."

He said, "Naw, I'm still a Raiders guy," and he thought, *Oh my God, she even knows about the Raiders.*

ZHAO HAD BEEN tired when she arrived in Cleveland; by the time she left, after killing Osborne, she was beyond exhausted. She pressed south into the night, was dazzled by the lights of Columbus, but continued into the dark beyond.

At Cincinnati, she quit. She spotted a hospital parking structure, slotted herself between a couple of pickups, crawled into the back of the 4Runner and fell into an agitated sleep. She woke before noon, dug out some toothpaste and a bottle of water, cleaned out her mouth, washed her face with a towelette she'd bought at an all-night convenience store where she'd stopped for gas.

She had to eat something besides crap and took the time to drive through a McDonald's: a couple of cheeseburgers, fries, and more caffeine. Feeling better, she was back on the interstate when Carter called.

Carter said, "Your experience with Bill Osborne has probably freaked you out, so I don't want to sound too . . . directive . . . but I've got a spot where I think we could get together."

Zhao had two immediate unspoken responses: gratitude that she wouldn't have to think about a rendezvous, and suspicion that Carter might be setting her up. She'd insisted the night before on someplace public. If Carter now wanted to go somewhere private down in her hometown . . .

Trying to sound a bit eager, she said, "I am so . . . grateful for your help, Andi, honest to God, this has been the worst week of my life. At least SFO helped out. I don't know what Bill . . . anyway, where should we meet?"

"To be honest, I don't want to meet in my hometown . . . if you should get caught, I don't want the feds thinking too hard about Bitcoin money in New Orleans. Anyway, what would you think about a Macy's store in Birmingham, Alabama? You should be able to get there today without any trouble, as long as you got some sleep last night. I've never been in the store myself, but we'll figure out a spot to meet when we get there."

Zhao felt the relief flooding through her . . . tinted with a tiny remnant of suspicion. "If you've never been there, how'd you find it?"

"Looked it up on Google Maps."

Good answer, and believable, Zhao thought. "Okay. I'll find it on my phone . . . Is there only one Macy's store in Birmingham?"

"I don't know," Carter said. "This one is in the Riverchase Galleria."

"Let me call you back in five minutes—I'll tell you when I can get there," Zhao said. "I just left Cincinnati."

She spent five minutes thinking about Macy's as a meeting spot and looking up the Riverchase Galleria on her phone as she drove. The place did exist, and it did look busy, and it was a little more than seven hours away.

Even better, it would be less than three hours from the Atlanta airport, the single busiest airport in the country. With her good primary phony ID, which she'd already flown on, and a Covid mask, she could get almost anywhere in the country with one set of security checks.

She called Carter: "That Macy's looks perfect. I'm about seven hours away."

"I'm about six from my house and I can leave in a few minutes," Carter lied. "Call me when you get close."

"And we'll meet in the store."

"Absolutely. I'll hand you a leather backpack and keep walking . . . I kinda don't want to hang out and be seen with you, in case . . . you know. I put in a hundred K."

"Aw, Andi . . . thank you. I'll see you about eight o'clock. I understand about not being seen with me. I'll call you when I get there."

WHEN CARTER RANG off, Sonnewell was admiring: "You did that very well. Very well."

"Thank you. But . . . are we being too cavalier about this?" Carter asked.

"Yes. So far. We'll tighten up when we get to it. At least I did with Wiggins. Right now, we could turn around, go back home, and nothing happens. Even if we go to the mall, you could just hand over the money . . ."

Carter rubbed her nose, shook her head. "I think we'll do it. And I'm tightening up. But, we can call it off at the last minute. We'll keep that option in mind."

On the way out of New Orleans, they stopped at a Home Depot that Carter said should be renamed "The Murder Your Wife Depot"—everything you need: clubs, knives, saws, shovels, ropes, tubs, contractor-size heavy-duty plastic trash bags.

Sonnewell bought a crowbar, as long as his forearm with a crook at the end to add swing weight, and two pairs of thin translucent painting gloves. Carter went through the self-checkout, buying a razor scraper.

Back in the Panamera, they headed north toward Birmingham.

"Mind if I sleep?" Sonnewell asked after they'd chatted for a while.

"Go ahead. This is not the most scenic trip in America."

Sonnewell did sleep, peacefully and deeply, which Carter thought too trusting, because she was automatically paranoid. He woke instantly when Carter patted his thigh. "We're there. Almost."

THEY CIRCLED THE mall, spotted the Macy's, and parked at an angle to the entrance. They carried their hats until they were well away from the distinctive car, then put them on; they saw a few people wearing Covid masks, and Carter pointed them out, saying, "Must be the local Democrats."

"Like one in twenty," Sonnewell said. They put on the masks, and trying not to be too obvious about it, looked for cameras without seeing any.

Macy's was a Macy's, like most other mall Macy's. Two floors. They walked through both, separately, then met at the entrance to the main mall. Riverchase Galleria wasn't the largest of shopping centers, but the design was attractive, with an arching glass dome overhead and an expansive interior courtyard. They bought a cup of cinnamon sticks at an Auntie Anne's, and Sonnewell asked, "Well?"

"I saw a couple of possibilities, but they both had problems," Carter said. "Not entirely disqualifying, but we'd have to be careful."

"Then I may have the spot," Sonnewell said. "The Ralph Lauren display. What we'd have to do is, we'd have to see her coming. No matter what direction she comes from, I could hide on the other side of a curving display wall. You could stand at a place where she'd have to have her back to me. I step out, and *whack*. There's good cover, nobody immediately around, no clerks. If somebody's shopping there, that could be a problem."

"Then that's a problem . . ."

"Yeah, but nobody was shopping there while I was looking around. Nobody the whole time. I could not find a camera looking at the Lauren display section . . . If somebody did come in to shop, you could leave, call Vivian and tell her you were running a little late, you'd meet her there in a few minutes. Then you could come in from a good angle, get her looking away from me . . ."

"I'd have to see it. The shopper thing worries me."

"So circle back and take a look. I didn't see anything better."

They split up again and Carter went back to Macy's, looked at the Ralph Lauren display, decided that, like Sonnewell, she hadn't seen anything as good. Back together in the courtyard, she said, "I think that's the place. I didn't see any cameras either and there was nobody shopping. Maybe we should feel sorry for Ralph Lauren."

"I think he's probably doing all right," Sonnewell said. "No need for pity."

CARTER CALLED ZHAO: she said she was an hour out, or a little more. Actually, Zhao was no more than forty-five minutes out, but she wanted to show up early. She thought the money pickup should go fine, but her paranoia was acting up.

She saw the mall from the interstate, circled it as Carter and Sonnewell had done, found a parking space less than fifty feet from Carter's car, though she didn't know that. She walked into the store, wearing a ball cap and a mask, and started looking for the Ralph Lauren display.

Sonnewell was watching the entrance from the mall when Carter called and said, "I think she's coming. I'm almost sure it's her. Better get in place. Now! Now! She's looking around, she's coming."

Sonnewell was still wearing the canvas overshirt, and had the crowbar down a pantleg and the hook over his belt. He kept the phone to his ear and his head tipped down, saw Carter looking for him as he came up to the Lauren section, and she nodded to her left.

He went right, around the edge of the display and pushed into a rack of men's jackets. Carter said, "She's coming . . . I'm coming now, I'm going to wave at her. If she comes right in, her back should be to you . . . it's gonna work, it's gonna work, there's that one clerk, you see him?"

"I see him, he's a nonfactor," Sonnewell said, looking across the sales floor at the checkout stand. "There's a woman coming to talk to him, I don't think he could see us anyway, his back will be toward us . . ."

"She'll see me in a couple of seconds, I'm going to put my phone down. You'll hear me say it . . ."

When she said, "I can't believe what Bill did," Zhao's back would be toward him.

Zhao came through the men's department, looking around, saw the Ralph Lauren display. Carter had her back to Zhao but could see her in a dressing mirror. When Zhao got close, Carter looked up, took a step back, and asked, "Is that you?"

"That's me," Zhao said.

Carter walked around a display table and lifted the buckskin backpack onto it and asked, "If you want to take a look, fine, but I want to move on out. Nice to see you, Vivian. I hope you make it. Please don't call me again, I'm scared enough as it is."

"I won't. Let me take a peek, I have to tell you . . . I mean . . ."

"I can't believe what Bill did," Carter said. She was six feet from Zhao, across the display table. Zhao looked up at her, with no hint that Sonnewell had stepped out and with a second fast step, was three feet behind her, coming fast. He lifted the crowbar and smashed it down on the crown of Zhao's head.

Zhao went down as though she'd been hit by a cannonball. Sonnewell looked around for any sign of alarm, and saw none. "She's dead," he said, quietly.

"Yes, I think so," Carter said. Zhao was lying on her back, behind a sweaters table, blood flooding onto the carpet around her head. Her body was invisible from anywhere more than a few steps away. She was staring sightlessly at the ceiling. Carter took the razor scraper, with a four-inch handle, from her purse. She knelt beside Zhao and pressed the razor blade to her throat, and pushed hard, the blade cutting through Zhao's windpipe and going almost to her spine.

"That should do it," Carter said, pulling the blade out and standing up. "No coming back from that."

"Then let's go . . ."

"You need shorts?" Carter asked. "Ralph Lauren has those very attractive wide-band boxer briefs that I . . ."

"You're fucking hilarious," Sonnewell said, taking her arm above the elbow, pulling her out of the Ralph Lauren section and toward the mall exit. "Let's not go straight to the car. Let's go out a side exit and find a place to take the hats off."

"Your wish is my command," she said.

"Then I gotta another wish for you," Sonnewell said, with a growl. "We'll talk about that later. Let's get out of here."

ZHAO'S BODY WAS in the deepest part of the Ralph Lauren section, behind and slightly beneath the sweater table. February could get cold in Birmingham, but people really weren't shopping for sweaters anymore. That's why Zhao's body, long dead, wasn't discovered until the next morning, a half hour after the store opened.

By that time, Sonnewell and Carter were sleeping comfortably under the million-thread-count Egyptian cotton sheets in her waterfront condo in New Orleans. Sonnewell cracked his eyes early, because he was the early-rising type, no matter where he was. Carter was lying a foot away, naked under the sheets, her head turned slightly toward him. She was breathing deeply, but not snoring at all.

After lying still for a while, he reached out and slowly edged the sheet down, exposing her body above her thighs.

Without opening her eyes, she said, "I felt that, you pervert."

"Is that a complaint or a compliment?"

"Let me think about that," she said, now opening her eyes. "Are we done killing people?"

"I dunno," Sonnewell said. "I'm tempted to continue, but this Five shit has to stop. You could probably get away with killing assholes for a long time, because basically, nobody cares when they get killed. Not even the cops. If you were very, very careful, and made sure you weren't creating a pattern, and kept the techniques varied. . . ."

"No press releases," she said.

"And no press releases . . . then I think you could probably kill a lot of assholes."

Now she opened her eyes. "What's that old movie, the one with the Nazis and the girl getting on the plane, there's this guy in a funny hat and Hubert Humphrey says something . . ."

"Humphrey Bogart, sweetheart," Sonnewell said, "Not Hubert Humphrey. Bogart says, 'I think this is the beginning of a beautiful friendship.'"

Her hand slid down his chest toward his groin. "Yeah," she said. "That's the one."

THIRTY-ONE

Marty Meyer had been small-rich before Bitcoin—fifteen million, including a three-bedroom West Side apartment from which you could see a narrow slice of New York City's Central Park, including parts of three trees. He'd made his money as a commercial real estate dealer.

Meyer was a tall man with a wintry look about him: thin, not quite bony, he had an angular face, close-cut sandy hair with a touch of gray at the temples, and pale gray eyes. Friends had said from time to time that he looked like Vladimir Putin, but taller, and thinner.

When he invested in Bitcoin, it had already gone to five dollars per coin. He wasn't exactly late to invest, but he was not in time to grab easy billionaire status. On the other hand, he did have some money that he could afford to throw down the toilet without missing it much, so he did it.

He cashed a chunk of Apple stock and bought four thousand Bit-coins for a little more than $20,000. He sold at $45,000 per coin, tak-ing out a hundred and eighty million dollars before taxes. After paying the taxes, which hurt like hell in New York, where heavy state income taxes get piled on top of federal capital gains taxes, he was still banking more than a hundred and twenty-five million.

He used some of the money to buy into the leafy enclave of Saga-ponack, in Long Island's Hamptons. He hadn't lived there long before realizing that he shared the neighborhood with Woodrow Orion Rap.

Even before he joined the Five, he suspected that one day he would kill Rap.

He even knew how he'd do it.

Rap was a fascist and if there had been a regular fascist party in the United States, he would have been a Fascist with a capital *F*. He was a believer—which didn't make him unique in the world, but did make him an enormous asshole.

Meyer's grandparents had missed the German concentration camps by the skin of their teeth, getting out of Amsterdam two days after the Germans invaded the Netherlands. After a brief stop in En-gland, they'd made it to America, where Meyer's parents had been born. Only one of his many great-aunts, and none of his many great-uncles, and few of their children, survived the Shoah.

Meyer was not an observant Jew, but he had no time for fascists (or Fascists) in whatever form they might take.

And Rap, in his opinion, was among the worst of the worst. No goose-stepping here, no Hitler salutes, no "88" tattoos, just the sub-tle, steady promotion of a philosophy that was nothing other than the lowest, anti-Semitic, anti-black, anti-immigrant, Hitlerian kind of fascism, dished up as free speech.

So. How would he kill Rap?

With a rifle. Specifically, with a single shot from a highly accurate AR-15 firing .223-caliber bullets and mounted with a red-dot optical scope. The shot would go in through the top of Rap's left ear and out the other side, having first penetrated a two-foot-square window in the bathroom off Rap's bedroom.

Rap would enter the well-lit bathroom to pee, as he did every single night before going to bed. He'd stand over the toilet facing the wall behind the toilet, the left side of his head framed perfectly in the window.

He *looked* like a target.

MEYER HAD ALWAYS had an interest in guns, though he'd never been a hunter. Even before striking it rich with Bitcoin, he was the owner of six hundred rugged acres in Maine's Great North Woods, where he'd go to shoot, and to sail a Sunfish on a small lake.

After moving to Sagaponack, and realizing that Rap was right there, no more than nine backyards away from his own house, he'd begun shooting more seriously.

He had gotten to the point where he could reliably put three shots in a space no bigger than a poker chip at a hundred yards, as long as there was no crosswind. After he'd begun to seriously think about killing Rap, he bought a stack of double-paned windows at a Lowe's in Bangor and had spent time shooting through the glass.

He found there was some small deflection of the bullets, but only some of the time, and not enough to really matter. Instead of going through the precise middle of Rap's ear, he might go a quarter inch to one side or the other, or that much high or low; not enough to make a difference.

And he decided to shoot full metal jackets, which should reduce the deflection even more, in case the window glass was especially thick.

Sitting in a tree one hundred and eight yards from the window, as measured with a golf range finder, and using a large maple branch as a rest, killing Rap should not be a problem—if he only had the guts to do it.

Meeting with the Five had helped with that. He wasn't a psycho like the others, but there wasn't a dumb one among them, and their discussions of motives, opportunity, techniques, and evidence had bolstered his resolve. And he liked the whole thing with the press releases: he wanted Rap's death to be a warning to the other fascist assholes in the world that a man with a gun might be coming for them.

He was shocked by the deaths of McGruder and Osborne, but if Vivian Zhao's posts in the chat room were honest—and he thought they were, and the television reports seemed to support her stories about those shootings—he thought he understood them.

He also thought that whether he understood them, whether Zhao might be coming to kill him, he still wanted Rap. Zhao he could deal with later.

One cold winter morning he made himself a cheese and chicken sandwich for lunch, with excellent small-batch sourdough bread and stone-ground organic mustard, and sat down with a bottle of beer to eat lunch. He clicked on CNN, and halfway through the sandwich was told that Vivian Zhao had been found murdered in a Macy's department store near Birmingham, Alabama.

He'd said to himself—he was thoroughly divorced—"My God: MSY."

He no longer had to worry about Vivian either blackmailing him or killing him. He resolved to go that night: put that slug right through Rap's ear.

VIRGIL WAS ASLEEP when Orish called. He picked up his phone, saw her name, and asked, "What happened?"

"Somebody murdered Vivian Zhao in a Macy's store in Birmingham, Alabama, probably last night just before the store closed. Her body was found this morning."

"Whoa," Virgil said. "MSY. Getting rid of her. Any sign of a struggle, anything we can use to . . ."

"Nothing. Not a damn thing," Orish said. "There are cameras in the store, but none were looking at the spot where she was killed. Agents on the scene are telling us that it had to be two people—it looks like she was hit from behind and never saw it coming. The theory is, she was speaking to one person, maybe MSY, and another person hit her with a steel bar, could be rebar or something like it. Then, to make sure she was dead, somebody used a razor blade to punch a hole through her windpipe. That was probably unnecessary. She was most likely killed instantly by the blow; her skull was shattered."

"I'll tell Lucas . . ."

"I already have. He said he was going back to sleep. He seemed . . . unexcited."

"That's Lucas. He tends to keep his eye on the target," Virgil said. "Zhao is dead and therefore, no longer relevant."

"Our question is, will this stop the killings?" Orish asked. "Will JFK back away from whatever he's planning? We don't think we can take the chance, but I don't see this stakeout continuing for more than another week or ten days. Everybody just blew a bubble of relief and relaxed . . . like JFK was no longer out there."

"I'll let you guys work that out. Maybe nothing will happen."

"What are you going to do?" Orish asked.

"You mean, right now? Go back to sleep," Virgil said.

"Keeping your eye on the . . . relevancies."

THAT AFTERNOON, AFTER eating his lunch, Meyer went down to his basement workshop and took a long look at his AR-15. Once used, he'd dispose of it—if he used it tonight, by dawn the next morning it'd be in the ocean. He'd bought it off the books from a Maine redneck who needed cash to move to Texas more than he needed the AR, so no purchase of a .223 could be traced to him.

The question in his mind was, had Osborne left anything behind that might identify him? Were there cops out there watching over Rap, as one of the nation's most identifiable assholes?

Had Rap or his network bought personal protection? Meyer suspected he had. Driving past Rap's place was something he normally did just to go shopping for food, and he'd seen a couple of large men who did not look like a yard maintenance crew. They looked like New York City cops. Or Mafia goons. One or the other. But they didn't look like the type that would be stalking around the neighborhood at night . . .

The question of personal bodyguards was important. He had to decide whether to attach his bump stock to the AR or leave it as a single-shot weapon. He'd bought the bump stock at a gun show—perfectly legal, at least for the time being—no license or registration necessary. Attached to the AR, it would give him what amounted to a fully automatic weapon. Similarly equipped weapons had been used to kill 60 people and wound 411 more in a Las Vegas mass shooting in 2017.

Meyer had experimented with the bump stock several times, shooting along a ravine on his Maine property. He'd made two findings: for all practical purposes, you could empty a magazine as quickly as a fully automatic military M16, and the people who said that bump stocks couldn't be fired accurately were only partly right.

They couldn't be fired as accurately as a dedicated automatic weapon, perhaps, but they were more than accurate enough to put thirty rounds in a bushel basket at fifty yards in two or three seconds . . .

And while he didn't want to kill any bodyguards Rap might have, a bump stock–equipped gun would be a deterrent that might allow him to escape pursuit, if there were any. Really, how many people want to chase a machine gun through a wooded landscape in the dark?

A bump stock–equipped rifle could be fired as a single-shot, with no loss of accuracy, but they had one problem. They bumped. That's not where they got their name, but he noticed when practicing in Maine that it was hard to move around without the stock rattling, which it had to do to operate. Any effort to muffle the stock affected its operation.

After considering the pros and cons, he decided to go big. He took the AR apart and fitted the bump stock to the gun, a process that took him four minutes. And if he was going to take the bump-stocked gun, he should take extra mags, he thought. Otherwise, there was no point in the bump stock.

Five should do it, he thought, thirty rounds apiece . . . He had a warm hunting coat; the mags would fit in the pockets. He didn't need any other survival gear, aside from long underwear and gloves, because Rap *was* only nine dark backyards from his own house.

When he decided he was ready, he drove his BMW three blocks to a house owned by friends, and parked the car in the driveway. His friends were in Florida for the month, and he'd promised them he'd occasionally leave a car in the driveway overnight. That, together with some lights on timers, might convince a burglar that the house was occupied.

It would also give him a second place to run to, should Rap actually have a security team that might give chase. He would not want to lead them directly back to his house . . .

After parking the car, he walked back home. The day was . . . ordinary. He thought it should somehow be different, because this was a major turning point in his life. Shouldn't there be some kind of sign? Some talisman? But the day stayed stubbornly ordinary.

LUCAS AND VIRGIL ate dinner at a heavily disguised McDonald's off Highway 80, the place so heavily disguised that they hadn't at first recognized it as a McDonald's even as they were looking at it.

"How much longer are we going to do this?" Virgil asked, when they settled into a booth. "I've got things to do at the farm, the twins . . ."

"The new novel."

"Yeah, the novel . . ."

"This is boring, but I'll be another week or ten days, I think," Lucas said. "I do believe Rap is the target and that JFK will be coming for him, and soon. I think he'll try to stay on schedule. But, if you want to go home, go."

"I can't. I promised Weather I'd take care of you," Virgil said.

"I appreciate that, Virgie, but like you said, you've got things to do. I really am thinking about your new novel. This is something way different than those magazine articles you write. This is serious."

"Ah, I'll stay as long as you do," Virgil said. "Actually, I only slept until about two o'clock this afternoon and got three solid hours on my laptop. Sitting in a motel with no twins to take care of, no horseshit to shovel . . . it's got some nice aspects to it."

Lucas leaned in and ticked a finger at him: "A lot of cops need a second career. They burn out on the shit we do. The shit we have to put up with. I got lucky with the software company—that made me enough money to free me up forever. Get me in a place where I only do stuff that interests me. You're not in that place, and I don't see you running around rural Minnesota for another twenty years. You gotta push the writing. See where it goes."

"You're starting to sound like Frankie."

"Frankie is an extremely intelligent woman," Lucas said.

"That's one reason she likes you so much," Virgil said. "She knows you think that. She told me so."

THEY PICKED UP Orish at the motel. She'd declined the opportunity to eat dinner at McDonald's, going instead to a vegetarian diner. She appeared wearing black jeans, a heavy black ski jacket, black

gloves, and dark brown boots. She was wearing a military-style holster on her right leg for her Glock 19.

"You're not coming outside with us," Lucas said when he saw her.
"We need the communications coordination. We need you talking
in our ears."

"I want to be ready to go out if I'm needed," she said. "You know
I'm not silly, but I want to be ready."

That settled that. They drove back to Rap's in the dark, parked in
the garage, met with the other agents for an abbreviated tactical
meeting—they would be doing nothing that they'd not done the night
before—and one at a time, slipped out of the side door and into Rap's
yard. Virgil and Lucas went last, adjusting their night-vision goggles,
penetrating the hedges behind Rap's house, to their stands from the
night before.

As they walked out, Virgil said, "Ten days. This could get old in
ten days."

"Pretend you're deer hunting. You do that voluntarily, in worse
conditions than this."

"See you in the morning," Virgil said.

And they sat.

RAP'S TELEVISION SHOW came on at ten o'clock on the days he
was working, and ran until midnight, in every time zone—the first
broadcast recorded to be rebroadcast at ten o'clock across the country.
Cranked from his two hours on the air, he usually stayed up until one
o'clock, cooling off. The late hours became a habit. That put him standing over the toilet between midnight and one o'clock, on most nights.

Meyer tried to nap. He couldn't think why he was doing that, because he was awake enough, but lying in the dark, visualizing the night to come, seemed a better option than watching some inane television show. He was up at nine o'clock, dressed head to foot in a hunter's night camo. He checked the rifle, checked it again. Each round in the five mags had been wiped down with alcohol to remove prints and DNA, part of the Five training. Now he wiped the mags themselves, in case he had to drop one. He would not touch them again, except with gloved hands, and the gloves had also been carefully wiped.

Starting to choke up a bit. The other members of the Five had told him that would happen.

He turned on an upstairs bedroom light, and then a light in the pear tree in the backyard. The light was weak, but the yellowish cast would act as a beacon to bring him home, should he get disoriented. He would be moving through shadows at the edges of the yards, where the light wasn't a factor.

He went out at eleven o'clock, moving slowly along a rehearsed route that took him across the backyards of three neighbors. All had cameras, but not pointed at their backyards. He'd done this a dozen times, rehearsing.

Staying in the shadows, he crossed a hedge at a thin point, let himself through a low wooden fence at a gate, crossed the next yard, crawled through an opening in the hedge marking the boundary between two lawns, sat and listened for a minute, then walked along a back hedge and up to a twisted old sugar maple tree. Someone, decades before, had retained the lower branches rather than pruning them, and now they made a platform both for tree-climbing kids and killers armed with AR-15s.

He climbed to the ten-foot level, where a secondary branch made a good gun rest. He put the rifle over the rest, looked through the red dot. He couldn't clearly see Rap's bathroom window, because it was dark, but he knew where it was: he had a clean shot.

Leaning back against the tree trunk, he straddled the limb, and watched.

"LUCAS TO VIRGIL: did you hear something from out in front of your position?"

Virgil buried his chin in his coat and said, quietly as he could, "No."

"I thought I heard a rattle, like maybe a trash can lid, but I didn't see anyone moving around the houses."

Virgil said, "Didn't hear anything."

"Okay."

AT MIDNIGHT, THE shift changed, and the four agents at the corners of Rap's yard traded places with four incoming agents. From his tree, Meyer couldn't tell what had happened. He could see by the headlights that a car had stopped at Rap's, and then shortly thereafter, had left. A pizza delivery? He didn't know, but thought about it, and couldn't see how it mattered. Nothing was moving below him or around him, as far as he could see.

There wasn't much light to see by, but there was some, from house windows, and a couple of driveway lights.

INSIDE RAP'S HOUSE, Orish did a communications check with the four new agents. As she was finishing with that, Rap stuck his head in the parlor where she was working, and said, "I'm going to bed."

"All right. You've got the shades down in your bedroom . . ."

"Yes, we got them down right after dark. If you leave before I get up tomorrow, know that tomorrow night will be the last night. I'm out here for a couple of days. I've got a doctor appointment in the city that I gotta make the day after tomorrow."

"We'll need to set up around your house . . ."

"Don't want to take that chance," Rap said. "I'm going to bag out at the Four Seasons. My guys will be there with me. If you want to stick a couple of agents in the lobby or the hall . . ."

"We'll discuss it tomorrow," Orish said. "Sleep well."

"Yeah, I don't do that," Rap said.

MEYER, IN HIS tree, had begun to wonder if perhaps Rap had gone back to Manhattan. He'd seen no sign of life in the house, and then, as he was wondering, the lights came on in the rooms that he believed were Rap's bedrooms. He could feel the muscles tighten across his back. Maybe this was crazy? Maybe he should climb down . . .

The bedroom shades were pulled, but some light filtered through them. A shadow crossed one of the shades and he put the red dot on the bathroom window. He'd chosen the smallest diameter red-dot optic he could find, because he got better accuracy with it.

With the gun resting comfortably, he clicked the safety off; a round was snug in the chamber, the red dot on the dark bathroom window, he waited . . .

Not for long.

The light clicked on and Rap stepped up to the toilet, looking down at it, his head right there, his ear right there. Meyer took up the slack on the trigger, took a shallow breath, held it . . . Yes? No? . . . He pulled the trigger.

Crack!

The gun jumped and when he got it back on target, Rap's head had disappeared. The red dot was not magnified, so he couldn't see if there was a hole in the window . . . And even as he thought that, he heard men's voices screaming . . .

"Gun! Gun!"

ORISH HEARD A window shatter and a millisecond later, the sound of a distant gunshot. She blurted, "Oh, Jesus," and ran up the stairs to the second floor and into Rap's bedroom; he wasn't there. She turned and ran into the bathroom and found Rap's body crumbled on the floor in a toilet booth.

A rose-colored stain decorated the wall opposite the shattered window, blood blown from Rap's head. The stain was punctuated by a single small bullet hole.

Rap, she knew at a glance, was dead, and she screamed into her headset, "Rap is down, Rap is down."

LUCAS HAD SEEN a wink of light that appeared to be well off the ground, and instantly afterward the *crack!* of a rifle that he unconsciously categorized as a .223: anything larger would *bang!* or *boom!*

Virgil had also seen the wink of a muzzle flash, and he shouted, "Thirty or forty yards ahead, your side, Lucas, your side, I'm going, I'm going."

Lucas shouted back, "I'm going . . ."

They both could hear the other agents shouting, two saying they were going to the street, two more moving through the backyards toward Virgil and Lucas.

Meyer was astonished by the rapidity of the response, and realized, as he climbed down from the tree, that the shouting men were not only cops, but were close. He heard one crashing through a hedge and he pointed the AR in that general direction and pushed the forestock of the AR forward, to activate the bump-stock function, and pulled the trigger and kept it pulled.

Thirty rounds ripped out of the muzzle of the gun and he dropped the magazine, got another from his pocket, slammed it home, and turned to run.

Virgil saw the winking of the AR and the ripping sound of the automatic fire and thought *shit!* and dropped facedown on the ground, the shotgun beneath him. Lucas, on the other side of the yard, had crashed through a hedge and fired two shots as the shooter opened up with the full-auto burst and a bullet hit his right arm like the blow of a baseball bat and he went down, and he shouted, "I'm down, I'm hit!"

And Meyer was hit in both legs but was still operating; he heard the shout and ran through a hedge opening and then thought: *Not to the house. Gotta go for the car.*

If they tracked him right to the house, he'd be screwed. Near panic, he turned right, limped through the side yard of a house toward the street and had cleared the house when a man screamed, "Halt! Stop!"

He pivoted and saw two men running toward him, the leader forty yards away, the second man trailing by five yards. One of the men slowed, lifted a handgun and fired two shots, *bang! bang!* but neither shot touched him. He lifted the rifle to his eye and let the bump stock run, dumping all thirty rounds at the two men and they both went down and he ran hard up the street.

WHEN LUCAS SCREAMED that he was hit, Virgil scooped up his shotgun and ran toward him, picking out his body partly through a hedge. "How bad, how bad?"

"Could be bad," Lucas groaned. "In the arm, the arm doesn't work, doesn't hurt much but it doesn't work . . ."

"Let me see, let me . . ."

"No, no, go get him. Get him!"

"You sure . . ."

Lucas struggled to get to his knees and shouted, "Go! Go!"

Virgil went, running toward the tree where he thought the shots had come from; he could see no movement through the night-vision goggles, kept running, and then saw what looked like a stick figure motion disappearing behind a house, running out toward the adjacent street.

He cut behind the house he was passing toward the street and saw two agents run by in the street and a moment later one of the agents shouted something he couldn't make out and then he heard two pistol shots as he cleared the house, and then again the ripping noise of a machine gun and both agents tumbled to the ground.

The shooter had slowed to reload and Virgil, though he thought the man was at least seventy or eighty yards away, emptied his shotgun at him, six fast pumps that sent a total of seventy-two .33-caliber pellets downrange. The man turned, stumbled, went down, struggled back to his feet, went down again, swiveled on his butt, and as Virgil ran farther into the yard, he saw the man's muzzle coming around. He dodged behind a tree and was immediately knocked down by a blow to the head.

Lying on his back, his body partly exposed, he had no idea what had hit him, or how badly he was hurt, and then he took another blow to a thigh. The shooter then turned and started to run away, but limping badly, and Virgil found another magazine and jammed it into the shotgun, pushed himself up and stumbled after him.

Up ahead and to the left, a woman shouted from the dark, then opened fire, and Virgil thought she must be firing at the shooter. A moment later, the machine gun opened up again, three short bursts, and Virgil kept running, his right thigh burning, and it occurred to him that he'd been shot not once, but twice. Blood was streaming down over his goggles from his head wound, obscuring his vision, and he ripped the headset off and ran into the dark.

Somebody was calling him: "Virgil, Virgil, coming up behind."

Virgil half turned, saw Lucas lurching toward him, his right arm flopping uselessly, like a broken wing, and Virgil shouted, "Man, stop, stop, sit down, you're hit," and Lucas shouted, "Fuck it," and kept coming.

From the angle of the last gunfire, a man was shouting, "Officer down, agent down, we got an agent down we need a medic, a medic . . ."

Virgil heard the same words on his headset, and then the man called, "Everybody's shot. Everybody's shot . . ."

Virgil and Lucas ran on, past the lit porch of a way-too-large house and Lucas shouted, "You're bleeding, Virg, you're bleeding bad . . ."

MORE GUNFIRE, PISTOL shots and a lot of them, then an agent shouted, "I think I hit him . . . I think . . . agent down, help me, help me!"

Lucas and Virgil ran that way, Lucas with his Walther in his left hand, Virgil limping, his leg beginning to scream with pain. Lucas shouted at the agent, who he could make out with his night-vision goggles, "We're coming up on you from the right—from behind, from the right."

They moved up in a hurry and found an unwounded agent crouched over a groaning woman, lying on her back, hands clenched over the stomach area of her body armor, and the agent said, "Nancy's hit, got her in the stomach, I think I might have hit the guy over by that red house, you can see the red in the light . . ."

"C'mon," Lucas said, "Let's get the motherfucker."

The agent said, "I can't, I'm out, I emptied out my magazine and I dropped the other one back there somewhere, I can't find it . . ."

Virgil said, "I'm going," and Lucas said, "I'm right behind you," and they spread a bit as they ran toward the red house.

MEYER HAD BEEN hit in the legs and the pelvis with buckshot and feared that he might have lost his testicles because he seemed to be bleeding heavily there and the pain was intense enough to blur his vision with involuntary tears. He'd dumped the third magazine into two pursuers and had seen one go down as bullets flew by him, none hitting him.

He thought, in the back of his mind, that he was done; they had him. Better to die here than to look at life in prison. He was lying at the corner of the red house, looking for pursuit. He could hear people shouting, but nobody coming after him, and he pushed himself to his feet and tried to think what to do next.

As he was moving away from the house, he heard somebody shout, "There!"

He turned and brought the rifle up and thought he saw movement in the dark, still thirty or forty yards away but getting closer. He brought the gun up and opened fire, dumping the full magazine out in the area of the movement.

Somebody screamed "No!" and Meyer turned to run, as best he could, but he hadn't turned his head more than a few inches when he saw the heavy muzzle flashes of a shotgun and instantly felt impacts in his chest and stomach.

He staggered backward and fell on his butt but was still sitting upright. The movement was getting closer as he tried to fish a magazine out of his pocket. He found one, dropped the empty, and tried to get the magazine into the gun.

He was doing that when the movement resolved itself into a blond man with a long gun and he lifted the rifle barrel toward him . . .

LUCAS GOT HIT a second time, outside his right nipple, actually *felt* a rib shatter and he shouted "No!" and got hit again in the leg and went down and Virgil saw the winking of the automatic weapon and when it stopped he thought he might have five seconds for the shooter to reload and he ran as hard as he could, dragging his damaged leg, toward the last place he'd seen him.

As he came up, the man lifted the barrel of his rifle toward Virgil and Virgil shot him in the face with the twelve-gauge, from ten feet, and followed it up with an almost involuntary pump and second shot to the chest.

Certain now that the shooter was dead, he turned back to help Lucas. He fell, halfway back, got up, fell again, crawled the rest of the way, dragging a leg.

"How bad?" he asked, when he got to Lucas.

"I dunno," Lucas said. He was lying on his back on frozen grass, his voice thick with pain. "Got me in the chest. Need . . . help . . . can't even see your face anymore, Virgie, it's all covered with blood. Could you roll me up on . . . roll me up on my side, I think, don't want blood in my lungs . . . What happened . . ."

"I killed him," Virgil said. "You're breathing okay, I don't think it got your lung." He raised his head up as if about to howl at the moon, and he did howl, "Help! Help us! Help us!"

ORISH CALLED THE night duty officer at FBI headquarters and told her to get every ambulance in the area to Rap's house—that there'd been a major firefight and they had agents down. Then she ran outside with her pistol in one hand and a flashlight in the other, turned out of the house and dashed up the street that ran parallel to the backyards.

A minute out of the house she saw the first lump on the blacktop, shined a light on it, and found herself looking into the dead face of an agent named Terrill. She groaned, ran on, found a second lump, another dead agent named Wilson.

She began not to weep, but to gasp, or groan, a rhythmic kind of vocal anguish that was completely involuntary. She heard a series of pistol shots and then a burst of automatic weapon fire and ran that way, and a moment later, the *boom! boom!* of a twelve-gauge. And then silence, for a moment, then men screaming for help.

They got him, she thought.

She found an agent named O'Malley crouched over another one named Nancy Nguyen, Nguyen literally humming to distract herself from the pain. She said, "Ambulances coming . . . Hear them?"

And they could hear them, some long distance away, but coming. She said to O'Malley, "Stay here. Where are the others?"

"They went that way." O'Malley pointed, and she ran that way, gun still in her hand, nearly stumbled over Virgil and Lucas. Virgil's face was a mask of blood, crimson in the light of her flashlight.

Virgil said, "Lucas is hit at least twice, maybe three times. I don't know what's going on with my head, but I got shot in the leg, I can still move it around . . ."

"Where's the shooter?"

"Dead," Virgil said.

She made Virgil stretch out his leg and used a pocketknife to cut through his pant leg. She found a small entrance wound on one side of his thigh, looking almost like a big pimple, trickling blood, and a bigger, bloodier hole on the other side, with blood streaming out. Not pumping out. She said, "No artery."

Lucas groaned and said, "Goddamn chest . . ."

She cut his coat off and looked, said, "I can't do anything here but it's just on the edge, Lucas, I don't think it got a lung . . ."

"Hurts."

"I think he's got a broken arm," Virgil said. "Right arm was flopping."

Virgil lay down on the ground and then there were more flashlights coming. Not medical care: local residents.

Orish didn't bother to shoo them away. Instead, she called, "FBI. We've got a lot of people hurt, the ambulances are coming, please get them back here."

People ran away to do that and the sirens were closer.

Virgil asked, "What about Rap?"

Orish said, "Dead. One small window without a shade, so small nobody thought about it. He turned on a light and stood in front of it. To pee. "

Virgil: "People are dead because Rap had to pee?"

"Yes." Orish sat down between them, and now she began to weep. "Because Rap had to pee. Because he had to pee."

THIRTY-TWO

Lucas pressed his face to the cold earth and waited. He hurt every time he so much as twitched, so he tried not to twitch. He knew Virgil was talking but couldn't quite make out what he was saying. The EMTs thought he was in trouble because of the bloody chest wound and unceremoniously hoisted him onto a gurney and ran him to an ambulance, which hurt more than a whole collection of twitches.

The world began getting hazy on the way to the hospital and he lost track of time, but registered the ambulance ride, his transfer to a well-lit hallway, the ceiling tiles clicking past his half-open eyes during the short trip to an emergency operating room where the light was even brighter than the hallway, and then it seemed like a dozen people were pulling and cutting his clothes off. A mask was slapped over his face, he felt a sharp prick as a line was linked into his arm, and then a cold wave—it felt freezing, icy—hit his chest and leg, and finally the anesthetic took him away.

A DOC CAME in carrying a medical version of an iPad and stood next to the foot of Virgil's bed, glanced at the iPad and said, "You're going in, probably in ten minutes or so. A nurse will be here to wash your leg again. Your head wound looks bad but it's superficial—your scalp is full of wood splinters, like shrapnel. It looks like a bullet hit a tree limb, close to your head. That was the blow you felt. We need to clean up your scalp. You'll have some stitches to deal with. Gonna itch."

"Hurts like hell right now," Virgil said. "Worse than the leg."

"Better than the alternative. If the bullet had been a couple inches lower, we'd be taking skull splinters out of a tree."

"What about the leg?"

"We can fix the leg," the doc said. "Something we don't often see here—the shooter was using solid military-style bullets. The wound is relatively small and straight through. Your biggest problem going forward will be the possibility of infection."

"What happened with Lucas?"

"The marshal? He's in the OR now. He was hit three times, we're giving him blood. Don't know yet how that's going, but everybody seemed confident that he's going to make it. We're pretty good with this stuff."

ORISH WAS SITTING in a corner chair when Virgil woke up, slowly for the first few seconds, then all at once, as though surfacing in a lake. He groaned, "Hello," his voice sounding rusty, and she looked up from her laptop and said, instantly, "You're gonna be fine."

He didn't hurt. The drugs had gotten really good, he thought. He asked, "What about Lucas?"

"He'll be okay. He'll hurt for a few months."

"What about everybody . . . ?"

She told him: Rap dead, shot through the head. Meyer dead, hit several times with shotgun pellets, the coup de grace coming from a shotgun blast in the face. Two agents dead, shredded by a blizzard of at least fifteen .223 slugs that went through their body armor like it was pudding. Another agent, Nancy Nguyen, seriously wounded, lifted by helicopter to a New York City medical center.

"The killer's name was Meyer, he lived not far from Rap's house. We never had a chance to stop him. He knew exactly what Rap was going to do—step in front of that little window to pee," Orish said. "He had the perfect setup, in an old maple tree—like a hunting stand. We found the cartridge case on the ground below the limb he was shooting from. He must have been stalking Meyer for weeks."

"He would have gotten away with it, if those Five lunatics hadn't stuck to their schedule," Virgil said. "If he'd moved earlier or waited a month, nobody would have known who the shooter was, and Rap would be just as dead."

Orish nodded and looked at her watch. "Your wife and Lucas' wife will be here in twenty minutes or half an hour, depending on traffic. Lucas' wife chartered a United business jet and they landed at an airport back down the island. Apparently, Lucas has money. I didn't know that."

"Yeah, he's a rich guy," Virgil said. After a moment, he asked, "How about you? Are you okay?"

She shook her head. "Not physically injured, but, there'll be an inquiry and my career with the FBI will be done. We not only failed to protect Rap, but we got a lot of people shot and agents killed."

"That's not fair," Virgil said.

She shook her head again. "The agency desperately needs somebody to blame. That's me. And I understand it. If it wasn't me, it'd have to be Assistant Director Kelly, and that won't happen."

"I'm sorry," Virgil said, because he knew she was right.

A NURSE CAME in and told Orish that Lucas was awake. She left, and twenty minutes later, Davenport's adoptive daughter, Letty, poked her head into the room and said, "You look like crap."

"Thank you. How's your dad? And where'd you come from?"

"He's okay now. He's got a lot of dope in him, but he's going to be very, very cranky in a little while," Letty said. In her early twenties, Letty was a pretty, mid-height woman, lean like a runner, with crystalline blue eyes. "I grabbed a shuttle up from D.C., and Mom had a limo meet me at LaGuardia and haul my ass out here."

"Letty Davenport, the Joan of Arc of the Rio Grande. I understand Mexico has nominated you for sainthood."

"Haven't burned me at the stake, anyway," Letty said. Her phone dinged with an incoming message, and she looked at it. "Mom and Frankie will be here in a minute."

"So I'm told," Virgil said. He moved his wounded leg and despite the good drugs, felt it and winced. "This is going to be a tiresome winter."

"No kidding. I'm gonna go meet the wives. I'll give you a kiss before Frankie gets here."

She stepped over to his bed and kissed him on the lips, held it for a second, and they both smiled, then she backed away, patted his good leg and said, "You guys are gonna be okay."

FRANKIE SHOWED UP, and after the usual fussery, a nurse helped Frankie get Virgil into a wheelchair, easing out of the bed onto his good leg. He was wheeled to Lucas' room, which was crowded with Weather, Letty, Orish, and a nurse.

Lucas turned his head, saw him coming and said, "You look like shit."

"Your daughter already told me that," Virgil said. "I'm happy to say you look worse than I do. I understand you've got another op coming up?"

"They didn't do the arm," Lucas said. "The bone's broken, up near the shoulder. They'll go back in tomorrow. They tell me I'll get a metal plate and a bunch of screws and a big fuckin' ugly scar."

"I can fix that," Weather said. "We could do it in the laundry room."

THEY TALKED ABOUT the shoot-out, what they'd all done and seen. Orish swore them to secrecy and told them that as far as anyone could tell, four FBI agents had fired twenty-eight rounds at Meyer and hadn't hit him even once. "They x-rayed the body at the medical examiner's. It appears that all of Meyer's wounds were from shotgun pellets."

Just as bad, she said, was that one of the agents, who'd been chasing Meyer right into the storm of rifle fire, had dropped one of his magazines while trying to reload after emptying the first magazine, then hadn't been able to find the dropped magazine. "He had two more on his belt but didn't take either of them out. He said he didn't think of it, the magazines on his belt, because he was trying to track Meyer and help Nancy at the same time."

"They all had guts, every one of them," Virgil said. "Every one of them."

Orish looked from Lucas to Virgil. "You two were using different brands of ammo with slightly different pellets. We found separate tracks of shucked-out shotgun shells. If you're interested, it appears that you both hit him."

"I don't know what to say," Lucas said. "I mean, what the fuck are we doing? We're fighting people who have machine guns."

"Not technically machine guns," Orish said.

"Yeah, tell me *not technically.* I was there," Lucas said. "One man, a nonprofessional, took down five of us—six, if you count Rap—killed two of us. Call it what you want, a bump stock turns an AR into a machine gun."

Orish nodded. "The guys Meyer killed were wearing Level IIIA armor because it doesn't have hard plates. The plates are too heavy if you might have to chase someone down. The IIIA armor was like toilet paper up against the AR. They should have been wearing Level III or IV. But . . . they weren't. If they had been, they might be alive, but they probably wouldn't have caught Meyer. None of the Five killers had used a rifle, so . . . they made a call. *We* made a call."

LUCAS HAD THE operation on his broken arm the next morning, with a titanium plate wrapped around the break and held in place with eleven screws. One of the doctors told him the bullet hadn't touched the bone, but after he was hit, he apparently windmilled the arm backward, trying to break a fall, and broke the arm when it hit the frozen ground. Lucas didn't remember that.

The break was clean and the bones weren't displaced, and ordinarily might heal itself, but because of complications created by the chest wound, the arm operation was necessary.

The chest shot had broken a rib, taking a chip out of it, and that would bother him for weeks. The same bullet poked a hole through the scapula, the shoulder blade, in his back, with radiating cracks. The scapula supported the same shoulder that had been broken, and the whole area would be wrapped and supported for at least a couple of weeks as the scapula healing began.

The third wound, to his lower leg, broke the long thin fibula bone. That had also been repaired with a metal plate, and he'd have to keep weight off the leg until it healed.

VIRGIL GOT OUT of the hospital four days after being shot, and he and Frankie flew commercial back to the Twin Cities. Lucas stayed on Long Island for another week, before flying home.

Frankie got her time on television, though it was Channel Three out of the Twin Cities, not a national morning program, and was less than the festive affair she'd imagined. Weather was with her as an interviewer questioned them, with simulated sympathy, about the emotional hazards of marriage to cops. Both Weather and Frankie dressed in conservative slacks with jackets, and button-up blouses well buttoned up; neither one cried.

They'd been invited after both Virgil and Lucas declined; the women accepted because they had things to say about guns.

Weather looked into the camera lens and said, "I work on gunshot wounds several times a year. Mostly people shot in the face or the hands. I try to help them as much as I can, but sometimes there's not much I can do. The victims, and a lot of them are children, are often disfigured for life. Many are permanently handicapped. For what? For nothing."

And Frankie: "I'm a farm woman and I've had guns all my life, rifles and shotguns. I'm a hunter. But this stuff, what our husbands ran into, the bump stocks and ghost guns and silencers . . . this is crazy. The people with this stuff aren't hunters or sportsmen or competitors; they want to kill somebody."

VIRGIL SPENT FOUR months at the farmhouse, recuperating from the leg wound on full pay, and writing *Fire and Rain*. "You're so lucky you got shot," Frankie said. "It's like a free vacation to write another novel."

"Yeah, just plain old good luck," Virgil said.

The finished manuscript was well received by the publisher, and his agent began negotiating for a three-book follow-up contract. "Brace yourself for the big bucks," she said. "Getting yourself shot in Suffolk County didn't hurt. I know, it was awful—but a lot of the top people in publishing have houses out there, so they all know about it. They're intrigued."

"Maybe I should try to get shot again, just before the publication date," Virgil suggested. "We could do it in Manhattan."

"Just don't get hit in the hands," she said. "You'll need those to type."

The conversation, Virgil thought, had lasted at least forty-six seconds, a new record.

ORISH WAS CORRECT about her career. The FBI did a lengthy investigation and formed three in-house committees to review armor standards and combat training, including a new emphasis on night fighting. Orish got mild criticism for not covering the bathroom window, but mild as it was, it effectively signaled the end of a promising career.

Her father and one of her brothers were both prominent politicians in Pittsburgh, Pennsylvania. After consultations with both men, and local friends, she decided to run for Allegheny County sheriff. With the support from the retiring sheriff, she was expected to win.

A STORY IN the *Daily M*... revealed that the Bitcoin donations given by the Five to four d'...erent charities had been accepted by them all. An anonymou*...* executive of one of the charities pointed out that if they didn't ...cept it, the money would sit there uselessly. "There are too m...y suffering people out there not to use this resource."

IN LATE FEBRUARY, Frankie and Virgil drove from the farm to St. Paul to visit Lucas, who was hobbling around with the help of a crutch. Mallard knew that they were getting together for the first time after the shoot-out and sent them a Zoom link so he could join the party.

"One thing that bothers me is that the Five actually had six members, and four of them are dead—McGruder, Osborne, Meyer, and Zhao," Mallard said. "But the other two are still out there. We've had a team looking for them, for more than a month, and not a sniff. Not a clue."

"You know they're probably in New Orleans and San Francisco and were big winners in Bitcoin. That should knock down the search parameters," Weather said.

"Not enough," Mallard said. "San Francisco is a particular problem. There are literally hundreds of thousands of techies in the area, and many, many Bitcoin winners. There are fewer in New Orleans, but enough to be absolutely . . . baffling."

"Virgil and I have a thought for you," Lucas said.

Mallard: "What's that?"

"While it might be a problem," Lucas said. "It's not our problem."

THE FIRST WEEK of March, New Orleans: blue skies with puffy clouds, light wind coming off the lake. The city was winding itself up for Mardi Gras, adding to the ineffable lightness of its being.

Andi Carter picked up a smiling George Sonnewell at Lakefront Airport in her sleek Panamera. He dropped his bag next to the car and pressed her up against it for a thorough "hello" kiss. That done to their mutual satisfaction, they stowed the bag and buckled themselves in for the ride to her condo.

Carter patted him on the thigh and asked, "What do you think, G?"

"He's even worse than we thought," Sonnewell said. "I'll show you some numbers tonight. But: the worst of the worst. He jammed through the merger of two retail companies, forced the companies to consolidate all their backroom operations at one site. Twenty-five hundred people got laid off in a small town in Indiana, and he took seventy million dollars out of the deal. I took a look at the town: it went from modest middle class to a slum, with no stops in between. Can't even sell your house there, because there's nothing to do, so nobody will move there. Nobody wants the houses."

"Can we get at him?"

"Yes. He's a huge Nuggets fan," Sonnewell said. "Never misses a game. He's got a ranch down southeast of the city and he drives himself in for the games. There's a bad intersection a couple miles from his ranch, where the ranch road intersects a state highway."

"Private road?"

"Not quite, but almost. Gravel and dirt. As far as I can tell, only three other ranches feed ont~ ... And you gotta stop at the intersection. It's a little down~ ..., with bad sight lines. You could get T-boned by a hay tru~' ... you didn't stop. There's an overgrown bank above the i~ ...section. A guy could get up on that bank with an AR-10 and completely thrash a car that stops below the bank. There are highways out of there in every direction . . . If you were going to design an ambush with a getaway, you'd design that intersection."

"Sounds like a plan," Carter said. "Gonna have to figure out exactly what your shot pattern would be. You'd want to get the tires as well as the passenger compartment, so it wouldn't roll onto the highway after we shoot it up. And we need an anonymous rifle. Maybe with one of those bump things, like Meyer had."

Sonnewell reached over to touch her shoulder. He was a happy man, with a good-looking woman who completely understood him. "There are guns everywhere, babe. Anything you want. You could buy an RPG if you wanted one. Maybe that's a problem, but it's not our problem."